Accolades for America's greatest hero Mack Bolan

"Very, very action-oriented.... Highly successful, today's hottest books for men."
—*The New York Times*

"Anyone who stands against the civilized forces of truth and justice will sooner or later have to face the piercing blue eyes and cold Beretta steel of Mack Bolan, the lean, mean nightstalker, civilization's avenging angel."
—*San Francisco Examiner*

"Mack Bolan is a star. The Executioner is a beacon of hope for people with a sense of American justice."
—*Las Vegas Review Journal*

"In the beginning there was the Executioner—a publishing phenomenon. Mack Bolan remains a spiritual godfather to those who have followed."
—*San Jose Mercury News*

DEATHWATCH WORDS

As far as Mack Bolan has ever been able to determine, the only remedy is still the application of his age-old motto: *Penetration, identification, destruction*. No quarter asked or given, no compromise, no negotiation. It is the only way. Terrorists come in two types—fanatics and mercenaries. Bolan has taken on both types. He will take on some more in Europe.

The Executioner is angry.

"Mack Bolan stabs right through the heart of the frustration and hopelessness the average person feels about crime running rampant in the streets."
—*Dallas Times Herald*

DON PENDLETON's
MACK BOLAN

Tightrope

A GOLD EAGLE BOOK FROM
WORLDWIDE.

TORONTO • NEW YORK • LONDON • PARIS
AMSTERDAM • STOCKHOLM • HAMBURG
ATHENS • MILAN • TOKYO • SYDNEY

First edition May 1989

ISBN 0-373-61415-2

Special thanks and acknowledgment to
Carl Furst for his contribution to this work.

Death overtakes the coward, but never the brave until his hour is come.

—Attributed to Napoleon I, 1769–1821

Life is a road that stretches between birth and death. I have a long way yet to go before I travel that last bloody mile.

—Mack Bolan

PROLOGUE

Mack Bolan lay on his belly among the stunted trees that afforded the only suggestion of cover for a mile in any direction. His cover, really, was the darkness. If there had been light, he would have been visible to anyone scanning the perimeter with field glasses. And he hoped that no one was scanning with a night vision scope.

Fortunately this barren land's brief span of daylight wouldn't begin for a while yet, as the sun rose for an hour, weak and white, then fell back below the low hills to the south without leaving any warmth.

There was little snow on the ground; the constant wind swept it all away. Where he lay, there was only an ever-shifting powder on the gravelly frozen ground. Any footprints were quickly obliterated by the wind.

He was certain that no one was tracking. The helicopters that had passed overhead had done so in darkness. The pilots flew as low as they dared, sometimes only fifty feet above the terrain, and they switched on floodlights only for the last minute before they landed. Their choppers—three of them—sat dark and cold now, waiting.

The base was dark, too. It couldn't be seen from the air, not even by a recon satellite passing two hundred miles above.

He was equipped for his mission—up to a point. He had the right cold-weather clothing. He had cold-weather rations. He had a compass, binoculars, a knife and a nylon shelter. He had weapons. He shook his head ruefully.

They weren't suitable for this job, nor were they even his own. Only what "cooperating agencies" would allow and supply. Only what had come from "allies," or what he had stolen. He would be lucky if they hadn't betrayed him.

Bolan's thoughts were interrupted as a narrow band of light appeared in the distance. Then the doors slid back and he could see inside the low prefabricated hangar.

He'd been right. There it was, just what he'd known he'd find here. A Foxbat. A MiG-25. And since he was right about finding the Foxbat here, he was right about its mission. And about what he had to do.

They started to tow the Foxbat out with a quiet little electric tractor. Once it had been the most feared aircraft in the Soviet air force. Even now it was still a formidable recon interceptor, capable of speeds that few other aircraft could approach. It was a beautiful thing, with a long, needle-thin body between huge boxy airscoops, stubby wings and twin tails. Four air-to-air missiles hung beneath its wings. The canopy was up. A pilot was sitting at the controls.

As soon as the aircraft was outside the doors they slid shut, leaving the big jet in darkness for a moment, until some weak yellow lights on poles were switched on. Then, suddenly, two long parallel lines of lights came on: the runway lights. The Foxbat was leaving.

That left Bolan little time. He stood and began to trot toward the runway lights. The starter truck moved up to the Foxbat. Two men attached the cables, then waved at the pilot. He returned their wave and lowered the canopy. One engine whined, then caught, and the whine rose to a painful level, a high-pitched scream that penetrated the roar. The pilot started the second engine and doubled the noise.

Rebels in Afghanistan were given shoulder-launched heat-seeking missiles, Bolan thought wryly. One of them could easily stop the Foxbat while it was still on the ground. But the people who supplied shoulder-launched heat-seeking missiles to Afghan rebels hadn't seen fit to send one along with Mack Bolan on a mission that could make the difference between war and peace for the whole world.

Fortunately for the world, Bolan's best weapons didn't have to be supplied by anyone, and no one could take them from him. They were his: his dedication and determination, based on his life experience, his long training, his courage, his shrewd, practiced intelligence.

He didn't have to be told there would be hardmen somewhere on the perimeter of this small, crude air base. Also, there would be detectors: motion detectors, heat detectors, something. The guys in charge would be confident their cover hadn't been broken, assured that their installation here hadn't been discovered; still, their kind would not be stupid enough to leave what they had here vulnerable to chance discovery.

When he was a hundred yards from the runway he stopped. If he had come this far without being detected, then his best bet was to *let* them discover him, when it was too late for them to stop him. When the Foxbat swung into position...

He saw the muzzle-flash and threw himself to the ground, pulling the Finnish automatic that had been issued to him; the Lahti was supposed to be reliable in subzero temperatures. If his attacker's aim had been good, trying to throw himself out of the way would have been useless. But the man had to fire into the darkness, while he stood silhouetted against the glow of the runway lights. The roar of the Foxbat's turbojets overpowered the sound of both shots: the one the hardman had fired and the one that killed him.

The Foxbat had begun to move. The pole lights went out. Now the aircraft was only a shape moving in the darkness, partly outlined by the runway lights. Bolan could see the eerie blue-and-yellow plume behind its jet exhausts.

He got to his feet and began to move toward the runway. He had only a minute now. Seldom had odds been so stacked against him—not just to do what he had come here to do, but also to get out alive after. They'd been stacked by just about everybody, all along the way. Once again it was one man against a powerful combination. That was the way it had always been for him.

Staying back from the nearest runway light, so as not to be in its glow, he knelt and unstrapped from his body the weapon he had to use to try to stop this monster that would soon rush toward him on the runway. As it paused and the pilot made his final instrument checks, Bolan set himself. He was ready, as soon as that renegade pilot was. But the pilot took a full minute—time for Bolan to review one more time the inescapable logic of his situation and to wish he could find a flaw in it.

The chain of events, all logically bound together, had begun two or three years ago. The part that involved him had begun only a little more than a month ago on a dark, quiet street in London.

CHAPTER ONE

The man who swung himself over the edge of the roof and crouched in the shadows was stocky. He was late middle-aged, and though it couldn't have been seen in the darkness of this London night, he had a florid complexion. He might have been taken for a man too old and fat to have climbed five stories up a steel fire ladder in the narrow passageway between two buildings. When he was satisfied he was alone on the roof, he stood and spent a long moment examining the skirts of his long Burberry raincoat, making certain no grime was stuck to it—something more that suggested a man unsuited for the work he was doing.

But he knew what he was doing and how to do it. He unbuttoned the double-breasted coat. Hanging in an improvised leather holster under his left arm was the barrel of a rifle. Hanging in a similar holster under his right arm was the stock. He unbuckled the straps that held the holsters in place and dropped them to the roof. Now, when he rebuttoned his coat, he didn't seem quite so stocky, though he was still a heavy man, and he wasn't young.

With deft movements—the result of knowledge and long experience—he attached the barrel to the stock. The weapon was a Weatherby Mark V hunting rifle. He took two cartridges and pushed them into the magazine. Two was all it held; two was one more than he would need. Though the bullet was light for this kind of weapon, just five hundred grains, it would be driven out of the heavy rifle at a tremendous muzzle velocity, with phenomenal energy.

The man patted the weapon, then walked calmly to the edge of the roof and looked down on Half Moon Street. It was a little past 6:00 p.m. The November sun had long since set over the city, and no trace of its afterglow remained in the sky. It had rained a little earlier, and a light drizzle continued to fall intermittently. Traffic was heavy on Piccadilly, just to his left. It was never heavy on Half Moon Street, but a cab had just pulled up in front of the Green Park Hotel, and another was pulling away from Flemings Hotel on this side of the street.

He felt like having a cigarette, but he was unwilling to show the flare of a lighter to someone who might, by some remote chance, be glancing up just as he snapped it. As he sometimes did when he wanted a smoke and couldn't have it, he pinched a corner of his white mustache nervously and tugged at it.

Suddenly all senses were on full alert. As the man on the roof looked down on Half Moon Street, a figure came around the corner from Curzon Street, striding briskly.

The man with the Weatherby put aside his tweed hat. He would fire from a standing position, not on his knees with the rifle resting on the ledge. He fixed his target in his sights. As the man below began to cross in the middle of the block, in the open, the gunman took up the slack on the trigger and drew in his breath. Then he exhaled half of it and squeezed.

The slug literally exploded from the barrel with a bright, sharp muzzle-flash and a deafening blast. The man on the street was lifted off his feet and thrown back against a parked car. He was dead, but to be sure, the man on the roof worked the bolt and fired a second shot. It served only to make the body jump.

SIR MICHAEL LANSDOWNE strolled into Half Moon Street. A crowd had gathered, and officers of the Metropolitan Police were having difficulty keeping them back. Sir Michael had an aura of authority, a cultivated presence of command, something even of a threat. He would walk through crowds and people instinctively stood aside for him—which he did now until he had reached the open semicircle around the body lying on the pavement.

"Sir?" an officer asked respectfully.

Sir Michael pointed to a man in a black raincoat. "Chief Inspector Wilson, I believe," he said.

"Yes, sir," said the officer, and without further suggestion went to the chief inspector and told him the gentleman in the Burberry raincoat had asked for him.

Sir Michael snapped his lighter and lit a cigarette. Chief Inspector Wilson broke away from what he was doing and approached him.

"Sir Michael Lansdowne?" he asked. "Yes, of course. I recognize you. MI6, am I not correct?"

"Retired," said Sir Michael. "Here unofficially. Just walked into the street on my way for a drink in the Green Park bar, and— Well, what's this?"

"I'm afraid you probably know the gentleman, Sir Michael," said the chief inspector, nodding toward the body, which had now been covered with a rubberized sheet. "Mr. Richard Vauxhall. Also of MI6."

"My God. Dick? Hit by a car?"

"Afraid not, Sir Michael. Hit by two slugs from a high-powered rifle. Not a pretty sight, I'm afraid," he added, nodding toward the body. "Tear a man up badly, that kind of slug."

"Fired from where?" asked Sir Michael.

"Probably from that roof," said the chief inspector, pointing up. "We're trying to get into the building now."

Sir Michael stared at the rubber sheet and shook his head. "Tragic," he muttered. "Had a promising career ahead of him." He sighed. "You understand, of course, that his affiliation with MI6 must not be mentioned in anything that becomes public. Officially, you know, there is no such thing as MI6.''

"There is no such thing, Sir Michael," said Chief Inspector Wilson. "Sir George Harrington is on his way, if you'd like to speak with him."

"No. Indeed, you needn't tell him I was here, unless you want to. I have no official connection anymore. Retired."

"Very well, sir."

Sir Michael shook his head as he began to walk away.

THE MAN IN THE SHORT, quilted black coat stood looking at the Rhine, broad and placid, and half obscured by a patchy fog that swirled over its surface. He pulled his black cap down tighter on his head, jammed his hands deep in his pockets and blew an impatient breath into the fog. An hour after dawn. The old man should have been here by now.

Düsseldorf nightclubs opened only a little before midnight. Interesting things began to happen only after two in the morning. They closed at five. He had spent five hours at Die Kätzchen—the Kittens—and the Czech hadn't appeared. To maintain his cover, that is to play the role of the innocent enthralled by the charms of Die Kätzchen, he had spent 420 marks. He would have to justify it to a skeptical bureaucrat who would have a hundred questions. And apart from all that, he had no idea why the old man asked that they meet on the riverfront before eight in the morning.

Anyway, there he was, coming along the street—Dr. Johann Kleist. The old man—it was habit to call him that—walked with his back straight, his pace brisk, with a military bearing he was old enough to have learned in the bad days. He had been a witness to those days, if not a participant. He had never denied his membership in the Hitler Jugend—Hitler Youth—and many in the service wondered what ideas men his age retained from the fierce indoctrination they had received as boys.

He wore a gray overcoat with a black velvet collar, a maroon paisley silk scarf around his neck, with a black homburg, black leather gloves; and he carried an old-fashioned leather briefcase. That was why they were meeting—the old man was handing over some files he acknowledged he had carried away when he left the service. That was why this meeting was secret—because he had broken security by taking those files and was subject to a severe penalty. He'd been gone four months, and now he was returning files that no one had even noticed were missing.

He had been one of the few men who could have walked out of a service office with files in his briefcase. He had been a legend. It was said of him that he had killed with his bare hands. He had spent years in the Democratic Republic, his life in danger every hour. The Federal Republic had retired him with honor and a pension, and he lived in a protected compound outside the city, for fear that old enemies would come to take revenge on him even now.

"Guten Morgen, Herr Doktor Kleist."

The old man acknowledged the greeting only with a nod. He spoke business immediately. "You must carry this briefcase to the office immediately," he said, "and get it inside before too many people are around. Don't open it until you are in your own office. Put the contents in your safe. Later, as time allows, sort out the documents and file them appropriately."

"I will do as you say."

"Good." The old man handed over the briefcase. Then he pulled off the glove from his right hand and extended it for a handshake. "I am not sure anyone cares about these files anymore," he said. "Anyone on this side. I am certain the others care."

"Very likely."

"Well, then. Goodbye, Hohnzecker. And good luck."

"Goodbye, Herr Doktor," said Hohnzecker. He was sorry this might be his last contact with a legend.

The old man walked away.

What was in the briefcase might well be important material. On the other hand, maybe it wasn't. Their judgment, the older ones, was colored by mental habits of a lifetime. They found it difficult to adjust to a changing world. That was why they had to be retired, even though they protested they had years of service left in them.

To the office immediately, the old man had said. It was difficult to break the habit of taking orders from him. Breakfast would have to wait until the papers from the briefcase were in the safe.

People without knowledge would have guessed that the Düsseldorf office had to be a minor office of the service. That guess would have been wrong. Because of the high-tech industry centered around Düsseldorf, foreign visitors were in and out constantly; and some of them weren't what they pretended to be. Some of them were agents of foreign governments. Some were agents of private organizations with hidden operations and motives. The Düsseldorf office was, in fact, a major office. That was why the old man had been here. That was why he, Hohnzecker, was here.

The office was unmarked. From the street the structure looked like an ordinary office building, with suites rented to a variety of businesses. That was what the directory said. It was only when a visitor approached an elevator or the stairs that a security officer stopped him.

No one stopped Hohnzecker. Everyone knew him. He took the elevator to the third floor and used his key to admit himself to his department, then another key to open his office. A few people were around. The night staff would be leaving shortly. One or two of the day staff had already arrived. No one took any particular notice of the odd hour at which the department head had arrived. They were used to his unscheduled and unannounced comings and goings—as they were to his informal style of dress, this morning the downlined coat and black cap.

He sat down at his desk. A heavy locked box containing the decoded messages that had come in overnight sat in the middle. He would get to them in a minute. Right now—the briefcase. He pressed down the brass tab that unlatched it.

The explosion tore the front wall from the building. An avalanche of brick, wood and plaster fell to the street, together with furniture, telephones, typewriters and filing cabinets, which burst open and scattered papers over the rubble and pavement. The entire third floor was gutted. The roof was ruptured, and parts of it stood at crazy angles, pointing at the sky. The floor collapsed, and part of the third floor fell into the second. Fire broke out.

Fourteen people died, including three on the street. Thirty-seven were injured. Friedrich Hohnzecker had been killed instantly.

SMALL CARS WERE inconspicuous, which was what the man was determined to be. Let others be chauffeured about Paris in Citroëns; for him, a Renault was sufficient, and he sat in the front seat beside his driver, so they looked like a pair of businessmen, a couple of friends.

Guy, his driver, had just picked him up on the rue des Saussaies, as he came out from the Ministry of the Interior. He had spent an uncomfortable hour with the minister, and now he told Guy to take him to Pyramides, not the square by that name but a restaurant on rue St. Roch. Guy had anticipated this and had already turned into rue du Faubourg St. Honoré. It was his employer's habit to take his lunch at Pyramides whenever he had met with the minister. After a meeting with that disagreeable man, his employer considered himself entitled to a leisurely lunch; and after Guy had parked the car he would be privileged to join him. Unlike his employer, Guy looked forward to the twice-weekly sessions at the ministry.

He turned left at the church of St. Roch and pulled to the curb in front of the restaurant.

"Hurry, Guy. I'm hungry and may have ordered something before you join me."

Guy had pulled away from the curb and heard the roar of gunfire before he saw or suspected anything. By the time he could stop and turn to look, his employer was dead. What was more, it was impossible to see which of the dozen people on the street in front of the restaurant had killed him. From the sound, probably more than one had fired. Automatic weapons, maybe mini-Uzis that could be carried unseen under a topcoat, pulled out and fired, and hidden again before witnesses realized what had happened.

Guy pulled his own Ingram submachine gun from under the seat, but he knew it was a futile gesture. More people came running up. Some were walking away. By the time police arrived and could begin to question and search anyone, a crowd of a hundred would be milling about. He pushed the Ingram back under the seat and drove away. He would report to headquarters. It was just as well he not be questioned by ordinary police.

The dead man was Claude Crillon, second-in-command of GIGN, Groupe d'Intervention de la Gendarmerie Nationale.

GALEAZZO BASTIANINI was killed, together with his mistress, in the flat he leased for her in Via della Croce in Rome. He opened the door and admitted his killer, who shot him with a Beretta pistol, then shot the mistress. Bastianini was an officer of SISDE, Servizio Informazioni Sicurezza Democratico.

Colonel Adolfo Martinez, of Centro Superior de Información de la Defensa, died in the crash of a small plane. His pilot, who had been flying him from Madrid to Barcelona, took his usual sip of tea from the thermos he always carried in the cockpit. He never drank tea, someone had observed of him, until on his initial approach to the airport at his destination—lest the urge to go to the bathroom overtake him too soon. This sip of tea was his last. It was laced with cyanide, and he died instantly.

Rijnhard van Reujen of the Dutch counterintelligence bureau died on the highway between Schiphol International Airport and downtown Amsterdam. Shots were fired into his car from the cab of a truck.

ALL OF THESE MURDERS occurred within the space of fifteen days. During the same fifteen days a bomb exploded in a passenger waiting hall in the airport at Hamburg, and eight people died, forty-two were injured; another bomb exploded on the Via Veneto in Rome, killing two, injuring five; and one exploded on a cross-Channel ferry between Calais and Dover, with no deaths and only one injury, because the bomb, set deep in the hold, had been meant to sink the vessel but wasn't powerful enough.

Terrorism had subsided a little over the past couple of years, partly because governments had learned more about how to counter it, partly because it had proved ineffective for achieving the terrorists' purposes. Now, the world's press moaned, it was back. People went about the streets of major cities with a little less confidence. International travel declined perceptibly. A general malaise and nervous tension settled over Western Europe.

CHAPTER TWO

Hal Brognola stood at the window of his Justice Department office, looking out at the snow swirling in a vicious wind: the kind of day Washington too often imposed on the people who had to come there. "It's no wonder," he said, "that the British diplomatic service traditionally allowed hardship pay to people assigned to Washington."

Mack Bolan sat in a leather-covered armchair, facing Brognola's desk, patiently waiting for the big Fed to finish the obligatory words of greeting, with comment on the weather, that usually preceded some kind of bad news.

Bolan had flown in from San Diego, responding to Brognola's word that something urgent was coming down—a drop-everything sort of urgency—and asked Bolan to fly to Washington on the first available flight. So he had come. He had come and had endured the usual Washington routine of a confidential visit to the Justice Department, where officially no one knew he was in town.

If not for the risk Hal himself took in bringing him to this office, Bolan wouldn't have come. On the other hand, he respected the big Fed; Hal Brognola was one of the few men he entirely trusted—a trust that was reciprocated, that both of them had learned from long and hard experience.

"Look, I appreciate it, Striker," Hal said. "I know what you're doing in California. I—" He flipped open a file folder. "I have a report here from the DEA. Coke importation across the Mexico-California border is down forty-two percent in the past two months, they say. Though how they know that, I'm not sure."

"They don't," said Bolan bluntly.

"Yeah. Anyway, they say it's down, and they take credit for it. I have my own idea where the credit should go."

Bolan shrugged. "It's history. What have you got?"

Brognola walked to the window. "Look, Striker...I'd like you to watch a videotape. It's of a meeting I attended last week, in London. It's something so important that even what you've been doing in California is small by comparison."

Bolan shrugged. "I don't get to watch much TV," he said.

Brognola closed the venetian blinds to lower the light level in the room, then switched on a television set and VCR. "I'll explain as we go along," he said. "In particular, I'll identify the people for you."

The picture that came up on the screen was in color, at first a picture of an empty conference room. Bolan noticed that the TV set and VCR were European; the scan standard was finer, and the picture had more detail and sharpness than one saw on an American set.

Abruptly the chairs around the table were filled. Whoever had been running the camera had stopped it as the men came in, then started it again when they were all seated. There was Brognola, sitting at one side of the table, by far the biggest man in the room. The other three were all talking at once. No one had yet assumed control of the discussion.

Brognola stopped the tape, leaving a still picture on the screen. "All right. The small man with the yellowish-white mustache is Sir George Harrington. British military intelligence—MI6. When you meet him, you'll see he walks with a limp. Took a piece of shrapnel in the hip in Belgium in 1944. He's just short of mandatory retirement, but at the moment he's firmly in control of MI6. A resourceful, imaginative man."

"I've heard of him," said Bolan dryly.

"He's very sharp, Striker. He made his beginning at MI6 as a cryptanalyst. He's a mathematician by education."

"Plays by the rules, as I hear it," said Bolan.

"Maybe," said Brognola. "Anyway, the tall thin man with the cigarette is Henri Leclerc. The French like to be mysterious about their intel agencies, but Leclerc is attached to GIGN, which is their crack antiterrorist outfit."

"The one that kills people," said Bolan.

"Unofficially," said Brognola, nodding. "That's a big issue in France. The socialists have tried repeatedly to abolish GIGN—which has existed under several other names—and haven't quite succeeded. Leclerc is a rather direct man. He operates a little like you."

Bolan studied the face on the screen. Leclerc looked a bit like a young Charles de Gaulle.

"The fourth man," said Brognola, "is the German."

"That's Reinhard Kremer," said Bolan.

"You got it," said Brognola. "Bundesnachrichtendienst. He's the youngest man in the meeting. He's given credit for destroying two of the most vicious terrorist gangs that were operating in Germany a few years ago. He's supposed to be cold and ruthless."

"I've met him," said Bolan. "Cold is the word."

So good was the television picture that Bolan could see that Kremer had aged a little. Still, his face was smooth, and his frosty blue eyes, squinting narrowly, still flaunted his austere cynicism as though it were the badge of his profession. Bolan himself had eliminated the core of the Brauner Gang, in the course of rescuing Linda Nordholm; and when he had tried to pursue a few of its lesser members—the kidnappers themselves, actually—he had found nothing but their blood. Kremer had found them first.

"Okay," said Brognola. "Let's listen to the meeting."

"Gentlemen—" This was Sir George Harrington. "Let's get down to business if we may. Let me summarize briefly what you already know. Within the past six weeks each of us has lost a valued colleague. Our colleagues have been murdered in highly public ways, with the result that the whole world knows. Other nations have also lost valuable men. Besides, terrorism is on the rise. That we are not faced with a set of coincidences is, I think, persuasively evident. It seems obvious, to me at least, that these assassinations and terrorist acts have a common purpose, a common author."

"What purpose?" asked Leclerc without taking the cigarette from his mouth.

"A purpose already achieved in part, I would suggest," said Sir George. "Destabilization."

"An easy word," muttered Leclerc. "We bandy it about a great deal."

Leclerc spoke fluent, if accented, English. As Bolan remembered, Kremer didn't; his English was heavily accented and slow. It was odd, in fact, that he had been sent to this meeting. But finally he spoke.

"My government is threatened," he said. "We may have to call elections."

"What's distressing to me," said Brognola, leaning his elbows on the conference table, "is that high-ranking officers of the most capable and respected Western intelligence and counterterrorist agencies have been murdered, and those same agencies—whose business it is to counter this kind of thing—can't identify any of the murderers."

"You are not, I suppose," said Sir George loftily, "suggesting we are not trying hard enough."

"Of course not," said Brognola.

"We are analyzing," said Kremer. "All these murders are having similar features. In our case, in Düsseldorf, our operative Hohnzecker is carrying the bomb into the office himself, in a briefcase, we think. If he is not wishing to commit suicide spectacularly, why is he doing this? Who is he trusting so much he receives a bomb from that man's hands and is carrying it into our office? And in Italy Bastianini is unlocking and opening the door. It is not broken. Why is he opening the door to the man who is there for shooting him? Someone he is trusting, no? Colonel Martinez in Spain—the same. Someone is knowing everything of the habits of the pilot of the colonel's airplane, to the least detail."

"A good point, Reinhard," said Sir George. "Our Dick Vauxhall was murdered by someone who knew his daily habits very intimately."

"The same with Crillon," said Leclerc.

"What American police call a common MO," said Brognola.

"Now," said Kremer. He was warming to his subject; that came through vividly on the television screen. "No more. Just these. Someone is wishing to kill just these men—Vauxhall, Crillon, Hohnzecker and the others, just them. What characteristic are they having in common?"

"A rhetorical question?" asked Sir George. "Or do you have an answer?"

"If I am having an answer," said Kremer, "I am having my man in custody."

"I am reluctant to mention what these coincidences suggest," said Brognola. "I'm afraid they suggest your victims may have been murdered by colleagues."

"Traitors in our agencies?" asked Sir George indignantly. "Frankly, you Americans are always ready to jump to that conclusion."

"I don't jump to it, Sir George," said Brognola. "I do ask you to consider the possibility."

"It has happened," said Leclerc. "You have had defectors, notorious ones, Sir George."

"So have we," said Kremer.

"Are we to believe," asked Sir George, "that six European intelligence agencies have traitors in them, who would murder their colleagues? If that is true, perhaps we should dismantle our entire apparatus. It would appear we are all hopelessly compromised."

Brognola stopped the tape. "You can see the problem," he said to Bolan. "Six agencies—British, French, German, Italian, Spanish, Dutch. If—"

Bolan shook his head. "Kremer made an important point. Six intel agents. All high-ranking. They must have had something in common. And whatever that something in common was, it was important enough to somebody *inside or outside* their agencies to get them killed. But it could have been somebody outside. What those six guys had in common was that they made the same mistake—they formed habits. If somebody wants to kill a man—wants to badly enough—that somebody can tail him for a while and learn his habits. A lot of hits have been set up that way."

"Bastianini?"

"The guy outside the door could have said he was delivering a telegram. Or flowers. He could have said a hundred things."

Hal Brognola nodded, then smiled. "Yeah. I wish I'd had you with me in London."

"London is one of the places where I'm not very welcome," said Bolan.

"Maybe," said Brognola. "Let's listen to some more of the tape."

"Extraordinary situations," said Brognola on the screen, "call for extraordinary measures."

Sir George Harrington smiled broadly. "Extraordinary situations," he said, "sometimes call out very ordinary clichés."

Brognola laughed, but only briefly. "One of your problems is that everyone who might participate in your investigation is almost certainly known to the people you're trying to identify. What you need is an outsider."

"I suppose you mean an American," said Sir George.

"I have one in mind," said Brognola.

"Let me hope you are not having in mind Bolan," said Kremer.

"As a matter of fact, that's just who I do have in mind," said Brognola.

"Bolan?" asked Sir George.

"The man the Americans call the Executioner," said Kremer. "An outlaw."

"Surely—" said Sir George.

"The most effective man we could send," said Brognola. "You know him, don't you, Reinhard?"

The German nodded. "When the Brauner Gang are kidnapping the daughter of the NATO air commander, this man is rescuing her. Of this gang, he has identified the leaders, and he is killing one of them every four hours. Not a word to them. He just is killing one, every four hours. They release her." He shrugged. "We have been knowing where she is, but we have been afraid of moving in, for fear they are killing her. When she is with us, we move in. They are shooting. We are shooting." He shrugged. "No more, the Brauner Gang."

"You mean, he just killed people he suspected were the leaders of the gang?" asked Sir George.

"Not suspecting," said Kremer firmly. "*Knowing.* Very bad people. Narcotics. Prostitution. Politics."

"Not an unusual combination," remarked Leclerc.

"But how did he *know* how to find these people, who to kill?" asked Sir George.

"We could have been knowing," said Kremer, "if we had been as free as this man is. Free, I mean, to use our judgment, to pursue animals like the Brauner Gang in ways we know but are forbidden to use. He operates outside . . . outside—"

"Outside the law, you mean?" asked Sir George?

Brognola smiled. "Let's say parallel with it," he suggested. "He is always on the *side* of the law. He doesn't always operate within it."

"With which of your agencies is he associated?" asked Sir George.

"With none," said Brognola. "He is independent."

"Then who controls him?" asked Sir George.

"No one," said Brognola. Then he shook his head and amended his statement. "Actually, he controls himself. You shouldn't think of him as a man out of control. Reinhard called him an outlaw just now. He's not really. He's not a renegade. He did work for us once. He believes he's more effective working independently. And he's right. Experience has proved him right."

"Affords you what you Americans call deniability, eh?" suggested Sir George. "You can always deny you ever heard of him."

"As you can," said Brognola.

"So you are offering us this man's services?" Leclerc asked.

"If he will accept the assignment, yes."

Sir George Harrington rubbed his hands together. "Makes a problem for us, you know."

"Not for you, Sir George," said Brognola. "I met with the prime minister this morning. I brought a message from the President. The prime minister will telephone you, perhaps yet today. You'll be authorized to use Bolan's services, or you won't—depending on the prime minister's decision. Similarly the other governments represented here will receive a personal offer from the President. That the President has intervened personally tells you how important he thinks this is."

Brognola switched off the VCR and television set. "The prime minister," he said to Bolan, "authorized Sir George to accept the President's offer. I went on to Paris and Bonn. The French and German governments have also accepted."

"The President offered, they accepted," said Bolan dryly. "What option does that leave me?"

"The same option you always have," said Brognola. "But I think you foreclosed on your option years ago."

"Yeah," said Bolan. "So... you think this deal is more important than the cocaine coming in through—"

"I do," said Brognola firmly. "I think it's possible this is the most important assignment you've ever been asked to take. I don't know what's going down, but I have a feeling, just a gut feeling, that it's something big."

"I like your gut feelings," said Bolan.

"We've made some arrangements," said Brognola. "The British did impose a condition or two. The first, or course, is that officially they refused to accept you and have never heard of you. Then they turn that around and say an agent of theirs will contact you within an hour after you arrive in

London. You can pretty much do what you see fit, but you're to keep this man informed. They'll offer cooperation and assistance as you require it, but it'll be through this contact."

"A fatal flaw in the arrangements," said Bolan.

"We're going to have to work cooperatively on this one, Striker," said Brognola grimly. "I accepted the conditions because this deal is too important to—"

"Understood," Bolan interjected. "What else?"

"The British are providing you with an identity," said Brognola. "British passport, and—" he hesitated "—British equipment. That is, British-supplied equipment. I'm sorry, but I couldn't get them to let you bring in your own stuff, your own weapons. They promise that what they supply you will be the very best, but they don't want any new weapons, especially your type, coming into the country. Besides, they've put new checks on all ports of entry, and to let you through Heathrow with luggage that would go unchecked would signal too many people that a special guy was entering the country. As it is right now, the only people who know you're coming are the prime minister, Sir George Harrington and the man who'll contact you."

"Three too many," said Bolan.

Brognola shook his head. "This one's too big, involves too complex an operation, to be worked one hundred percent alone. We have to trust some people on this one, Striker."

Bolan counted off on his fingers. "The prime minister, Sir George, the contact man, Kremer and Leclerc. That's five already."

"Six," said Brognola. "You didn't count me."

Bolan smiled. "I never count you."

"Seven," said Brognola. "You didn't count the President."

"Eight," said Bolan. "I didn't count his wife."

CHAPTER THREE

By 9:00 p.m. Bolan was on an overnight flight to Heathrow. By eight in the morning—only three in the morning in Washington—the 747 was on its final approach to landing.

His passport said he was Ernest Bradley. He was wearing English clothes from the skin out, carrying English money, and in a crocodile-leather briefcase under his seat he carried a sheaf of letters, memoranda and reports that were supposed to identify him with a manufacturing firm in Manchester whose overseas salesman he was supposed to be. Overnight he had read all this stuff. On the shuttle from Washington to New York he had been briefed on his identity. He'd been told where he lived in Manchester, what kind of neighborhood he lived in, what family he had—no wife, no children, but a brother who worked for the same company—what schools he had attended, how he had come to work for British Cybernetics, Ltd., and when, and what the company made and where it sold it.

Nine. The bright young English diplomat who had accompanied him to New York and given him this briefing made nine people who knew his mission.

"Brad . . ."

She was awake. She had been an impediment to his study of the files in his briefcase—a young woman who would have been more than welcome to impede any other man in any other circumstances. Her name was Marilyn Henry. From the moment he'd sat down in his aisle seat in first class, she had turned her attention away from what she could see out the window and to what she saw sitting beside her. Within ten minutes she'd told him to call her Marilyn and asked if she could call him Ernest. He'd told her to call him Brad; he'd given her no explanation.

She had ordered champagne and told the steward to bring two glasses. He couldn't refuse it without being rude, or without also inspiring reason for suspicion in anyone who noticed him being rude to Marilyn Henry.

Her smooth blond hair hung to her shoulders. Her lips were full and colored with some sort of pink lipstick that caught the light and glistened. Her yellow sweater, under her dark gray jacket, was tight, stretched over her abundant figure like a body stocking. Her short dark gray skirt was tight, and in the seat it crept up and showed him a fascinating pair of legs.

She had talked, not senseless chatter but quiet conversation, about the flight, about her visit to America. She worked for an English publishing company and had been doing some business in New York.

Bolan wasn't unaware of the fact that women found him not just attractive but intriguing. Though they couldn't have guessed who he was and what he did, they were drawn to him at first by his hawkish good looks, a man exceptionally well put together and carrying no excess flesh. His face, of course, interested them: the strong, regular features, the powerful jaw and resolute chin, the blue eyes in which a perceptive woman would see sadness and gentleness but also anger and the faintest suggestion of menace. That perceptive woman might detect also the subtle marks that said his handsome face had been broken and put back together by surgeons. But Bolan bore his scars like a professional athlete, or the professional soldier that he was. They made him no less handsome. They added character to a face already handsome.

She had asked him where he would be staying in London. He had told her: the Green Park Hotel on Half Moon

Street. She had said they should get together for a drink while they were both in London. He had said he'd be glad to, if it was possible.

She'd drunk wine with her dinner and brandy after. He'd accepted the same but had drunk less than half of the brandy. When she'd gone to sleep, he'd opened the brief-case and begun to review the papers. Shortly her head was on his shoulder, and it was difficult to study business documents.

Now she was awake.

"Rainy," she said, looking down on the flat green land of southern England.

He looked past her at light gray, low-hanging clouds and glimpses of gray-green fields and shiny black highways. There was a certain tidiness about England, that you could see from the air. He had always identified tidiness as an English characteristic. He wondered if he would encounter that in Sir George Harrington or the operative from MI6.

"Here is my card," she said, handing him a white rectangle that said: Senior Editor, Heath & Blackstone, Publishers, St. Martins Lane, London. "In case you'd like to ring me up."

"I'll try to, Marilyn," he said. "I mean that sincerely. I'm afraid I may...well, I may be sent off on another sales tour very shortly. Confidentially, the company isn't doing as well as we'd like."

"Well..." She smiled weakly. "I'll know where to find you. The Green Park."

"I'd really like to see you, Marilyn," he said. He didn't want to put her off, certainly not to make her feel foolish for the friendship she had extended him, whatever dimensions the offer had. "I'll call you if I can."

The plane landed. They walked together through the airport, he helped her with her luggage, and as they separated in the main concourse of the airport, she kissed him on the cheek and said she was happy she had met him.

A moment later a young man walked up to him. "Mr. Bradley?"

Bolan was surprised, but he nodded. "Yes."

"I'm Tom Forbes," the young man said. "MI6. I've our car and driver outside. Can I carry one of those for you?"

"Thanks, but they balance," said Bolan.

He was prepared to dislike Forbes from the moment he saw him. It was something irrational: the fact that the young man had long girlish eyelashes. More than that, though; his handclasp was flaccid, and the cut of his clothes was somehow just a little too stylish. Such judgments had to be put away if men from different nations and backgrounds were to work together. Bolan decided to reserve judgment.

He was conscious that the suitcase he'd been handed at JFK weighed very little. He had been promised that the businessman's outfits in the suitcase would be supplemented with a combat blacksuit, and boots suitable for the kind of work he might have to do.

"We'll get you to your hotel first," said Forbes. "Green Park, is it?"

"So I'm told."

"You're going to need a showerproof."

"Pardon?"

"A raincoat."

"Maybe there's one in my bag."

The car was a Humber, a big, black, boxy vehicle, not quite a limousine, but still a big car, particularly for English streets. The uniformed driver pulled the big car out into the stream of traffic leaving the terminal.

A light rain was falling. Heavy traffic was moving east toward the city. It was, in fact, the morning rush hour. They weren't a mile from the airport when they were in a slow-moving stream of traffic that extended ahead of them as far as they could see.

"Bit of a jam, I'm afraid," said Forbes. "Well, anyway, have you developed any ideas about our little problem?"

Bolan shook his head. "Not yet." He thought the question odd. "I'm here to learn."

"And to teach, I understand," said Forbes. "We're to learn something of your methods."

"I've got no methods," said Bolan. "All I do is what I have to do, when I have to do it."

Forbes smiled. "Your reputation precedes you, Mr. Bolan," he said. "You're a great deal more sophisticated than that."

Ten. If Forbes called him Bolan in the presence of the driver, then someone else was in on the secret. Either that or Forbes was a careless fool.

His thought may have communicated itself to Forbes, even if he hadn't put it in words. Maybe Forbes read his silence. He fell silent himself and stared gloomily at the rain, which was falling harder.

Traffic seemed lighter in the right lanes—in England these were the center lanes—but the driver clung to the left. In a moment Bolan saw why. The driver pulled off the divided highway and onto a narrower road. This one led north.

"A shorter way?" Bolan asked.

"Yes," said Forbes. "Yes, he's quite good. He knows his way."

Sure he does, Bolan thought wryly. If this driver knows a better way to Half Moon Street, then why don't a thousand other drivers know it, too? Bolan leaned back and pretended to relax, but he had been alerted. Something was screwy here.

He glanced casually at Forbes. He was carrying a pistol in his armpit. But why? And on his home turf?

The word last night at Kennedy had been that someone from MI6 would contact him at the Green Park Hotel. Not at Heathrow. They weren't heading into London. They were leaving the city.

Bolan extended an arm past Forbes, as if he were pointing at a stone church. "Isn't that . . . ?" he began. And he drove his left fist into Forbes's ribs, while with his right hand he reached inside his jacket and grabbed his pistol, a Walther PPK.

The driver was armed, too. He pulled a heavy military revolver from under the seat, then hit the brakes as he turned to fire at Bolan. The Warrior fired the PPK through the back of the seat. The slug punched through, and the driver screamed and doubled over.

Forbes grunted and grabbed at the pistol in Bolan's hands, but the Executioner jerked it away and slugged him across the cheek with it. Forbes fell back against the door as the Humber ran off the road and came to a stop against a grassy slope.

Bolan pushed the driver away from the wheel, then climbed over the backrest. He sat in the driver's seat and backed the car off the slope, waving cordially to cars going past. Nothing was wrong. A momentary loss of control. He drove into a paved parking space in front of a pub.

"All right, pal," he said to Forbes. "Let's see your MI6 identification."

Forbes, whose cracked-open cheek was bleeding profusely, shook his head.

"Thought so. Okay. Come around here. You're going to drive."

"Can't."

"You're going to," said Bolan. "Your driver friend isn't going to, for sure. And I'm not used to driving on the left. So get around here. *Now!*"

Forbes lurched out of the rear and staggered around the car. Bolan grabbed the driver by his clothes and hoisted him over the back of the seat and onto the floor behind. Then he took his pistol, which had fallen to the floor, and shoved it under his belt.

"All right. Drive, Forbes, or whatever your name is. *Drive.*"

"Where?"

"Into town somewhere. Where I can get a cab."

"You're going to kill me," said Forbes as he settled himself behind the wheel.

Bolan turned down the corners of his mouth and shook his head. "No way. No reason. So drive."

"Where . . . ?"

"Make it Hammersmith."

It took the effeminate young man half an hour to return to the main road between the airport and the city. Bolan didn't know the town well, but when they reached Hammersmith he nudged Forbes and pointed to a northbound street. Forbes pulled the Humber to the curb where Bolan indicated—a quiet street of homes and small shops.

"Out. Open the boot."

When the trunk was open, Bolan reached for his luggage. He opened the suitcase and put the driver's Webley revolver inside. Then he put Forbes's Walther in the crocodile leather briefcase.

"In," he said, pointing to the empty trunk of the Humber. "Give me the keys."

Forbes climbed in. Bolan closed the lid and checked to make sure it was locked. Confident, he tossed the keys as far as he could into the middle of a playground between two apartment buildings.

Picking up his luggage, he walked back toward the Hammersmith Flyover and Talgarth Road. A taxi came along. He hailed it and asked to be taken to the West London Air

Terminal—a bus station where buses from Heathrow discharged passengers who then took cabs and subway trains to their eventual destinations. There he caught another taxi and told the driver to take him to the Green Park Hotel.

IN THE HOTEL ROOM he examined what MI6 had provided in his luggage. The kit was rather complete, for a civilian businessman—a blue suit, a tweed jacket, wool slacks, white shirts, a Scottish wool sweater, socks and underwear and an extra pair of shoes, plus toiletries. A raincoat was neatly folded in the suitcase, too—with a crumpled Irish tweed hat. The only thing wrong with the disguise they afforded was that everything was new, which any alert security officer would have noticed if the luggage had been searched. So MI6 was smart but not too smart. Or maybe—more likely—they knew he would go through Heathrow without a search and anything after that was beyond their concern.

Now, at least, he had two pistols. The Walther was a 7.65 mm German automatic, developed in the 1930s to be carried concealed by police officers. The Webley was a .38-caliber British military revolver, too bulky to be carried unnoticed under a man's suit jacket, but a reliable, heavy weapon he was pleased to have. Of course he only had the ammunition in the Walther's clip—save the one shot he had fired—and in the Webley's chambers.

He laid the Webley on the toilet seat by the tub while he took a bath. Not a shower, a tub bath—a man could be surprised in a shower; the water made too much noise. After he had bathed and shaved, he stretched out on the bed naked to wait for the call from the real MI6 operative who was to contact him.

He slept, but not soundly; he remained alert. Still, he slept enough to restore his sharpness for the expedition into the streets he would have to make soon, whether MI6 called or not.

He checked his money. MI6—or maybe it had been Hal—hadn't been ungenerous with cash. He had eight hundred pounds—more than thirteen hundred dollars—in fifty-pound notes. On the other hand, he had noticed the rate for the hotel was seventy pounds a night. London wasn't a cheap city. Eight hundred pounds was ample for a week. After that he would have to think about where to get his next eight hundred.

He called room service and had a meal brought up. Given a choice, he would have rather gone out, but he needed to be where his contact could reach him.

Seven o'clock. Eight. No contact. Nine o'clock. He wondered if the contact could be waiting on the street, for some reason unwilling to enter the hotel and expecting him to come out. At ten, he decided, he would go out, whether the contact had called or not. He didn't like to spend a night in a hotel room without knowing all the ways in and out, so he would make a quick recon of the neighborhood.

More than once he had jolted a triggerman by knowing more about the streets, alleys and rooftops than anyone imagined he could know. The recon was instinct with him; he did it everywhere he went. And he saw things other men didn't see. Long experience had whetted his powers of observation.

He put on the tweed jacket, the sweater and a pair of dark slacks, plus the raincoat. The Walther fit nicely into the deep right pocket of the raincoat, out of sight yet handy. Because it was raining he jammed the Irish tweed hat down on his head and was amused at his image in the mirror. It was all right. He looked English. At least he didn't look terribly American.

He went down by the stairs, not what the English call the lift, to have a look at the ways people could get in and out of the Green Park Hotel. It was a small hotel, with maybe a hundred rooms, five floors. As he expected, there were service doors onto the street, not intended to be used by guests. Also there were windows from which a man could drop to a ground-floor rooftop and then drop into a passageway behind the hotel. He came out into the lobby and handed his key to the desk clerk.

The desk clerk was a girl. "Rainy night, sir," she said.

He nodded, and went out through the revolving door into a cool, drizzly night. Instinctively he moved away from the hotel door, out of the light. He paused on the wet sidewalk beyond the light and looked up and down the street. This was Half Moon Street, only one block long. At the end of the block to his right was Piccadilly, one of the main thoroughfares of the city. To his left, Half Moon Street came to an end in a street whose name he didn't know, another quiet, dimly lit neighborhood street. He knew Piccadilly from past experiences in London, and he decided to walk there and look around. If he remembered right, there was an underground station not far away, and the London underground would be a quick, handy way of transportation.

He checked the cars parked on the street. Someone was sitting in one on the opposite side and a few yards north. That alerted him. It might be nothing, but why would someone be sitting in a car on this quiet street at this hour? Maybe it was his contact. Well...if the man in the car wanted to make a move, let him make it quick. Bolan strode decisively toward Piccadilly.

He remained alert to the man in the car, the more so when he heard the door open and close. He glanced around. The man crossed the street and walked into the light at the hotel door.

It wasn't a man. It was—

"*Bolan!* Get down! Get down!"

It was a woman, and she was running toward him, shrieking at him. Get down, she'd said. He crouched.

Just in time. He heard the sharp crack of a heavy-caliber rifle, and a bullet smacked through the glass of the parked car beside him, spraying shards across the sidewalk. The woman fell to her hands and knees. Another crack. The car rocked on its springs from the impact.

Bolan had the Walther in his hand, but the shots had come from a roof on the other side of the street. He couldn't see the gunman. Likely he wouldn't be able to hit him even if he could see him.

The woman gestured to him to crawl toward her, keeping behind the cars parked along the curb. He duck-walked. She remained on her hands and knees, but she had a pistol in one hand. She was studying the rooftops, and she looked as if she might try a shot, if only to scare the rifleman. But she shook her head, as if to say the rifleman was probably gone. Getting to her feet, she continued to scan the tops of the buildings, all the while holding her pistol at the ready. "He's gone," she finally said, pulling off the plastic scarf that protected her head from the rain. Her smooth blond hair fell to her shoulders.

"Marilyn!"

She smiled. "MI6," she said. "Welcome to London."

CHAPTER FOUR

Marilyn Henry, which was her real name, lived in a small but expensive-looking flat in a Georgian building overlooking Lincoln's Inn Fields. On the ground floor was a real estate agent's office, the first floor was occupied by the office of a firm of lawyers, and the second floor, what an American would have called the third floor, had two apartments: Marilyn's and another.

She had insisted he come here. "Things I'm supposed to give you are in my flat," she had told him.

That proved true. She had a pistol for him, with a cleverly designed harness and quickdraw holster. He realized as he strapped the fine leather around him that his clothes had been tailored to hide the pistol. It would take a smart operative to detect the gun.

The pistol was a Lahti, a 9 mm parabellum automatic of Finnish manufacture. It looked like a Luger.

"But it isn't," Marilyn explained. "When the Finns fought the Russians in 1940, they needed a military automatic that wouldn't fail in arctic cold. I know it's not what you're used to, but it's what MI6 thinks you should have—a highly reliable, accurate 9 mm automatic. I've got four extra magazines for you, all loaded, plus another hundred rounds in boxes. MI6 would be most pleased if you could return the weapon with no rounds fired."

"I've already fired a round today," he said.

"Yes, and I'd like the popgun," she said. "The driver died this afternoon, even though it was only a 7.65 slug that went through his lung. He didn't get medical attention soon enough."

"You know about that?" Bolan asked.

"One man got away—"

"He got away?"

"He got away before the police arrived. Pushed the rear seat forward and crawled through from the boot. He wasn't interested in calling for help for the chauffeur, either, and the man bled to death."

"Who were they?"

She shook her head. "Rented car. The dead man was a two-bit London hoodlum. The man who got away..." She shrugged. "His fingerprints were on the wheel. MI6 was advised by Scotland Yard that a man identified by them as Dieter Schellenberg, an agent of the German Democratic Republic, was the other man in the car—the one who got away. And the third man..." She smiled.

"How do you connect it to me?"

"I didn't until you pulled the Walther on Half Moon Street—and just now told me you fired a round today. Then it made sense. Schellenberg met you at Heathrow. He was taking you...somewhere in the Humber. He underestimated his man." She smiled again. "As many people do, I suspect, until they get to know you."

Bolan went to his raincoat, which he'd laid aside when they entered her apartment, pulled the Walther from the pocket and handed it over. "The mission is compromised, in any case," he said. "Schellenberg met me at Heathrow. He knew who I was. So did the hoodlum, the driver. And tonight...the shots from the roof. Is there anyone in England who doesn't know I'm here? Was my arrival announced on the BBC evening news?"

"Whoever is running Schellenberg knows you're here," she said. "I would suppose that same whoever is also responsible for putting the sniper on the roof. In fact, it may have been Schellenberg.''

''That was a very timely warning you gave me,'' said Bolan

''I was extremely conscious of that roof,'' she said. ''It's very likely the same roof from which the shots were fired that killed Richard Vauxhall. Seeing you walking along where Dick was walking when he was shot, I . . . well, I suppose unconsciously my eyes were drawn up to the rooftops.''

Marilyn had been in and out of her kitchen while this conversation was going on, putting glasses and a bucket of ice on a tray and bringing them to the small marble-topped table that sat between her love seat and her tiny fireplace.

''Know how to light a few coals?'' she asked.

''Uh, I suppose.''

''Please, then. A bit of wadded newspaper, a few sticks of kindling, some coal from the bucket. While I pour us a drink.''

Bolan tried to avoid liquor while he was working. He didn't like ingesting anything that might make him less alert or interfere with cool, logical thought. On the other hand . . . he'd had nothing since the drinks with Marilyn on the airplane last night. He had a strong suspicion he wasn't going back to the Green Park Hotel tonight.

''I'm sorry about last night,'' she said. ''Sir George Harrington's idea. They sent me to New York. I spent the night before last in an airport hotel. They'd set up seat assignments so I'd be next to you. All that was arranged. Then I was to use my charms to get close to you.''

Bolan squatted before the marble fireplace, building the fire as she'd told him. ''You're good,'' he said. ''I didn't suspect.''

''I'm glad to know the famous Executioner isn't infallible,'' she said. ''You'd be less of a man if you were.''

He looked up from the little stack of paper, wood and coal he had arranged in the fireplace. "I've never been interested in proving how much of a man I am," he said. "I don't need to."

"People you cared about—" she started to say.

"Are dead," he finished.

"And wouldn't be if—"

"If other people had done their duty," he said coldly.

"So you do yours."

He nodded curtly. "I do mine."

He struck a wooden match from a box he had found on the hearth. The flame caught in the paper and ignited the little sticks of kindling. He pushed the screen back across the fireplace.

The Scotch she had poured was smoky and heavy, a satisfying taste. He sipped, then took a swallow.

"Mack..." She paused, obviously reconsidering what she had been about to say. "Uh, Dick Vauxhall was a fine man. He wasn't killed because of anything wrong with him. He was assassinated. It was political, something to do with who he was and what he did."

"Did you know him?" Bolan asked. "I mean, personally."

"Yes. Not very well. But I did know him."

"Tell me about him."

She shrugged, then reached for the bottle and refreshed her drink. "Well," she said with a sigh. "He was one of the younger men in the office. I mean, he was young among the higher ratings. Rumor was that Dick Vauxhall would have become chief, sooner or later. He was an able man. What is perhaps more to the point, he was well connected."

"Politically, you mean?"

"Ah, yes, but it was a matter also of family connection, school connection—you know, the sort of thing that counts for a great deal in England."

Bolan smiled, showing a little bitterness. "Or anywhere else," he said.

"That's the kind of man he was," Marilyn said. "Every day he left the office about the same time, walked to Shepherd Market, spent twenty or thirty minutes with a prostitute, then went to a pub for a beer, and finally walked through Half Moon Street on his way to the Green Park tube station. Someone knew his habits."

"And no one knew mine," said Bolan, "and still somebody was waiting on a roof for me. It's not quite the same thing, is it?"

"Schellenberg knew what flight you were coming in on. He knew—"

"He knew what hotel I was staying at," said Bolan.

"The problem could have originated with the German or the Frenchman, with BND or GIGN. But they didn't know what hotel we'd put you in."

"The leak's in MI6," said Bolan.

"YOU ARE ABSOLUTELY CORRECT, Mr. Bolan," said Sir George Harrington. "Your mission has been compromised. I shouldn't be surprised if you elect to terminate it right now."

Bolan shook his head. "I don't scare that easily."

"Mr. Brognola told me that," said Sir George.

The two of them sat alone in a windowless conference room in a building on South Audley Street. It was a secure room, the MI6 man had explained. They could talk there in complete confidence and not be overheard.

"Tell me about Marilyn Henry," said Bolan.

"Well, to begin with, I trust you'll forgive me for imposing her on you in such a dishonest way. It was her idea that she have a good look at you before identifying herself as your contact. I had to agree. She formed a very favorable impression of you. I hope you formed an equally good one of her. She is a very capable young woman.''

"Background?''

"Londoner, born and bred. She attended a good boarding school for girls, then London School of Economics. She took her civil service examinations some six years ago and applied for work with the Foreign Office. She was recruited for MI5—domestic intelligence, you understand. Two years ago we stole her from MI5. She had been studying German in a night school, we learned, and had developed into quite an effective linguist. Well, that, of course, puts her in our jurisdiction, foreign intelligence. We sent her to Germany. She was most effective on the job we gave her there. I believe I should not reveal the details. She became available for reassignment lately. She is a perfect contact for you, Mr. Bolan. You are going to need her.''

"I work alone.''

"Do you indeed? If you'd been working alone last night, you'd be dead.''

"Maybe.''

"Think again, Mr. Bolan. You are working in a country you don't know very well, in circumstances where your identity must be kept a complete secret and you can't win cooperation on your own. Mr. Brognola talked to me for a long time about you, about your history and your methods. He made me an admirer of yours, almost as strong a one as he is himself. I am glad to have you here to help us. But let us help you, too.''

It was time to concede the point—keeping his reservations. Bolan nodded. "Okay.''

"Mr. Bolan . . . Let us use the name Bradley. We may as well form the habit. I—''

There was a knock on the door. Sir George rose and went to it. The room was locked from inside, and he peered through a lens in the door before he opened. He received a tray bearing a pot of coffee and cups, plus some small pastries, which he brought to the table.

"Coffee, Mr. Bradley?"

"Black," said Bolan.

Sir George nodded, and poured, then poured for himself and added generous amounts of cream and sugar to his coffee.

"The shots fired at you last night," he said, "were fired from the same roof where the shots were fired that killed Richard Vauxhall. What is more, it could have been the same rifle."

"Could have been?"

"Yes, a .460 caliber. Probably a Weatherby. But the bullets were so deformed by their impact with the steel bodies of the two automobiles that ballistics tests are impossible."

"Okay. But who knew I would be on that street at that hour? I didn't know myself."

"To what conclusion did you and Miss Henry come last night? I believe you had ample time to discuss it."

Bolan wondered if she had reported to him. Or did Sir George have Marilyn watched? It didn't matter.

"Our operatives submit a log every day, Mr. Bolan," said Sir George. "It would have been dereliction for Miss Henry to fail to note that she was in your company from a quarter past ten last night until a quarter past nine this morning."

"So you know what we talked about."

Sir George smiled. "The reason for your mission. You seem to have conveyed no significant information. She reported none."

"Who put me in the Green Park Hotel?" Bolan asked. "If you'd put me in, say, the Hilton, no one could have fired a shot at me on the street outside."

"*I* put you there, Mr. Bolan, because I regard it as a pleasant small hotel," said Sir George crisply. "What I would like to know is, how many people knew I put you

there. And how did they know? I called the hotel personally."

"Schellenberg knew also," said Bolan.

"He did? Damn! Schellenberg, incidentally, seems to
have effected a mysterious disappearance."

"Want to bet he shows up again?"

"Let us hope not," said Sir George. "Petty, weaselly little fellow."

Bolan nodded. "What about the driver? You say you
know who he was. Right now he's our only connection."

"Thought you'd want to know," said Sir George. "His
name was Tom Forbes."

"That's what Schellenberg said his name was."

"A handy alias. But that was the driver's *real* name. He
used to hang about the gambling clubs in the West End, or
the strip joints in Soho when he was down on his luck. A
sort of garden-variety, jack-of-all-trades malefactor. Burglar. Driver. Bully boy. He was well-known in the cells at the
Old Bailey."

"Known to Schellenberg and maybe to whoever Schellenberg works for," said Bolan.

"Yes. It's a line of inquiry, perhaps one you can pursue
more effectively than we can. And you just might run into
Schellenberg, too."

At the hour when Bolan was meeting with Sir George
Harrington, Dieter Schellenberg was in a painful position.
Excruciatingly painful. He hung upside down from the
ceiling of a room in Bayswater at the end of a rope that
bound his ankles. He was naked. He had hung there for two
hours now, and the pain had become unbearable.

The men drinking coffee and eating pastries pretended to
ignore him. One of them had said to him that he could escape his predicament if only he were strong enough to raise
himself, to seize the rope, and then to untie the simple knots.

But he wasn't that strong. And every minute he hung with his head down he grew weaker.

The cut on the side of his face, opened by the American's backhand blow with the pistol, had begun to bleed again. Schellenberg's hands were free, and he had just wiped his cheek with the back of his hand and been horrified by the great smear of red blood he had rubbed off.

He groaned.

"Do you want coffee, Herr Schellenberg?" asked one of the men at the table.

There were four of them, all English, all of them scornful of him as a German. They spoke of Germans as cruel and ruthless people. Their own cruelty and ruthlessness exceeded anything any German had ever conceived. Their men had hung him here and left him alone for a very long time while his pain intensified, but there was no one to hear him plead for release. Then these three men had come in and sat down to their coffee. He'd made his plea. They had ignored him.

He couldn't hear their conversation. The room was large, and they sat on the opposite side before the broad window. But they were talking intently. He heard something about helicopters, something about their capacity to carry heavy loads. They referred constantly to some kind of small pocket notebook one of them carried. They hardly glanced at him. He moaned. Still they didn't glance at him.

One of them was florid and had a white mustache. One was tall and thin and bald except for some strands of slicked-down yellow hair. One was a handsome man with a distinguished appearance who refused to take any notice of Schellenberg. One was short, rotund, completely bald, and hungry. The florid one wore tweeds, the others dark blue English business suits, like bankers in the City.

At last one of them stood and came closer—the thin, bald one. He picked up his umbrella and prodded Schellenberg sharply on the hip. It made Schellenberg turn at the end of the rope. He turned until the rope twisted a little, and then the rope untwisted and made him turn the other way. Turning upside down made him nauseous.

"We warned you, Herr Schellenberg," the man said. He sneered over the word "herr." "We don't tolerate failure."

"The man . . . is a devil," Schellenberg protested thinly.

"The man . . . is a man. That's all. And you knew what you were supposed to be doing, while he didn't. You were two. He was one. Failure, Herr Schellenberg."

Schellenberg drew a deep, painful breath. "He struck me. For no reason, just abruptly. He hit me."

"He wouldn't have if you'd had your pistol in your hand."

"I was waiting until he knew—"

"Obviously he did know. Carelessness. Failure."

"Please . . ."

The Englishman stepped back and swung the umbrella in a hard backhand stroke across Schellenberg's mouth, splitting his lips, breaking a tooth, loosing a spray of blood.

"Don't whine, you kraut bastard!"

Schellenberg nearly fainted from shock and agony, but he heard one of the other Englishmen speak in a calm, high voice. "Don't kill him. Be careful."

"Schellenberg," said the tall one. He poked him in the belly with the point of his umbrella. "We can dispose of you here. We can send you back with a report that you're useless. Or we can give you another chance. Obviously you don't wish us to dispose of you. You might, though, think you can go home and argue your case with your superiors. Or you can try to show us you're not the clumsy, stupid fool we think you are. What would you rather?"

Schellenberg gasped. "Another chance, please!"

IN FINLAND many highways came to within a kilometer of the border and there stopped. On the Russian side they stopped five or ten kilometers back. Only at a few towns did the highways meet. There were only a few border crossings. One of the crossings was between the Russian town of Vyartsilya and the Finnish town of Tohmajarvi, fifty kilometers northwest of the northernmost reach of Lake Ladoga.

As he drove the heavy truck along the twisting, icy highway toward the frontier, Mikhail felt a pang of fear in his gut. This was the eighth time he had driven across the frontier between the Soviet Union and the wretched little republic of Finland. Seven successful trips. And now he was a rich man—if he succeeded the eighth time.

He didn't know what he was carrying across the frontier. He had never known, only that it was something illicit and that he would suffer if he were caught. Sometimes he told himself the reward was worth the risk. Other times he told himself he was the world's stupidest fool. If he died somewhere in the freezing cold, behind the wire of a camp, he was a fool. If he lived to swim on warm beaches in the south of France, or even in America, he was brave and shrewd.

Mikhail was a big man, with the broad, flat peasant face his fellow peasants trusted. He had a mouthful of stainless-steel teeth. His nose was red and purple-veined from drinking liter after liter of vodka, as much as he could buy. He was a simple optimist. How else could he take this risk?

And there was the glow of lights. The border. The frontier station.

He brought the truck to a stop short of the barrier, beside the log hut, opened the door and stepped down, his right hand clutching his documents.

"Comrades," he said to the two soldiers who emerged from the hut.

Bad luck. One of them was young. An older man didn't care to freeze his hands pawing around in the back of a battered old truck. A young soldier might still think of duty.

"Oil again?" asked the older man.

"So they tell me," grunted Mikhail. He handed over the documents. "Might be a load of vodka, if we're lucky. I can drink a barrel of it myself. You and the young comrade can share another. Who would miss two barrels?"

The older man laughed and scanned the documents without much interest. The younger man stepped to the back of the truck and shone his light through the gap in the canvas at the ranks of barrels.

"What is it?" he asked.

"Oil," said Mikhail. "Used oil. It's oil that's been in engines for months, so it's full of dirt—or so they tell me. It's too dirty to be filtered anymore. It's no good to us anymore. So we sell it to the Finns, and they have some way of cleaning it partly, and they burn it in stoves. Or so I'm told. This is—" He raised his voice and spoke to the older man. "What is this, comrade, my seventh or eighth load of the stuff?"

The young soldier frowned. "You have a wrench?" he asked.

Mikhail showed the older man a glittering stainless-steel smile. "He wants a wrench, comrade. I tell him there's no vodka, but . . . In the toolbox, comrade. I'll open it."

Mikhail handed the wrench to the young soldier.

"You do it," the young man said. He didn't want to soil his gloves on a dirty barrel.

Mikhail nodded. "Which one, comrade? Which barrel do you want opened?"

The young man pointed at a barrel. Mikhail climbed up in the back of the truck and applied the wrench. He grunted and turned the cap. He turned it a dozen times, and it came loose. The young man climbed up and shone his light into the opening.

"Oil," said Mikhail. He thrust a stubby finger into the viscous black fluid and held it up. He wiped it across the top of the barrel, leaving a smear. "Dirty oil."

"That one," the young solder said, pointing to a barrel in the second rank.

Mikhail screwed down the cap on the first barrel, then opened the second one. "Oil," he said again, showing the thick stuff on his finger.

The young man frowned. If now he decided to plunge a stick into the barrel, he would discover the secret, that each barrel contained about fifteen centimeters of oil, then a false bottom, and under that whatever contraband Mikhail was hauling across the frontier. Mikhail tried to look bored while the young soldier pondered.

The younger man glanced down at the older one, who stood behind the truck, amused. He shrugged and nodded at Mikhail. Mikhail replaced the second cap.

"Well, comrades." He presented his personal document, his permission to cross into Finland for twelve hours to deliver his load.

The old soldier waved the pass aside. "Until tomorrow, comrade," he said. "If I'm asleep when you come back, don't wake me. Unless you bring a pretty Finnish girl. Then you can wake me. I'll get up and look."

"Yes, look," said the younger man. "And that's all you'll do."

Mikhail laughed as he climbed into the cab again. It would go easy on the Finnish side, he knew. He had crossed the frontier successfully for the eighth time. The last time. Under the seat of the truck he was carrying the money. And they would give him more at Joensuu. They would put his barrels on an airplane there. He had often wondered what was in the barrels and where they flew them.

CHAPTER FIVE

Mack Bolan walked through the narrow, littered streets and the garishly lit passageways of Soho. He couldn't help but be amused. From pimply twenty-year-olds to shuffling men in their seventies, hunched and bundled up in their overcoats though the evening wasn't really cold, men browsed, reading the promises on flamboyant posters, listening to the stage-whispered propositions from the entryways to tiny, smoky showrooms—all as if they'd never been suckered before. These weren't innocents. They *had* been suckered before. But their optimism was indestructible.

Bolan had come to be propositioned. He was wearing the blue suit and the raincoat, with the hat he thought made him look moronic, and he carried the briefcase filled with the papers about the company in Manchester. Maybe it wasn't possible for him to look like a sucker, but he was trying. In the harness under his suit jacket, the Lahti rode heavily, a reassuring weight. He hadn't fired it, of course, but in the hotel room he had tried pulling it from the holster, had aimed it, had unloaded it and experimented with the action. It was a finely machined, well-balanced, smooth weapon. This one had been modified for him, Marilyn had explained. The sharp front sight, which might have interfered with pulling it fast from the holster, had been removed. He figured he'd be using it at close range, if at all.

Yeah. If at all. If he could attract the scum he wanted to confront.

He paused before a glass-enclosed poster beside the door of a narrow brick building. COUPLES! the red-and-blue

poster shrieked. GUYS AND GALS! BED SHOW! NOTHING LEFT
TO THE IMAGINATION! He stood there. Chances were—

"You don't want that, sir."

He glanced to his right. A small man stood beside him—
maybe Pakistani.

"Not good. Not pretty girls. You want to see *pretty* girls?
Doing it? I know a better place."

The little man in the tan suit was only a runner, Bolan
understood. But he was the key to moving on a step.

"How much?" he asked. "How much is this going to cost
me?" That was what a sucker would ask. "I mean . . . how
much?"

The small man shrugged. "That," he said, sneering at the
poster, "costs ten quid. Would you spend fifteen quid for a
real show?"

"Plus drinks, plus—"

The little man smiled. "You know how these things are.
Suppose I say twenty-five quid buys you a split of champagne, a pretty girl to sit with you and talk, and a show like
you won't see in this place. That's all—twenty-five quid.
You're a sophisticated man, plainly. You know you can
spend more. Okay, twenty-five buys you what I have said.
For sure. You want to spend more . . ." He shrugged dra-
matically. "Your choice."'

"Where?" asked Bolan.

"You come with me."

He followed the little man north toward Oxford Street,
away from the lights and crowds of the most tawdry part of
Soho, into a neighborhood of shops and restaurants. As
they walked, he kept an eye on the street behind them, alert
for muggers, alert too for someone who might step out of a
door. More likely the small man meant to take him where
more than the cash he was carrying could be extracted from
him, where before the night was over he might offer a credit
card to meet an immense bill. That was the way of it: a more

profitable and less risky business than mugging—backed, of course, by a threat that would move him to sign a hugely inflated bill.

"Here, sir."

Okay. The establishment was below, in the cellar under a restaurant supply house with a window filled with meat-slicing machines and other restaurant kitchen devices.

The small man knocked on a door at the bottom of a short flight of concrete steps. The door opened. A burly man dressed in a wrinkled tuxedo, with a soiled shirt, nodded at Bolan and beckoned him in.

"It's twenty-five quid," the man said curtly.

Bolan peeled a note off his wad, letting him see that the fifty-pound note he was offering them was by no means all the money he had.

"Want me to keep it on account or give you change?"

Bolan glanced at the little man who had led him here. "He said twenty-five pounds. Right or wrong?"

The burly man nodded. "Sure. If you want something else, let me know."

Bolan received two tens and a five in change, and the burly man led him through a curtain and into a small room lit in pink and choking with cigarette smoke. He pointed at a table set with two chairs, and Bolan sat down.

On the improvised stage—nothing more than a small round platform under a bank of theatrical lights, with a mattress in the center—an emaciated young man simulated an act of coitus with a plump, pale girl. What he was simulating would have been impossible in his condition; and besides, as Bolan decided at a glance, no one could possibly care if he did it or not.

A bare-breasted girl sat down with him. She brought the half bottle of champagne and two glasses. Like the little man who had brought him here, she was perhaps Pakistani; anyway, her skin was dusty—he found that word better than "dusky" to describe it—and she studied him with dark, thoughtful eyes. She poured the champagne. The little bottle just filled the two glasses, and she raised hers, toasted him silently and drank half of it.

"Canadian?" she asked.

Bolan shrugged. "Could be. Tom around tonight?"

"Tom?"

"Tom Forbes."

She shook her head. "I don't know. Forbes? I don't know him."

"He told me this is where I would find him."

He saw her eyes rise. That was all the signal she gave, just a quick ceilingward glance; someone was watching her closely.

A goon in a tux came to the table. "More champagne?" he asked.

"Tom said to meet him here," said Bolan. "Tom Forbes."

"Never heard of him," said the goon. "You want another bottle of champagne? Or not?"

Bolan shrugged. "Tom said he'd buy."

"No Tom is buying this one, mate," said the goon. "So are you, or are you not?"

Bolan looked at the girl, as if to let her make the decision.

She smiled at him. "It would be nice," she said.

Bolan nodded. "Okay. One more."

The goon left.

"We could have our champagne in a private room," the girl said. "Very nice. A couch, you know, where we can sit together."

Bolan glanced toward the slothful couple on the mattress. "And miss the show?" he asked.

For the first time she smiled. "We can do better than that," she said.

Bolan sighed inwardly. Here it was again: an intelligent little girl, somehow exploited, turned into whatever she was in this place. He wondered if she was hooked on something. Or if she just had to make a living somehow in a city that opened itself to people from all over the Commonwealth and then closed around them, made them anonymous and demanded they make some kind of living, no matter how. It was what all big cities did: lured people, then robbed them of their humanity.

And always, the exploiters. The goon was back with the champagne.

"Tom Forbes doesn't come in?" Bolan asked.

The goon shook his head. "Never heard the name."

But of course he had. It was plain enough that the repeated inquiry after Tom Forbes had excited his curiosity, maybe a degree of apprehension.

Bolan drank a little of the champagne with the dusty-skinned girl. She, too, had become leery of him. Maybe she thought he was a policeman. She studied his face as she sipped the champagne, and he could tell that she saw something that interested her, yet frightened her. In her line of work the very last thing she wanted was anything that rattled the cupboards. She didn't even press him again to accompany her to a private room.

"Here you go," he said after about twenty minutes. He handed her a fifty-pound note and the change from the one he had given the man at the door—seventy-five pounds. That ought to cover the tab and leave something for you. "See you around."

The goon stiffened as Bolan walked toward the door, but the girl waved the money and nodded, and he relaxed, Bolan saw. He also saw the goon pick up a telephone and speak urgently.

So far so good.

Hardmen were the same anywhere. If they'd been any good for anything else, they wouldn't have been hardmen; and what they did and how they did it generated in them a dull self-confidence. A man whose business is hurting other people, or anyway threatening to, forgets he'll someday meet a man just as hard as he is. They swaggered. They were used to getting most of what they wanted, just by their menace. Some of them were smart, but most of them weren't. The two who followed Bolan into Wardour Street had no idea he was anything but the dumb businessman he was miming, and they were too dull-witted even to try to guess who he was, what he was.

Fine. Bolan turned into a street that was dark, where no one was walking but a dim figure far ahead of him. He knew the hardmen would make their move, and they did.

"Uh, hey!"

He turned.

"Friend of ours wants to talk to you."

Bolan shrugged. "I don't want to talk to him."

"Uh-huh!" The spokesman for the two flashed a knife. "But he wants to talk to you."

Bolan pulled the Lahti and with a quick backhand slash broke the hardman's jaw. As that one fell, Bolan put the muzzle to the face of the other one. He staggered backward against a brick wall, and Bolan jammed the pistol into the hardman's mouth, breaking teeth.

"What's the name of the man who wants to see me?" he growled.

"Uh-uh-uh," the man said through his bleeding mouth.

Bolan pulled the Lahti back. "His name is what?"

"Ah, ah . . . Harper. Bobbie Harper."

"He the fat guy in the club?"

The hardman shook his head. "No. He's the boss."

"So. Well, I've got a message for the boss. You tell him my name is Ernest Bradley. I'm at the Green Park Hotel,

room 304. You tell him I want to see him there, tonight, at
eleven o'clock. You tell him I'm the man who shot Tom
Forbes. You tell him if I have to come looking for him, he'll
wish I hadn't.''

THE TIME HAD COME to stop playing Ernest Bradley.

London was the perfect place to buy the clothes and
equipment he needed but couldn't carry with him. And since
MI6 was dragging their heels about supplies, Bolan had decided to buy them. He had visited shops in Jermyn Street
before his expedition to Soho. His purchases had sharply
reduced his supply of money, but Bolan had walked out of
the east shop on Jermyn Street feeling more comfortable,
with working clothes and equipment in neat packages.

He wasn't so naive as to suppose that Bobbie Harper
would appear at eleven. No matter. He had walked across
the street during the afternoon and taken a room at Flemings Hotel. And it was to Flemings that he returned after his
visit to Soho.

In his room in his new hotel, Bolan stripped off the
clothes of a businessman and suited himself in the comfortable blacksuit with watch cap, boots and web belts—to
which he added the leather harness that carried the Lahti.

With a nylon rope he had bought, he lowered himself
from his room to the narrow passageway behind the hotel,
retrieving the looped rope and attaching it to his belt. He
slipped along behind the hotel and office buildings and
reached a passageway he had already noticed during his soft
probe—to Half Moon Street. He stood in the shadows and
waited for a taxi to pass through the street, and then he
trotted across into the shadows and into another passage.
Three minutes after he had left his room in Flemings he was
on the ledge of the window outside his room in the Green
Park Hotel.

They were out there, three of them waiting for Mr. Ernest Bradley to return to the Green Park. He had seen them as he crossed the street. He knew what they'd do.

Bolan jimmied the window open, slipped into the room and settled down to wait. He didn't have to wait long.

Bolan heard a knock on the door, followed by the unmistakable sounds of the lock being picked. A heartbeat later the door opened.

The hardmen stepped in first. The room was dark, but the light from the window showed them that the bed was empty. Harper stepped in and closed the door.

"No lights," he said to the first hardman, who had reached toward the switch. "We're going to surprise the guy, don't forget."

Harper stretched out on the bed, plumping the pillows comfortably behind him. One hardman sat in the upholstered chair, the other on the straight chair at the writing table.

It was only after they were relaxed and their eyes began to adjust to the dark that they realized there was a fourth man there. Dressed all in black, he stood in the open door of the bathroom. He held a pistol in his hand, and the muzzle was leveled at them.

"Who the hell are you?"

Bolan pegged the man as Bobbie Harper, and he was frightened.

"We'll talk," said Bolan. "But first things first. Coats off. I want to see if you're carrying."

The hardmen weren't armed. Harper was. He was carrying a Browning pocket automatic. Bolan took it.

"All right. Now you do exactly what you're told, and everything may come out all right."

They obeyed orders. They looked at Bolan, heard his voice and obeyed.

The hardmen took off their belts. The first one sat down on the floor and the second one covered his head with a blanket from the bed and secured it with his belt, tightened around his neck. Then Harper did the same to the second hardman. They sat with their knees drawn up and their hands clasped around their knees. Harper returned to the bed and sat as he'd been before, with his legs stretched out in front of him.

"Forbes worked for you," said Bolan.

"You're not asking me. You're telling me."

"Okay. I'm telling you. Forbes and Schellenberg kidnapped me. I think they were supposed to kill me."

Harper shook his head. "I wouldn't know."

"What are you, just an employment agent for hoodlums?" Bolan asked.

Harper shrugged. "I'm in several lines of business," he said.

"What lines of business?"

"Well . . . you know. I've got my clubs."

"Let me guess. You deal in coke, pot, maybe heroin. You've got—what, twenty?—little girls turned out, some of them addicts. You probably lend money at fifty percent interest a week. And gambling. You must make a lot of money."

"What difference does it make to you?" Harper asked. "Just what have you got in mind? You came looking for me tonight."

"I want Dieter Schellenberg," said Bolan.

"I can't deliver Dieter Schellenberg," said Harper.

"Want to bet?"

"How am I going to find Schellenberg? If he's in trouble, how can I find him any better than you can? Do the police want him? How the hell can I find him if they can't?"

"What was the deal for Forbes?" Bolan asked.

"Schellenberg wanted a driver, a man he could rely on if something bad happened. That's all. He wanted a tough man."

"So why did he come to you?"

Harper shrugged again. "He knew I've got…resources."

"He lost your resource," said Bolan. "He got him killed. Doesn't he owe you?"

"What do you mean?"

"You're supposed to return resources you hire," said Bolan. "You rent a car, you're supposed to return it. If you don't, you pay."

Harper grinned. "I hadn't thought of that."

"Anyway," said Bolan, "you can find Schellenberg. In fact, I wouldn't be surprised if he hasn't been in contact with you since he lost Forbes."

"Like hell he has. I swear to you he hasn't."

"I want him."

Harper raised his chin a little higher, and he regarded Bolan with a cynical leer. "Well, maybe you and I can work together," he said.

"I doubt it."

"No? Aside from the fact that I'm sitting here, outsmarted for the moment, and you've got my gun and yours, give me a reason why I should do anything for you."

"A man like you is vulnerable," said Bolan.

"Right now I am," said Harper. "What makes me vulnerable after I leave here? You're smart and tough, and I underestimated you. But you underestimate me if you think you can put me in this position twice. You can kill me, I suppose, but that won't get you Schellenberg and whatever else it is you want. If you aren't going to kill me, sooner or later you have to let me go. And after that, why should I do anything for you?"

"Have it your own way," said Bolan.

"You'd better come up with a payment," said Harper. "You talk about Schellenberg owing me for Forbes. Okay, if I deliver Schellenberg, what's the price?"

"We'll see," said Bolan.

CHAPTER SIX

"It's twenty-five quid," the man in the shabby tuxedo and soiled shirt said curtly. He didn't recognize Bolan as a man who had been here earlier tonight. The place was still open at one in the morning, which wasn't surprising.

As before, Bolan offered a fifty-pound note.

"Want me to keep it on account or give you change?"

"On account," said Bolan. He decided to let the man think he had a true sucker here.

The man led him through the curtain and into the pink-lit room. Bolan sat down at a table nearer the stage than the one he'd had before and was given the same tiny bottle of champagne. He was wearing his raincoat. He glanced around. So were most of the men in the room.

On the stage a sweating black man was doing what the anemic young man had been unable to do before, this time to a plump black girl.

Again a bare-breasted girl came to Bolan's table. This one was blond and pale. "Like to take a bottle of bubbly to a private room, luv?" she asked. "We could 'ave a lot of fun."

"Bubbly," he said. "I had something else in mind."

"Oh? And what's that?"

"I was thinking of sniffing a line or two," he said.

He saw the sign go to the man who was watching from across the room. It wasn't subtle. The girl lifted her head and cast the man a significant glance. He came.

"What you got in mind, guv?" the man asked. He was a tall, bald, emaciated man, pallid, with a thin, shiny scar across his chin. Bolan shrugged. "Thought I'd rather sniff a line—I mean, rather than drink champagne."

"We don't have nothin' like that here, sir," the man said coldly.

"Funny. Bobbie said you did."

"Bobbie?"

"Bobbie Harper."

The man drew a deep breath. "Well . . . tell me something, sir. What does Bobbie look like?"

Bolan smiled. "He looks like a greaseball," he said.

The man tried to suppress a grin. "All right, sir," he said. "You can come with me. You want to buy a line for the young lady, too?"

"Sure."

They followed the pale, thin man across the front of the stage—where the couple was laboring mightily and generating a spatter of applause—and toward a door to the rear of the room. The bare-breasted girl touched Bolan's hand. He couldn't imagine it was a gesture of affection and wondered if she were warning him of something.

He need not be warned. Dressed again in his businessman's clothes, he was carrying the Lahti in its holster and also Harper's Browning. Even if they had been warned, he was ready.

The rooms behind were also dimly lit with pink bulbs. A narrow hallway passed several doors, the cribs, Bolan supposed, where some of the girls were servicing their customers. The thin man opened a door toward the end of the corridor.

"Two lines," he said as he gestured that Bolan and the girl should enter the room.

"Four," said Bolan.

The room was small, square and furnished with a narrow cot and a table with two chairs. Another one of the pink bulbs burned in a ceiling fixture. Bolan glanced around. The only exit was through the door.

"You can pay?" the girl asked quietly.

"Yes. How much will it be?"

"A 'undred quid," she said, regarding Bolan steadily. "You a copper or somethin'?" She didn't wait for Bolan to respond. "Don't try anything foolish with these people, mister."

He studied her solemn face. This young woman wasn't a girl. She was thirty years old, likely. Her blond hair was coarse. She wore a little lipstick on her thin lips, badly applied and askew.

"Hooked?" he asked.

She nodded.

"What's your name?" he asked.

"Martha," she said.

"Okay, Martha. If something tough goes down, just get out of the way. Don't try to help."

She sighed. "These guys are—"

"Don't worry about it," he said, patting her hand.

The emaciated man returned. "I'll need a 'undred pounds from you, guv," he said as he put a small plastic envelope of white powder on the table.

"Right," said Bolan.

He reached inside his raincoat and jacket, and instead of money he withdrew the Browning automatic.

The chair legs shrieked over the floor as Martha pushed herself back from the table. The thin man's eyes narrowed, and he stiffened, but he didn't seem entirely afraid.

"Recognize the Browning?" Bolan asked. "Bobbie's. I told you I know him."

The man flushed. "What you want?"

Bolan pushed back his chair and rose. "I want to see where this came from," he said, nodding at the envelope that contained a little cocaine.

"I—"

"No argument," said Bolan.

The man backed cautiously toward the door. Bolan followed, and Martha came along behind. In the corridor the man kept backing away, his eyes fixed on the Browning that Bolan kept pointed at his belly. At the end the man reached behind him and opened a door. They entered a crude office.

"Let's see what you have," Bolan said.

The man opened a drawer in an old wooden filing cabinet, reached in and pulled out a plastic bag. It was filled with maybe a kilo of cocaine.

"Open it," said Bolan.

The man opened the bag on the desktop. Bolan wet his finger on his tongue and touched it to the white powder. He tasted it. It was cocaine.

With the Browning he waved the man aside. He checked the drawer. He found two more bags.

"Pick them up," he told the man.

The man lifted the bags one by one and pressed them against his body.

"Ohh..."

Martha had been startled by the appearance of another man. It was the heavy guy who tended the door, the one in the shabby tuxedo and dirty shirt. He had a pistol in his hand.

It would have been well for the heavy man to shoot fast. He didn't; he raised the muzzle toward Bolan, but he seemed to be waiting for a signal from the emaciated man; and in the instant that he hesitated he died. The Browning spat with a small, sharp crack. The slug hit the heavy man in the throat. He crumpled and fell.

The emaciated one gaped. Martha staggered back against the wall.

"Let's go," said Bolan. "Where's the nearest bathroom."

The man pointed.

It was a filthy bathroom with black stains on the toilet bowl and a litter of wet paper towels on the floor. Bolan pointed at the bags of cocaine, then at the toilet.

The man shook his head. "Like *diamonds*!" he croaked. "This stuff is worth—"

"I know what it's worth," said Bolan. "Flush it."

While Martha stood behind, watching in appalled fascination, the emaciated man poured the contents of the first plastic bag into the toilet and pushed down the handle. A fortune disappeared in the swirling water.

Bolan gestured with the muzzle of the pistol, and the man poured in the second bag of cocaine. They had to wait for the tank to refill. Bolan nodded. The man pushed down the handle again, and a second kilo of riches went down the drain.

And then the third.

"You stay in here," he said to the man. "Guess when it'll be safe to come out. Too soon..." He shrugged. "Stay until you think it's safe."

He pushed the door shut. He turned and seized Martha by one hand. "You want out of here?"

She was stunned—stunned to have seen a man shot, stunned to have seen three fortunes in cocaine flushed down a toilet—and she shook her head. She looked up into Bolan's face. "Where am I going to get it? You just flushed down enough to keep me going for—"

"Years," he interrupted. "You want to try to get along without it?"

Martha lowered her eyes. She shook her head.

"Then good luck," said Bolan. "Your friends are going to be short of the stuff for a while. For a while. They'll get more."

She nodded. "Yes. There's always more."

THE DESK CLERK HAD a message for him when he returned to the Green Park Hotel a little after 2:00 a.m. There was a telephone number. The message read: "Please call Mr. Harper, no matter what the hour."

When he dialed the number, Harper answered. "Bradley? I'll do what I can. Leave me alone, and I'll try to find Schellenberg for you."

Bolan didn't think it necessary to respond. He just put down the telephone.

Sure Bobbie Harper would help him—if he couldn't kill him first. Bolan decided not to stay in the Green Park Hotel that night. Possibly they were already watching, and since they knew he had come in through the bathroom window before, it wouldn't be safe to go that way again. He put on the blacksuit.

Darkening the room, he opened the door. The hall was lit, and silent. With doors on both sides, and with its several turns, it afforded plenty of easy cover for a triggerman. But if anyone was waiting, Bolan reasoned, likely he was outside.

The big soldier walked along the hall. At two-thirty in the morning he was unlikely to confront anyone, but a hotel guest who came upon him in the blacksuit with two pistols in view would have a shock. Or a maid or waiter. Or a night watchman.

As he passed the doors to the elevators, he could hear one of the cars moving in the shaft. It might not be coming to the floor, but it was time for him to move. He opened the door to the stairs, stood for a moment to see if the lift was stopping on his floor, and when he saw it wasn't moving on, headed for the roof.

His earlier recon was valuable now. He knew how to get to the roof. He knew the door was locked from the outside only. He knew that a matchbook left in the latch would let him back in whenever he wanted. So, jamming the latch with the folded matchbook, he closed the door and stepped out into the night.

Traffic was still brisk on Piccadilly, moving fast now that it wasn't so heavy. From the roof he could see to the west the towers of the Hilton Hotel and of the Inn on the Park, plus the bulk of the Park Lane Hotel, and to the south he could see the roof of Buckingham Palace above the trees of the Green Park, and in the distance the tower of Big Ben. The neighborhood here was Mayfair, and people were still coming out of clubs, and taxis were still hurrying through narrow, twisting streets.

London was still a safe city, compared to most big American cities. You could be squeezed for a bundle in a place like he'd twice visited tonight, and you could get your lights punched out if you didn't pay up. You could pick up some nasty microbiology from the hookers. All kinds of little scans were run, for tourists particularly. But you wouldn't get mugged on the streets. Not likely. London's scum worked a little different.

So, okay. What was down there?

He edged his way around the roof, checking everything below. Not what was on the street, where lights shone from the doorways of the Green Park and Flemings, but in the alleyways behind in the dark corners.

Okay. There was one. Down behind in the passage where the trash and garbage was hauled out of the hotel. He could see the tiny orange glow on the tip of a cigarette. Why would a man be loitering there, smoking, in that damp, smelly place at this hour?

Bolan decided this man was no ordinary street hoodlum. He wore a hat and a raincoat. And he was alert. He kept looking around; even in the near-darkness, Bolan could see how nervously the man kept checking all around him, as if he were afraid someone might be about to attack him from behind.

If there was one, there had to be another one. If this one was watching for a man coming out the back of the hotel, where was the one who was watching the front? Bolan reexamined the shadowy doorways of Half Moon Street. They were empty, but—

Inside. Behind a glass door. Only a shadow, but a moving shadow.

That made two of them.

He wasn't sure what he should do about them. He could take them out. That should rattle Bobbie Harper. Two assets.

But maybe they weren't from Harper. It wasn't Harper, after all, who'd sent Schellenberg to pick him up at Heathrow; and it wasn't Harper who'd put a sniper on that roof across the street.

Roof. Yeah. He peered at the roof. Oh, yeah. A man on the roof. These weren't Harper's boys. These were the real guys, the ones he was here to see.

Something else. Why were they here now? Were they expecting him to go out again at this time of night?

Simple enough. Somebody in the hotel, like the night clerk or the night porter. Somebody underpaid who could use whatever was offered for something as innocent as just keeping a generous man informed as to when Mr. Bradley went in and out.

And Mr. Bradley had had an interesting night. In and out. Three gentlemen had inquired for Mr. Bradley; and when they were told he wasn't in, they had pretended to go down to the men's washroom but had instead gone up to the third floor. They had come down half an hour later, looking angry. Then a postmidnight telephone call, which he had returned.

Mr. Bradley seemed to be an active man. Maybe he was going out again tonight. A good time to drop him.

Bolan replayed the scenario in his head as he crossed the rooftops all the way to Curzon Street. Getting down would have been a problem, except for the rope. He lowered himself into the passageway behind the last building. It was a place he had scouted earlier, a little walkway behind a pub in Shepherd Market.

He edged around the corner of the pub. Shepherd Market was deserted, though the red lights still burned inside the open doors of the flats where the hookers worked. He hurried through the passage into Curzon Street, past two little cafés and a vegetable market. He waited for a cab to go by, then watched the street for a minute, to be sure no one was close—no one who would be startled by the sight of an armed man in black prowling the streets of Mayfair. Then he crossed and double-timed back to Half Moon Street.

He was on the east side of Half Moon Street, and the man lurking in the doorway couldn't have seen him. Now he worked his way along the street toward that doorway. A taxi came past. He crouched on a door stoop until the lights passed on.

And he reached that door, where the man watched from inside the glass. Bolan lunged at the door, jerked it—it opened in—pushed it, and came at the man hard.

The man fumbled inside his raincoat, digging for hardware, when the single solid blow caught him on the tip of the chin. Bolan caught him before he crumpled, and lowered him to the floor.

He had a gun all right: a 9 mm Luger, which Bolan tucked into his web belt.

What he wanted was access to the roof. Maybe the man on the roof down the street was the man who had shot Vauxhall, who had taken a shot at him. This was an office building. There was an elevator, but Bolan took the stairs. He checked on each floor as he went up. Every floor had offices. All were dark at 3:00 a.m.

On the top floor there were two apartments. Someone was asleep—presumably—behind those thin wooden doors.

Access to the roof? Where was it? Always in these buildings there was a way to get on the roof. Could it be inside one of the flats?

He checked the center hall end to end. No. The trapdoor onto the roof was inside one of the flats.

Windows. At the back of the building the hall window opened in a flat brick wall. There was a pipe running up that wall, but it was too far from the window for a jump to grab it.

Front window. Maybe. An ornamental cornice just above, within reach. Bolan opened the window, found handholds around the frame and climbed out onto the sill.

Securing himself with his left hand, he stood on tiptoe on the sill and grabbed the cornice with his right hand. It felt gritty. Carved stone—carved a century ago, maybe—and softened by the atmosphere of a big city. He tugged at it. He couldn't be sure it wouldn't break away with his weight. He tugged and tested. It held.

Holding on with his right hand, he threw up his left, grabbed and raised himself off the windowsill. The cornice held. He pulled himself higher, threw over a leg and rolled onto the roof.

He didn't have much time. The man he had slugged would crawl out onto the stoop and alert his confederates at any moment.

He crouch-walked across the rooftops until he reached the building next to the one where he knew the rifleman waited. He crawled across that roof.

The man was intent on the street below, crouching near the edge of the roof, staring down.

Bolan watched him for a moment. The man was wearing a long raincoat and a crumpled tweed hat. Like the man in the passageway behind the hotel, he impressed Bolan as something other than your typical hardman. Even though he was crouching, he bore himself with a rigidity, a self-confidence that suggested something quite different from the demeanor of the mafioso hoods Bolan had fought so long, something different from the hopped-up terrorist types he had fought recently. This man was a professional.

Professional something.

Professional hit man, from the look of it—because there was the rifle. It was a Weatherby. A man who chose a Weatherby .460 Magnum was a man who knew something about weapons. A man who could handle it, and fire it accurately, was an expert marksman.

So here was the man who had killed Vauxhall. And here was the man who had fired two shots at him—or maybe one at him and one at Marilyn.

Bolan leaped over the short wall that divided two roofs and charged at the rifleman. The man heard him coming. He didn't reach for the big rifle; he went inside his coat for a pistol. Bolan got to him before he could pull the pistol. He drove a fist into the man's face with all his strength.

Stumbling back, the rifleman hit the wall with the backs of his thighs. For an instant he tottered, then toppled backward and fell. He didn't scream. He grunted, as if in astonishment to find himself falling and not quite aware of why he was falling or what would happen in one more second. He struck the pavement below with a sickening, crunching thud.

Bolan stared down, surprised that the man had fallen. He picked up the Weatherby and dropped it. It landed with a crack on the sidewalk beside the sprawled, silent body of the man who had used it to kill.

Let the police find them together.

No. The police wouldn't find them. Two men rushed out of the darkness. A car backed down the one-way street. In a moment the two men had loaded the body and the rifle into the car, and in another moment it was gone.

CHAPTER SEVEN

The men who had hung Dieter Schellenberg by his heels were gathered in the walnut-paneled parlor of a town house in Belgravia, just west of Buckingham Palace. They were the same group except for one.

"This is what comes of independent operations," said Sir Alexander Bentwood, owner of the residence. "Damn it, gentlemen! Insubordination—"

"He underestimated the American," said Edward Holmesby-Lovett. "He was flush with success, I'm afraid."

"Over Vauxhall, you mean?" said Sir Alex. "An insufficient reason for a man to grow self-congratulatory."

"I am glad he was able to do it," said Holmesby-Lovett. "I know *I* couldn't have."

"And *I* wouldn't have," said Sir Alex.

Sir Alexander Bentwood was, by common consent, one of the most handsome men in England. Tall, with silvery-gray hair, a tanned complexion—the result, not just of frequent holidays in warm climates but also of lying under a bank of ultraviolet lamps once a week at his club—and regular features, he was trim and straight and wore clothes perfectly tailored to his frame. Edward Holmesby-Lovett, in contrast, was short, plump and bald. Cherubic in appearance, he had a cherubic personality: a ready smile, a quick wit.

"He was right to try to eliminate Bolan," said Cobden, the one who was tall and thin, whose baldness was less than complete only by virtue of some strands of yellow hair that lay across his pale scalp in orderly parallel lines, as if he had glued them in place. He was also the one who had struck the hanging Dieter Schellenberg across the face with his umbrella. "It is foolish to think we can do anything else about him."

"It was insubordinate," snapped Sir Alexander Bentwood angrily. "I want to handle the Bolan problem another way. And it's settled. I don't want to discuss it further."

"Well, we shall have it your way," said Holmesby-Lovett. "Anyway, I should hope we have the decency to mourn the man. Sir Michael was my friend for the past twenty-five years, and I for one regret his loss deeply."

"I regret he didn't succeed in eliminating Bolan," said Cobden.

"How is his death being explained?" asked Sir Alex.

"A doctor on our payroll has certified that Sir Michael died suddenly of a heart attack whilst sipping a bedtime glass of port," said Holmesby-Lovett. "An undertaker in our employ has laid him out nicely, so the injuries to the body are invisible. Friends will view him. There is, of course, no family—except, I think, a son in America, who will not return for the funeral and wouldn't make an inquiry if he did."

"What of Schellenberg?" asked Sir Alex.

"Served faithfully enough last night," said Cobden. "Quick with that car. If they'd had to rely on Finley, they'd have been in trouble. Bolan's blow to the face injured him seriously."

"Then Schellenberg's reprieved?" asked Holmesby-Lovett.

"He's valuable for small work," said Cobden.

"Fine. I should like to talk about big work," said Sir Alex. "The last shipment crossed the border safely—the balance of the electronics. Installation will require several weeks."

"So long?" asked Cobden.

"Patience," said Sir Alex. "When work of this delicate nature is being done by conscript technicians, it must be checked, rechecked, and rechecked a second and third time. They are resentful, you know."

"Shanghaied people do tend to bear some grudge," Holmesby-Lovett observed with a casual air.

"But the work is being done," said Sir Alex firmly. "It will be finished in a month. And then—"

"Then what?" asked Cobden sharply. "What are we going to do with the damn thing?"

"Some word from Washington," said Sir Alex. "Only a rumor at the moment. But if it proves true—and my contact assures me it will—then we shall have an opportunity greater than any we ever dared hope for."

"Word from France, then?"

Holmesby-Lovett spoke. "Something spectacular is about to happen. Perhaps yet today. Followed by something more spectacular tomorrow."

"Bolan, then," said Cobden. "That goddamn American..."

"The Executioner," said Sir Alex. "Let us hope he doesn't prove to be *our* executioner—as he did, unwittingly I suspect, prove to be that of poor Sir Michael."

"Unwittingly?" asked Cobden.

"Yes. The man is a dolt," said Sir Alex. "Last night, for a brief moment, Mr. Bolan had his hands on a man who could have compromised everything, had he been taken and interrogated by methods I suspect Mr. Mack Bolan knows well. Instead, he threw him off the roof."

"So what do we do about him?" asked Cobden.

"For the moment, I think," said Sir Alex, "we let him stumble around trying to discover what is happening. If he seems to be finding out—and I assure you we will know if he begins to find out—then we may have to rid ourselves of him."

Cobden shook his head. "We've tried twice."

"Sir Michael tried twice," said Sir Alex. "When *I* try, Mr. Mack Bolan will be negated."

THEY SPOKE ITALIAN. They were eating Italian and enjoying themselves. Most of them still sat at a table behind a thick glass door—bulletproof—that overlooked the Corsican coastline. Their table was set with an abundance of food and wine, and to have shown reluctance to eat and drink would have been an offense.

An offense to Vittorio Muro, who had left the table a few minutes earlier and now sat apart on a balcony that overlooked the dining table, the terrace and the view of the sea. Benito Calabrese sat with him. The two old friends were sharing a special bottle of wine, listening to the animated conversation at the table.

Vittorio Muro was old enough to remember bitterly the German soldiers who had occupied his Corsican village. As a child he had been taught to hate the French; as a young man he had learned by his own experience to hate the Germans. His name wasn't Muro. It was the name of his village. It had been convenient all his life to call himself Muro, like the old aristocrats who called themselves by the names of their towns. He had long since achieved a status where no one dared question whatever he might call himself.

He wore English clothes: an olive-colored tweed jacket in fine Scottish wool, a white shirt with narrow blue stripes, a pinned-down collar, a narrow striped necktie. Benito and the others below at the table wore silk suits, silk shirts, flamboyant styles. By his clothes and by his manner and speech, Vittorio Muro underscored the difference between himself and all the others.

The talk at the table was about money, always money. With them, money was always discussed in American dollars or English pounds. Who knew what a franc might be worth tomorrow? Or, worse, a lira? Swiss francs and German marks were stable, but business was done in dollars and pounds. The Americans and English were entitled to their legendary arrogance on this subject.

"I wouldn't let Joey go home," said Benito Calabrese quietly.

"I *must* let him go home," said Vittorio Muro. "A matter of honor. A practical matter, as well. They know they're safe when they come here. From each other. From me. If there were ever an exception, they would never come again."

"Safe also from a decision of the table, Don Vittorio?"

"Yes. Who would come to answer to the table if he couldn't be assured—absolutely assured, Don Benito—that he wouldn't leave here safely?"

"I'll raise the question if you want."

"I'm grateful for the offer," said Muro, "but it won't be necessary."

The Joey they were talking about was Guiseppe Castiglione, boss of the Genoa waterfront and one of the two men who shared Milan—shared it uneasily, so long as both lived. He was only forty years old, young for his status; and, as wasn't uncommon among young men risen fast to wealth and power, he was cocky and impatient. Somehow, reflected Vittorio Muro, Joey Castiglione could swagger even while he was seated.

Sitting at the table also were Johnny Cimone from Las Vegas, Basilio Massa from Marseilles, Fredo Rovigo from New York, Giorgio Lazzero from Naples, and Ricciotti Ciano from São Paulo. Not all the men asked to come had been able to come. Their reasons were good. Vittorio Muro wasn't worried that anyone had neglected to come.

"He can't create a problem?" asked Calabrese. His thoughts, his eyes, were still on Joey Castiglione.

"There will be no problem," said Muro.

"He hasn't married, either."

Vittorio Muro shrugged. "Perhaps it's just as well."

"I should tell you," said Calabrese, "that he isn't the only one who's curious to know how you're spending the assessment."

"You're curious yourself, Don Benito," said Muro with a faint smile.

Calabrese shrugged. He was Muro's age but was a simpler man: grown fat on the good things life had brought him. In Palermo where he was the boss of bosses he had a little stable of girls to keep his nights warm and happy.

"I'll be happy to tell you what I've done with the money," said Muro. "I won't tell *them*."

"You don't have to tell me, Don Vittorio."

"I can tell you," said Muro, "as a matter of friendship. I can't tell them. I won't establish a precedent that requires me to account to them. They must trust me. If they don't—"

"They trust you."

Vittorio Muro raised his glass and sipped the rich red wine he loved. "The world is a changing place," he said. "Always changing. Not all changes are for the good, or for the bad, but all changes a man isn't prepared for are bad. It's essential to anticipate changes. I've reason to think there's going to be a major change in the way the world is run. I've used the assessment to promote that change, also to put us on the right side of it. I've put some interesting people under obligation to us. Our investment may pay a thousandfold return. Or—" he shrugged "—it may pay nothing."

"Politics," said Calabrese.

"Politicians," said Muro. "I've invested in some important ones. If they seize power in the next few months, as they plan to do, the world will be astonished. But we won't."

"Half a billion dollars..." mused Calabrese. "Who've you bought? The President of the United States?"

Muro smiled. "If these people succeed, the President of the United States will be insignificant. Anyway, the investment. Is anyone down there—" he nodded toward the table "—suggesting we couldn't afford the assessment?"

Calabrese shook his head.

"I didn't think so," said Muro. "Look at those two Americans—Cimone and Rovigo. Did you ever look at their reports? They don't touch drugs, no aspect of the drug trade. They don't touch prostitution. No loan sharking. None of the old-time waterfront rackets. They almost never use muscle. The Cimone family owns a billion dollars worth of real estate. Rovigo...the Rovigo family controls forty-seven separate corporations in every line of business you could imagine. I assessed them a hundred million dollars apiece."

"A hundred... But Don Vittorio, I sent you only—"

"Don Benito, you sent what I asked of you. Your businesses don't generate the kind of income the Americans' businesses do."

"I'm grateful that you understand," said Calabrese.

"The Latin Americans are ruining our drug trade," said Muro. "That's something I expect our newly purchased friends to remedy. They will eliminate the sources of cocaine—by military force if necessary. In fact, it will probably be by military force."

"What do these people call themselves?" asked Calabrese.

"The White Front," said Muro. "Whites as opposed to Reds—with maybe an overtone of racism mixed in."

A blond girl with a 1960 lacquered hairdo rapped on the doorframe and waited to be asked onto the balcony. Muro nodded at her, and she came to the small table. "Luca," she said quietly.

"Tell him to join us."

In a moment Luca Ampezzo came out. He bowed to Vittorio Muro and waited to be invited to sit down.

"Sit down with us, Luca," said Muro. "Have a glass of wine."

Ampezzo was a self-possessed, quiet man with a dark complexion and a heavy dark beard that required at least two shaves a day. He was tall and well put together and had a strong, regular face.

"Tell me, Luca," said Muro. "Do you think you could rid the world of Mack Bolan?"

Ampezzo stiffened and inhaled. "If he didn't know I was coming," he said. "If I were lucky. If he's not immortal, as they say he is."

Muro nodded. "I think you're right. It would be the most difficult job I could possibly ask of you. Think about it. Someday I might ask you—and I want you to feel absolutely free to refuse. You have my word on this, Luca. If I ask you and you tell me it's a risk you don't want to take, I won't hold it against you."

Ampezzo nodded and lifted his glass of wine.

"Right now, an easier one," said Muro. "Joey Castiglione."

Ampezzo's only reaction was another measured nod.

"Three days after he gets home," said Muro. "Not before. You understand he must get home safely to Genoa or Milan. Then we'll let him have three days. Then . . ."

Ampezzo nodded again.

THEIR ORDERS WERE to use code names. Between him and Fritz, that was silly, since they had worked together before and knew each other well. Nevertheless, Fritz and Willi. And the girl was Trudl—which was also silly, because from her accent it was instantly obvious that she was no Trudl; she was a Marie or Josette.

Trudl was young and pretty. She might almost have been what they were pretending to be. The blond hair hanging halfway down her back hadn't been grown in three weeks in preparation for this operation, as his beard and Fritz's had been. And somehow she managed to achieve a defiant air in the cheap, ill-fitting, dirty clothes they had been ordered to wear.

He and Fritz had never ridden motorcycles before, and neither had she. But Trudl had taken to hers as if she had ridden one ten thousand kilometers. She sped through the streets of West Berlin, taking the corners in a crazy tilt, looking as though she must surely crash to the pavement. Fritz had crashed once. He had crashed twice. His own first crash had almost put him out of the mission.

For this assignment he and Fritz had had to learn, not just new roles but also new status. No one had told them so, but they had discovered, as the plan unfolded, that they were nothing but guards and helpers.

Trudl was the center of the mission. Trudl was the expert.

It had been frightening at first to watch her handle the C-4 plastique as if it were so much modeling clay. She had shoved the detonators into it as if she were pushing pencils into loaves of bread. The dexterity with which she twisted wires together suggested that she had been twisting them together for years. He and Fritz had learned to admire her work. She knew exactly what she was doing.

Why Trudl, though? Neither of them had dared to ask why the charges had to be set by a young Frenchwoman. Surely the organization included a German who could have done the same.

"Now, let's understand," she said in her odd, nasal-accented German. "I'll place one charge. Willi places the other. Fritz is on guard. I want to survive to collect my fee for this work, gentlemen. I am carrying a detonator. Each of you has one. But we're not giving up our lives for this job. If one or two of us is arrested, no one sends the detonator signal until the arrested one or ones is out of the area. Is that clear?"

Willi nodded. He was resentful. So far as he was concerned, he was ready to give his life for what they were doing. But Fritz wasn't. Like Trudl.

"Fritz, you have an alarm transmitter. Let me see it."

Fritz obediently pulled the little transmitter from his pocket, while Willi burned with indignation that she would drill them like this, as if they were schoolboys—and that Fritz would submit to it.

"Good," she said. "And you have a detonator transmitter."

Fritz pulled it from his pocket. She had smeared it with white paint, to be sure he would distinguish the one from the other, even if in panic.

"What we're about to do," she said, "isn't difficult. All that could make it dangerous for us is fear."

Willi was checking his pistol. He had a Luger inside the shabby workingman's jacket he wore. Old-fashioned, it was still simple, reliable and effective. He liked it. Fritz was more modern. His weapon was a Beretta.

He had seen Trudl's weapon and knew she didn't intend to be taken alive. She carried an American pistol, a .357 Magnum revolver. A heavy, bulky thing, she could stop an automobile with it; the bullet would crack an engine block. It was difficult to believe she could handle it. But he had learned not to doubt what Trudl could handle.

They sped through the streets on their motorcycles. She had laughed when she assured them that even a flaming crash against a wall wouldn't detonate the C-4 plastique. It was stable, she said, except against the sharp shock of the detonators.

A part of the plan was that they were to be seen. That was why they were wearing beards and shabby clothes. Be seen! He couldn't imagine it. He had guessed why. He didn't want to speculate on it.

They sped into Kurfürstendamm, the chief downtown commercial street of West Berlin. It hadn't been so important in the old Berlin, but it was in the split Berlin. Out of the rubble the West Berliners had built a new commercial center that bore an unfortunate resemblance to Fort Worth or Houston, except for the reminder at the end of the street—the bomb-shattered black ruin of the Kaiser Wilhelm Memorial Church, left standing as a reminder of the horrors of war.

In late morning the street was choked with traffic. It was strange how West Berliners favored fast cars, like Porsches, when they had only the city's streets and peripheral roads to race them on—the highways being denied them since their city was inside the East Zone. On the sidewalks, hurrying pedestrians elbowed one another. Kurfürstendamm wasn't unlike Fifth Avenue in New York, except that exclusive shops needed more room than the street itself afforded, so shopping malls opened off the street, and many shops were to be found in enclosed malls just off the street.

One of them was called Frühling, meaning "spring." It was an appropriate target on this morning when a light snow was falling on Berlin.

Trudl, Fritz and Willi were a little dismayed by the snow shower that turned the streets slippery and made them hazardous for inexperienced motorcycle riders.

Even so the three reached the Kaiser Wilhelm Church a little after eleven, which was their target hour. They parked

their motorcycles and ambled along Kurfürstendamm toward the Frühling mall.

The center store of the mall was the department store
named Frühling. It was something like an American Saks
store, a merchandiser of high-quality clothes for men and
women, not appliances and furniture. One walked in
through an air door, where streams of warm air blowing
down from above and sucked into vacuum slots in the floor
prevented cold, wet air outside from entering the store. Inside, walking on a thick pile carpet, breathing air perfumed
through the ventilating system, one was presented with in-
viting displays of merchandise.

Christmas wasn't far away. Frühling was crowded with
shoppers.

Trudl and Willi were viewed with hostile suspicion in
Frühling. A shabby, bearded man and an unkempt girl
weren't the kind of people the store expected to spend
money. What was more, the floorwalkers noticed, they went
directly to the bathrooms. That was to be expected—street
people coming into a nice store to use the toilet. If they did
and went out, it would be all right. That much could be tolerated. If they stayed afterward and became nuisances—
begging or trying to distribute peacenik literature or something of the kind—they would have to be put out, firmly.

Willi urinated. He needed to. Maybe he wouldn't have a
later opportunity. He washed his hands and put his towel
litter into the wastebasket. Then he glanced around. The
only other man in the room was intent on his stream. Willi
shoved the bomb into the wastebasket.

Trudl was waiting. She nodded, and the two of them
hurried out of the store—hurried because their orders were
to hurry at this point, to be *seen* hurrying. They hurried toward the street.

"All right," she said.

They stopped.

She pulled out the detonator transmitter. She looked at him for a moment. Then she raised her arm and yelled, "For peace and freedom!"

Frühling erupted. Willi was astounded, appalled, by the force in their two packages of plastique. He had expected an explosion. Two explosions. He hadn't expected the store to erupt in fire and smoke, its display windows blown across the mall, its roof rising like the lid of a box.

The people who had heard Trudl cry "Peace and freedom!" hardly noticed that she and Willi hurried out of the mall onto Kurfürstendamm.

Fritz was waiting. The car was waiting. They scrambled into the big black Mercedes, and the driver pulled away from the curb.

Trudl had taken the front seat. She began to pull off her clothes, laughing and throwing the shabby costume of a peacenik out the window. Underneath she was stylishly dressed in a black cashmere sweater with a rope of pearls around her neck. The driver handed her a mink jacket that waited beside him on the seat.

She looked at Willi and Fritz in the rear. "Change!" she snapped. "And throw those rags out. Also the pistols. We've got a long way to go, and we're going with different identities."

CHAPTER EIGHT

"Sorry to be late," said Sir George Harrington. "I'm afraid some of us have had a most distressing experience this morning. The funeral of a colleague. Sir Michael Lansdowne. Retired only this year—in February, I believe it was. Not yet sixty years old." He stopped and shook his head. "Distressing. First to lose Dick Vauxhall, murdered, now Sir Michael, heart attack. Most distressing."

They were meeting in the secure conference room. No one was allowed to bring in a briefcase. No files were brought in. No notes were to be taken in the meeting. No record was made of who was present or what was said. There were five persons in the room.

"I believe all of us know one another, except perhaps... Let's see. Perhaps Mr. Brognola doesn't know our operative, Marilyn Henry. She's Mr. Bolan's assigned contact in this country, and I believe she has so far served him well."

Sir George glanced at Bolan. "And, uh, Mr. Bolan hasn't met Sir Alex. Mr. Bolan, this is Sir Alexander Bentwood, deputy foreign secretary. Sir Alex has been briefed as to who you are."

Sir Alexander nodded at Bolan. "You have impressive credentials."

"As do you, Sir Alexander," said Brognola. "Years of valuable service in the intelligence community. Admiral Turner used to speak highly of you." This was for Bolan's benefit, a bit of introduction.

"I thought highly of the admiral," said Sir Alexander.

"So," said Sir George. "We know one another. And we meet to face difficulties. I wish it were a happier day."

"May we have from you, Sir George," said Sir Alexander, "a briefing on the incident in Berlin?"

"Yes," said Sir George. "Followed, I regret to say, by a briefing on a similar event in Paris."

"Paris?"

"Only this morning," said Sir George. "I'll advise you fully."

Marilyn had made a point of sitting beside Bolan. Earlier, outside the room, she had chided him playfully about spending a day and night away from her, pursuing things on his own. "That's the way I work," he had said.

"I'm not altogether sure I want to know what you've done," she had rejoined.

"In West Berlin," said Sir George, "the death toll is now fifty-eight. More than two hundred were hurt, many seriously. The quantity of explosive detonated is clear evidence that the intention was to kill. The loss of property is...immaterial. Half as much plastique would have destroyed the store. Half as much would have spread terror and confusion. The amount detonated can only mean that the criminals meant to kill as many people as possible."

"To what purpose?" asked Sir Alexander.

"To destabilize the government of the Federal Republic," said Sir George.

"More than that, I suggest," said Brognola. "Not just to destabilize the West German government. To destabilize Western Europe. If there was another incident in Paris this morning, that's more evidence of the purpose."

"From what source?" asked Sir Alexander Bentwood. "What are we talking about? A KGB destabilization?"

"I doubt that," said Brognola. "Although it's always possible. But isn't it inconsistent with the current Soviet effort to normalize relations?"

"Glasnost," said Sir Alexander. "In my judgment, that's just a word intended to dull us into reducing our state of alert, to let them take a major advantage of us before we get our wits together again."

"You don't trust *glasnost*, Sir Alexander?" asked Bolan.

"Do you?" asked the Briton directly.

"No, I don't," said Bolan. "Any more than I trust a mafíoso in a three-piece suit with a silk handkerchief in his breast pocket. He's still a killer. And the Soviet regime is still a—"

"Despotism," said Sir Alexander.

Bolan nodded. "There are a thousand things they could do to demonstrate their good faith if they really mean to convert their tyranny into something approaching a decent government. They haven't done one."

"Not one," said Sir Alexander. "I'm glad we agree so completely, Mr. Bolan. You and I can work together very happily, I think."

Bolan said nothing.

Sir George had sat with his hands clasped before him on the table throughout the exchange. "Let me brief you," he said, "On the explosion on the Kurfürstendamm."

"Please do," said Brognola.

"Two young men and a young woman," said Sir George. "On motorcycles. Stolen motorcycles with fake registration plates. Beards, long hair, dirty clothes. Just before the explosion the young woman shook her fist at the sky and yelled something about peace and freedom."

"Peaceniks," said Sir Alexander.

"To the contrary, Sir Alex," said Sir George Harrington. "Professionals. Agents of . . . well, agents of somebody or other."

"I grant you," said Sir Alexander, "that their effort to make themselves look like peaceniks was a bit unsubtle. But—"

"Conclusive evidence," said Sir George.

"Which is?" asked Brognola.

"It was our friend XY again," said Sir George. "The signature was clear."

"Meaning?" asked Bolan.

Sir George turned in his chair to face Bolan.

"Bomb fragments," he said. "Specifically, bits of wire twisted together. The connections between the radio receiver and the detonator. Those little twisted connections tend to survive the explosions, and if you search carefully enough, you can retrieve them. I hope you understand that when our agencies investigate terrorist explosions they literally vacuum the area and sift through everything they find."

"And what do these bits of wire tell you?" asked Bolan a little impatiently.

"If we had two bits of wire, I could demonstrate. But use your fingers and pretend you're twisting two pieces of wire together. Please do it, Mr. Bolan."

Bolan mimed the manipulation. He didn't need to imagine. He had done it.

"Look at what you're doing, Mr. Bolan," he said. "You would hold the two ends of wire in your left hand and use your right to twist them. That's what you are showing. And you twist . . . clockwise. See. Aren't you?"

Bolan nodded. "Okay."

"But if you're left-handed—"

"Right," said Bolan. "You'd twist counterclockwise."

"Exactly. Then you might—or you might not—bend the twisted pair double as insurance against their becoming untwisted. Would you do that, Mr. Bolan?"

Bolan shook his head. "I guess not. I'd trust my—"

"But XY does, invariably. XY twists counterclockwise, then bends the twisted pair back against itself. He did it in Hamburg and Rome. Then in Berlin. And this morning in Paris."

"You've found the evidence of the twisted wires already?" Brognola asked.

"A bit of luck, that," said Sir George. "Also, the French investigators knew what they were looking for. Bits of wire torn loose from a bomb don't fly far. Not heavy, you know. This kind of evidence is usually found within a few yards of where the bomb was. Anyway, they found the signature wire. Our friend XY set off this explosion, too."

"And where was it?" asked Sir Alexander.

"In a metro station," said Sir George grimly.

"Which one?" asked Marilyn.

"Gare St. Lazare. Commuters coming out of the railroad station, into the metro station . . . the worst possible case. They haven't finished counting the dead. It's worse than Berlin."

"Destabilization," said Brognola. "The chancellor is on the carpet in the Bundestag this morning. He's going to hear demands for beefing up security forces."

"What do they want, a new Gestapo?" asked Sir George.

"That's just the problem," said Brognola. "There are those in Germany who do. There's always been that element."

"Surely you exaggerate," said Sir Alexander. "All they want is effective suppression of terrorism and subversion. Counterterrorist agencies on the Continent have become far less effective in recent years, as the result of new socialist and peacenik restraints, also because a new, more naive generation has succeeded to control of the agencies. We've seen a bit of controversy on that score even here, haven't we, Sir George?"

"Well…I suppose we have, actually. The younger chaps coming along are very different from what we were in our generation."

"Softer," said Sir Alexander. "They call us old cold war warriors, think there never was a menace, that we made it all up, or at any rate feared a menace that was never real. *They* know how to do it better. Cozy up to the Soviets. Fight crime with social programs. Be comfortable."

"Was Richard Vauxhall one of them?" Bolan asked. "One of the new types, I mean?"

"Yes, I suppose he was," said Sir Alexander.

"BEGINS TO FIT together, doesn't it?" Brognola said to Bolan as they walked toward the American embassy.

They had decided to walk, to have a chance to talk alone where there was little chance they would be overheard, either in person or by something electronic.

"It's been developing for a long time," Brognola went on. "The old security agencies in France, Germany, Italy, Spain—not so much here in England, but you did hear what Sir Alexander said about a new generation coming on—have been purged of the old cold war types. Some of them are gone just by attrition—old age, mandatory retirement, illness, death by natural causes. Some were retired early— pressured out to make room for a new generation."

"You think Richard Vauxhall was murdered because he represented the new generation? Marilyn tells me he was likely to have succeeded Sir George Harrington."

"I think it's possible," said Brognola. "In France the Mitterand socialists abolished Action Service," said Brognola. "They replaced it with GIGN, but the change had little impact on tactics because the old personnel just moved over into the new agency. The only way they could change tactics was by changing personnel, and they've been doing it. There is evidence that a few bitter men, some still inside

GIGN and others recently detached from it, have formed a private action group. There is evidence that something of the kind has happened in Germany and Italy."

"And if those groups got together—"

"Right. If they got together and decided to use their experience and special knowledge to destabilize governments, they'd be hard to stop."

"They could sponsor terrorism, with the idea that their countries would have to call them back to power to stop it."

Brognola nodded. "It's a theory. But it would explain the murders and the acts of terrorism."

"So all I've got to do is find out if the theory is true, and if it is, to penetrate one or more of the groups, and then—"

"Then to destroy the conspiracy," said Brognola. "The possibility that the theory is sound is what has prompted the several governments to let you work your way in their countries. When the antiterrorist agencies themselves—people in them, anyway—become the sponsors of terrorism, who fights the terrorism?"

"I do. And I guess I'm not alone."

"No, but you've got to be very careful who you trust."

Bolan laughed. "When did I ever do it any other way?"

When he returned to the Green Park Hotel, carrying another two thousand pounds that Brognola had requisitioned from embassy funds, he found two telephone messages, one to call Bobbie Harper, one to call Marilyn Henry.

He called Harper first. "Your man isn't around his usual haunts," Harper said. "He has his tastes, you know. Usually he's to be found where they're to be satisfied. Not for the past two days. Or three. I'm not a policeman, you know. I've got men looking for Schellenberg, but I can't take the town apart."

"Keep trying," said Bolan coldly. Schellenberg was his only contact with the conspiracy. Harper was his only help in locating the man. "I want him."

"Look, Bradley. You cost me half a million pounds. My man tells me you're a cold-blooded killer. I don't need a guy like you against me right now. So I'm doing what I can. I don't need to be reminded that you want Schellenberg. I know. I don't need any reinforcement."

"You got a deal," said Bolan. "Till you drag your feet."

"I'm not draggin' my goddamn feet! I'm doing what I can."

"Good. Keep in touch."

Then Bolan returned Marilyn's call. "Dinner," she said. "Some things to talk about. Also, Anglo-American relations."

"Okay. Where and when?"

They had dinner at Tiddy Dol's, an traditional English-style restaurant in Shepherd Market. The roast beef was superb. The wine was excellent. After dinner they sat over Stilton and port, with apples and grapes. It was the kind of meal he rarely took—rarely had time to take, rarely would have eaten anyway; a man who ate and drank like this wouldn't be fully alert. That consideration didn't seem to trouble Marilyn who, as he had noticed before, placed comforts higher in her scale of values than he did.

She said they had things to talk about. In fact, she had none. He understood, after a little while, that she had just wanted to be with him; and he guessed she would ask him to return with her to her apartment.

His guess was right. Her invitation was direct. He accepted it.

They took the underground to Holborn Station, then walked down Kingsway a short distance and turned left into the darker, quieter streets that bordered the small, square,

wooded park called Lincoln's Inn Fields. Marilyn took his
arm as they walked in silence for a while.

The muted report of a sound-suppressed pistol broke the
quiet. He heard the whip of the bullet. His reactions were
quick. In an instant he drew the Lahti, dropped into a
crouch and moved to position himself between Marilyn and
the triggerman.

Marilyn was down! She lay on the sidewalk, her body
drawn up in the fetal position.

"Marilyn!"

"I'll be okay," she whispered hoarsely.

All right. If she was going to be okay, then he was going
after the gunman. He sprang over the waist-high iron fence
that bordered the Fields. His man was somewhere in the little park.

The Fields wasn't entirely dark. The city's night glow—
the dim reflection of its million lights on low clouds—shed
a pinkish light. The gunman had to be behind a tree. Waiting for the chance to escape. Or to fire another shot.

On the ground, likely. Crouched. He had an advantage.
Bolan was between him and the street. Bolan could be silhouetted against the lights inside some of the houses that
faced the Fields. Apparently he wasn't silhouetted right
now. Otherwise the guy would have taken another shot.

Bolan moved forward, into the park, away from the
sidewalk and fence. He expected to draw a shot, crouched
to offer a small target and was half-surprised when the shot
didn't come.

The triggerman didn't have many options. He hadn't
run—Bolan would have heard him—so he had to be close.
He had to be behind a tree, and there were just three big
enough and close enough.

He had to know Bolan was moving toward him. He had
to make his move.

Bolan would let him.

Crouching, alert, his eyes sweeping the indistinct shadows, Bolan unfolded the raincoat. He poised, then tossed it man-high to his left. And his idea worked. The silenced pistol spat angrily—a shot at the fluttering raincoat.

Now Bolan knew where the gunman was—behind the tree to his left. And the man would be peering at the coat, unsure if his bullet had hit his target. Bolan moved to his right. And closer.

There he was. A shadow against the tree trunk.

Bolan knelt and took careful, steady aim. If he missed, the bullet would be stopped by the tree; he couldn't risk letting it loose to fly into one of the houses facing Lincoln's Inn Fields. The shadow moved. Bolan fired.

The Lahti cracked authoritatively. The 9 mm slug ripped through the bark of the tree, sending a shower of chips flying. Then it crashed into the shadow.

The triggerman screamed and stumbled backward. That made him an open target, and Bolan put one in his chest.

At the sound of running feet, Bolan whirled with his gun extended.

He lowered the weapon when he recognized Marilyn.

"Are you all right?" Bolan asked, surprised she was on her feet, astonished that she could run through the dark and reach him.

She nodded. She was heaving, gasping. "We've got to get out of here. We don't want to have to explain this to the Metropolitan Police."

"He's carrying no ID," said Bolan. "But look at this." He pointed to the ground beside the body at a short, odd-shaped automatic pistol. "A CZ," he said. "A Czech pistol. Chambered for the 7.62 mm Soviet army pistol cartridge. Who is this guy?"

"What are you thinking about? KGB?"

"What *am* I thinking about? What am I *looking* at?"

Marilyn glanced around. The sound of the two shots from the Lahti had raised the neighborhood. Lights were on that hadn't been on before. People stood at their doors, peering into Lincoln's Inn Fields. "Time to move," she said. "Someone has surely called the police."

Bolan stood up. "Okay. But I've got as many questions to ask as they've got."

They hurried the short distance to Marilyn's apartment.

Once inside, Bolan stood at her window, looking at the police working their investigation in Lincoln's Inn Fields. It was the same everywhere—flashing lights, men officiously going about their business. They would collect a vanload of what they called evidence, impressing themselves and the reporters with their skill and thoroughness; and they wouldn't find out who killed the man who lay dead with his pistol not far from his hand, or why he had fired two shots himself.

"Who was he shooting at?" Bolan asked.

Marilyn shook her head. "I supposed you. But maybe not." She lifted her shoulders and shook her head, shuddering. "Maybe at me."

"Yeah. If so, why?"

She shook her head again.

"Where do you stand in your organization?"

"If the question is, am I in line to become director or deputy director of MI6, the answer is no."

"Are you identified with the new people? Were you identified with Richard Vauxhall?"

"Not particularly."

Bolan let the curtains fall back across the window. "For a moment I thought the man might be Schellenberg."

Marilyn didn't respond. Bolan stared at her. Her sleek legs extended from beneath her short skirt. Her cashmere sweater was full of her. But her face was flushed.

"I guess I better go back to the hotel," he said gently.

She looked up, as if startled. "No," she said quietly.

CHAPTER NINE

A telephone call from Sir George Harrington woke Marilyn. Bolan was in the kitchen making coffee. After a moment she came in.

"Sir George wants us to fly to Paris as soon as possible," she said. "Henri Leclerc has his claim on your services, too, and wants to see you. I'm to go with you. We'll be flown over in a little RAF jet. Sir George would like to be able to tell Leclerc that we'll be there before noon."

The twelve-passenger Falcon jet landed at Orly, south of Paris, at 10:22, thirty-six minutes after takeoff from the former fighter command field in Kent, just south of London. A car pulled up to the jet as soon as it taxied in, and they were met by the tall, saturnine Major Henri Leclerc. They entered his car, an armored Citroën, and the chauffeur sped away, off the airfield.

They didn't pass through passport control or customs, and Bolan carried two pistols under his coat, the Lahti and the Browning pocket automatic he had taken from Bobbie Harper. Marilyn had strapped herself into a leather harness that carried a Beretta 951 under her dark blue blazer. He had noticed her also strapping a little nylon holster to her leg, well above her knee and under her skirt. She was carrying a tiny .22-caliber Beretta automatic there.

"I would like to have your assistance, Mr. Bolan," Leclerc said as the Citroën weaved in traffic on the highway leading into the city from the south. "Your President offered your assistance. We accept it." He favored Marilyn with a gallant smile. "Of course we will be happy also to have the assistance of a charming representative of MI6."

Marilyn returned his smile with a sidelong glance and a half sneer.

Leclerc noticed her reaction. Bolan could see how it went into his mental file—aggressive English girl agent, tolerate her.

"You've been fighting terrorism as long as I have, Mr. Bolan," said Leclerc. "I didn't know your name until it was brought to my attention by Mr. Brognola, but since the explosions in Berlin and Paris I have been in constant contact with Reinhard Kremer—whom you know, I understand—and he all but demanded I call for you. He wanted you in Berlin, in fact. But then the XY bomber struck here in Paris. We think the bomber is still in the city."

"Why do you think so?"

"Let me show you some photographs," said Leclerc.

The driver took the cue and passed a small leather case over the back of the front seat. Leclerc opened it and extracted five photographs. While Bolan looked at them, Leclerc lit a strong French cigarette.

"Do you know any of those, Mr. Bolan?" he asked.

Bolan frowned over the pictures. He sighed and nodded. "Okay. This one calls himself Josef Schmidt. In American that would be Joe Smith. I doubt that's his name. Anyway, I've seen him. He tried to kill me in Hamburg one night."

"You're sure this is the same man? What sort is he?" pressed Leclerc.

"I'm sure," said Bolan positively. "If you're looking for an idealogue, look for somebody else. Schmidt is a hardman, works for pay. He doesn't believe in anything."

"He's in Paris," said Leclerc. "The bomb in Gare St. Lazare was carried in a briefcase, probably by a man in a conservative suit. He abandoned his briefcase and hurried up to the street. A young woman noticed that he'd left his briefcase behind and tried to run after him, to remind him. She couldn't keep up with him. She went back down into the station and was injured in the explosion."

"And she remembered and told you?" asked Marilyn.

"She remembered vividly," said Leclerc. "She will remember him for the rest of her life, for the loss of her leg. She identified Schmidt from this picture. We showed it to her because we know him as you do, Mr. Bolan—as a professional criminal whose services can be procured for any purpose. Also, a German. The first bomb was set off in Berlin. The connection . . . Anyway, it was a good guess."

"Half of what we do is a matter of good guesses," said Bolan.

"Schmidt did not work alone," said Leclerc. "There were three of them in Berlin. Likely there were three of them here. We thought you might recognize another one of them if you saw him."

"If I see him," said Bolan. "Paris is a big city."

"Not so big," said Leclerc. "Like any other city, it is a collection of neighborhoods where people know people. And, of course, we have our resources.

"You have the use of a flat in the Sixth Arrondissement," said Leclerc. "It will be a convenient place in which to take refuge and rest when you wish. It belongs to GIGN. The neighbors will stare at you. They are supposed to do that—and report to us anything out of order. All of them are paid. All of them are trustworthy. You know Paris, do you not?"

"A little," said Bolan.

"I know the city," said Marilyn.

"You know St. Denis?"

She nodded.

Leclerc nodded. "It is an industrial area. Schmidt is remembered there. He was the gunman for a small ring of counterfeiters who worked in a small print shop in St.

Denis—five years ago. These people tend to return to their haunts."

"Unless the other two had their haunts in some other neighborhood," said Marilyn.

"He had a woman there, though," said Leclerc. "We wonder if he wouldn't return to her if he had a few days in Paris and was confident no one would identity him as the St. Lazare bomber."

"Possible," said Bolan.

"The best idea we have, for the moment," said Leclerc. "We did not anticipate Miss Henry, but for you we have supplied a set of blue coveralls, which you will find in the flat. They are the kind that French street workmen wear. They will make you a good disguise."

Leclerc had described St. Denis too negatively. It wasn't so much an industrial neighborhood as it was a neighborhood where working class people lived, crowded with the stores and cafés and bars that served working class people. It wasn't a glamorous area, but it was no slum.

Bolan visited the bars, leaning on the zinc-topped counters and sipping sparingly of the hard red wine the male patrons were drinking. Bolan had only a working knowledge of French. Marilyn was never far from him. Dressed in what she had picked up in a flea market, she played the part of a working class hooker, wearing a short skirt and a dark blue quilted nylon jacket with a fuzzy gray collar of imitation fleece. A GIGN agent, also in disguise, was always within sight.

They set to work in St. Denis late in the afternoon when they arrived from London. They spent the next day, and the next, on the streets and in the bars and cafés of St. Denis. They reached the point where they ceased to look for Josef Schmidt but just looked for people they thought suspicious.

Leclerc insisted a man like Schmidt would never be found on the streets late. He persisted in entertaining them evenings in good small Parisian restaurants. He was confident of his border checks, he said. Schmidt was still in France.

SCHMIDT WAS INDEED still in France. His code name in Berlin had been Fritz. Trudl, also known as XY, was Aimé Rafil. Willi was Heinz Knochen.

Schmidt was what Bolan thought he was, a mercenary criminal.

Aimé Rafil was a professional bomber, trained by Mossad, then a traitor to Israel and its intelligence agency because she could demand and receive fees far in excess of anything Israel would have paid her. She'd had dual citizenship, Israeli and French. Now she didn't claim either. She had millions of francs stashed here and there and was planning to retire.

Aimé had fended off the amorous approaches of both men. Though she was as erotic a creature as either of them had ever seen, she wasn't interested in men. When she had the time, when she wasn't involved in a project, she returned to a small flat in Nanterre where Brigitte waited for her. Of that she could be confident. Brigitte would wait. It was for Brigitte that she let her hair grow long and wore her skirts skimpy. It was for Brigitte that she mimed the sexpot French girl. Brigitte knew how to appreciate her, as did other Brigittes, and she played to them.

Heinz Knochen was a onetime devotee of Germany's Green Party. Then BfV—Bundesamt für Verfassungsschutz, the Office for the Protection of the Constitution— had turned him and made him a spy against the Greens. Now his political philosophy was impossible to define, except that he was certain he had one and was ready to die for it.

Aimé Rafil and Josef Schmidt were scornful of the ideologically confused Heinz Knochen. Still, they found him useful. He was brave. Anyway, the people who paid them were fond of him and insisted he should be a part of all their operations. He had been with them at Hamburg and at Rome and this week in Berlin and Paris.

Bolan's recollection of Schmidt was correct. He had been involved in a counterfeiting operation in St. Denis, and he did have friends there. He had one in particular—a stunning part-time hooker, part-time nude dancer, who called herself Michele Villette. Josef was fond of Michele for reasons not difficult to understand. Michele was fond of Josef because somehow he earned a lot of money, which he was never reluctant to spend. She wore jewelry he had given her—wore it, in fact, with nothing else when she was strutting on the stage of some small club, wore it even when she was in bed with a client.

Days, Michele was to be found on the streets or in the stores and bars of St. Denis. She didn't make much money. She lived in a small flat above a grocery on rue Suger. It was confining, and so she went out. She made small purchases in the shops, and she went into bars for glasses of cheap red wine. She wasn't known as a prostitute in her home neighborhood, and she never accepted propositions there. Anyway, the workingmen and shopkeepers couldn't have met her price. The kind of men whose propositions she would accept were to be found on the grand boulevards.

She didn't have a telephone, either, and when Josef wanted to see her he had to go looking for her.

BOLAN KEPT HIS HEAD down, as if he were staring drunkenly into his wine. Schmidt stood just inside the door to the smoky little bar. Someone grunted at him to close the door—he was letting in the cold—and he stepped inside and up to the bar. He was looking dapper. His hair was slicked back on his bullet-shaped head. He wore a handsome camel overcoat with a maroon silk scarf. He was smoking a long, thin cigarette.

Bolan touched the Lahti. It hung in its harness inside the blue coveralls. He reached up with his left hand and shoved his beret down the side of his head in order to hide his face from Schmidt.

At the far end of the bar Marilyn was talking to a shopkeeper, shaking her head against the invitation Bolan could guess the man was making. He signaled her with his eyes, but she was occupied with fending off the shopkeeper and didn't notice. The man from GIGN was on the street just outside, but Bolan couldn't signal him, either.

Schmidt seemed to exchange quips with the bartender as though they were old friends. Bolan heard him mention the name Michele. The bartender shook his head and shrugged. Schmidt turned away from the bar and strode to the door, as if annoyed.

Bolan lifted a hand to get Marilyn's attention. He tossed his head toward the door. She understood, broke away from the shopkeeper and hurried after Schmidt.

Outside, she signaled the GIGN man. Both of them followed Schmidt. Bolan came out of the bar and trailed after them, keeping well back.

They were good, he was glad to see. When Schmidt stepped inside a little store for a moment, the GIGN man hurried ahead, and Marilyn stopped and seemed to study the goods in a shop window. When Schmidt came out, they were ready for him, whichever way he turned. He continued north, walking past the yawning, smoking GIGN man who ambled into step behind him. Marilyn crossed the street. A little later Schmidt crossed over. Marilyn was leaning on a storefront, apparently searching for something in her purse, and she let Schmidt walk a little distance from her before she walked after him. The GIGN man followed, too—but on the opposite side.

Bolan went to the motorcycles they had parked just off the main street. He expected Schmidt to go to a car eventually, so he started the bike and took up the tail, keeping fifty yards between himself and Schmidt.

Schmidt walked in and out of half a dozen shops and bars; then, looking irritated and walking faster, he went to a Peugeot parked at the curb.

Bolan closed the distance. The GIGN man was calling for help on his radio. The Peugeot pulled away from the curb and into the traffic. Bolan would have liked to stay back, but he would lose him for sure if he didn't follow close.

Schmidt was a bold driver. Swerving back and forth between lanes, he sped south toward the center of Paris. Bolan didn't know the area, but he knew Schmidt could enter the autoroute just a little farther south—and if he did that, he would speed away from the little motorcycle; Bolan doubted he could keep up with the French car if Schmidt took it onto the superhighway.

Schmidt didn't enter the autoroute. Just short of the entry ramp he bore right and headed southwest. Then he turned left and headed due south again. Traffic grew heavier. Bolan recognized the Périphérique ahead, the circle road that went all around the central city. They crossed over it on a bridge and were in the streets.

Here the advantage switched to Bolan. The motorcycle was more maneuverable than the Peugeot. Anyway, Schmidt had to stop for lights. Bolan let a car slip between him and the Peugeot, to make himself less conspicuous, and he followed as Schmidt entered a street that sloped upward.

They were ascending the Butte de Montmartre. Bolan could see the white domes of the Basilica of Sacré Coeur ahead and above.

Traffic stopped. There was no light, but a truck was blocking an intersection ahead. Another motorcycle roared up beside Bolan.

It was Marilyn! Her face was red from the cold air that had blasted against it all the way from St. Denis, and her skirt had been blown back to her hips, uncovering the little .22 automatic she wore between her legs. She grinned at him and pointed—meaning that she would take up the chase and he should drop back. He nodded.

She was right of course. He'd been back there too long; Schmidt could notice. Schmidt would know him if he turned and stared. Marilyn was right.

The streets grew narrower and steeper. Ahead the street ended at a long flight of stone stairs; one would have to walk up from there. But Schmidt turned right, Marilyn followed and Bolan made the same turn and saw them ahead.

Then, abruptly, Schmidt pulled to the curb. Marilyn, obviously experienced in tailing subjects, passed him without a glance and turned right into another street. She knew Bolan was behind and would see where Schmidt went.

Bolan stopped. He watched Schmidt leave the Peugeot and cross the sidewalk. Schmidt had a key. He let himself in through the locked door of a narrow, four-story brick building. From the look of it, it was probably a residential building containing a flat on each floor.

"What's behind? Did you see when you came around?" Bolan asked when Marilyn caught up with him again.

She shook her head. "I'd guess this building backs up against the one behind it," she said.

"Then there'd be only one way out of it—through this door."

"Probably," she said. "Though maybe you can go all the way through and out onto the next street."

Bolan glanced around. It was noon. Pedestrian traffic wasn't heavy, but there were people on the street—women carrying their morning purchases of bread, cheese and wine, one old man smoking a heavy pipe. They were bundled up against the cold. The sky was blue, and white billowy clouds sailed across on a stiff wind.

"First things first," said Bolan. He walked to the Peugeot, knelt down on the street beside it, out of sight from the windows of the building where Schmidt had gone, and—while passersby stared at him in amused curiosity—let the air out of the two left tires.

Marilyn stood staring at the windows of the building. "Are you going to call Leclerc?" she asked when he returned from the Peugeot.

Bolan shook his head. "We'll wait here until Schmidt comes out. We'll nab him and take him to Leclerc. GIGN has ways of finding out things from people, and they'll find out where the other two are."

"Maybe they're in there," she said.

"I wouldn't be surprised."

"Let's hope they are," she said. "If they're still here, they haven't gone off to plant another bomb in another city."

Bolan glanced at his watch. "You can go get something to eat," he said. "And bring me back a sandwich. We're apt to be here a long time."

"I'll stay with you," she said.

They eased back a short distance to where they wouldn't be readily visible from the windows. Marilyn hooked her arm through his and squeezed affectionately. It reminded him of how angry he was at someone who had tried to kill her—or anyway had nearly killed her by firing a shot at him. She didn't require much protection—a young woman who was carrying one Beretta inside her jacket and another between her legs—but he felt protective toward her.

Their wait seemed long, but it was only about twenty minutes. The door opened. Schmidt came out to the Peugeot. He stood beside it for a moment, his lips moving as he cursed under his breath. Then he walked back to the door.

"*Schmidt!*"

Josef Schmidt spun around in the doorway to find Bolan crouched in the street, legs wide, pistol aimed and braced with left hand clutching right wrist.

Bolan hadn't figured Schmidt would surrender. He wasn't surprised when the German threw himself to his left and down, rolling on the sidewalk and drawing a pistol from the big pocket of the camel overcoat. He jerked the trigger and fired one shot without aiming, meaning probably to unnerve Bolan and spoil his aim. The bullet spanged off the pavement and whined for an instant before it hit the brick wall of a building.

Schmidt scrambled to his knees to aim a second shot— just as Bolan's 9 mm slug blasted into his throat and threw him on his back.

Shrieking people dashed for cover as Marilyn ran to Schmidt, kicked him over and grabbed for the keys he had been carrying. She ran to the door and unlocked it.

Bolan followed her as she kicked the door open. But it wasn't what they had expected. It wasn't the entry hall to a block of flats.

A small brown-wrapped package, thrown from a door to the rear, skidded across the floor. Bolan threw Marilyn out the door and into the street just before the package exploded. Marilyn rolled into the gutter, and Bolan rolled on top of her. Shards of glass flew over them, rattling against the Peugeot.

Bolan was on his feet and back through the door before the plaster stopped falling inside. He fired two shots through the door from which the package had been thrown, then he ran through and into the next room.

Next room. There wasn't a room and a next room anymore. The plaster walls were down, the lathing hung limply.

The ceiling of the first room had bumped up, then fallen heavily. The air was white with dust.

These had been workrooms. This was where the terrorists had assembled their bombs. He recognized the supplies and equipment—all too familiar.

And they were still in here.

"Mack..."

"You can get killed in here."

Her Beretta hung loosely in her right hand; her eyes darted around. She put the index finger of her left hand to her lips, then she leveled the Beretta at the shattered plaster wall to Bolan's left and squeezed off a shot.

The slug punched through the wall and then through flesh. Someone beyond screamed.

Two shots came back, barely missing both of them.

Bolan threw his weight against the broken wall, and it collapsed. On his hands and knees on the floor of the small room beyond, a man looked up in terror. He had a pistol in his hand, but he tossed it across the floor, out of his reach, and dropped onto his belly. His clothes were red and sticky with his blood.

Bolan stepped through the wall. Marilyn followed. She nudged Bolan and pointed toward the front of the building. At the front of the long narrow room, which was a sort of hallway, a stairway rose toward the next floor.

Stairway. Always a problem. Someone could fire down on you as you climbed.

Bolan took a moment to pull the clip from the Lahti and to insert another one, full. Marilyn had fired only one shot, but she took a loaded clip from her pocket and shoved it under the tight knit cuff of her jacket, where it could be pulled out and jammed into the automatic in an instant.

Stairway. Where he needed automatic fire. Bursts. The Lahti fired smoothly, with entirely controllable recoil, and

hit what you aimed it at. Eight shots, one at a time. If he'd
only had his Beretta 93-R . . .

"You know how to do this?" he asked.

She nodded. "Keep them worried."

"Right."

Yeah. Worried. He stepped into the narrow stairway and
squeezed off two quick rounds at nothing in particular, just
to the right and up. Marilyn fired two through the ceiling,
also just to the right of the stairs. Somebody up there had
something to think about.

Bolan charged up. He heard Marilyn's feet pounding on
the stairs just behind him. She fired twice more, her slugs
going nowhere, just smashing plaster and kicking up dust.

A hole appeared in the wall ahead of them at the head of
the stairs. Someone had fired cautiously, not moving out
where he could get a clear shot. It had come from a doorway to the right and at the front of the building.

Bolan rolled onto the floor at the top of the stairs, aiming the Lahti at the door from which the shot had been fired.
Marilyn began firing through the wall, shots at two-foot intervals. She pulled her clip and jammed in the full one.

Another package skidded from the door. Marilyn ducked
down, and Bolan threw himself down the stairs. The bomb
had been timidly thrown, by someone afraid to step into the
doorway. It exploded with a roar, blowing an immense hole
in the floor at the front and blowing out the window at the
front of the hall.

A man stepped out and leveled a revolver at the head of
the stairs. He fired at Bolan as he scrambled up again, and
Bolan rolled over and triggered a round at him. The man
grabbed his belly, stumbled forward and fell through the
hole in the floor.

Marilyn shoved her way past Bolan. She ran for the front
of the hall, circled the hole in the floor and reached the door
just as a young woman stepped out.

The young woman had yet another package in her hand. Shocked to see Marilyn so close, she opened her mouth and screamed wildly—until her scream was choked off by the explosion of blood from her lungs into her mouth. Marilyn shot her once at point-blank range.

HENRI LECLERC WAS BEAMING. *"Félicitations,"* he said. "They were the mass murderers of Kurfürstendamm and of Gare St. Lazare. You have performed a service to mankind." He swelled and grinned. "A service to France especially. Not a man of ours was within a kilometer of that house. The newspapers are speculating it was a shoot-out between two factions of a terrorist organization."

Mack Bolan didn't share Leclerc's enthusiasm. He was glad they had executed the terrorist bombers, but he could never congratulate himself. In the first place, they had been human after all. In the second place, whatever had produced them would produce more like them. He had thought once you could better the world by exterminating the animals that killed without conscience, for money or for their petty causes, whatever they might be. He knew better now. There would be others.

"Schmidt, you knew," said Leclerc. "You were right. That is who he was. The man downstairs was José Byass, a Spanish hoodlum with a long criminal record. He's alive, incidentally. But interrogating him will be of little value. He was a hireling, like Schmidt. He doesn't know who he worked for. He took orders from the woman."

"Who was she?" asked Bolan.

"The most interesting," said Leclerc. "But first the other man. He did not survive the trip to the hospital. A shame. He was Heinz Knochen, a German political activist, at one time an agent of BfV. I am curious to know who he was working for."

"And the woman?" pressed Marilyn.

"Aimé Rafil," said Leclerc. "She was XY. The bombs she threw at you had the signature twist to the wire. A very big bomb she was assembling in the cellar had it, too. She was a Parisian. She went to Israel in 1979, worked on a kibbutz, was somehow recruited for Mossad and was trained in antiterrorist tactics. She became an explosives expert. Then she defected." He shrugged. "There is more money in murder than in preventing murder."

"So we know who they were," said Bolan. "What we need to know is who hired them."

CHAPTER TEN

The aircraft was a real bastard. That was why only a few of them had been made, why his employers had been able to buy this one cheap.

On the other hand, it was well suited for what he was doing with it. He swept over the waters of the Mediterranean at little more than a hundred meters, making more than fourteen hundred kilometers per hour, well short of supersonic but still fast.

It was an unbelievable airplane. More than forty years old, it had begun life as a North American F86-F Sabre. The Americans had flown it in Korea before he was born in what they called MG Alley, where its pilots had shot down scores of MGs.

That was an odd thing. No matter how good the MGs became—and some of them, he knew from experience, were very good indeed—the Americans regularly bested them in combat.

Anyway, this Sabre and maybe fifty others had wound up in the hands of an American company in California, which had gutted them of the jet engines that had filled most of the fuselage, put a pointy nose on where the airscoop had been, installed two business jet engines on the outside and the rear, put fuel tanks inside the fuselage, reconfigured the wing fairings a bit, replaced the avionics, painted and buffed the whole bird and offered it to Third World air forces as a subsonic fighter, recon aircraft and fighter pilot trainer. They named it Mink.

It had been a good idea. The trouble was the Mink wasn't a well-behaved airplane. It was tail-heavy. If you didn't know what you were doing, you could scrape the bottom of the rear fuselage on the runway, both taking off and landing. It wanted to skid in turns. It required an unusually gentle hand on the controls; overcontrolling was usually fatal.

After a dozen or so Latin American and African pilots died in it, the Mink was unmarketable. But it was a very competent machine in the hands of a skilled, experienced pilot who knew how to handle a hot, temperamental airplane; and his employers hadn't used bad judgment in buying it.

He and the Mink made a good match.

At low altitude it didn't make its full speed, but in three hours he had flown two-thirds of the length of the Mediterranean. Most of the way he had navigated by compass and by his long experience in flying over this part of the world. The Mink was equipped, however, with an inertial navigation system, which allowed him to fly point-to-point with great precision without relying on radio navigation signals.

At fourteen hundred kilometers per hour and a hundred meters above the water, he had crossed the Malta Channel, then swung a little north to pass between Pantelleria and Sicily. He had seen the lights of towns around the Gulf of Tunis and the sky glow of the city of Tunis itself.

He carried no radar, guns or rockets. Panel lights blinked to show him he was being queried by radars all the way. Probably supersonic fighters high above had him on their scopes. He had never been attacked—and this was his twentieth or twenty-first flight over this route. He was, after all, flying over international waters, which he had every right to do. It was a touchy part of the world. Everyone was interested in avoiding what would be called "an incident." Besides, the people he worked for distributed money lavishly to make sure not too many questions were asked about his weekly flights.

All he really worried about was the American carrier task force that prowled the Mediterranean. Its pilots were touchy about unidentified aircraft that approached too close to the big carrier. Before each flight he got a briefing on the last sightings of the task force, but if sometime he accidentally flew into its zone, he could expect the air to fill with heat-seeking missiles.

The lights of Cagliari glowed on the horizon to his right. Sardinia.

He flew on west until he crossed eight degrees longitude, then five minutes more west before turning north.

Not more than fifty kilometers off the Sardinian coast, he could see the lights of the towns and villages along the shoreline—pinpoints like stars, blinking like stars. Gradually, cautiously, he let the airplane lose altitude until, when he passed Cape Falcon, he was only fifty meters above the water.

He roared over fishing boats, probably over a few yachts, too. Some of the fishermen sent up greetings with bright battery-powered lights. They had seen him before, and he had lent an element of mystery and romance to their drab lives—a roaring jet airplane skimming the waves among them in the predawn dark.

Now came the tough part. Corsica was French. The government of France was more alert than the government of Italy, and had a grim attitude about aircraft intruding into French airspace. He turned the nose of the Mink a little to the east. If he hugged the coastline, the mountains would shield him from all radar except that specifically set along that coast. This approach had worked so far. The French expected violations from the east, not from the west—which was why he had rounded Sardinia and made this western approach to Corsica.

Corsica was mountainous. Mountainside lights loomed above him, to the right and straight ahead. Mountains rose to fifteen hundred meters, within a few kilometers of the coast. He edged closer to the coastline, reduced speed and turned due north.

He was looking for the Gulf of Valinco, and nothing but eyeballing was going to find it for him. The few flights he'd had to abort had happened on nights when coastal fog obscured the gulf. It wasn't easy to find in the dark. Radar would have been immensely helpful, but his radar signal, scanning the coastline and mountains, would have alerted every French defense station between here and Paris. He peered at the lights in the villages and at the looming bulk of the island.

And there it was. The narrow entrance to the little gulf—unless he was wrong. He turned the aircraft sharply to the right and flew straight toward the mountains that ringed the gulf. If some night he was wrong...

But once again he wasn't. To his left was the mouth of the Taravo River, flowing down from the mountains through a narrow valley where he would now fly.

North and east. A Corsican river valley, climbing into the central massif of the island. A mountain to his right rose almost two thousand meters. One to his left rose twelve hundred. Good. They shielded him. He raised the nose a little and began a slow climb. He was almost home.

Not home, really. Among the Corsicans. They were Italians, not French. They were a conquered people, as his people were. That made them fierce, as unfortunately it hadn't made all of his people, only some of them. But for all their fierceness, they lived as a conquered people. They had learned ways of coping with their status. They enjoyed a degree of independence. They took their vengeance. But still they weren't free. For well over two hundred years they had lived this way. How could they endure it?

He pulled back the stick, pushed in the throttle and climbed abruptly. Then just as abruptly he cut power. A fire burned in a field on a slope ahead. He studied the sparks rising from the flame. He'd had to teach them to put dry wood in their fire and make sparks. By watching the sparks he could tell which way the wind was blowing. Wind from six-zero. Good. He extended his wing flaps, then his landing gear.

He switched on his landing lights for a moment, wincing at the long bright beams that stabbed the darkness. They were a signal only; in truth they interfered with his view of the landing site, and like most pilots he rarely used them more than momentarily.

The Americans had built the Sabre to operate off short fields, and the Mink had no trouble with a short landing on rough ground. He cut his power almost to nothing and let the plane settle. The ground came up. He felt the ground effect, the compression of air between his wings and the ground just below them. Then he raised the nose, and the Mink settled down comfortably.

"WELCOME, MAJOR."

The man in the fleece vest handed him a cup of strong black coffee. Others similarly dressed, some carrying short shotguns, ran around the fire, throwing on water. Two men in dark suits were opening the sealed door in the bottom of the fuselage.

Sealed. No matter how many times he flew for them, they remained distrustful. He sipped his coffee gratefully. Distrustful. Well . . . how far would he trust *them*? With a million pounds? Not likely.

"It's in order, Major," one of the suits said to him. "And here is your money."

He never counted it. Not in their presence. They didn't trust him, but it was a matter of honor with them that he should trust them. And so far they had met their obligations promptly and in full.

"The padrone wants to see you," one of the suits said. "I have a car waiting. By the time we reach the villa, it will be the time when he wants to see you."

The major nodded. He glanced at the Mink, which they were now covering with foliage—a useful precaution only against the most primitive visual observation. He had developed an affection for the aircraft, and he would have preferred to stay with it until it had been properly serviced. But the Corsican waited.

The car was a Mercedes. His employer seemed to own nothing else. It was an armored Mercedes. Rich men used armored automobiles in the Corsican mountains. If the padrone had no enemies who would dare touch him, the armored car was a precaution against some mountain man who might not realize whose car it was.

It was a two-hour drive to the mountaintop villa. As the suit had said, they arrived at the hour when Don Vittorio Muro was sitting down to his breakfast. The table was set for two, for the don and the major. It was behind the glass doors that overlooked the terrace and the long view.

"An easy flight?" asked Don Vittorio. It was a polite question, politely asked; obviously it was a successful flight, or the major wouldn't be here, and that was all the don cared about.

The major shrugged.

"So. None of them are easy, are they? You think we should appreciate that, Major Alani, and believe me we do. I do. I have every confidence in you as a pilot."

Major Alani nodded. He appreciated the assurance.

"In fact, supreme confidence," said Don Vittorio. He drew a deep breath. "You told me you once flew a Foxbat. Is that true?"

It was true. Major Sayed Hadji Alani had flown a Foxbat for the Egyptian air force. He had flown in combat against the Israelis. That is, he did after he was supplied with a second aircraft. His first Foxbat had been destroyed when the Israelis attacked without warning and knocked out almost the entire Egyptian air force before it could get off the ground. He remembered running in frustration across the tarmac toward what had been his beautiful, gleaming jet fighter, now literally broken in two. But he'd had his revenge later in the air over the Sinai and over the Canal. He had shot down three Israeli Mirages.

Then . . . Anwar Sadat had betrayed the cause of the Arabs. Sayed Hadji Alani was a bitter man.

"Could you still fly a Foxbat?"

Major Alani nodded. "It's something you don't forget. In a few minutes I could—"

"You would be paid one million pounds," said Don Vittorio Muro.

"It's a combat aircraft," said Alani.

"It's a reconnaissance interceptor," said Don Vittorio. "Its purpose is to find enemy aircraft and shoot them down."

"You want me to shoot down—"

Don Vittorio interrupted with a quick gesture of his hand. "I want to introduce you to certain people. They will pay you half a million English pounds for *attempting* this mission, another half million if you succeed. It will be a very dangerous mission—difficult and dangerous, requiring skills and courage of the first order. If you carry it out successfully, not only will you be a wealthy man for the rest of your life—no need to fly opium base to Corsica for me—but you will have done something spectacularly damaging to your people's enemies."

"*My* people's enemies?"

"Yes. This mission is political. I know you find a political element in the flying you do for me, since the heroin we make from the opium base isn't shot into Arab veins, but into the veins of Americans—"

"Into the veins of the imps of Satan," said Alani.

The don nodded patiently. "But this is nothing—in terms of damaging the Americans—compared to what you will have the opportunity to do now."

"Exactly what is it I will have the opportunity to do?"

Don Vittorio paused while the cook put a big platter of eggs and sausage on the table, and he himself used a spoon and fork to heap two plates with generous portions. The major knew that these sausages were beef sausages, and the eggs hadn't been cooked in the fat of pigs. The don liked American-style breakfasts, but he respected Major Alani's sensibilities.

"This mission isn't mine. Friends of mine asked me if I knew a first-class pilot in whom they could place their confidence to carry out an historic mission. I thought of you and recommended you. But only they can tell you what the mission is. Even they won't tell you until you are committed."

Major Alani was hungry. He was hungry and tired after flying a tough, demanding run. He welcomed a new job. Sooner or later, this one was going to go bad. It offered no margin for error, and any one of a thousand accidents could occur. He hadn't been sure how the Corsican padrone would take his resignation, but now he himself was offering something different. The major began to eat hungrily, his spirits lifted by the conversation.

Don Vittorio had always liked the major. On the other hand, he would be glad to get rid of him. He was a skilled pilot. None could be better. But he was a believer. Not only that, he was a believer in something the don couldn't begin to understand. It was difficult to place as much confidence in him as he hoped the Egyptian believed he did.

"I must tell you, Major," said the don. "This mission could make you a martyr. But I think you will agree, when you know what it is, a man with your dedication could not find a better martyrdom."

Major Alani nodded and went on eating. The don had judged his man. Talk of martyrdom would only inspire him.

The major ate rapidly. Military people learned to do that—also people who had been hungry, though Don Vittorio wasn't sure that applied to Major Alani. He cleared his plate and emptied his cup.

"If you want to meet the people who are offering this mission," said the don, "I will have you flown to Rome this evening. You can talk with them and make your own judgment."

The major nodded. "I will go."

"Good. Then . . . you have flown a long distance, come a long distance from the field. I am sure you need sleep. Federico will show you your suite. In your bed you will find someone attractive. If you like her . . . she is yours. If not . . . well, a man needs his sleep. Anyway, she will be there to serve your needs, whatever they are. Maybe when you are rested . . ."

Major Alani grinned boyishly. Europeans . . .

They stood. Don Vittorio Muro extended his hand. Major Sayed Hadji Alani shook it.

"Do we have a deal, my friend?" asked the don. "At least one that you will seriously consider?"

Major Alani nodded emphatically. "In the name of Allah, the most compassionate, the most merciful . . ."

ROME WAS A CITY of conspiracy. With its centuries-old history of conspiracies, it was the perfect place to hide a conclave. What schemes had been hatched here, the Egyptian major mused as he rode in a careening little Roman taxi toward the mysterious address he had been given. The Caesars...the Popes...the ghosts of knife-wielding assassins and subtle conspirators joined in the dark streets. It was a city in which nothing was what it seemed.

Much less the villa where the taxi took him. Once past the hardmen who guarded the gates and doors, Major Alani walked along a corridor paved with mosaic tiles, between marble-paneled walls lined with odd busts in niches, past potted palms and huge oak doors, until at last he was admitted through double doors and welcomed into a cavernous salon.

A log fire roared and crackled in a huge marble fireplace that dominated the room. Three men sat in huge chairs that faced the fireplace. All of them were nattily dressed in suits with white shirts, vests and neckties. Each of them was drinking what looked like whiskey and soda.

"Ah, Major Sayed Hadji Alani," one of them said, and he rose, put his glass aside and came across the room. "You speak English, I believe? It is the only language that is common to all of us. I am Aldo Vicaria. Let me introduce you to Herr Doktor Johann Kleist and to Mr. Edward Holmesby-Lovett."

The two men looked up and acknowledged the major with smiles, but they didn't rise or extend their hands.

Vicaria was a handsome Italian, probably sixty years old. His white hair was thick and looked as if it had the daily attention of a barber. His eyebrows were black and bushy. His face was tanned.

"Major," he said, "I understand you do not take alcohol. Would you like coffee or juice?"

"Coffee, please."

"Good. Join us. Have a chair. The fire takes the chill and damp off the room, does it not?" Vicaria pressed a button on the wall beside the fireplace to summon a servant and then pointed to a chair.

The Englishman interlaced his fingers and studied Alani with a forthright, appraising stare. He was a heavy, jolly-looking man, the major thought. The German, too, was making his judgment—a less friendly appraisal—but apparently neither of them found any defect by their superficial examination. He was a compact, muscular man, forty-two years old, with an olive complexion, soulful dark eyes and a luxuriant black mustache.

"You fly for Don Vittorio Muro," said the German. "You flew a Foxbat in combat for the Egyptian air force. And you resigned your commission because—"

"Because Anwar Sadat sold out the Arab cause and entered into an unholy alliance with the Jews," said Major Alani.

"Who do you regard as your enemies?" the German asked bluntly.

"The Israelis above all," said the major. "Then all those who help and support them in their evil designs. The Americans, chiefly."

"Maybe the British and the French also," suggested the Englishman, lifting his brows high and showing his great, bulging blue eyes.

"We will tell you frankly," said the German crisply, ignoring the Englishman's comment, "that we have no interest in the Arab cause. Or the Israeli cause, either, for that matter. We need a skilled pilot to carry out a difficult flying mission for us. We will pay well, and I suggest that be your motive for accepting the mission—if you accept it. What we want you to do will damage the Americans. Grievously. If you find satisfaction in that, so be it. But our pilot must be anonymous, must never be identified. If you're interested in making some kind of statement, forget it. You will be a mercenary soldier."

A maid—a timid young girl wearing a very short black dress with a white apron and starched white cap—came in and heard an order to bring coffee.

"You have a Foxbat?" asked the major skeptically, once the girl had left. "Where did you get it?"

"Never mind where we got it," said Vicaria. "It is in first-class condition and is entirely capable of flying the mission."

"And the mission is—"

"We can't tell you now," said the German. "It is dangerous. After it is completed, you must eject from the Foxbat, which will not have enough fuel to return to its base, and let it crash into the sea. We will be waiting for you and will pick you up from the water. You will be wearing a locator transmitter, and a high-speed boat will rush to get you. You must realize, though, that we might not get to you in time before you drown or freeze. We will try. This is not a suicide mission. But you may lose your life. For that reason we will pay your money to anyone you designate in the event you should not live to collect it."

"Don Vittorio will act as your agent with regard to the money," said Vicaria. He smiled faintly. "He is your guarantor. You could not have a better one."

"If I accept—"

"If you accept, we will hand you half a million English pounds, tonight, in cash," said Edward Holmesby-Lovett. "We suggest you let Don Vittorio hold it for you, but that is your judgment to make. You will return to the don's villa and wait for our orders. Shortly we will fly you to the base from which you will fly the Foxbat. We assume you know the aircraft well and will want to participate in the final checkout."

"What if I don't like the mission?" asked Major Alani. "When you tell me what it is, I mean."

"We assure you of three things," said Holmesby-Lovett. "One, of payment. Two, that it isn't a suicide mission, that elaborate preparations are being made to save the pilot. Three, that you will be striking an enormously hurtful blow against the United States. But you must trust us—or Don Vittorio."

Major Alani nodded thoughtfully. "Great causes are worth great risk," he said.

When Major Alani was gone, Kleist, Vicaria and Holmesby-Lovett sat engrossed in thought for a long, silent moment, each one frowning, none of them drinking from their glasses.

Holmesby-Lovett spoke first. "He's all that was promised, but I have a serious reservation."

Kleist nodded. "I, too. If he is stupid enough to think we are going to pull him out of the water, is he intelligent enough to fly the mission?"

"I suggest two answers to that question," said Vicaria. "First, we must remember we are dealing with a fanatic. He is intelligent and brave, but his mind has a flaw, a block one might say. Given the right stimulus, Major Alani reacts instinctively. Given the opportunity to strike at what he hates, he blinds himself to everything but the attack. Second, he may understand perfectly well that we have no intention of saving him from drowning—and be willing to do it because it will be the martyrdom that earns him an eternity in paradise."

"A magnificent animal," said Kleist. "Trained from his childhood to respond to certain stimuli in a certain way."

"Programmed is, I believe, today's fashionable word," said Holmesby-Lovett. His concern half dispelled, he reached for his glass. "And when he learns what the mission is—"

"He will react like a machine!" Kleist exulted. "I think Don Vittorio has done us a wonderful service."

Vicaria nodded thoughtfully. "Everything is falling into place. When we began to build the Foxbat, I could never have guessed we would have such an opportunity for it! I thought something...much smaller. But this..." He raised his glass. "Gentlemen! To success! Success beyond our wildest dreams!"

MIKOYAN DIDN'T KNOW where he was. He had never known, not since he had been brought here. He could only guess. It was somewhere cold, somewhere above the Arctic Circle. And he was prisoner of a conspiracy so unrealistic that he couldn't imagine what the criminals who held him expected to accomplish. Their resources were astonishing. They were capitalists obviously, and they seemed to have unlimited funds.

The word impossible meant nothing to them. He had imposed requirements he had been certain they couldn't meet. They met them. Materials. Personnel. Whatever he said he needed, they supplied. Brought it here somehow, to this remote frozen place from which the sun had long since retreated.

He wasn't sure, but he suspected they had originally thought he was a son or grandson of the Mikoyan of the Mikoyan-Gurevich design team who had designed the MiG aircraft. They knew better now. Mikhail Nikolaievich Mikoyan wasn't related to that famous man, nor to Anastas Ivanovich Mikoyan, late of the Politburo.

Or maybe they hadn't been deceived. Whoever had been his father or grandfather, Mikhail Mikoyan was one of the finest aircraft engineers the Soviet Union had ever produced. He had gone to Prague, to a meeting of aircraft designers, and suddenly... kidnapped.

He sensed that his only chance to survive was to do exactly what they told him. He was kept here by grim, hard men. If he intentionally built a failure into their Foxbat, he would die. Maybe painfully.

So they had their Foxbat engineer, and they had their Foxbat. Incredibly they had brought it here piece by piece, and God knows where they got the pieces. Some of them were from different stages in the development of the aircraft and didn't fit together. Some of the parts weren't Foxbat parts at all. Some of the parts weren't even of Soviet manufacture. This Foxbat would fly with components from such diverse aircraft as French Mirages, British Harriers and North American F-16s. Particularly the electronics. His crew had learned much about American electronics in the past few months.

Incredibly, too, the Foxbat that was now in final stages of assembly in the hangar would be a competent aircraft, capable of everything a Foxbat was supposed to be capable of.

But today, like every day, there was a problem.

The armorer, Sobolensky, shook his head. "The AAMs," he said. "Too long in storage, too long neglected. Fifty percent chance they will work."

The Frenchman, one of their masters, walked across the hangar floor and looked at the four air-to-air missiles laid out on trestles. Though he peered inside the open panels at the electronic innards of the infrared-guided missile, obviously he could tell nothing by looking. "You're sure of this?" he asked.

Sobolensky nodded. "From twenty or thirty kilometers and coming directly up from the rear, they might find their target. Shooting from an angle, shooting from a greater distance..." He shrugged. "Every component has aged. Connections are corroded. If we disassembled everything—"

"Mount the Phoenix missiles, then," said the Frenchman curtly.

"What? An American missile fired from—"

"Do it," said the Frenchman. "You'll need to mount only two. They have an effective range of more than two hundred kilometers, and they deliver a bigger load of explosives."

Mikoyan nodded. "Why not?" he said to Sobolensky. "Firing from so great a range, the Foxbat will be doing exactly what it was designed to do—stand off at a great distance and launch AAMs. If the target is escorted by fighters, they will have no chance of overtaking." He smiled. "And no chance of interfering with the American missiles."

"You should have recognized from the first," said the Frenchman to Mikoyan, "that the American Phoenix is a weapon superior to the Russian Acrid. So overcome the problems. Mount the Phoenixes and devise a link between their guidance system and the Foxbat's radar. You have work to do, you and your crew. We have little time left. Analyze quickly. If you need any kind of part, let me know within twenty-four hours. *Twenty-four hours,* Mikoyan."

CHAPTER ELEVEN

"Your messages, sir."

Bolan took his key and three telephone messages from the clerk behind the desk at the Green Park Hotel. He had been in Paris just four days, but returning to London he felt as though he had been away for a month. Oddly—oddly, that is, for London in winter—the sun was shining brightly. It was a crisp, bright blue day. The little RAF jet that had flown them over from Orly had climbed only to fifteen thousand feet and swept over the Channel under a few scattered clouds.

The MI6 car had dropped him here and had carried Marilyn on to headquarters. He had promised to come there after he had bathed and changed his clothes.

In the lift he scanned his messages. The first was routine, a call from Sir George Harrington, asking him to telephone him when he arrived. The second was from Bobbie Harper, who also asked to be called. The third read: "The friends of Aimé will not let her death go unavenged. You and Marilyn are in trouble. Dieter."

Dieter. Dieter Schellenberg. Gutsy. No, not gutsy. Obedient. Yeah. A little man taking orders.

But odd orders, Bolan figured. They didn't think he'd scare, did they? And if they really meant to make another attempt to kill him, why warn him? It didn't make sense.

He called Bobbie Harper.

"I've located your man for you," Harper said crisply. "He's a man of fixed habits, can't seem to stay away from them very long. If you still want him, you can have him."

"I want him. Where is he?"

"He showed up in a place of mine night before last. He's got a favorite girl. He wanted to see her again, but I had her tell him she wouldn't be available for a few days and he should call. He called last night. He'll call tonight, I wager. She can be available, if that's how you want it."

"That's how I want it," said Bolan.

"Barring something odd, he will be at this place at nine. It's in Bloomsbury. Do you want to write down the address?"

Bolan did so, hung up, then called Sir George.

"Well done in Paris, Bolan. Well done. I'm afraid it doesn't get us any closer to the power behind the murders and bombings, though. I've a message for you from Mr. Brognola. He's in Bonn. He said he should like you to come there, perhaps tomorrow. Try to make yourself available, he said."

After he hung up, Bolan dialed Marilyn's number. He felt he owed her an explanation as to why he might not be able to see her that night. When she answered, he could sense the excitement in her voice.

"Sometimes I work alone, Marilyn. In fact, usually I work alone. And this evening, what I'm going to do, you couldn't possibly help me with. In fact—"

"In fact, I'd be in your way," she interrupted.

"Let's don't say it that way."

"All right, Mack. Let's don't say it that way. Will you call me when you're finished?"

"It may be dawn."

"All the more reason to call."

"Okay. I'll wake you up."

"I won't be asleep. Not until I hear from you."

Bolan sighed loudly just after he put down the telephone. Marilyn was beautiful, smart and brave. She could be a complication in his life. In all kinds of ways.

Like right now. He couldn't be sure she wouldn't come to the hotel and insist on joining him. He decided to leave early, just after seven. He'd have dinner somewhere and then walk to his appointment.

He hid the Lahti under the mattress and slipped Bobbie Harper's Browning into the holster, where it would ride very loosely but would be quickly available if he needed it.

He walked to his appointment. During his few days in Paris the Christmas decorations had been put up in London. Spectacular on Regent Street. It seemed as if a million people were on the streets that evening, crowding one another happily, bustling in and out of stores, shopping, popping in and out of pubs, eating in restaurants, laughing, smiling...

They reminded Bolan of his mission. They represented it in a very real way. It was to them that he had dedicated himself—to make it possible for innocents to scurry about their Christmas shopping, to enjoy life in peace and freedom. They didn't even have to think about the handful of men and women who had pledged their lives to defend their peace and freedom.

Maybe he and Marilyn had saved the lives of scores of these very people. Maybe the bombers they had shot to death in Paris—who had been busily manufacturing more bombs at the very hour when he and Marilyn found them— had meant to come here next, to set off a murderous explosion in one of the big stores on Regent Street.

He ate a light dinner in a small Italian restaurant in Soho. Then it was time to move on to his appointment with Dieter Schellenberg.

BOBBIE HARPER'S old-fashioned bordello was in Bloomsbury, only a few blocks from the British Museum. The whorehouse was in a redbrick Victorian house facing a small wooded park.

The woman who opened the door looked at him with a curious, unfriendly expression and waited for him to speak. She was apparently the madam of the house. She was in her forties, a ravaged-looking woman who had probably worked as a whore until wrinkles and sagging flesh diminished demand for her. She wore black, a short silk dress reminiscent of the twenties.

"Ernest Bradley," he told her. "Bobbie Harper sent me."

She nodded and stepped back from the door. He entered a narrow, dimly lit hallway, and the woman pointed at a set of oak double doors to the right. She stepped past him and knocked, then opened the doors.

Harper was waiting for him in the madam's parlor. He sat at an antique round oak table covered with a fringed red cloth. A bottle of whiskey sat before him, and a little remained in his glass. He looked up at Bolan from beneath his sleepy eyelids, his eyes flickering alertly under his long, effeminate lashes.

"Well . . . Mr. Bradley. Our friend hasn't arrived yet. But he will. He called and made his appointment."

Bolan nodded as he drew up a chair.

"While we wait, I was hoping you might be willing to discuss a business proposition with me."

Bolan shrugged. "I'm willing to discuss anything," he said.

"Good. You once said to me that if I located Schellenberg for you, you would consider doing me some service to repay me for what you cost me. Are you willing to hear a proposition?"

"Why not?"

Harper ran a hand along the side of his head—along, in fact, his swept-back, abundant hair. He wore his hair like an American motorcycle cowboy of a couple of decades ago. It was a type Bolan detested.

"A man of your particular talents could do me an important service," Harper said. "To balance the books between us, so to speak."

"A hit?"

Harper nodded. "Then it would be peace between you and me. And that's something you might want, Mr. Bradley. I told you I am a man who evens scores. Right now I think you're well ahead of me. If you do this job for me, I'm willing to call things even."

"I'm not leaving the country," Bolan said. "You know where to call me. I'll be taking Schellenberg with me when I leave here. But you can call me tomorrow or the next day."

Harper smiled. "All right. I lied to you. Schellenberg is here now. I wanted this chance to talk with you before I turn him over to you. So...I will telephone you tomorrow. Now Priscilla will take you to Schellenberg."

Harper went to the door and knocked once. The woman who had met Bolan at the door opened it immediately; she had been waiting. She beckoned with a finger, and Bolan left the room and went with her.

Without speaking a word, she led him up a narrow flight of stairs, then up another. The hallways on each floor were identical—dimly lit, with rows of oak doors opening to either side. It was as though the house had been built for a small hotel, or for the bordello it had become. She stopped before a door, raised a hand and signaled for silence. Then she seized the knob, turned it quickly, pushed the door and stepped back.

Dieter Schellenberg was in bed with a pretty blond girl. He sat almost fully erect, propped up with pillows. She reclined beside him. A sheet covered both of them to their shoulders.

Bolan came alert. Schellenberg wasn't shocked, wasn't outraged. Something...

The girl threw back the sheet. Schellenberg was fully clothed, and in both hands he held a pistol pointed squarely at Bolan. The girl was clothed. She reached under the sheet and pulled out another pistol.

"Well, Mr. Bolan?" Schellenberg said.

He couldn't reach for the Browning. He had come expecting a trap but not one sprung like this. He sensed movement behind him, but before he had time to turn, he felt a blow to the back of his head. Though he was stunned and disoriented, Bolan wasn't unconscious. It was wise to pretend to be, though.

The man who had struck him from behind knelt over him and pulled the Browning from the holster. He handed it up to Bobbie Harper.

"I prize this, actually," said Harper. "Glad to have it back."

Five of them stood over him—Schellenberg and the blonde, Harper and the hardman who had just taken the Browning, and Priscilla. Bolan lay facedown. The pain at the back of his head was all but unbearable, and he could feel wet blood on his neck.

"Be careful with him," said Schellenberg. "He may be faking unconsciousness."

"I can make sure of him very easily," said Harper, leveling the Browning at Bolan's head.

"Don't even think of it, Harper," said Schellenberg coldly. "He's mine."

Bobbie Harper sneered. "Well, now," he said. "I have a claim on him."

"*Harper.* Haven't you gotten it through your head yet who you're dealing with?"

"I want to be paid," said Harper sullenly.

"That's correct. If you obey your orders, we'll allow you to live. That's your payment."

"I'm not sure you're in control here, Schellenberg," sneered Harper.

The blonde, who still sat on the bed with pistol in hand, turned the muzzle almost lazily toward Harper's hard-man—he was one of the two who had visited Bolan's hotel room—and pulled the trigger. Her Beretta was silenced, and it simply burped its 9 mm slug into the man's chest. As he toppled, she turned the muzzle toward Harper.

He threw out his hands, away from the Browning he had tucked inside his jacket. "Okay," he muttered. *"Okay!"*

Priscilla was horrified and slumped against the wall.

"All right," said Schellenberg. "Eva has made my point more effectively than I could. Now, Harper, I have more work for you. First, I want you to get rid of that corpse there. In the river, hmm? Then I want you to lodge Mr. Bolan— Incidentally, you do understand that he's Mack Bolan? I mean, you have heard of the American they call the Executioner? All right. He is to stay here temporarily. We haven't made a final decision as to what we're going to do with him."

"Bolan..." Harper muttered. "He's worth a goddamn fortune. I know people who—"

"After we're finished with him, we may let you sell him," said Schellenberg. "Tomorrow Mr. Bolan begins an ordeal by interrogation. He's the most valuable capture we've made in years—so valuable that interrogators are flying in just to question him. My superiors couldn't believe we'd succeed in taking him alive. It was a crude operation, Harper, but simple and effective."

"What will you do to him?" Harper asked. "I need him alive."

"When we're finished with him, he'll be alive. There may not be much left of his brain, but he'll be alive."

"How long will you keep him here?"

"Two or three days. I'll send people to guard him. Eva will stay here to supervise."

Harper stared at the unconscious Bolan. "When he comes around, he—"

"He'll be most dangerous," said Schellenberg.

"But he won't come around for a while," said Eva. She knelt beside him.

Bolan felt the sharp prick of a needle. She hadn't even bothered to pull back his sleeve, much less to locate a vein; she had just shot him with something. He felt it almost instantly.

"You owe me, Schellenberg," said Harper. "And you don't dare kill me. You'd have to kill too many others. You couldn't keep it secret."

"You'll be paid. Don't worry."

"You'll still be at the place on Craven Street?"

"Craven Hill," said Schellenberg. "Eighteen twenty-four. And you may..."

The voice trailed off for Bolan. He heard a distant humming that grew louder, and then nothing.

SIGHT RETURNED FIRST, even before the pain at the back of his head. Bolan became aware of light, then blacked out again, then became aware of light shining on his closed eyes. He separated his lids slowly, cautiously. The light was the bulb in the ceiling fixture in the room where he had seen Schellenberg just before...

Then he felt the tight steel cuffs on his wrists. He was a prisoner. If he was alive, he was a prisoner. His hands were behind and above his head. He was lying on the floor in a corner of the room, and the link between his handcuffs had been passed behind a steel or drainpipe that came up through the floor and went on through the ceiling. His ankles, too, were tightly clamped in leg irons. He was stark naked.

Eva was lying on her back on the bed, her head propped up on the pillows, reading. She didn't know he had come out of it. He closed his eyes again. That she didn't know he was conscious was his only advantage.

He'd been slugged hard. The dull pain was an insistent, deep throbbing. Under that he felt the sting of raw flesh.

Slowly he opened his eyes again. The girl was still reading. He glanced around, moving only his eyes, not his head—even though moving his eyes was like rubbing his throbbing head with chain. The room was almost bare. It was nothing but a whorehouse room, furnished with a bed, a sink and a stand on which clients hung their clothes.

Probably some of the rooms below were better. They had brought him up here because no one worked on this floor anymore. Below, likely, the house's usual traffic was moving in and out.

Likely... likely if it was still night. He had no idea what time it was. He could have been out a whole night. The sun might be shining outside. No. There was a window just beyond his outstretched feet. Though it was covered with a curtain and a paper blind, he could see no light on the blind, so it was still dark outside.

But what time was it? What difference did it make?

They hadn't killed him. They hadn't moved him. Schellenberg had said someone was coming to interrogate him. Someone who had to fly in. Schellenberg's superiors.

Schellenberg had been clever this time. That note of his, or had it been from him, really? Probably. A dare. A ploy to make Bolan angry, less cautious. He—

Eva put down her book. He closed his eyes.

"You're among us again, Mr. Bolan, aren't you? Don't try to deceive me. It makes no difference anyway."

He opened his eyes. She was beautiful. She had a provocative figure. Her eyes were blue, her hair naturally blond—as he could tell from her blond and almost invisible eyebrows and lashes. She was no bimbo. She'd pointed that pistol of hers at him with a cool detachment that had told him she would fire without hesitation.

She cocked her head, looked him up and down and grinned. "I'm sorry we meet in such circumstances," she said. "You're obviously a real man—with scars you didn't get from women's fingernails. But...every man has his price, every man his Achilles' heel. What was yours? Hate? Too much hate to be cautious?"

He closed his eyes. "I have to go to the bathroom," he said.

"I suppose so," she said. "We thought you might."

She rolled off the bed, went to the basin and lifted out a stainless-steel bedpan. She squatted beside him and pressed the bedpan against his crotch. He urinated. She emptied the bedpan into the sink and rinsed it out.

"Later you'll require additional care," she said. "I'll have help. For now, you may as well relax."

Relax. Sure. He twisted his body to relieve cramps in his back and legs. The cuffs were strong and tight. There would be no slipping them, no breaking the link. The pipe was solid. The leg irons—just bigger handcuffs, actually—were tight, too. There would be no escape. The blonde could go to sleep if she wanted to.

"I CONGRATULATE MYSELF," laughed Dieter Schellenberg. "If you won't congratulate me, I congratulate myself. *Bolan!* Ready for interrogation. Chained up and waiting."

"I want to see for myself. Write down the address. You say you left Eva to guard him?"

Schellenberg scribbled. "Eva. She shot one of Harper's men tonight, just to impress Harper with the situation. Come now. I'm to be congratulated, am I not?"

"Where's Bolan? I want to see him."

Schellenberg shook his head. "He's *mine.*"

"To whom is your loyalty, Dieter?"

Schellenberg stiffened. He raised his chin, and his lips hardened in a twisted grin. "To the Deutsche Demokratische Republik!" he barked. "To the Ministerium für Staats-Sicherheit!"

"The wrong answer, Dieter."

The 9 mm slug ripped upward through his throat and exited from the back of his neck, splattering the wall with his gore.

BOLAN STIRRED. Had he slept? Or lost consciousness again? Had the blonde slept? She was slow, he thought, in responding to the discreet rap on the door. He glanced around. Nothing had changed. The light still burned in a fixture on the ceiling, glaring on his eyes. It was still dark beyond the curtain and window blind.

"Miss Zhulev, someone at the door."

Zhulev. So that was her name. She spoke irritably to Priscilla, the madam. "What do you mean, someone at the door?"

"Someone asking for you by name. A woman. At the door. I didn't let her in."

"She wants to see—"

"Eva Zhulev. I asked her twice. She's emphatic."

Eva Zhulev glanced at Bolan, then came to him and checked his handcuffs. They were tight. He could attest to that; his hands were beginning to tingle. She stood before him for a moment, staring at him as if satisfying herself that she could leave him alone for a minute or two.

He could all but read her mind. She glanced next at Priscilla. Should she leave Priscilla as his guard while she went downstairs to see who was asking for her? No.

Decisively Eva Zhulev left the room, slamming the door behind her, leaving Bolan alone.

He tested the handcuffs. He could barely turn his wrists an inch inside the imprisoning steel, much less slip a cuff down over his hand. The link between the cuffs was secure and strong. He seized the pipe in both hands and tugged on it. It wouldn't budge.

He stood. At least he could relieve his muscles by standing. But when he stood his hands were behind his back, one on each side of the pipe. His ankles were joined by a chain about twelve inches long. But that was immaterial; so long as he was cuffed to the pipe he couldn't move.

Bolan flexed his muscles for a minute or two, then sank to his knees and back on his haunches.

Impossible.

Eva Zhulev didn't return. No one came. He couldn't guess how long she was gone, but he was surprised at how long it was.

Suddenly he heard a thump outside the window. It came again, and with a tinkle the glass broke and fell onto the sill, some on the floor. A gloved hand pressed back the blind. A face behind a black mask. Then the gloved hand tossed a key on the floor between his legs.

Bolan scrambled. He let himself down on his side and twisted his body to bring his face close to the key. Pulling against his shoulders, he stretched his chin toward the key. The pain in his shoulders burned, but he got his chin on the key and slid it back. In another second he had the key in his mouth.

He struggled to a sitting position, twisted his neck and dropped the key down his back. He groped for it until he found it. Ten seconds later he was free from the handcuffs. Five seconds after that he was free from the leg irons.

Pulling back the blind, he looked out into the dark. The window faced on a brick wall. He unlatched the window and shoved the sash up. There was no ladder, no rope. How had the man—? If the man in the mask had done it, he could do it. But how? A rope that he'd pulled back? Why would he have broken the window and tossed in a key and then pulled up his climbing rope?

No, he had supposed Bolan would see how it was done.

Okay. The distance to the brick wall opposite the window was about three feet. Sure. He had pressed between the two walls. And he had assumed Bolan could do the same. Anyone with mountain climbing training knew now to do it.

Yeah. In boots, heavy clothes... Maybe he hadn't noticed Bolan was naked. Maybe he just hadn't guessed he could be and so hadn't brought clothes.

There was no time to think about the reasons and possibilities. Bolan climbed out. He sat for a moment on the windowsill, then pressed his heels hard against the brick wall opposite. He slid to the left, and after a few seconds was wedged in the three-foot space between the two brick walls, held from falling by the pressure of his legs pressing his heels and back against the walls.

Below—a drop of twenty-five or thirty feet into litter, likely broken glass. Above, maybe ten feet to the edge of the roof.

Bolan began to squirm, working his way up. It took the skin off his back. He was lucky that the bricks were rough. They were wet, and if they had been smooth he would have slid down. But because they were rough, they abraded his back painfully.

It was raining. London. A bright clear day had to be followed by a rainy night. Cold rain.

He couldn't think about that. His upward progress was slow. Eva Zhulev would immediately see which way he had gone, and she would kill him if she saw him out here, he had no doubt.

He needed minutes to inch his way up the ten feet, leaving his skin behind on every brick. He kept groping for a handhold, and when at last he could reach the edge of the roof of the building opposite, he grabbed it and let his heels fall. He hung then on his strained shoulders, half-numb hands curled around cold, rough stone. He hung and breathed heavily, then made the effort. He lunged up, almost lost his grip, then managed to throw himself on his belly onto the ledge. A moment later he slithered into the water standing on the roof.

A black-clad figure three roofs away stood for a moment watching him, then abruptly disappeared over the edge.

Something odd was going on below. Bolan crawled to the edge of the roof and looked over. A police car and an ambulance were on the street in front of the bordello.

Not his problem. His problem was that he was on the roof of a building in Bloomsbury, in the rain, with dawn surely not more than two or three hours away, stark naked and shivering.

He couldn't ask for police help. Too many questions. If he could get to a telephone, he could call Marilyn; she was expecting his call. But how did a naked man get to a telephone in the middle of London at four or five in the morning? He couldn't say where he was. Sooner or later Schellenberg and whoever was behind him would come looking—and he had left a trail. He had to get off this roof.

He had to get out of this neighborhood. It was impossible to return to Mayfair, to his hotel. London was one of those great cities that never slept, and between here and Mayfair were many wide, well-lit streets a naked man couldn't possibly cross.

He had to steal clothes. There was no other way.

He stood, acutely conscious that anyone who saw him would be alarmed. He could only hope that on a rainy night no one was casually looking around the gloomy rooftops of Bloomsbury. He wiped the rain from his face, some off his belly and hips also—an instinctive gesture with no purpose.

How many times had he entered guarded enclosures in the night? It should have been easy. He had defeated alarm systems, evaded fanatic hardmen, crossed over walls topped with sharp glass, climbed up and down buildings, slipped through windows. And—when he considered it rationally—the only disadvantage of his nakedness was that he was without equipment or a weapon. In truth, he had his best resources with him—the inner ones he had evolved into a unique weapon.

He jumped the three feet to the roof of the bordello. They would hardly expect him to return there, and the citizen whose clothes he might take from there would hardly be an innocent. But as he searched the roof it became apparent there was no access to the building from the roof. No door. No skylight.

Someone working on the roof had left a plank, though. That was handy. A heavy eight-foot plank made him a shaky bridge across a passageway between this building and the one behind it—better than an eight-foot jump from one slippery wet roof to another. He didn't walk across. He hung beneath it and went across hand over hand.

On this roof there was a skylight. Not only that, it was a skylight fastened shut by a loose, rusty latch. When he pulled up on the frame, the latch gave a little, then gave more, then broke. Bolan peered into the room below. It was an office. He could see desks, filing cabinets. No clothes, apparently.

Even so, it meant getting in out of the rain. He lowered himself and dropped quietly to the wooden floor.

Telephones. He picked one up and dialed Marilyn.

No answer. There was a clock on the wall. It was past 5:00 a.m., and she didn't answer her telephone. That was frightening. Maybe Schellenberg's friends had captured her, too. Another reason for working alone—you didn't have to worry about someone else getting hurt.

He found the bathroom and used paper towels to dry himself. Then he searched the office for clothes. Nothing. Not a coat, not even a hat or scarf. The offices belonged to an insurance firm, from the look of them. So here he was, dry, with access to a telephone, but still naked.

He opened a door into a hall and went out. Other offices. He searched through those. Still nothing. He found a cashier's till behind a counter and took out a few pounds, which he stuffed in an envelope. He didn't like taking money, but if he could ever find clothes he was going to need a taxi.

He went down a flight of stairs to another floor. More offices. Another firm, apparently, with locked doors. Insurance firms. Estate agents. None of them likely to have a spare suit of clothes hanging about.

He went down to the ground floor. Shops. A tobacconist and a stamp- and coin-collectors' shop, each of them with burglar alarm tape conspicuous on the glass.

He went to the rear door of the building. That, too, was secured by an alarm, but the box was just inside the door, and he opened it and turned the alarm off. Careful to leave the door unlocked, he ventured into the narrow passageway he had crossed at rooftop level on the plank.

The passage was paved and wide enough for small trucks to back in and make deliveries. The doors facing it were steel-reinforced and likely secured by alarms. He peered through windows. In the darkness of the rooms beyond, he could see nothing.

The rain, stronger now, pelted his naked body with cold water. Clothes, damn it! He had to find—

Lights! Red. A small van was backing into the passageway. He crouched in a doorway and watched. An early-morning delivery? Not likely. At five? No, not likely. A burglary, very probably. And a bit of luck.

"Macht schnell."

German burglars? A man gestured to his companion to hurry around the back of the van. In the dim light from windows above, Bolan could see that the two men were dressed in gray coveralls. They carried something indistinct, but he couldn't identify it in the bad light.

"Hier. Diese Tür." Here. This door.

They were going in the whorehouse. Through the back door. One of them knocked.

Bolan slipped along the wall, closer to the van.

The door opened. A woman—Priscilla. "You're too late. You're too goddamn late. He's gone."

"What do you mean, gone? Where's Eva?"

"God knows. Hauled away to hospital. A woman came to the door and asked for her. She left your man and went to the door. It was none of my business, so I went about doing what I'm supposed to do. The next thing I know, the police are at the door. Eva is lying on the sidewalk in front of the house. I ran upstairs to see about the man . . . and he was gone!"

"Impossible!"

"Look for yourself. I've been trying to reach Bobbie—"

"Telefoniere Schellenberg! Schnell!"

One of the Germans pushed his way past Priscilla into the house. The other opened the rear doors of the van and reached inside for something. Bolan was close enough to recognize an Uzi submachine gun, even in the dimness.

The German cradled the Uzi and busied his hands lighting a cigarette. That was his mistake. As the flare of his lighter obscured his vision, Bolan sprang from the shadows and drove a fist into his nose, another into his throat, a knee into his crotch.

CHAPTER TWELVE

Whoever had killed Harper had worked him over pretty thoroughly first, then dispatched him brutally with a shot to the throat. He lay on his back on his bed in a drying stain of his own blood. His nose was broken, maybe also his jaw—certainly many teeth. His eyes stared at the ceiling, still suggesting his final instant of terror. He wore the top of a pair of black silk pajamas. The pants lay on the floor nearby. Whoever had worked on him had fired a shot between his legs, nicking his genitals. He had bled heavily there, and the pain must have been beyond imagining.

The fear more.

Bolan sat down and stared at the body for a long moment. It was odd, this death. Almost peaceful now—though it had been accompanied by pain and terror some hours ago. Harper had lived well in a comfortable flat. He had a view of Regent's Park. Probably his neighbors hadn't guessed how he made his living.

Rain still fell. It pattered on the windows of Harper's bedroom. The gray light of a rainy day filled Harper's rooms and seemed to cry out for someone to switch on a warm light.

Schellenberg and Harper had argued, Bolan remembered from the moments before he had passed out. Harper had blustered. It had been his final mistake, probably. Schellenberg had said Harper didn't know who he was dealing with, and surely that had been true. Even a man like Harper, who saw a side of life hidden from most citizens, hadn't guessed what people like Schellenberg—and his Eva—were capable of.

Maybe Harper got what he deserved.

IT WAS NOT EASY to move. The skin on Bolan's back was marked in a lattice pattern of cuts and abrasions. The back of his head was swollen, and the swelling was split and still oozed blood. He had astounded the desk clerk at the hotel by appearing in a pair of workingman's coveralls, at six in the morning.

The two Germans had been carrying a straitjacket in the van. And a leather gag and blindfold. They had obviously been sent to move him from the bordello in Bloomsbury to some place where they were going to work him over good.

But they hadn't counted on the experience and skill of a man like the Executioner. He had left Hans lying in the passageway, minus his coveralls. And he had driven the van to Shepherd Market, where he had abandoned it. The Uzi was too valuable a weapon to be abandoned, and he had taken the time, before he went to the hotel, to go into the passageway behind and stash the submachine gun and its two 32-round magazines. Then, from his room, he had gone down to the passage by the route he had used before and retrieved the Uzi, putting it in his suitcase.

While he was showering, trying to ease some of the pain with a lot of hot water, the telephone rang. Marilyn. She was relieved to reach him. He was relieved to hear from her. She said she had slept through the ringing of her telephone at 5:00 a.m. Had he been out all night? What was he doing now?

He told her he was going to sleep. Then he finished his shower, dressed, pulled the Lahti from under the mattress and went out to see Schellenberg.

Craven Hill. The address was that of a three-story brick house, one of a dozen identical ones in a row, sharing walls.

"Excuse me," he said to a man in a blue smock who was delivering milk to doorsteps along the street. "I'm looking for a Mr. Schellenberg. Do you happen to know—"

"No, sir. There's no Mr. Schellenberg on this street. They're not all my customers, but I believe I know the names of everyone on the block. No Mr. Schellenberg 'ere."

"Oh. Well, who lives in number 1824 there?"

"That would be Mr. 'oward, sir. Mr. Walter 'oward."

"Young fellow," said Bolan. "A German, in fact. Maybe just a little bit . . . how shall we say? A little bit girlish-looking?"

The delivery man grinned. "Well, sir, not to be quoted, I suppose we might say so."

"Ah, well, thank you."

Bolan walked into Paddington Station and found the telephone directories and public telephones. Walter Howard. Okay. He put in a coin and dialed the number. Mr. Howard didn't answer.

If Mr. Howard was there, he would answer the telephone. He had too much going to let the telephone ring. Unless he had another number.

Bolan decided to enter. If Schellenberg was expecting him and had another trap set, frontal assault would be best. Sometimes decisive boldness overcame the cleverest trap. But he had a sense this wasn't a trap.

Of course, maybe the milkman was wrong. Maybe Mr. Howard wasn't Schellenberg.

Bolan went to the door. Through the glass he could see a long hallway that led from the front to the back of the house. He pulled the Lahti—which he was now carrying under his belt, since he had lost the holster with his clothes last night—and jammed it against the glass by the knob. The muzzle of the pistol cracked a big jagged hole in the glass but didn't make much noise. He reached through and turned the latch from inside.

The room to the right was a Victorian parlor, furnished in a style Bolan had always found oppressive. Schellenberg lay on his face on the floor. The back of his head had been blown against the wall.

"YOU'VE BEEN BUSY," said Sir George Harrington. "I believe you're entitled to a day off, since tomorrow you must fly to Rome to meet Mr. Brognola. He's moved on from Bonn."

They sat around a conference room table at MI6 headquarters—Bolan, Sir George and Marilyn.

"Running off on your own in the famous Bolan style damn near got you killed last night," said Marilyn.

"Apparently I wasn't on my own," said Bolan. "Somebody tossed me a key. If not for that—"

"You might be fortunate to be dead," said Sir George. "I've a sense they intended to drain your mind of every fact it contains—after which they would have dumped the empty container in the Thames."

"Chemicals..." said Bolan.

Sir George nodded. "Chemicals. If one doesn't care what permanent damage one does to a mind, certain injections can eliminate the will to keep any kind of secret."

"Schellenberg," said Bolan. "He was the only contact we had. I mean, it was only through Schellenberg that we might have gotten a finger on whatever's going on."

"Actually," said Sir George, "we have another. Eva Zhulev. She was taken to Middlesex Hospital last night. Crushed trachea. Someone chopped her across the throat. Quite viciously. Meant to kill her, I suppose. But she survived. As soon as she's recovered a bit, we'll interrogate her."

"Who is she?" Bolan asked.

"A secretary at the East German Trade Mission. Actually, we've suspected since she entered this country that she's an agent for MfS."

"She killed Harper's man last night," said Bolan. "About as cold-blooded a killing as I've ever seen."

"It's just as well she's in the hospital," said Sir George.

"Chained to the bed, I hope," said Marilyn.

"We'll fly you to Rome," Sir George told Bolan. "Also, we'll replace what's missing from your kit."

"I should like to go, Sir George," said Marilyn.

"Mr. Bolan?"

"Hal Brognola and I will meet alone," said Bolan. "That's how it has to be."

Marilyn smiled. "I'll just stand by to keep you out of trouble," she said.

"I DON'T KNOW, big guy," said Hal Brognola. "She seems to stick to you like glue. I can understand if she has a thing for you, but are you developing something for her?"

They were sitting in Brognola's room at the Cavalieri Hilton in Rome. From the windows they had a view of the Vatican gardens and the dome of St. Peter's. The little RAF jet had flown Bolan down from London that morning—with Marilyn, too. She had checked into a room on another floor of the Cavalieri and was waiting for him. She said they were entitled to a night in Rome.

Bolan didn't immediately answer Brognola's question. He pondered over it for a long moment, then he shook his head. "You and I know it can't be," he said. "I made my decisions a long time ago."

"Perhaps an interlude. After this thing's over, we could arrange for the two of you to go somewhere. Every man's entitled to R and R. Maybe after a month with you up close, she'll change her mind."

Bolan shook his head again. "Not funny, Hal," he said.

"Sorry... anything I can do. I mean, anything."

"You're right, actually," said Bolan quietly. "A woman would have to have a hell of a lot of understanding. She wants to go along, to be a part of everything. I can't work with a partner, Hal. Besides, we've been through this many times before."

"We've run a check on her, I might as well tell you," said Brognola. "MI6 thinks the world of her. She's been with them for nine years. She spent time in East Germany. She speaks fluent German. Linguist. Athlete. And quite capable of killing, they say. It seems she has done it on a mission or two. If you were going to take on a partner, you could do worse. There's no woman who would understand better."

"No," said Bolan firmly.

"Then be careful, big guy," said Brognola. He had an open file folder on the coffee table between them, and he glanced at his file. "Eva Zhulev—"

"She got away from them," said Bolan.

"What?"

"She walked out of the hospital yesterday evening. They couldn't believe it. Because of the injury to her throat, she was on oxygen and breathing through a tube, and she pulled it out, got up and walked away. They hadn't guarded her because they figured she couldn't breathe without the tube."

"Another brave woman," said Brognola.

"And disappeared," said Bolan. "Obviously she got in touch with her buddies at the DDR trade mission. Maybe they actually helped her get out of bed. Anyway, she's gone, and MI6 doesn't know where."

"They're looking, I suppose."

"Sure. But that's not the big question, as far as I'm concerned. I want to know who saved my neck at the whorehouse. How did that person know where I was? And who killed Schellenberg? And Harper? And why was somebody torturing Harper?"

"Do you assume all this was done by the same person?"

"If so, somebody had busy night," said Bolan.

"Have you considered the possibility," asked Brognola, "that the scene in the whorehouse was faked, that everybody involved meant for you to escape?"

"Sure. But then why were the two principal guys killed within hours?"

Brognola shook his head. "I don't know. I can't guess. Correction—I *refuse* to guess. I've got some new intel, just in. A bomb went off this morning in Gare du Nord in Paris. The big railroad station. Casualties...they don't know yet. It's as if they were thumbing their noses at us. You knocked off one bomber team. They run in another. Henri Leclerc is demanding that you and Miss Henry return to Paris to deal with this team the way you dealt with the other. I said no. GIGN has no idea who set this bomb, and we can't spare you to do detective work. His answer, of course, is that you're doing detective work in London, why not in Paris? The French are—"

"Furious," said Bolan.

"Right. But that's my problem. I'll deal with Henri Leclerc. For today, here, I have something else. It's something even Miss Henry can't be told."

"No problem," said Bolan dryly,

"Well...find something to occupy her time. Because you and I have something to do a little later today. Now there's someone I'd like you to meet." He opened the door to a connecting room and a stocky man entered. Brognola made the introductions.

Vladimir Pavlovich Telpuchovski offered Bolan a firm grip. He smiled, showing a stainless-steel tooth. And he nodded, his great bearish head bobbing up and down, his piggish little eyes beaming under his huge, bushy black eyebrows.

"We have things to forgive each other, my new friend," he said to Bolan. "And we *must*! Nations must. Men must."

Telpuchovski was a professional survivor, skilled at bending with the political winds; his mind worked like a computer, reaching into a memory that seemed to have no limit, calling up bits of information everyone but him had forgotten, then relating them to other bits and assembling the facts necessary to make a shrewd judgment.

He let Bolan see the one he made now. It appeared on his face, to be read. To the facts he called out of his memory he added a personal assessment; and obviously he found Mack Bolan a formidable man, cool and calculating, yet filled with anger—a man not to be crossed.

"May I call you Mack? I will tell you something in confidence. I have told Hal. Now I tell you. A month ago a man was assassinated at his dacha in the hills just outside Moscow. You have heard of Grigori Petrovich Parotikin?"

Bolan nodded. He had heard of Parotikin. The new man, reputedly—the man the general secretary had appointed to change the image of the KGB. Some people believed he was running the agency now. Was Telpuchovski saying Parotikin had been murdered?

"Grigori Petrovich answered a knock at his door and was shot in the face," said Telpuchovski grimly. "I have trusted you with a state secret of the gravest import. Do you understand why the assassination is so ominous?"

"Murder is ominous," said Bolan. "Assassination of a government official is more ominous."

Telpuchovski lifted his glass of vodka out of the bowl of ice that Brognola had ordered from room service. "These dachas," the Russian explained, "are in a secure area. It is surrounded by a guarded fence, and entry is only through a guarded gate. What is more, no one had climbed the fence.

How do we know this? Because there were no tracks in the snow either outside or inside the fence. The trees have been cleared back for twenty meters on both sides of the fence. No one could approach the fence without leaving tracks in the snow. Conclusion—"

"Someone who lives inside the compound killed Parotikin," said Bolan.

"Exactly," said Telpuchovski.

"How many people live there?" Bolan asked.

"About four hundred," said Telpuchovski. "Officials of the party and state. Some retired officials. Their families, of course."

"The significance," said Brognola, "is the similarity between this killing and the killings of Richard Vauxhall in London, Claude Crillon in Paris, Friedrich Hohnzecker in Düsseldorf, Galeazzo Bastianini in Rome and Colonel Adolfo Martinez in Spain."

"Yes," said Telpuchovski. "We are very much aware of those. That is why we contacted you, Hal, and that is why I am pleased at last to meet you, Mack. I am in charge of the investigation into the death of Grigori Petrovich Parotikin, and I, too, see the similarity between his death and the deaths of those others."

"All high-ranking officers of their countries'...let us say security agencies."

Telpuchovski laughed. "Espionage agencies, Hal. Why not?"

Brognola nodded. "All high-ranking officers of their countries' espionage agencies. All relatively young. All relatively new to their agencies. All—"

"All murdered," Bolan interrupted, "by people who knew them, at least knew their habits intimately, knew how to get to them. Not by strangers."

"Yes," said Telpuchovski. "The general secretary himself has ordered me to bring the Parotikin assassin to justice.

He agrees with me that all the men we have mentioned may be the victims of a single conspiracy. What is more, the bombings—"

"Destabilization," Brognola interrupted.

"Our governments," said Telpuchovski, "are not accustomed to taking one another's word. But the general secretary has sent the President a personal message, assuring him that this series of murders and bombings are as mysterious to us as they are to you." He shrugged. "You can believe it or not."

"The President and the general secretary are going to meet to talk about it," said Brognola. "This won't be a summit meeting. It will be a secret meeting. Officially the President will be in California. Officially the general secretary will be in the Crimea. No newspeople will be with them. *None.*"

"Where are they meeting?" asked Bolan.

"Stockholm," said Brognola.

"When?"

"About the end of the month, probably," said Brognola. "They agreed to the meeting early last week, but these things take time to arrange."

"Yes," said Telpuchovski. "Especially when they are secret."

"It isn't secret, of course," said Bolan. "Lots of people know."

"We are setting up the most complete security imaginable," said Brognola.

"Cooperatively," said Telpuchovski.

"A wealthy Swedish businessman has given us his country estate just outside Stockholm for the meeting," said Brognola. "The President wants to see you there, Striker." He turned to Telpuchovski. "Mack works unofficially. Officially the President doesn't know him."

"Officially neither do I," said Telpuchovski.

"Vladimir has some intel for us," Brognola said.

Telpuchovski nodded at Bolan. "In that bomb factory on Montmartre, you or Miss Henry shot a man named Heinz Knochen. Am I right?"

"I was told that was his name."

"Yes. Well, it was his name. He was an inveterate political activist, a believer. To him it made no difference what he believed, so long as he had something to believe in, a cause. He started as a Green, an unwashed, unshaven street demonstrator. But—" the Russian paused and smiled sarcastically "—the Bundesamt für Verfassungsschutz captured his enthusiasm, and he became a spy against the Greens."

"Inconsistent," said Brognola.

Telpuchovski shook his head. "It made him feel important. Conspiracy. He loved conspiracy. So, if betraying his Green Party friends to the BfV made him feel important, how much more important he would feel if he betrayed the BfV! He tried to contact our friends in the German Democratic Republic. He tried to contact us." The Russian shrugged. "We didn't want him. And neither did the BfV anymore. They are not so stupid. They found out what he was doing. They dropped him. He was bitter. That is why he became a bomber. More correctly said, that is why he became an errand boy for Aimé Rafil. A dangerous connection. He survived three months after he first contacted her."

"Who was she working for?" asked Bolan impatiently.

Telpuchovski smiled at Bolan, a tolerant smile that responded to Bolan's impatience. "If we knew that, sir, we would stop all this foolishness. But I have some information that may be useful to you. When Heinz Knochen tried to insinuate himself into the confidence of the West German counterespionage agency, the BND, his contact was Friedrich Hohnzecker, the BND bureau chief for Düsseldorf—the man who was assassinated by explosives."

"How do you know?"

"When Knochen offered himself to us, we decided to watch him for a while. Likely he would offer his services to someone else, we supposed. And if he did, he might become an agent for the BND or—who knows?—even for the CIA. That would have been useful to know, wouldn't it?"

"All right," said Bolan, again impatient.

"We knew where Knochen stayed when he was in Paris," Telpuchovski continued. "A flat in Montparnasse. We didn't know about the bomb factory on Montmartre. *You* found that. But we do know that Knochen left Paris early in the morning before Hohnzecker was killed. He had brought an expensive new Mercedes to his street in Montparnasse the night before. He carried a briefcase into his building—one we had never seen before—and left the Mercedes on the street overnight. He left before dawn and returned not much before midnight."

"Time to have driven to Düsseldorf," said Bolan.

"Time to have driven a thousand kilometers—which is how far he drove, approximately," said Telpuchovski. "We checked the odometer on the car. It is a thousand kilometers, approximately, from Paris to Düsseldorf and return."

"So he could have delivered the bomb," said Bolan. He shook his head. "But they didn't find the signature, the wires twisted in the left-handed way Aimé Rafil always twisted them. This bomb was different."

"Very different," the Russian agreed. "This bomb was not detonated by radio signal."

"That's right," said Brognola. "The Düsseldorf bomb was detonated by a fuse and blasting cap. Almost certainly a short fuse was chemically ignited. When Hohnzecker opened the briefcase, probably he broke a vial of nitric acid. That would be one way—"

"But you didn't follow him," Bolan said to the Russian. "So we don't know where he went. And we're not going to find out, because he's dead."

"The Mercedes," said Telpuchovski, "is owned by a German manufacturing company in Düsseldorf. It is there now, back performing its usual function of carrying corporate officials to and from the airport and such. We are curious—aren't you?—as to why a reputable manufacturing company would lend a valuable automobile to a gang of murderers."

"Want to find out, Striker?" asked Brognola.

CHAPTER THIRTEEN

It wasn't easy to convince Marilyn that she had to return to London without him. When he refused to tell her where he was going or when he would be back in London, she turned unattractively peevish, and he saw a side of her he hadn't seen before. He couldn't blame her, actually; but, though he agreed with the decision not to include her in his mission to Germany, it was Brognola and Telpuchovski who didn't want her going. She was known in Germany, Telpuchovski said. On both sides.

Reinhard Kremer was waiting when he came off the airplane at Düsseldorf. "It's essential to work with the locals," Brognola had said. It was convenient, anyway, if you wanted to carry a weapon into the Federal Republic. Kremer greeted him as an old friend, then hurried him around immigration and customs and drove him to the Breidenbacher Hof, a fine old hotel in the center of the city.

"I have been preparing for you a briefing on NUG," said Kremer. NUG meant Nordländische Unternehmungs Gesellschaft, roughly Northern Enterprises Corporation, the company that owned the Mercedes that had been driven from Paris by Heinz Knochen. "The chief executive officer is a man named Willi von Voss. Sixty-seven years old. In 1945 he is holding the rank of Obersturmführer in the Waffen SS. You know what this has been?"

"He was a first lieutenant in the SS," said Bolan.

"Waffen SS," said Kremer. "Military SS. He is fighting on the Russian front. He is never a concentration camp bully. On the other hand, he is being of necessity a dedicated Nazi. So, after the war he is denazified, by order of a court. After this he is avoiding politics always. He is never a member of a party. He is a businessman only. However, he is employing many of his former associates of the SS, including some who are serving prison terms in 1946 and 1947 for their offenses. No big war criminals. But we are watching Herr Voss most closely all the time. And his associates.''

"So, do you have anything on him?" Bolan asked.

"No. Not until we are learning from a source you know that an automobile belonging to NUG is being driven by Heinz Knochen from Paris and back to Paris. Even if Heinz Knochen is not one of the bombers in Paris and Berlin, why is an automobile owned by this company being driven by him?''

"You haven't found out?" asked Bolan.

Kremer shook his head. "No. Our Soviet friends are deciding to give us this information already this week only. As you know. Well, I am knowing one more piece of information you may wish to know. We are checking the border station at Aachen, the most likely point for Knochen to be crossing. No Knochen is crossing there. But the Mercedes is crossing, eastbound before noon, westbound early in the evening, the day before the death of Hohnzecker. It is as the Russian is saying. And it is being driven by a man with a West German passport with the name Otto Schörner. This is the name of a man who is dead.''

"How did he die?"

"Of cancer. We are examining the doctors closely. A year ago. Of cancer.''

"Did he have any relationship with NUG?" Bolan asked.

"His wife is working for the company already for many years. A stenographer.''

"What does the company manufacture?"

"Small motors," said Kremer. "You find them on motorcycles, powered lawn mowers, skimobiles...others you find pumping water for irrigation, generating electricity, compressing air. Gasoline engines, mostly. A few small diesels. They export them everywhere."

"A significant international trade," said Bolan.

"They export everywhere. Import steel from Sweden. Machine tools from Czechoslovakia. And so on. Their people travel widely, selling, negotiating contracts for materials. They attend trade fairs. An international business."

"Highly respectable, huh?"

Kremer nodded. "So respectable that the former head of the Düsseldorf bureau of BND is one of Herr Voss's directors. Very respectable. Very honest business. Always complying with trade regulations. No political connection."

"Except that a man with the passport of a deceased employee drives a company car from Paris to Düsseldorf and back on the day before Hohnzecker was murdered with a bomb," said Bolan. "And the man calling himself Otto Schörner is Heinz Knochen, who was killed in the Paris house where bombs were put together."

"Something is wrong, hmm?" said Kremer.

LIKE INDUSTRIAL CITIES everywhere, Düsseldorf spilled its business and industry into the surrounding countryside, and many companies that called themselves Düsseldorf companies were actually situated in towns like Neuss, which was on the west side of the Rhine, across the river from the city. NUG was at Neuss. It was a good corporate neighbor, having established a small industrial park and built its manufacturing plant and executive office building within the park, separated from the town by landscaping that all but hid its forbidding fence.

Bolan did a soft probe of the place that afternoon, driving the inconspicuous Opel that Kremer had provided for him. He was traveling as Ernest Bradley, representing British Cybernetics; and he went to the gate and offered his card, saying he would like to speak with Herr Willi von Voss. Word was sent in, and the executive offices sent back word that Herr Voss wasn't available and that Herr Bradley should write and state his purpose in asking for an appointment, after which one might be arranged.

The park was more secure than seemed appropriate for a manufacturing company in the business of making small motors to power lawn mowers. The security system was designed to be low profile, but it was high profile to Bolan. He identified infrared detectors all around the periphery. A man, or even a big dog, moving near the fence would trigger an alarm. The detectors were supplemented by video cameras and powerful floodlights mounted on poles well inside the fence. Turned on, the lights would illuminate the fence; and the cameras, remotely controlled, would swing back and forth, scanning the bare ground inside and outside the fence. Infrared detectors, lights and cameras were concealed in pods on trees twenty meters or so inside the fence.

Yeah. Herr Voss didn't want his premises penetrated, and he didn't want his neighbors to know how anxious he was that his premises not be penetrated.

Bolan made a quick mental sketch. He would return for a hard probe under cover of darkness.

HE HAD BEEN UNABLE to bring the Uzi, which remained in his hotel room in London. But he had packed the blacksuit and the equipment he had bought in London.

Under his left arm was a shoulder rig that held a Puuko knife hanging handle-down—the correct position for drawing it quickly. The Lahti rode on his hip in a black holster. Extra clips of ammo were tucked in pouches on his belt.

Over his right shoulder and under his right arm was a twenty-foot coil of strong nylon rope, dyed black.

He wore a raincoat as he drove the Opel out from the center of the city, just before midnight. It was cold, with low clouds blocking the moonlight. He drove the Opel past the NUG park and into a side road to the west, to a place he had chosen during the day as a good place to leave it. It was just midnight when he entered the field outside the perimeter fence and began to work his way toward the north boundary of the park and the railroad siding on which NUG took deliveries and made shipments.

Business must be good. The factory was lit; a night shift was working. There were even lights in some of the windows of the building he had identified during the day as the executive office building. As he worked his way along the line of trees and shrubs that separated the industrial park, he saw that a string of railroad cars remained on the siding. That was good. He had hoped for that.

Though the railroad siding ran outside the fence, it ran inside the barrier of trees and shrubs—therefore, probably it was inside the guard line of sensors. The string of cars sitting on the siding might, though, be a weak point in the security system. He doubted the sensors were focused on the cars. If they were, every time a brakeman moved on the cars he would trigger an alarm. Probably instead the security system depended on someone keeping a watch on the cars.

Bolan stayed well west of the line of trees and shrubs—and west of the sensors mounted among them. He was almost in the backyards of an apartment subdivision that backed on the NUG complex. A low chain-link fence marked the rear boundary of the subdivision. A shallow drainage ditch ran between that fence and the NUG tree line. It made it possible for him to work his way north while keeping low and out of sight.

Dogs barked—one so loud and insistent that someone switched on the lights in his backyard and peered from his window. Bolan kept moving. The last thing he wanted to encounter was a curious resident.

At length he reached the railroad track. It ran inside a fence a little higher than the one that guarded the back-yards—to keep children away from the tracks, he supposed. He lunged over it without any trouble.

Now he was on the track. He could see how it ran through a gap in the NUG trees. Far ahead, well inside the guarded area, it reached a loading dock. Lights blazed there. Workmen were loading or unloading cars, crossing and recrossing the dock with little yellow electric tractors that pulled small carts. The train they were loading or unloading consisted of maybe a dozen little four-wheeled European boxcars and a tiny electric locomotive. The locomotive stood just inside the line of trees, with the cars strung out behind it.

Two men stood on the track, one an armed guard, the other apparently the locomotive driver. They were sharing some food and drink, maybe sandwiches and coffee, and chatting. Neither was alert.

Bolan dropped into a low crouch on the north side of the railroad track and moved east toward the gate. The track, like any other railroad track, was elevated a little on its ballast and was edged on either side by a shallow depression meant to carry away rainwater. The men standing on the track had a view of the depression on either side, but it was in deep shadow except where the dim yellow headlight of the locomotive laid down a patch of weak light. Bolan approached to the edge of that patch.

He couldn't pass. He wouldn't take out the locomotive driver and the guard; he had no reason to believe they were anything but two middle-aged men doing innocent jobs. But he couldn't crawl past them.

For several minutes he lay there watching, waiting.

The locomotive driver laughed, then punched the guard playfully on the shoulder and climbed up into the locomotive. The engine whined, and the little locomotive inched forward the length of one car. It passed between Bolan and the guard.

The patch of light moved forward, too. It fell on Bolan. He pressed himself to the gravel beside the track.

Then the engine stopped whining, and he guessed the driver was climbing down again, to take up again his interrupted snack and talk. He was climbing down the other side and couldn't see the north side of the track.

Bolan took the chance and scurried forward. He was inside the line of trees. The locomotive and cars were between him and the guard, between him and the fence.

He rose and trotted back about three cars. He supposed there must be guards patrolling the area between the track and the northern line of trees, but for the moment he had alerted none of them. He seized a grab iron on the nearest little boxcar and climbed to the top.

From there he had a view. Just south was the perimeter fence, with its sensors, cameras and lights. Ahead, to the east, the string of cars extended past the loading dock, which was flooded with light. The dock was a wide gap in the fence, and beyond the fence a wide door opened into a big warehouse. It was brightly lit inside. As many as twenty men were working on the loading dock and just inside the warehouse. He could now see that they were loading, not unloading, the boxcars—hauling out wooden crates and dragging them into place inside the cars. Three armed and uniformed guards walked about the loading dock, watching the work. They carried submachine guns, Heckler & Koch MP-5s, from the look of them.

Motors? For lawn mowers and skimobiles? NUG was shipping little motors under the eyes of guards armed with submachine guns? Yeah. Sure they were.

The way they were loading, the cars at the front of the train had been loaded first, and as each car was filled, the locomotive pulled the train forward, bringing another car up to the loading dock. The doors were sealed as each car was loaded.

Even so there was a way in. Each car had a hatch on the roof. Bolan opened the hatch and dropped into the little boxcar.

Stacks of heavy wooden crates filled the car almost to the roof, giving him space to crawl but not to stand. He closed the hatch, then took from one of his pouches a small flashlight. Cupping his hand around the lens so as to confine the beam to as small an area as possible, he read the legends stenciled on the crates—addresses of companies and individuals in cities all over Western Europe.

He pulled the Puuko knife from its rig under his arm and pried up the lid of one crate. Two little gasoline motors. He tried another crate. Two more motors.

Okay, but why were the cars being loaded under the guns of ugly-looking, gimlet-eyed guards?

He crawled forward in the car and chose another crate. So. Now it made sense. In this crate, the same size and shape and labeled the same as all the others, he found six Heckler & Koch submachine guns. Addressed to a corporation in Brussels.

Another crate. Motors. Another. More motors. Another—paper-wrapped blocks of C-4 plastique, addressed to Amsterdam.

Amsterdam. The new bomb factory? Replacing the one he and Marilyn had closed in Paris?

He pulled two one-kilogram blocks from the crate and stuffed them under his belt, one on each hip. No one would supply him grenades, so he supplied two for himself. He had no detonators, but the stuff would go off if he fired a shot into it.

Bolan crawled back to the hatch. He switched off the flashlight and put it back in his leather pouch. Then he eased up the hatch and peered out.

Something had changed. Floodlights had come on. The roof of the plant was brightly lit. A small orange wind sock hung from a pole, conspicuous in the beam of its own special light.

He heard the helicopter before he saw it. It came low, from the west, over the suburban rooftops. It hovered for a minute above the roof of the plant, then gently lowered and came to rest. It was a big helicopter, painted black.

The rotor swung to a stop, and three men hurried forward to the door just as it was opened. Three men climbed down. There was handshaking all around, after which everyone hurried across the roof to a door, went inside and disappeared down a flight of stairs. The floodlights went out, leaving the helicopter standing as a looming black silhouette, vaguely threatening.

Must be a group of buyers come to hear a bid on some little motors, Bolan thought wryly.

The question was, how was he going to get in?

Maybe he didn't have to. Maybe all he needed to do was go back to Kremer and tell him he had found explosives and automatic weapons in boxes labeled motors. But somehow Bolan didn't think that would do the job. Kremer was no fool, and he wasn't afraid to take direct action—as he had proved in the matter of the Brauner Gang. If he didn't know what was going on here, surely at least he suspected. And if he hadn't done anything, it had to be because Herr Voss had political influence.

Maybe that was why Brognola and Telpuchovski—even Kremer—wanted him here. Maybe they counted on him to do something Kremer didn't dare do.

Bolan crawled along the top of the cars toward the loading dock, then let himself down to the track again on the side of the cars opposite the dock. There, between the cars and the tree line, he was in shadow. He stared around for men patrolling the open ground. Nothing. If they were there, he couldn't see them.

They had finished loading another car and were ready to have the next car pulled up to the center of the dock. The little locomotive whined and strained and moved the string of cars forward.

Good. That meant they wouldn't move the cars again for a while, and he could crawl under. He rolled over a rail onto the center of the track and inched his way along on his belly. The fence was only some ten feet from him here. Looking up, he could see the sensors—motion detectors probably, or body heat sensors.

He scanned the fence. The sensors were mounted at regular intervals, about forty feet apart. Each pod seemed to contain two sensors, one pointing in either direction. That meant each one had a detecting range of about twenty feet, probably a little more; otherwise there would be a dead spot between them.

The detector pods nearest the loading dock were only about ten feet back from the edges of the concrete platform. That meant they covered the platform itself. The dock was set in a gap in the fence, but the electronic security system covered the dock and would detect anyone moving on it.

Which meant it was turned off right now! Otherwise the men working on the dock would set off an alarm. Probably only the two nearest pods were turned off—separately switched. But that was enough.

Bolan crawled forward between the rails under the coupling between two cars. He came to the wall of the loading dock, which stood about five feet above the level of the ground, high enough to match the floors of the boxcars. That made it possible for him to crouch at the bottom of the loading dock wall, his shoulders touching the wheels of a car, and remain out of sight to anyone on the dock—except someone who came to the edge and peered down.

Pressed against the bottom of the loading dock wall, he crawled toward the fence. He was ready for the shriek of an alarm. If it happened, he would scurry back under a boxcar and come up on the far side.

But the alarm didn't shriek. As he had guessed, the sensors that detected movement, or the infrared signature of a living body, were dead around the loading dock.

He reached the fence.

For a long moment he lay there and listened. He could hear the conversations above—in German. Though he couldn't understand all they said, he could hear that their talk was casual. No one was alerted.

Bolan examined the bottom of the fence. Herr Voss—or his security experts—had relied entirely on their sensors. The fence reached the ground; it wasn't anchored to it; it didn't extend below ground and wasn't anchored in a concrete barrier.

He began to scrape at the earth. With the knife he dug quickly. In a couple of minutes he had made a hole under the fence and could scramble under. In another minute he was under the fence and inside the compound that contained the secrets of Nordländische Unternehmungs Gesellschaft.

CHAPTER FOURTEEN

In a sense he was trapped. He was inside the security fence, but he was also in the narrow, lit strip of land between the fence and the wall of the plant and its connecting warehouse. Pressed against the bottom of the loading dock wall, he was in the only space not clearly visible to the guards on the dock. What was more, he had no reason to think that space wasn't patrolled. It might be only a matter of minutes before he was spotted.

He had thought the situation through before he dug under the fence. He didn't like the solution he had come up with, but it was the only one he had.

He pulled one of the packages of C-4 from under his belt. He unwrapped it. C-4 looked like putty. In fact, in some of its most effective uses, it was pressed into a narrow space, say the crack between a door and its frame. It could be pressed into an angle in a framework, say a bridge, and it would stick there. The stuff was sticky, it could be shaped, and it was safe to handle.

He shaped the block into a ball, then unholstered the Lahti. Rising on his knees, Bolan gave the ball of plastique a hard underhand toss along the wall of the manufacturing plant. It landed quietly and rolled. Good. It was forty feet or so from him. No one had noticed.

He steadied the Lahti in both hands and took aim on the ball of explosive. He fired. The blast erupted in a roiling brown cloud of smoke, dust and debris. It punched a hole in the wall of the factory and tore a long rip in the fence. For a moment the alarms wailed, but then sparks bounced from broken wires along the fence, lights flickered, the alarms ceased and the lights went out.

There was darkness and total confusion. Bolan sprinted along the wall and sprang through the new hole into the manufacturing plant. The confusion there was even greater. No one had been hurt, apparently, but the plant floor was obscured by smoke and dust, and the universal instinct was to run away. Everyone was running and yelling, scrambling for the exits. Bolan wasn't noticed—or if he was he was taken for someone whose clothes had been blackened by the awful explosion.

He took a moment to orient himself. The manufacturing floor—an acre or so—was laid out as an assembly line. The line was moving, in fact. No one had thought to stop it. A hundred little motors were advancing past abandoned work stations and cramming together in a jumble at the end of the line.

On the west wall there was an exit door. Bolan jogged toward it, opened it and went out into the darkness. He moved south along the wall, rounded the corner and worked his way east to the office building.

The office building was like every other building of its kind—a depressing collection of cubicles and offices, desks and chairs, desktop computers, typewriters, filing cabinets, plus a variety of weak little attempts to personalize work space with family pictures, calendars, prints, potted plants. Everything was dimly lit by the exit lights at the ends of the corridor.

Bolan entered an office and looked down from a window. He could see at least twenty armed NUG security men running around the grounds, in and out of the factory and the warehouse. He moved away from the window and exited the room, walking quickly along the corridor until he came to the elevators.

The lights indicated that one car was at the ground floor, one at the fifth. People upstairs would be watching those lights.

He pulled his knife and forced it between the right-hand set of doors to the elevator shaft. The doors yielded. He forced the doors back and leaned into the shaft.

The right-hand car was at the bottom. The left-hand one was above. He could see both cars, dimly, in the little light that made it into the shaft. As he stood there studying the shaft, it suddenly dawned on him—the roof.

He unslung the rope from over his shoulder.

The two elevator cars ran in four vertical tracks. The outside tracks were mounted on the walls of the shaft; but the inside tracks, between the cars, were attached to horizontal beams that ran from the front to the rear of the shaft, one about every ten feet.

He tied one end of the rope around the knife, then gave the knife a toss. It passed over the beam and beyond it, then swung back toward him. He reached out and caught it.

With the rope doubled over the beam, Bolan swung out and hung. He let himself down until his feet rested on the next beam below. He untied the knife and tied a strong knot in the rope, which he then pulled tight on the beam above. He climbed the rope, got a grip on the beam and pulled himself over it. Standing on that beam, he tossed the rope over the next one up.

In two minutes he stood on the small steel platform used by the personnel who inspected and serviced the elevator machinery. It was above the level of the roof in a brick extension of the elevator shaft. A door opened onto the roof.

Bolan stepped out onto the roof. It was flat except for the extensions of the elevator shaft and stairwells. He was alone there.

Looking down, he saw guards climbing over the little locomotive and the string of boxcars. Patrols prowled the

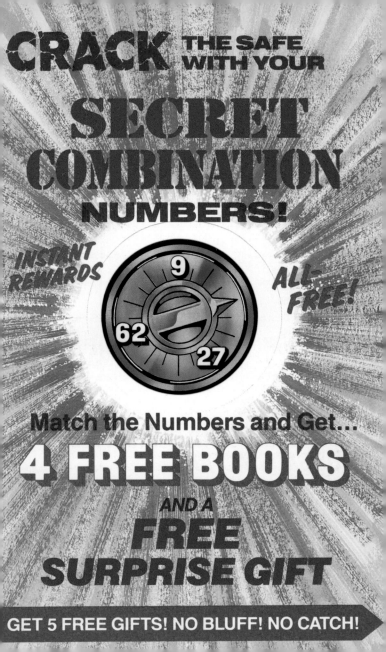

MATCH THE SECRET COMBINATION NUMBERS ...AND RECEIVE FIVE FREE GIFTS!

HOW TO SCORE <u>5</u> INSTANT FREE GIFTS:

1. The Combination Lock on the front cover is yours. First, CHECK the numbers on this Lock against the three numbers on the right.

2. If you have a MATCH, Peel off your Combination Lock from the front and attach it in the space provided across.

3. RETURN the attached card and we'll send you your Free Gifts: 4 of the hottest Gold Eagle novels ever published—*FREE*—plus an <u>extra</u> Surprise Gift—*FREE!*

"UNLOCK" YOUR BEST DEAL EVER!

Once you've read your free books, we're betting you'll want more of these DYNAMITE stories delivered right to your home. So we'll send you six brand-new Gold Eagle books every other month to preview—Two Mack Bolans and one each of Able Team, Phoenix Force, Vietnam: Ground Zero and SOBs.

OUR IRON-CLAD GUARANTEE OF SATISFACTION!

As A Gold Eagle subscriber, you come FIRST. That means you ALWAYS get: 1. **Brand-new,** action-packed novels 2. **Hefty savings** off the retail price 3. **Delivery** right to your home 4. Hot-off-the-press books **before** they're available in bookstores 5. The right to cancel **at any time!** 6. Free newsletter with every shipment.

PLUS MORE FREE GIFTS FROM TIME TO TIME!

DON'T MISS THIS IN-CREDIBLE ALL-FREE OFFER!

The Secret Combination Lock is in your hands now. Find a perfect match...and get yourself FIVE FREE GIFTS! RUSH YOUR REPLY CARD TO US TODAY!

Free Surprise Gift!

We can't tell you what your Free Surprise Gift is—that would spoil the surprise—but it is also yours FREE when you return the card below with the Combination Lock attached. And like the 4 Free Books, your Free Surprise Gift is yours to keep even if you never buy another Gold Eagle book!

STAKE YOUR CLAIM TO 5 FREE GIFTS! MAIL THIS CARD TODAY!

Yes, my Secret Combination Numbers match! Rush my 4 Free Books and Free Surprise Gift. I understand that I am under no obligation to purchase any more books. I may keep these free gifts and return my statement marked "cancel." If I do not cancel, then send me 6 brand-new Gold Eagle novels every second month as they come off the presses. Bill me at the low price of $2.49 for each book—a saving of 11% off the total suggested retail price for six books—plus 95¢ postage and handling per shipment. I can always return a shipment and cancel at any time. The Four Free Books and Surprise Gift remain mine to keep forever.

166 CIM PAP2

Name _____
(Please Print)

Address _____ Apt. No. _____

City _____

State _____ Zip Code _____

Offer limited to one per household and not valid for present subscribers. Terms and prices subject to change without notice.

GET YOUR FREE GIFTS NOW! MAIL THIS CARD TODAY!

BUSINESS REPLY CARD

First Class   Permit No. 717   Buffalo, NY

Postage will be paid by addressee

Gold Eagle Reader Service

901 Fuhrmann Blvd.
P.O. Box 1867
Buffalo, NY 14240-9952

NO POSTAGE
NECESSARY
IF MAILED
IN THE
UNITED STATES

fence and the line of trees and shrubs beyond. The black helicopter remained on the roof of the plant, guarded by hardmen with submachine guns cradled in their arms.

He had come to find out who that helicopter had brought here. He would do it by lowering himself from the roof and having a look through the window.

WILLI VON VOSS was a tall, emaciated man. His long head, home to a few strands of yellowish-blond hair, was otherwise bald with brown liver spots. His wrinkled face was long, too. His lips were thin, the mouth wide. His hands were thin, the fingers long and mobile, like the hands of a concert pianist. Taken as a whole, he wore the expression and had the air of an innocent, benevolent grandfather. He stood, at the moment, at the window, looking down impassively on the spectacle of his security force searching the grounds for whoever had set off the bomb.

The telephone rang, and he stepped away from the window and picked it up. *"So...so...ja...Natürlich. Ja."*

He turned to the men around the conference table, who had interrupted their conversation to wait for whatever report he was receiving. He spoke to them in English, the only language they had in common.

"My security people believe the bomb was thrown, perhaps from some sort of launcher. At any rate, no one suspicious has been seen inside the grounds."

"And why would anyone throw a bomb?" one of the men at the table asked.

"We've had many complaints about the helicopter landing at night. The noise. There may be some very militant people in the neighborhood."

"If the bomb had exploded in the wrong place—"

"Yes. Then we should have had an explosion! But it didn't..."

Voss sat down again at the table. He wasn't presiding over the meeting but took his place in the middle of the table.

"Very well, then," said the man who sat at the head of the table and was presiding. "I wish to return to my inquiry of a few minutes ago." The man was Deputy Foreign Secretary Sir Alexander Bentwood. "It has been my distinct impression that these aircraft don't have the range to fly the mission that has been proposed to us. I should like more assurance on that point."

"You shall have it, my friend," said Dr. Johann Kleist. "You shall have it, though I wish you had more confidence in your associates. Do you really think we would have proposed this mission without checking thoroughly into the problem of range?"

"Indeed, I should hope not," said Sir Alexander. "You may, however, understand that I have seen—"

"Sir Alexander," Dr. Kleist interrupted. "The Israeli F-15s and F-16s that bombed the Iraqi reactor flew from the Sinai to Baghdad and returned without refueling—only a bit less than two thousand kilometers. The Foxbat has less range than the F-15, but it has enough—roughly sixteen hundred kilometers. Remember, it doesn't have to return."

"The fuel?"

"It is in place," said Dr. Kleist. "What the Russians call Y-6. All we lack is the methanol that is injected to give the Foxbat bursts of extraordinarily high speed. That—" he swung his arms around in a gesture "—is in one of those boxcars out there."

"Undamaged," said Voss. "Even if it were lost, the mission can be flown without methanol."

"But we take no chances," said Aldo Vicaria. "With a water-methanol injection, the Foxbat can exceed mach 3. Releasing the American Phoenix missiles with which it is being fitted, it can fire from two hundred kilometers and turn away before the escort can know what's happened."

"Phoenix missiles," said Edward Holmesby-Lovett. "American missiles on a Soviet interceptor...that makes a bastard of our aircraft, doesn't it?"

"I know something of aircraft," said Jean Henriot. Because he spoke English only with difficulty, he had kept quiet during much of the conversation. He was a square-faced man, gold-rimmed spectacles astride his reddish nose, a slash of black hair fallen across his forehead. "Our Foxbat is that which Mr. Holmesby-Lovett has called a bastard. But it has been ingeniously fabricated and will surpass the performings of other Foxbats."

"Without flight testing?" asked Holmesby-Lovett.

Henriot nodded.

Voss clasped his hands on the table before him. "Gentlemen," he said, "I suggest to you that rarely in the history of human endeavor has so complex and demanding a project been carried out in so short a time. Think of it! In the course of six months we have acquired the bits and pieces of one of the world's most sophisticated warplanes, from a thousand sources, most of them from sources that didn't want to give them up—"

"Some of them," Sir Alexander said, chuckling, "don't yet realize they *have* given them up."

"And the necessary technicians," Voss went on. "Kidnapped from under the very noses of security forces specifically detailed to protect them." He nodded toward the Russian at the foot of the table. "Herr Potapava," he said.

"*Gospodin* Potopova," Sir Alexander corrected him.

Von Voss nodded. "Tovarishch Potopova," he said with a little smile.

The Russian was a shrunken man who seemed to have sunk down into his heavy wool double-breasted suit. The oldest man at the table, his beady little eyes peered myopically at the conferees from behind tiny, round, steel-rimmed eyeglasses. He was bald. He understood less than half of

what they said and had been giving his attention mostly to
a bottle of Château Lafitte Rothschild, which sat before
him, now nearly empty.

Voss picked up his telephone and spoke sharply to the
person on the other end of the line.

"Speak of the purpose," growled Potopova. "Speak of
the day."

"More explosions," said Sir Alexander. "Destabilization. Then...then the day. The day, Gospodin Potopova,
will be fixed in Washington and Moscow."

Maybe he understood, maybe he didn't. Potopova nodded. He lifted the bottle and poured the rest of his rare
French wine into his glass—frowning over the emptiness
inside the green bottle.

A door opened. A pretty blond girl, nude except for a
brief pair of white panties, came in carrying another bottle
of the costly old wine. With a quick smile she put it before
the Russian and was rewarded with a broad, gold-toothed
smile. She glanced at Voss, saw the signal to leave and hurried out.

"Minor matters, gentlemen," said Sir Alexander Bentwood. "An administrative decision, if you don't mind."

THE BUILDING WAS steel and glass. All of the facade was
glass. Even so it wasn't all windows. Part of the glass covered structural components. Part of it covered windows.
Bolan had attached his rope securely and let himself down
the west wall. He'd had to climb back up. He couldn't come
down in front of a conference room window and hang there
grinning at the meeting of these conspirators, like some
disoriented window cleaner. He was in the dark, but once he
was outside the window of that lit room he would be a conspicuous figure, from inside and from the ground below.

Now he inched his way down, a little to the south of the
lit room. He rotated his body and entwined his legs in the

rope, so he could turn upside down and hang with only his face exposed to the light when he swung over and looked into the lit room. It was a painful, awkward position he couldn't hold very long.

In fact, his view of the room would be punctuated by the moment of the pendulum he had become for this operation. He had to swing over, look and swing back; kick himself over for another look, then swing back.

His first view was what he had expected—an elegant conference room, old and middle-aged men engaged in what was obviously an intent confrontation. He didn't get enough of a look to recognize any of them.

After his first look, he took a moment to scan the ground below. If one guard down there saw him, he could be shot off his rope in a moment. He had a sense that he must be conspicuous up here—an odd black-clad figure hanging upside down on the gleaming glass facade of a modern office cube. But no one was looking.

He pushed with his feet and swung over to the window again.

The hairs on the back of his neck stood up. He knew one of the men at the table! He was sure he did. But before he could focus on the face and be certain, he swung back and lost sight of the room. He kicked and swung toward the window again.

The man he knew—a Frenchman! He'd met him...yeah, Henri Leclerc had introduced him. What was his name? Jean Henriot, Leclerc's immediate superior! What the hell was he doing here?

There was no time to stop and ponder. Bolan kicked and swung himself across to the window once again. Apart from Henriot, he wasn't sure. The man at the head of the table, who seemed to preside, had his back to the window. That leonine head looked somehow familiar, too; but Bolan couldn't make the identification.

The others, well, all of them were distinctive men, never to be forgotten. But who were they?

Then he swung across and something had changed. They were all staring at a woman. He'd gotten only a glimpse and couldn't guess. A blonde. Something odd...

He had to right himself for a moment. His blood had run to his head and begun to disorient him. He turned up and secured a better purchase on the black nylon rope, then took a moment to look down.

Nothing. All the security effort had moved to the blasted-open hole in the fence. Except, he could be sure, the hard-men protecting the meeting in that conference room.

Every muscle in his body begged him to return to the roof, to rest them before he turned himself upside down and swung across that window again. He shook his head, as if speaking to his own body, and turned himself over for another look.

"So, FRAULEIN ZHULEV," said Edward Holmesby-Lovett. "Once more we confront a failure. I believe you understand we don't tolerate failure. Ours is a cause too important to allow it to be the victim of incompetence."

Eva Zhulev, stark naked, with her hands cuffed behind her, stood facing the conferees around the table. She was blindfolded. Her throat was swathed in bandages.

"Your friend Herr Schellenberg failed twice. Twice, Fräulein. And you... you let the American escape."

"I swear I didn't," she croaked. Her voice was impeded by the hard blow she'd taken across the throat.

"Then where is Mr. Bolan?"

"I was attacked—"

"After you left the room where you had been ordered to remain," grunted Holmesby-Lovett. "No matter. You abandoned your prisoner, went down to the street and—"

Eva Zhulev gasped. "Someone helped him...."

"Of course someone helped him," said Holmesby-Lovett. "But could that someone have helped him if you had been in the room with him, where you belonged?"

The naked young woman tugged against the handcuffs that held her arms behind her back—though apparently more in frustration and anger than in fear. *"Meine Herren—"* she muttered.

"We tend to give people one additional chance, Fräulein Zhulev," Sir Alexander Bentwood interrupted her. "If we may have from you an assurance that you won't fail again—"

EVA ZHULEV! Bolan recognized her, even with the black blindfold over her eyes. He wouldn't forget that cold face too soon.

He swung back.

Jean Henriot. Eva Zhulev. One of the men in there was undoubtedly Herr Voss. And the man at the head of the table, whose face remained always turned away, almost as if he was determined it should be, was disturbingly familiar.

He could hear nothing. He wasn't likely to learn more. It was time to return to the roof and escape from the NUG industrial park.

He turned on the rope and climbed upward. In a moment he was on the roof again, and he lay down and relaxed the tortured muscles that had held him upside down for ten minutes.

Weapons. Explosives. On their way to destinations all over Europe. A meeting in the middle of the night. A Frenchman, officer of GIGN. Eva Zhulev, naked, in handcuffs. All elements somehow of one story. And nothing small.

It was time to get out.

Bolan withdrew the second block of C-4 plastique from his belt and reentered the elevator shaft, letting himself down with his rope. He stopped at the second floor and pressed the sticky plastic explosive into a corner between a steel beam and the brick wall. At the ground floor he pried open the door. He braced himself in the doorway, for a shot and also to be able to throw himself away from the door when a bullet hit the explosive. Then he aimed the Lahti at the lump of C-4 above him.

The explosion was more spectacular and terrifying than lethal. It blew the elevator doors across the hallways on every floor. The brick machinery house on the roof jumped up a foot or two, then collapsed, and the elevator machinery fell into the shaft. The car that had been at the fifth floor fell to the bottom. Brick and mortar, bits of roofing and flooring, wheels and shafts and beams and cable, all tumbled down the shaft in a sustained roar, generating a thick cloud of dust that poured out into the halls.

Bolan ran past the ground-floor security man, who held a telephone in his hand and was mumbling into it, dazed. His eyes followed Bolan, but he seemed not to notice him.

Out on the grounds Bolan looked back. Some of the glass panels had been jarred loose from the facade of the building, giving it an odd checkerboard look. The lights went out. The building fire alarms jangled.

He sprinted to the perimeter fence, used his rope to help him quickly climb over, dropped to the outside and ran for the line of trees that separated the NUG park from the highway. Alarms shrieked. Lights came on, flooding the area in a bluish white glare. He crossed the highway and trotted into the darkness beyond. No one was following.

CHAPTER FIFTEEN

Bolan crossed the Rhine at Nijmegen, still driving the Opel supplied by Kremer and the BND. The two explosions in the NUG compound had given BND ample excuse to look more closely inside the industrial park—for which Reinhard Kremer was most grateful.

In spite of the fact that a bomb had gone off in Rotterdam the very morning when Bolan crossed the border and then the river, the Dutch border control was casual. He had stopped ten kilometers short of the frontier and taped the Lahti, his extra magazines and the Puuko knife inside the engine compartment. But the border people hadn't so much as opened his suitcase. It was a matter of principle that the border should remain open, and the two governments—Federal Republic of Germany and Kingdom of the Netherlands—adhered firmly to the principle.

The Rotterdam bombing wasn't the only terrorist act that had occurred in Europe in the past two days. Besides that, a bomb had exploded in the cargo hold of a Swiss Air 727 en route from Zurich to Munich, destroying the airplane and killing eighty-three passengers and crew. The Rotterdam bombing had been in a mall in the center of the city, tearing a restaurant to pieces and killing thirty-four people.

Bolan had received an encrypted wire from Brognola. When decoded, it read:

Read your message re C-4 to Amsterdam. Pursue. Rotterdam and Swiss Air bombings give new import to terrorist use of explosives. Take a shot at that, then let's get back to what the hell is going on.

Even peaceful, prosperous little Holland wasn't exempt from the new terrorism. In fact, Rijnhard van Reujen of the Dutch counterintelligence service had been one of the first European counterintelligence agents murdered in the new outbreak.

If you didn't care about who lived or died, you could do just about anything, to anyone, for any reason. That was terrorism. And, so far as Bolan had ever been able to discover, the only remedy was to find the terrorists and annihilate them. You didn't negotiate. You didn't compromise. You just identified them and got rid of them. It was the only way.

They came in two flavors—fanatics and mercenaries. He had taken out a lot of both kinds. He would take out some more in Amsterdam.

Bolan was angry as he drove to the small, inconspicuous hotel Kremer had suggested. It faced a canal and you could park the car in front. He nosed the Opel up against the low pipe barrier intended to keep cars from rolling into the canal. The hotel seemed to have about twenty rooms, occupied chiefly by elderly people who dozed in the chairs around the fireplace in the little lobby.

They dozed there, he discovered, because the rooms were cold. His was furnished with a huge, tall bed heaped with comforters. The bathroom was cold, too. The old desk clerk had suggested he could warm his bathroom, if he wished, by filling the bathtub with hot water. That would make it comfortable, he had said.

But Bolan wasn't there for comfort, and he didn't expect to be in his room much. His window overlooked the street and canal. Rooms across the hall had no windows, because the hotel backed up against another building.

He unpacked, strapped on the harness and settled the Lahti into its holster. Wearing his English tweed jacket and one of the pairs of slacks, plus the new coat they had provided to replace the one he had lost in Bobbie Harper's whorehouse, Mr. Ernest Bradley left the hotel ten minutes after he checked in and went to look for the address he had read on the crate of C-4 in the boxcar in Düsseldorf.

He didn't want to ask for the address. He stopped at a newsstand and bought a street map. Even with the map he was unable to locate the street. He stopped a policeman finally. The address, the officer explained, was that of a houseboat permanently moored on the Amstel River. The street name was the name of the quay, actually. The number was the number of the boat.

He walked to the river. It wasn't far, through narrow streets paved with cobblestones, between tall narrow houses. A light snow began to fall. When he reached the river, a sharp wind was whipping the icy snow, stinging his face. The river was wide, the water gray and choppy. Boats lay in the water along both quays, their lines stretching up the river for a considerable distance.

The boats looked like hulks at first glance. They were typical Dutch boats, short, squat, heavy-looking, lying low in the water. Some of them looked like warehouse boats, their cabins locked and cold-looking. Others were clearly homes.

Bolan strolled along the waterside, checking the boat numbers. It took him only a few minutes to find it. The boat looked like most of the others—black-painted hull streaked with rust, white cabin, smoke curling out of a pipe. The curtains covered the windows. He could see light, nothing more.

A case of C-4. To this address?

He couldn't risk having it noticed that he was staring. He turned away from the boat and walked back along the quay, toward the bridge he had crossed, toward the center of the city. The stinging snow crystals turned to big flakes that began to soften the hard outlines of the city.

People began to hurry. Wherever they were going, they wanted to get there before the streets turned slippery. Purposeful, careful of their footing, they walked with their heads down, watching their feet, shielding their faces from the snow.

Bolan did the same. Only with him it was always a little different. Nowhere could he afford to be careless. Never could he afford to be less than alert. He noticed faces. He studied postures. He watched people's strides.

With him it was a subconscious thing to be alert, observant. He wasn't sure when he noticed that a man coming toward him was different. But he was, and Bolan stiffened and put his hand to the Lahti.

The man walked past him. For an instant his eyes flitted over Bolan's face without showing any reaction. Then he fixed his gaze straight ahead and walked on.

Bolan stepped into a doorway of a little tobacco shop—purposefully, as if he were going inside. He saw the man turn and glance back.

Maybe he recognized Bolan. Maybe he didn't. It made no difference. Bolan recognized *him*.

Myrer. Hermie Myrer. What was he doing in Amsterdam?

"Hermie!"

Better men than Hermie Myrer had been shaken by that voice. Mack Bolan wasn't a man anyone ignored when he spoke in anger. Myrer stopped and turned around.

Bolan stepped out of the doorway and walked up to the man.

Hermie Myrer was frightened, and he wasn't a man easy to frighten. There was a gun under his heavy, short gray coat—Bolan would bet on it. His bald head was covered by an Irish tweed walking hat. His intent little brown eyes looked up at Bolan with an expression of suspicion mixed with frustrated malice.

The chief problem with the American system of justice was that animals like Hermie got out of prison eventually.

"What are you doing in Amsterdam, Hermie?"

"Nothin' that's any of your business."

Bolan smiled. "How do you know my business?"

Myrer filled with breath. "I know you," he muttered. He looked around nervously. "What you're interested in, I'm not interested in anymore."

"What? Narcotics?"

Myrer shook his head. "I have nothing to do with that business anymore. I'm on parole. I touch that stuff one time, I'm back inside. No way, Bolan. No way."

Bolan shrugged. "Okay. So what are you doing in Amsterdam?"

"Hey. None of your business. Nothin' that's got anything to do with you."

"What's the name on your passport?"

"When did you start enforcing the passport laws?"

Bolan didn't like the way Myrer's eyes kept shifting, looking past Bolan, looking for something. Looking for...?

Driven by an instinct born of long experience, Bolan abruptly seized Hermann Myrer by both shoulders and spun him around, trading places with him—putting Myrer's back to the gunman who fired an instant too late and hit Myrer instead of Bolan.

Myrer yelled and staggered. He was hit in the left shoulder. The wound wasn't fatal.

Bolan held him as a shield and pulled the Lahti.

Nothing. Whoever had fired didn't fire again. Or appear. The crack of the single shot had been muffled by the heavy snow, and if anyone had noticed, no one reacted.

Bolan was left standing alone in the heavy snowfall, the wounded Myrer slumped against him, moaning.

"If I had any sense at all, Hermie, I'd shove you into the river," Bolan muttered.

"Please..."

"Yeah. Please."

Bolan poked at the entry wound behind Myrer's shoulder. He judged the slug had gone through the fleshy part of the man's body, clipping his shoulder blade maybe, but missing the chief bones.

"I'll walk you to where you can stumble over to a policeman, Hermie."

"No... for God's sake, no, Bolan. Help me!"

THE 7.65 MM SLUG had hit Myrer in the back of the armpit. It had grazed a rib, maybe cracked it, exited a couple of inches left of the nipple, gone into his arm, grazed the bone, exited and stopped in the sleeve of his heavy coat. Bolan stripped him and laid him in a tub of hot water. He had no bandages, nothing with which to treat the wounds against infection. He called room service and ordered a bottle of brandy. Part of that he poured on the wounds, part down Myrer's throat, and he tore up Myrer's shirt and underclothes and made bandages. He'd learned the techniques in Vietnam. He'd bound up far worse with much less.

"No blood on the towels, Hermie," he growled. "None on the bed. If you want to bleed, bleed in the tub. You don't want the Dutch police to know. Neither do I. And you can bet this hotel reports any gunshot wounds they see any evidence of."

"Bolan..." Myrer whispered. "Why?"

"Why would I help you? Why would your buddies shoot you?"

"They didn't mean to."

"Maybe. But they'd have walked away and left you on the street for the police. You owe me one, Hermie."

Myrer lay back in the tub. Bolan had let out the water, which had been pink with blood, and Myrer shivered.

He was a contemptible little man. As a reward for years of unquestioning loyalty and obedience, the Rovigo family in New York had made him a middleman in their heroin business, selling to him at a price that allowed him to make an immense profit when he resold to street pushers. They gave him a small territory in upper Manhattan, and Myrer prospered.

He prospered not least because it was understood that he would visit cruel punishment on anyone who tried to muscle in. In his glory days he reputedly punished six ambitious young men—always with the permission of the Rovigo family. When a Colombian muscled in on one of his street vendors, Myrer dutifully sought the permission of Fredo Rovigo, then shot the Colombian through the head.

But it had been a mistake. The new Colombian dealers had their own ways of protecting their interests. They shot down four of Fredo's soldiers. Fredo responded as Fredo always did—he declared war and sent his soldiers against the Colombians en masse. Three more Colombians died. When the Colombians struck back, they killed, not just two more of Fredo's soldiers, but their wives and children as well. That was the Colombian way—which New York had better learn.

Fredo sought peace. The Council ordered him to seek peace, even if it meant surrendering the narcotics trade entirely. The Colombians made peace. One of their terms was the head of Hermie Myrer. They meant his head, literally, but he was allowed to bow his head instead of taking a bullet through it. He was allowed to get himself arrested and to cop a plea. He went to Attica for a ten-to-twenty and was paroled after seven years.

Bolan might have eliminated Myrer in his glory years. He came to New York to do just that, then learned that the problem he had come to look into hadn't been a Hermie Myrer move or even a Rovigo move but had been done by the Travoliani family. He'd found good enough reason for blasting Myrer but had turned away to pursue something far more important and had all but forgotten Hermie Myrer.

Except that Bolan never forgot.

He turned on hot water and let it splash into the tub around the shivering little man. "Don't get your bandages wet, Hermie," he said.

Myrer stared disconsolately at the red stains on the strips of shirt around his arm and shoulder. Then he looked up at Bolan with the best he could manage of what had once been a tough sneer. "Never thought the Executioner would play nurse," he said.

Bolan stood with his back to the wall, looking down at the naked little man in the steaming hot water. "You know what I want to know, Hermie," he said. "So why don't you start telling me?"

"What do you want to know?"

Bolan shook his head. "We're not going to play it that way. No twenty questions. You tell me what you know—what you think I might want to know."

"If I don't?"

Bolan shrugged. "You know me, Hermie."

Myrer bowed his head. "There's no place I can hide," he said.

"I've got a car outside," said Bolan. "I don't need it anymore. It belongs to a man in Düsseldorf. You can drive it there. I'll call him and tell him you're coming. You'll get a little time out of that. If what we're doing works, he might decide to take care of you."

"Cop . . . ?"

"Ever hear of Bundesnachtrichtendienst?"

"Oh, Jesus!"

"You could make worse friends, Hermie."

Myrer stared down into the water. He reached up and turned off the stream of hot water. "I got nobody else," he said.

"That's how I figure," said Bolan. "If I put you out on the street..."

"They're a different bunch of guys," said Myrer. "Nothin' means nothin' to them. I don't know what the Christ they got in mind, Bolan—"

"Let's start at the beginning, Hermie. In the first place, *why you?* You don't fit into this. Why you?"

Myrer looked up. "Well, it's really funny, Bolan. I still don't understand it. One day about ten days ago, Fredo calls me in and says he's got a special job for me. I got to go to Europe to do it. He sets me up with a passport. My passport name's Myron Herman, incidentally. Bolan...I been in London, Paris—"

"Finger man," said Bolan coldly.

Myrer nodded. "You got it. Somebody wanted a guy who could recognize you. All I had to do was finger you. They don't know you, these guys I'm working with. They need a guy who knows what you look like."

"So they put you on the Amstel quay—"

"Yeah. They figured you'd show up. I been standin' out there in the friggin' cold all yesterday, all today."

"Why'd they think I'd show up here?" Bolan asked.

"I don't know. Well...oh, yeah, I did hear something. Somebody said something about how you'd cracked open a crate."

Yeah. Okay, Bolan understood. In the boxcar. The crate that was short two one-kilo blocks of C-4. Sure. It was where he'd gotten the Amsterdam address.

"You know what they're doing, Hermie?"

Myrer shook his head.

"That boat. You know the boat?"

Myrer nodded.

"It's a bomb factory. The bomb that brought down the Swiss Air 727 and the bomb that went off in the restaurant in Rotterdam—made on that boat. Maybe not, but very likely."

Myrer shook his head. "I never been mixed up in nothing like that. Hey, I wasted guys, but they were in the business, like me. That makes a difference, Bolan. Doesn't it? Citizens. Guys in the business. Different kinds of people. Right? Different to you and me . . ."

Bolan nodded. "Let's get to specifics, Hermie," he said.

"Like . . . ?"

"You tell me."

Myrer nodded. "Fredo said go to Europe. I didn't have a choice, did I? Hey, I don't think Fredo had any, either. Things being what they were, I don't think Fredo wanted to give me anything good. But they didn't ask him. They *told* him."

"Where'd you land in Europe?"

Myrer sighed unhappily. "Pan Am to London. I was met at the airport by a beautiful girl. Hey, she treated me like a king! And it was the first hint I got of what I was here for. She was like a police artist. We sat down, and she sketched out a drawing of you, based on what I said."

"They know what I look like," Bolan said.

"No, they don't. I mean, they talked about how maybe some did. But not everybody who was interested in you did. Anyway, they said you were good at using makeup and stuff. They said you'd showed up looking a lot of different ways. They said I was to finger you."

"Why London—aside from meeting this girl and helping her with the sketch?"

"I don't know. I was supposed to meet some old guy, pass muster with him, I guess. What I got was threatened. Fat old guy. He told me they'd cut my balls off if— Hell, I'm doing it!''

"Talked, you mean."

"Yeah, talked. A hundred thousand in small bills if I did my job. Somethin' awful if I ever talked about what I did."

"Paris?"

"I saw you hit that place on Montmartre," said Myrer. "I was sitting in a bar across the street, watching. I saw you come up on that motorcycle with the girl. I was supposed to call the people across the street if I saw you. I tried to. It was only then I found out you can't put a coin in a French pay phone. You got to buy a token. While I'm at the bar, trying to buy the damn token, Schmidt came out and all hell broke loose. I called my emergency number instead, but by the time the reinforcements got there, it was all over and you were gone."

"So you told them who hit the place," said Bolan.

"Yeah, but they'd have figured that anyway. They were expecting you. I was lucky they didn't cut my balls off for that one. I was their lookout, and I didn't warn them in time. I didn't tell them about the token and all that. I said you came riding up on a motorcycle just when Schmidt came out the door."

"So what are they doing, Hermie?" Bolan asked. "What's going down?"

"I don't know, Bolan. Honest to God, I don't know. But they're heavy hitters. I mean, like you never saw before. It's political, but it's also the organization, you know? Whoever's giving orders, it's somebody *big*. Money...they don't care about money. They spend whatever it takes."

"I suppose they don't know where I am," said Bolan. "This hotel."

"They didn't know you were in town till I spotted you and gave the sign."

"Lucky I recognized you, Hermie."

"Lucky for you," said Myrer bitterly. "If you hadn't, I'd be a hundred thou richer."

"You'd be dead," said Bolan. "If they'd got me, they'd have had no more use for you."

Myrer looked up. He nodded. "Yeah, maybe. Yeah, probably, come to think of it. But they want your ass, Bolan. You're getting in their way."

"You've met a lot of them, Hermie. Tell me about them."

Myrer sighed. He reached forward and turned the handle to run more hot water into the tub. "Okay. To start with, it was Fredo. I don't think Fredo has much to do with it. He was takin' orders. 'Find us a guy who could finger Bolan,' they said. He didn't have anybody else who could. So I get my ticket and my fake passport and a wad of bills, and off I go.

"The first one I meet is the girl in London. A blonde. She's sweet, she's a cute kid, and she's in it up to her throat. She treats me nice, does the drawing and takes me to meet the old fat guy. What can I tell you about him? Old fat guy. Red face. Rubbery lips. He tells me my job and tells me what'll happen if I don't do it right. They didn't seem to be in any hurry about anything. The put me up in a little hotel, and the girl comes around to be sure I'm not lonesome. Then all of a sudden everybody's in a big hurry. The girl turns me over to a tough guy named Bert—which wasn't his real name, you know—and Bert takes me to Paris and delivers me to the house on Montmartre."

"What was the girl's name?" Bolan asked.

"Sandra. Probably wasn't. Probably a fake name."

"Okay. Paris."

Myrer nodded. "You knew Schmidt. You saw the other two. You know more about them than I do."

"Okay. You said you had an emergency number to call. What was it?"

Myrer recited the number for Bolan.

"Go on. Who else did you meet in Paris?"

"Hard guys. Guys that acted like they'd cut your guts out if they could think of a reason. Two of them. Only one spoke English. They put me in a room—"

"Where?"

"Where? In Paris. I never been in Europe before. I don't know where in Paris. I don't know where I was in London, except that the little hotel they put me up in was called Bay something. Anyway, they didn't say I was a prisoner in that room, but I was. Till day before yesterday, when—bang!—get your ass in gear, Myrer, you're going to Amsterdam."

"Who shot you, Hermie?"

"He's called Joop. The Frenchies put me on a plane in Paris, and this Joop met me when I came off here. Young fellow. Not over twenty-five. Looks like a Dutchman, I guess you'd say. Eyes so light blue they're almost white. Yellow hair. Talks good English. Dresses snappy. But inside that beautiful overcoat he's got an odd little pistol, like I never saw before."

"A 7.65 mm something or other," said Bolan. "That's why you aren't torn up more. A small bullet."

"They took me on the boat. That's where I slept two nights. You may be right about their making bombs on the boat. I wasn't allowed down in the hold. The doors that went down there had heavy padlocks on them."

"How many of them are there?"

"I only saw two, Joop and another guy. They spoke Dutch to each other, so I didn't catch the other guy's name. Two girls came to see them last night, but I got the idea they were just friends, not part of anything. They talked Dutch, but the talk seemed all fun and jokes."

"How about guns?"

Myrer shook his head. "Maybe down in the hold," he said.

"Okay, Hermie. If you think you can drive, I suggest you get dressed and do it. The sooner you're out of this town, the better your chances will be."

CHAPTER SIXTEEN

The man who had fired at him and instead hit Myrer hadn't had a very good look at him, Bolan figured. It would be easy enough to alter the image the man probably retained in his mind. In a shop near the waterfront he bought a short blue coat of heavy wool, a gray wool turtleneck sweater, blue jeans and a black watch cap. In another shop he bought half a dozen cigars.

The point wasn't to try to cover your face. The point was for it to be seen and not recognized. Bolan hadn't shaved this morning, and his face was dark with bristly stubble, but he knew it would have been foolish to glue on a beard or mustache. The young man Hermie had called Joop would be giving second and third looks at every beard and mustache he saw, watching for the tip-off of glued-on hair. No matter how observant he was, though, he would associate the face he had seen with the gentlemanly English clothes that had accompanied it; and to see that face with a cigar clamped between the teeth, under a heavy knit watch cap, framed in the turned-up collar of a sailor's short coat, he would almost certainly fail to match it to his mental image.

The leather rig that carried the Lahti was well concealed under the coat, as was the rig for the Puuko knife. The black boots he wore with his blacksuit were proper boots to go with the coat, jeans and cap.

The snow lay four or five inches deep on the streets of Amsterdam as Bolan left the hotel and set out through the streets toward the Amstel quay and another look at the boat where Joop and his friend were making bombs. He trudged along the snow-covered streets, glad for his boots.

The homes on boats looked even more cozy as he saw them snow-covered. Their warm lights gleamed through lace curtains. Though they lay deep in cold water, he knew that only helped to keep them warm, since the temperature of the water never fell as low as the temperature of winter air.

Except for the boat where Joop and his friend made bombs. It was dark. A curl of dark smoke rose from the pipe. Maybe a thermostat-controlled oil stove was burning. Maybe they were in there in the dark, waiting for him. Maybe they were out.

Well, he had a way to find out.

Three boats away from their boat he crossed the plank and knocked on the door.

"Ja?" A woman—young, pretty, pregnant.

"Herr Schneider, alstublieft?"

She shook her head.

It was enough. All he wanted was for anyone watching to see him stopping at each boat.

He went on to the next one, and the one after that, knocking, asking for Herr Schneider, being told that no Herr Schneider was there.

Was he fooling anyone, or was the charade for nothing? He didn't know. He knew it was worth it.

He crossed the plank of the dark boat and knocked. No response. He knocked again. Nothing. As he mimed waiting for someone to come to the door, he glanced around, feigning casualness, examining the area for anyone watching.

He saw nothing.

He tried the knob. The door was flimsy. He glanced around one more time, then stepped back and jammed a foot hard against the wooden door. It splintered and swung in. With Lahti drawn, he stepped inside.

Nothing. They *were* out.

He pulled the door shut. That made it dark in the cabin, so he pulled back the curtains on the water side. Hermie had said there were padlocked doors into the hull. That was true. They were the same kind of flimsy wooden door he had just kicked in, and he shattered one of them.

They hadn't abandoned the place. It was a bomb factory, all right. He might have interfered with one shipment of C-4, but here was plenty more. Crates of it. He opened them with the knife. They had maybe three hundred kilos. Plus a dozen Heckler & Koch MP-5 submachine guns and maybe two thousand rounds of 9 mm parabellum. Detonator equipment—radio transmitters and receivers, delayed action fuses, wire and tape and innocent-looking boxes in which bombs could be carried. Flower boxes—light boxes in which a dozen long-stemmed roses might be delivered, would be perfect for a one- or two-kilo bomb. A baby carriage. It would carry ten kilos.

Death.

A priority. For the next quarter of an hour he opened crates of C-4, carried the packages up the stairs into the cabin and heaved them out a window into the waters of the Amstel River. River water didn't make C-4 any less deadly, but it made it unavailable to Joop and his partner. And he heaved the rest of what they had—handguns, the detonator equipment, their ammunition. He filled his pockets with boxes of 9 mm cartridges—a man could never have too much—but what he couldn't carry he threw into the river.

He was tempted to set a small charge, blast a hole in the hull and sink the boat. But innocent people lived on the boats moored at both ends of this vessel. Instead, he opened a hatch that opened into the bilge. A little water stood in there. He fired a clip from the Lahti through the rusting steel hull. Water spurted into the bilge. If Joop or his friend didn't come back soon, they would return to find their boat had settled gently to the bottom.

THE CIGAR-SMOKING SAILOR returned to the quay later in the morning. The decks of the former bomb factory were awash. Dutch policemen in high boots were aboard. The boat had sunk to the mud bottom and listed until the water ran in over the gunwales and finished the job of filling the hull. A small crowd watched the policemen. They weren't excited. Apparently it was nothing unusual for a boat to sink along the quay. All anyone was concerned about was being sure no one was aboard.

And there was Joop. Bolan knew he had his man. The blond young man wore a handsome camel overcoat. His throat was wrapped in a Burberry scarf, but he wore no hat, so the hair Myrer had described as yellow fluttered in the wind.

Bolan stepped behind him.

"Don't worry, Joop. They won't find anything. It's all in the water, scattered downstream on the current or sinking in the river mud."

Joop's hand went for his pistol.

"Don't," Bolan warned. "The muzzle against your back is 9 mm. Yours is only 7.65. Except for the fact that I want to talk to you, I'd just blow a gap in your spine and walk away. But I do want to talk to you, so you and I are going to walk away together."

"Bolan—" the young man grunted.

"You've heard of me. Then maybe you're too smart to try anything stupid, particularly giving your friend a sign to try to take me on. He might waste me. But think about living the rest of your life missing one or two vertebrae and a couple of inches of spinal cord. I hear guys like that can't even get it up, and I hear you put some importance on getting it up."

"I *want* to talk with you," the young man said.

"I bet. If you do, now's your chance. Just walk ahead of me. I'll tell you which way to go."

Bolan had looked around. He knew where he wanted to go—into one of the streets of the red-light district and a little bar he'd spotted, where off-duty girls anesthetized themselves with the Dutch gin called jenever and chatted with the locals and the plainclothes policemen who made sure they didn't solicit business in the bar. The place was small. It was warm. They fried fish, and the room smelled of it. It smelled, too, of good Dutch beer and good Dutch cheese. Bolan ordered beer and a plate of the fish.

"Where people enjoy life," Bolan said to Joop as they sat down at a table. "Like you ought to do. Like you ought to let other people do. Slip that little pistol of yours out and push it under my left hand."

Joop obeyed. Bolan recognized the pistol, a smooth little Mauser automatic. He slipped it into his pocket.

"My name is Joop Thijn," the young Dutchman said. "You seem to know that already."

"I patched up Hermie and sent him where he'll be safe."

Thijn smiled. "And where might that be? There will be no safe place soon. You are on the wrong side, Bolan. You should be with us. It's where you belong."

"You tried to kill me yesterday," said Bolan. "Was that to put me on the side where I belong?"

"My orders are to kill you," said Thijn coldly, his striking light blue eyes narrowing. "I'd have carried out that order if I could have. But only because everyone has despaired of recruiting you. Now..." He shrugged. "Well, maybe we can talk."

"Oh, you *do* talk?" said Bolan scornfully. "I thought you let your bombs talk for you. *Innocent people,* you bastard!"

"You're angry because you don't understand," said Thijn. "I know you're determined to kill me, but—"

"Like the animal you are," said Bolan.

"They call *you* that, Bolan," Thijn snapped. "The Executioner. How many men have you killed? Are you to be condemned out of hand for killing? Not when you have reason, I think. Not when you have a cause. War? In war people get killed. In Vietnam, your country—"

"I was in Vietnam."

"I know. And I know you didn't kill innocent civilians. Not intentionally, anyway. But tens of thousands of innocent civilians died at American hands—not because you Americans were unprincipled butchers, but because you were fighting for a cause you believed was right, and probably was right, and in war people—"

"What war are you fighting, Joop?"

"A good war. A just war. We who are fighting it call ourselves the White Front. Do you want to let me explain?"

"I've heard it all before, how a 'cause' justifies inhumanity. And I've heard romantic names—Red Anvil, Justice Commandos, the People's Liberation Army and a lot of other bullcrap names," Bolan sneered. "But I'll listen to it again. Am I going to hear an original idea?"

"Listen to me, Bolan," Thijn said quietly, leaning across the table toward him. "What have you fought for? A world where decent people can live and prosper in peace? That's it, isn't it? And who's been your worst opposition? Not the animals you wanted to rid the world of, right? Not them. In the end, your worst enemies have been the weaklings who'd rather just *let* a few thousand kilos of cocaine pass across your borders rather than do something effective to stop it. Or how about the sociologists who argue we should try to *understand* the terrorists rather than trying to stop them? What about it, Bolan? Who are your enemies?"

Bolan faced Thijn and listened, showing him nothing. He'd heard all this before.

"Who, Bolan?" Thijn persisted. "Who's going to make the world decent again? You reject the White Front? You belong to it, whether you know it or not. Who else, I ask you, is going to make the world decent again?"

Bolan shrugged. "When was it ever decent, with your kind around?" he asked.

Thijn glanced around the bar—whether to look for someone who would come shooting and save him, or just to see who was watching, Bolan couldn't be sure.

"You and I have more in common than you want to admit," said Thijn.

"The people we have in common have tried to kill me half a dozen times in the past couple of weeks," said Bolan.

"They're afraid of you," said Thijn. "They're afraid you'll damage the cause. They're afraid you're programmed like a computer, to act without thinking. I'd have killed you if I'd gotten the chance. I don't deny it. Because I'm afraid of you, too. But I also know you're a smart man. I also know you're potentially one of us, once it's explained to you."

"Explain it."

"The people I work for have fought on the front line in this great continuing battle, just as you have, Bolan. And recently... well, recently in almost every country, the weaklings have assumed power, and civilization is in retreat."

"For example," said Bolan.

"I give you an example," said Thijn. "In France SDECE—sometimes called Action Service—used methods not unlike yours to defend France against the animals."

"I remember," said Bolan dryly. "People disappeared in France. There was some disagreement about whether or not all of them could be called animals."

Thijn shrugged. "Then came Mitterand, he and his socialists. They *abolished* Action Service."

"And created GIGN," said Bolan. "And the veterans of Action Service formed the cadre for GIGN."

"Yes," Thijn persisted. "And as long as they survive, GIGN can be effective. But as they grow older and retire, they are being replaced by weak men. It is the same in all the countries of Western Europe. It is the same in the Soviet Union, for that matter. The men who had the courage to act effectively are being replaced by irresolute men who blather and fret and let the animals run wild. Terrorists. Fanatics. Barbarians. Criminals of every sort."

"Terrorists," said Bolan. "Criminals. How do you define people who set off bombs in crowded railroad stations and shopping malls, bring down airliners with explosives, try to sink a cross-Channel ferry? How do you define the people who've murdered—"

"Bolan!" Thijn interrupted in a shrill, impatient whisper. "Sometimes you have to adopt their own tactics to do something effective against the animals. It's what you do temporarily until you get things under control again."

"Is this how you would explain yourselves to the families of the hundreds of innocent people who've been killed in your bombings?" Bolan asked.

"How do you explain yourself to the families of the men you've killed?" asked Thijn with a sneer.

Bolan shook his head, containing his rage only by a hard effort of will. "Do you really think I'm like you, Thijn?" he asked. "Sure, I'm the Executioner. But I've never thrown a bomb into a crowd. If there were fifty terrorists in a room, and *one* innocent man, I wouldn't throw the bomb. If there were fifty terrorists in a room and one I suspected but wasn't sure of, I wouldn't throw the bomb. And that's why I wouldn't even *think* of joining you."

"But of course you're going to kill me," said Thijn almost calmly.

"No. No matter how much I'd like to."

"Then what are you going to do?"

"Hand you over to someone who'll know what to do with you."

"And who might that be?"

"I'll find out," said Bolan.

He led Thijn to the back of the little bar, where there was a telephone. He checked the men's room. There was no escape from it, no window. He told Thijn to go inside and stay there. He got an English-speaking operator and gave her the number Brognola had given him in Rome.

He knew how the system worked. The call went to an army communications center outside Heidelberg, where it was scrambled and transmitted up to a satellite, which transmitted it to a bank of hilltop dish antennas in Virginia.

"Hello." A woman's voice. Just "Hello."

That was the routine. No identification, in case someone called the number accidentally.

"This is Striker," he said.

There was a long moment of silence. The name Striker was being put into a computer identification bank. It hit. "Go ahead, Striker," she said.

"Put me through to Virginia," he said.

"You got it."

The next word was "Center." Another woman's voice.

"Striker."

"Go ahead, Striker."

"Run me a search on an outfit called the White Front."

"Hold on."

"I've got all day."

"Won't take all day. The answer is nothing. We've got nothing on the White Front."

"Run me a name. Joop Thijn." Bolan spelled the name. "Hold on."

Bolan glanced at the door. It was possible Thijn was carrying another pistol, maybe in an ankle holster.

"Striker, we have a record on your man Joop Thijn. Dutch. Blond, twenty-eight years old. Graduate of Leyden University, a degree in languages. Fluent English speaker, as well as fluent in German and French. Employed by the government. He's a case officer, Dutch counterintelligence."

Bolan walked out of the little bar, leaving Thijn in the men's room.

An agent of Dutch counterintelligence.

And in the meeting in Düsseldorf—Jean Henriot of GIGN. France. Henri Leclerc knew. He had to know.

In Düsseldorf it had to be obvious what NUG was, what Willi von Voss was doing—yet Reinhard Kremer had been unable to move against it and had been grateful when two explosions made it possible for him to move inside the NUG compound.

Maybe Brognola understood. The established security agencies couldn't move against this conspiracy that called itself the White Front. They were penetrated by it. That was why they were willing to call on the Executioner.

And let him take the hit, too, if it came to that.

Except, of course, Brognola. He kept some things to himself but never anything he thought might cost him the life and services of Mack Bolan.

Bolan was angrier than he had been for a long time. He had been tempted just to open that men's room door and put a bullet in Joop Thijn. And he would have, except that it wouldn't have contributed anything. The Dutch unit of the White Front had lost its plastique and its guns in the cold river waters of the Amstel. It would set off no new explosions for a few days. And Thijn might have died a Dutch hero, victim of some mysterious assassin who—

On the cold streets outside the little bar, Bolan decided to fade into the crowd of sailors and whores on the street and wait for Thijn to come out.

He waited a long time. Good. It couldn't be because Thijn was too timid to open the men's room door and check. It had to be because he had come out and used the telephone to report. Maybe twenty minutes passed before Joop Thijn came out of the bar into the cold, windswept street.

He didn't turn south, as Bolan had thought he might, toward the waters of the Amstel and the sunken hulk of the boat where he had made bombs. He turned north toward the harborfront, toward the central train station.

Bolan followed, keeping enough distance between them that Thijn would be unlikely to spot him on streets that weren't crowded yet abounded in busy people.

He followed Thijn into a street that ran perpendicular to the canals, which meant crossing little bridges at the end of every block. The sidewalks were narrow. The tall, narrow Dutch houses rose high on either side. Thijn strode purposefully, twenty-five or thirty yards ahead of him.

Abruptly Thijn ducked into a doorway. And Bolan instinctively erupted into action as an automatic weapon roared. He threw himself toward a doorway and onto his belly. He was pulling the Lahti and trying to get an aim when the first motorbike roared past, carrying a rider behind the driver. The rider swept a submachine gun back and forth, spewing fire, oblivious of the terrified pedestrians who dropped to the pavement to save themselves. A stream of slugs cut the wooden door behind Bolan, just above his head.

The motorbike driver hit his brakes. The machine skidded to a stop and spun. The gunman shoved the driver aside and leveled the muzzle of his weapon toward Bolan. He was too slow. A 9 mm slug from Bolan's Lahti blasted into his sternum and threw him backward, his heart and lungs exploding from the shock and pressure.

The driver had pulled a pistol. His face exploded from Bolan's next shot.

But there were more motorbikes. Three others screeched to a stop in the narrow street. Two more submachine guns erupted with a stream of fire. Bolan rolled out of the doorway just as a torrent of slugs chopped up the door and chipped furrows in the soft brick of the wall.

One gunner had the courage to jump from his motorbike and take a spread-eagle stance in the middle of the street. Rolling, Bolan missed him with his first shot, but the second plowed into his rib cage, and he toppled back with a scream, firing wildly into the air, his bullets hitting the facades of buildings high above and ricocheting into the sky. His driver gunned his engine and, skidding wildly, retreated out of the street.

But two gunmen were still firing. Bolan was in the middle of a hail of ill-aimed but deadly fire. He rolled around on the sidewalk, trying to avoid the slugs that chipped at the pavement and trying also to level the Lahti on another target.

He felt a burning shock in his left shoulder and knew he was hit.

He clutched the Lahti in both hands and leveled on a leather-jacketed gunman.

The man crumpled and fell. Bolan hadn't fired, but the man doubled, clutching his body, and dropped his weapon. The man astride the motorbike that had carried the wounded man grabbed inside his leather jacket and pulled an automatic just in time to take a slug in the gut and bent over, yelling.

Still another one braced himself and took aim with a submachine gun. Bolan dropped him with one shot to the gut.

The driver of the fourth motorbike retreated. Bolan rose to his knees and aimed the Lahti, but he didn't fire. The bike had reached the corner and turned.

Thijn bolted out of the doorway where he had taken refuge and ran toward the canal bridge at the far end of the block. As he ran a shot hit him. He staggered, but one of the motorbike drivers rushed to him, helped him on his motorbike and roared off.

Sitting on the pavement, Bolan pulled the clip from the Lahti and inserted another. His shoulder was throbbing, and the sleeve of his jacket was wet with blood, but he wasn't immobilized.

Someone had helped him. The same someone who now called out his name.

Marilyn.

"HOW'D YOU KNOW?"

He sat in hot water in the big tub in his hotel bathroom, and she washed the blood from his wound, poured brandy on it and bandaged him with strips of torn shirts.

He had asked the question immediately after she'd dragged him into the small Mercedes she had abandoned at the end of the street. She had refused to talk then. She'd asked him where he was staying and had driven directly to the hotel. They had been able to pass through the lobby and come up to his room without anyone noticing he was wounded.

"I saw you go aboard the boat," she said now. "You told Brognola you were coming to Amsterdam. He signaled Sir George. Kremer in Düsseldorf shared intel with us, too. Sir George and I agreed it was time for you to quit playing Lone Ranger. I arrived here last night. I didn't know where you were, but I supposed you'd go to the boat sooner or later. I've been following you ever since."

"We've got a bigger problem than we thought," he said to her, wincing as he prodded his shoulder, testing it.

"This isn't so bad, fortunately," she said. "Could have been. I'd guess this slug ricocheted into your shoulder. It's in there. We're going to have to get you to hospital, my friend."

"Hospital—"

"In London. Or in Germany somewhere. Not here. I—"

"No, not here," he agreed. "The man who ran away, the one in the camel coat that you put a slug into. He's an agent of Dutch counterintelligence."

She nodded. "We've suspected."

"They call themselves the White Front. They've penetrated GIGN—"

"Mack . . ." she said gently. "We've got to get across the frontier as soon as you can move. That intelligence agent will have put out the word on you—God knows what. I'm afraid to go through Schiphol Airport. If I can get you back into Germany, or across the border into Belgium—"

"We move *now*, then," he said.

CHAPTER SEVENTEEN

Marilyn drove south, not east. She crossed the Belgian frontier at Breda and headed for Brussels. The Dutch and Belgians were still casual about the border crossing and didn't seem to be looking for a wounded man in a rented Mercedes driven by an attractive young woman, so they passed across without incident—Miss Marilyn Henry, English publisher, and Mr. Ernest Bradley, salesman for a Manchester company called British Cybernetics.

Bolan's shoulder was oozing blood. Once they were over the border, Marilyn stopped and bought gauze pads, tape and an antiseptic powder.

As they drove toward Brussels they turned the car's radio to the BBC and heard the news that Harry Kilroy, identified by the newscaster as CIA station chief for Paris, had been killed early that morning. His car had blown up outside his flat in Montparnasse.

"Henriot," said Bolan.

"Hmm?"

"Jean Henriot," said Bolan. "He was at the White Front council meeting—if that was what it was—in Düsseldorf."

"How do you know?"

"I saw him. Through the window. He was the only man there I recognized. One of them had to be Voss. One or two of them had to be English. But—"

"But you didn't recognize anyone else?"

He shook his head.

"You struck a real blow in Düsseldorf," she said. "Voss is under arrest. BND moved in after the explosions you set

off. They found that NUG was operating as a warehousing
and shipping center for... well, for something. It's hard to
say what. They were shipping explosives and weapons. BND
took the addresses off the crates, and yesterday and today
there were raids on establishments in Italy, Spain and Nor-
way."

"They catch anyone?" he asked.

"No. Someone put the word out very fast. The places had
been abandoned."

"The men I saw at the meeting—"

"Scattered," she said. "By helicopter, some of them."

"The word circulates too fast," said Bolan. "They've
penetrated—" he sighed loudly "—Dutch intelligence.
GIGN. Who knows what else?"

NOT SINCE 1946 HAD Willi von Voss been held in custody.
He found it a distressing business, though not frightening,
since he had experienced it before. He occupied a clean,
bright cell. He was allowed to wear his own clothes, and his
valet was allowed to bring him what he needed—clothing,
toiletries, the small cigars he favored, tinned foods, even
bottles of wine. In his cell each morning he brushed his
teeth, shaved and dressed in clean underwear, a white shirt
and a conservative business suit, which he wore all day. He
spent his time reading and in writing memoranda for his
corporate staff. When he was taken out for exercise, he
walked briskly in the courtyard in his overcoat—astonishing the other prisoners by his dress and manner.

He refused to be interrogated. All he would say was that
his lawyers advised him to remain quiet. Their position was
that the contraband found in his warehouse and in the railroad cars on his siding were there entirely without his
knowledge. He confidently expected to be released in another day or so.

On the morning of his fourth day in prison he followed his routine. His valet arrived about ten, bringing a stack of reports for his attention, a small bottle of brandy and some cigars. Voss spoke to the man confidentially, in quiet urgency. The valet absorbed the message he was to carry out. He left after ten minutes.

Voss sat down at his table and began to scan the reports from his department heads. He shook a cigar from a little package, put it between his lips and lit a match. He sucked on the cigar to draw the fire into the tip.

Odd. The cigar tasted funny. Funny... No! In the last moment of his life Willi von Voss realized he had just inhaled a deadly poison. What tasted funny was cyanide. He gasped. He had no time to call for help. His throat and lungs were afire. He slumped over his table, then fell to one side onto the floor. By the time a guard noticed him on the floor he had been dead a quarter of an hour.

JOOP THIJN WISHED he could die. He had hung upside down and naked for more than twenty-four hours. How much longer than twenty-four hours, he didn't know. His feet were dead. He knew they would have to be amputated if he lived; they had been without circulation for too long. They were numb. His hands... there was a little circulation in his right hand anyway, maybe none in his left. The men who hung him here had used pliers to tighten wire around his wrists. Another wire had been forced through the tennis ball that had been shoved into his mouth to gag him, and that wire was twisted hard against the back of his neck.

His bullet wound had ceased to throb, though it had at first, painfully. He had gotten medical treatment for it and had been assured it wasn't permanently damaging. The next day he had received the summons, had reported as ordered, and within half an hour he was hanging here. They had ripped off his bandage. The wound had bled a little. It was the least of his problems now.

He had ceased to moan. No one noticed. In fact, they hardly came near him. He stank. He had urinated and defecated, and the residue of both functions was on him.

He knew where he was—on the top floor of a house only three blocks from where Bolan had survived an attack by eight men. He didn't know how many Bolan had killed. No one had told him. They had told him Bolan had gotten away.

There was an element of mercy in nature. He had lost consciousness for a while, two or three times. He had no idea for how long. He felt life slipping away. He could only wish it would retreat faster.

"Well, Herr Thijn. You don't look comfortable. What can we do for you?"

He had drifted out. Cruelly the voice brought him back. His eyes focused. A gray-haired man was sitting on a wooden chair he had drawn up. He spoke German, and he regarded Joop Thijn with detached interest.

"I say, what can we do for you?"

"Kill me," Thijn muttered hoarsely. "Short of that, a drink of water."

"Yes, of course, a drink of water," the man said to one of the two hard types who were always in the room. "We don't want Herr Thijn to die of thirst."

"Jawohl, Herr Doktor."

Thijn's eyes followed the man as he went to a sink in a corner of the large room and drew a cup of water. Then he noticed the woman. A young woman. Beautiful. Her throat was bandaged. She hung back, as if she were afraid, but her cold eyes showed him no sympathy. A young man stood a few paces behind the one the hardman had called Herr Doktor. Everyone was deferential to the older man. Thijn retained enough awareness to see that.

The hardman shoved the cup against Thijn's mouth, and he was able to suck in a little water before the man lost patience and tossed the rest across his face.

"It is important for the two of you to see what is happening to Herr Thijn," said the older man. "He lost his temper and his judgment. When Herr Bolan bested him, he called in *eight men* to kill Bolan—in a stupid street attack that terrorized a whole quarter of Amsterdam. Eight men. Four motorcycles. Four submachine guns. To kill one man. And they failed."

"He had help," muttered Thijn.

"And what help did he have the day before? The man we sent you pointed him out and you—" he paused to shake his head "—shot our man instead of Bolan. And let Bolan capture him. Then you let him capture *you*. And then you lost your reason, Herr Thijn."

Thijn couldn't see the man they called Herr Doktor. He had turned at the end of the rope from which he hung, and his face was toward a wall.

"Let's see what you've cost us in the past few days," the Herr Doktor continued. "Four men killed. Two wounded and taken by the police. Only two of your eight escaped. Fortunately they were nothing but hired gunmen and the two in custody don't know why they were called on to shoot down the American. Besides that, you lost the little New York mobster we brought over to help us identify Bolan. *And* you lost a boat loaded with explosives and weapons. Perhaps worst of all, you have heightened the police alert in half a dozen countries. Bolan knows who you are, and you can be sure whoever he reports to knows, too. You were in fact a valuable resource, Herr Thijn—and you cost us yourself."

So that was it. They counted him a spectacular failure, and they would let him hang here until he died. He had seen it done to another man, and he wasn't surprised when he was hoisted up by his ankles. He tried to remember how long the other man had lasted. He had begged to be killed. They had waited him out.

"So," said the older man. Now he was talking to the others, Thijn knew. "We have changed our strategy. Until now we tolerated the proposition that Bolan might be taken alive. It might have been useful to inject him with appropriate chemicals and interrogate him extensively. We might have found out how much Herr Brognola, for one, knows about us. But Bolan has learned too much, injured us too much. Now the policy is to kill him as quickly as possible, by whatever means may be most effective. Those were Herr Thijn's orders."

Thijn had turned again and could see the two younger people staring at him. He wondered if he had stared as coldly at the middle-aged Swede he had seen hanging like this. They weren't horrified, only curious. They were solemn.

"Fräulein Zhulev, you have failed once. You need not take this assignment. We are offering it to you because you have seen Bolan—indeed, you saw him rather intimately, I believe—and you will recognize him. But if you create a disaster, as Herr Thijn has done, then—"

"I understand, Herr Doktor," she said. "I would like to accept the assignment. The man Bolan is not invincible. We had him in our grasp, and if the assignment had been to kill him, we could have killed him easily. I acknowledge I underestimated him. I will not make that mistake again."

The Herr Doktor nodded. "And you, Herr Hastings?"

Hastings nodded thoughtfully. He was an athletic-looking blond man with close-cropped hair, a sharp chin, a prominent Adam's apple and an overall look of emaciation and intense solemnity.

"Well, then. You are not the only people assigned. You will go to England and try to catch him there. I need hardly warn you that Bolan is clever and ruthless. And…I thought it would be well if you had a look at Herr Thijn."

Eva Zhulev adjusted the bandage on her throat. "The woman," she whispered. "What about the woman?"

"The one who hit you? No, Fräulein. Your assignment is to kill Bolan. No one else. You are not to be distracted from your mission by looking also for your revenge against that woman, whoever she was. Even if you get the chance to kill her, you are not to do it. Do you understand me. *Forget* the woman."

Eva Zhulev nodded curtly. *"Jawohl, Herr Doktor."*

The older man stood. He nodded toward the door. "Wait for me below," he said.

For a moment he stood looking at Thijn, his nose wrinkling slightly. Thijn turned on the rope, involuntarily presenting his backside to the Herr Doktor.

"You insist there were two of them firing at your men," he said.

"Yes, I am sure of it."

"Then *who?*"

Thijn released a short, disconsolate breath. "I don't know," he muttered weakly.

The Herr Doktor walked across the room to where his two hardmen sat at a small table, reading a newspaper and sipping beer. They stood as he approached. "I can't spare the two of you to baby-sit him any longer," he said. He glanced back at Thijn, who had turned again and could see him. "Cut his throat."

"Jawohl, Herr Doktor."

Doktor Johann Kleist left the room, closing the door behind him, and walked down the narrow stairs.

THE EGYPTIAN WAS A MADMAN. Besides being a religious fanatic, even to the point of banging his head on the floor, he insisted on prying into every assembly and subassembly of the Foxbat; with the result that an aircraft that had been all but ready to fly was now twenty percent disassembled. I'm going to fly it, he kept saying. It's my life, he insisted. Mikoyan kept his own thought quiet—which was, What do you think happens to *my* life if this aircraft fails?

He had insisted on static tests, even though the Frenchman had forbidden them. The aircraft had been lashed down, the rear doors of the hangar had been opened and the engines had been spun up until they spewed a roar of fire out into the arctic night, just as the Frenchman had insisted couldn't be done, for fear the plume of flame would be observed from overhead.

And, sure enough, he found a fault. The big air inlets that scooped in air for the turbojets were fitted with doors, like lower lips, that were supposed to open and close as the throttles were advanced and retarded—opening wide as the aircraft operated at a low speed, as during takeoff and landing, and closing at high speeds. A sophisticated linkage connected the hydraulic system that pulled this lower lip up or pushed it down. Twice the linkage on the right inlet had jammed open. The solution was simple—the pilot could override the automatic mechanism and order the lip closed. But for a moment the Foxbat would yaw as one scoop remained wide open and the other closed. Mikoyan and the Frenchman had agreed this solution was good enough; the aircraft would yaw only for a moment.

But the Egyptian said no. It was all very well, said Major Alani, for ground mechanics to talk about something being good enough; but ground mechanics didn't have to fly the aircraft. Takeoff was a critical maneuver. Foxbats had been known to crash during takeoff.

The problem was in a finely machined little pivot coupler in the linkage. It was bent. It had worked back and forth too many times, giving a tiny bit each time, until now it was visibly distorted. If they tried to straighten it, it might break.

"If the service schedule had been followed," Mikoyan explained to the Frenchman, "it would have been replaced after three thousand hours." He shrugged. "Likely enough, this one *was* replaced. This is the throwaway."

"Sabotage," the Frenchman snapped threateningly.

Mikoyan shook his head. "The subassembly was delivered complete. The part had been installed long ago. You can check that for yourself. Look at how the distortion has rubbed a groove in the retainer."

"Why? Why would anyone—"

"A comrade sergeant-mechanic was ordered to keep, say, five Foxbats flying. If he couldn't do it, he couldn't explain he was short of parts; that would imply criticism of the supply system and in turn of the State and Party, which isn't permitted. So, faced with a broken pivot coupler and having no new one to replace it, he went to his junk box and pulled out a part that had too many hours on it but looked all right. What is more, he made no record of the fact, and when he got the new part he had use for it and didn't put it in an aircraft that was flying acceptably without it. And in time he forgot it. It's the system. Not sabotage."

The Frenchman grunted and scowled. "Can you machine a new one?"

"No. Just look at it. We can improvise many things. Not that. Either the Egyptian flies with this pivot coupler or the aircraft cannot fly until you can obtain a new one."

In a gasoline station outside Brussels, Bolan used a public telephone to place another call to the Heidelberg communications center. As Marilyn waited in the car, once again annoyed to be excluded from something, he reached Hal Brognola in Washington.

"Where are you, Striker? I notice you called about Joop Thijn. Well, Joop Thijn called about you, too. I guess that's no coincidence."

"This thing we're up against is called the White Front," said Bolan. "Thijn works for it. He tried to recruit me, and when I wouldn't fall, he tried to kill me. Big operation. Eight guys."

"Right. Thijn called. He said there'd been a hell of a shoot-out on the streets of Amsterdam. He said you were wounded. He said he'd been wounded trying to help you. He wanted to know where he could find you to help you."

"Sure he did," said Bolan scornfully. "He wanted another chance at me."

"He's missing, Striker."

"What do you mean?"

"The Dutch government has been in touch. After Thijn talked to us and asked about you, he turned up missing."

"I bet he did," said Bolan. "Since he couldn't kill me, he knew what word I was carrying. The C-4 from Düsseldorf was being delivered to him. He was running a bomb factory on a boat."

"Right. The Amsterdam police have fished a lot of C-4 out of the Amstel River. They're not what you'd call overjoyed."

"They'd rather it was being detonated in stores and restaurants?"

"Striker..." said Brognola hesitantly. "You're absolutely sure about Thijn?"

"I couldn't be more sure."

"How badly are you wounded?"

"I've got a bullet in my shoulder. Marilyn is here. She showed up in Amsterdam at the crucial moment. She's the one who wounded Thijn. The point is, I've got to get to a doctor and get this bullet out. Marilyn wants us to fly to London and have it done there. I'm not opposed, but—"

"Understood, Striker," said Brognola. "How far are you from the airport?"

"Say half an hour. We've got to turn in a rental car."

"I'll have somebody there. What kind of car?"

"Dark blue Mercedes. Dutch plates."

"My man will be at the rental station. Thirty minutes."

Bolan and Marilyn made it to the car rental station with five minutes to spare.

"You're . . . Striker?"

Bolan sized up the man before he nodded. A thirty-year-old man in brown overcoat and brown hat, with the open, innocent face of an honest agent who hadn't seen much but would do his duty even if he got hurt at it. A soldier. A Company man. In civilian life he would have been a company man, too—with a small *c*.

"I'm Bill Palmer. With the Company. Brussels station. And, uh, Miss Henry?"

Marilyn nodded at him.

"My car," said Palmer, nodding. "Let me get your bags."

He drove them, not toward the airport terminal, but along an access road that ran parallel to the main runways and a tall fence tapped with razor wire. The road had been plowed out, and snow was heaped on either side. Big jets roaring down the runway blasted up plumes of snow that trailed them and drifted on the wind.

"I've heard about you for years," Palmer said to Bolan. "I never thought I'd meet you."

"No big deal," said Bolan dryly.

But it was, for Palmer. He was in awe of Mack Bolan, and he couldn't hide it. He kept glancing at him, as if to burn the image of Bolan's face into his memory. Others did that. A man in Palmer's position could never talk about the day he met the Executioner. Officially he never had. But he would remember.

"There have been three more murders," he said.

"We know about Kilroy in Paris," Marilyn said. "We heard it on the radio."

"Well, besides that, someone killed Willi von Voss in his prison cell. And an agent of Italian intelligence, SISDE, was shot this morning in Rome."

Bolan glanced over the seat at Marilyn in the back. He didn't say what he had in mind; he knew she would understand—that they were dealing with rough characters.

"We don't know how to cope with what's going on," said Palmer.

Bolan didn't respond. He knew how to cope with it. There was only one way to cope with it.

Palmer turned the car toward a gate. Two uniformed guards unlocked and opened it. He drove through and toward a small jet that waited just off the taxiway. It was a Lear, marked with the green-and-blue logo of Fabricants Généraux.

SIR ALEXANDER BENTWOOD was waiting for them at Gatwick Airport—waiting with a Rolls-Royce and driver.

"He's deputy foreign secretary," Marilyn reminded Bolan as he looked down from the window of the little jet at the tall, distinguished-looking man standing by the car. "Specialist in intelligence. You remember him. You met him at the briefing with Mr. Brognola and Sir George Harrington."

"I remember him," said Bolan.

The bullet in his shoulder had begun to ache. He really didn't care that the deputy foreign secretary had come to Gatwick to meet him.

"Sir George wasn't able to be with us this afternoon," said Sir Alexander. "But the arrangements we've made were at his suggestion. We're taking you to Oaks, Mr. Bolan. My country house. A surgeon and nurse are waiting for you. Your wound can be treated properly and entirely confidentially."

"Not to hospital in London?" Marilyn asked.

Sir Alexander shook his head. "No. They're setting up a small operating theater in the house. If the wound is more serious than we think, we can move Mr. Bolan to hospital most expeditiously. If it is as we think, it can be attended to at Oaks."

Half an hour later Bolan lay on a table in the library of Sir Alexander's elegant seventeenth-century stone house. Though the table had been covered with a pad and with sheets, it was a dining table, carried in from one of the dining rooms.

"Not difficult," said the surgeon. "No great damage, Mr. Bolan. But because the wound is twenty-four hours old, and more, there is swelling and the beginning of infection that will have to be cleaned out. For that reason, you'll need to sleep through the procedure. Otherwise it would be quite painful."

Bolan watched apprehensively as the doctor inserted a needle in his arm and pressed down to inject something into his veins. He looked around. Besides the doctor and nurse, Marilyn was in the library. As the anesthetic began to take hold, Marilyn stepped up to the table and put her face down to his ear.

"I love you, Mack Bolan," she whispered as he blacked out.

CHAPTER EIGHTEEN

Gradually Mack Bolan became aware of his surroundings. He lay in a huge bed, his head deep in oversize soft pillows. He felt his shoulder. It was swathed in bandages. There was no pain. The room was lit only by the flickering yellow flames of a dying fire in a great stone fireplace. He could see paneling of old wood. The ceiling was elaborately beamed and carved. Grotesque sculpted figures stared down from the corners. The windows were of leaded glass, and beyond them the sun had set.

He felt around. His watch lay on an antique table by the bed. He reached for it and strapped it on his wrist. Twenty-two hundred hours. He looked for his weapons. Neither the Lahti nor the Mauser he'd taken from Thijn were anywhere he could see or reach.

He discovered he was dressed only in his undershorts.

How long had he been out? Six hours? Seven? Had it taken that long to dig a bullet out of his shoulder and cleanse and disinfect a wound? Maybe the operation had been worse than they had tried to tell him it would be.

He moved his arm. No more painful than it had been. He clenched and unclenched his fist. No loss there.

He pushed himself up and tried sitting erect, propped against the pillows. Nausea. A little dizziness.

He was sitting, still examining himself very closely, when the door opened and Sir Alexander Bentwood came in.

"Ah, Bolan," he said. "How are you feeling?"

Bolan shook his head. "A little weak," he said.

"Yes, the bullet was in a bit deeper than we had supposed. The doctor had to probe for it. Took him quite a while. You were under the anesthesia longer than he had planned."

"Damage?" Bolan asked.

Sir Alexander sat down. "No more than the doctor had thought," he said. "That's why he probed in the bullet hole rather than going in with an incision to get the bullet—to prevent additional damage to muscles and nerves. Quite a competent man, actually. We were fortunate he was available."

Bolan flexed his arm.

"Are you hungry?" asked Sir Alex. "I shall have some soup sent in. And you will be my guest for a few days."

"I can't stay," said Bolan. "I'll be ready to move in the morning."

Sir Alex rose and went to the fire. He poked at it and added a chunk of wood from a nearby wood box. "I hope you'll reconsider that," he said. "In fact, Mr. Brognola sent word for you. He asks you to remain here until you recuperate. He said to tell you he will fly over here in a few days to meet with you."

"I've got—"

"Mr. Bolan," Sir Alex interrupted. "The people you have been up against are quite ruthless, quite vicious. You have done them severe damage. I've no question whatever but that they have more than one team in the field, charged with no other assignment but to find you and kill you. If you're to survive against them, you will need all your strength. Please accept my advice—and Mr. Brognola's—and take a few days to recover."

"What I'd most like to recover are my two guns," said Bolan.

"I shall have them brought immediately. And something to eat? I recommend it."

"Yes, thank you."

Marilyn came in. She was carrying a large leather purse, slung over her shoulder, and she was wearing a plaid skirt, a dark blue wool sweater. She looked very English as she sat down on the edge of the bed.

"Feel naked without these, do you?" she asked, pulling first the Lahti, then Thijn's Mauser, from the purse.

Bolan hefted the Lahti. It had proved a reliable, accurate pistol, but he frowned over it and said, "Well, they're better than nothing. I wish I had my own."

"I've heard of your AutoMag," she said. "Can you really hit anything with a monster like that?"

"*I* can," he said. "You couldn't."

She smiled. "A mere woman," she said.

Bolan laughed. "It takes not just a man but a man my size to cope with the recoil."

"A cannon," she said.

"Got your popgun?" he asked with a grin as he reached over and pulled up her skirt.

She had it. Even here, where surely she was relaxed, she wore her Beretta strapped to the inside of her leg.

"Do you remember what I said to you as you were going under the anesthesia?" she asked.

He nodded. "I remember."

She shook her head. "It's stupid of me."

"Not stupid, Marilyn," he said, putting his hand on hers. "People ought to have a chance to be human. When they are, they—"

She placed a finger gently against his lips. "I know, Mack," she said softly. "I know all about you."

"And friends..." he whispered hoarsely. "So many...so many good guys. And women."

"April Rose," she said quietly.

For an instant his eyes hardened. Who had told her? Who *could* have? Not Brognola. He wouldn't. Not—

"For a few days, anyway," she said. "You can't go out and face it for a few days, Mack. For a few days you can have a normal life. I can stay here with you. Sir Alexander has cleared that with MI6. We can have a little time."

"While the White Front is on the move," he said grimly.

"You don't have any choice, really," she said. "That shoulder isn't fully functional." She sighed heavily.

"Something big is going down," said Bolan. "Something damn big."

"Yes," she said. "And the assassination of Mack Bolan is part of it."

"It's always—"

They were interrupted by the arrival of a servant bringing a tray. The servant offered to put the tray on the bed, but Bolan asked him to put it on a small table before the fire.

Marilyn went to the closet and returned with a robe. She helped Bolan into it. They sat down at the small table, and she ladled soup into a bowl for him.

"The salvation of the world doesn't depend on one man," she said. "If you're hurt, you have to stand aside for a bit. Someone else can handle it."

"I could have said that ten thousand times, Marilyn."

"There's a limit to the number of scars one man can carry."

"I haven't reached that limit."

"Do me a favor, then," she said quietly. "Promise me you won't jump out of bed in the morning and insist you're leaving, before you make a rational judgment about yourself, before the doctor has another look at you."

"Okay."

"You promise?"

He flexed his arm, testing it. Of course it *was* stiff and a little weak. He'd have to work on it. She was right that he'd need a day. Maybe more than one. "I promise," he said.

IN THE MORNING he didn't need to be reminded of his promise. He slept later than he meant to, until well after nine o'clock, and he didn't waken until Marilyn appeared with a tray of coffee.

Afterward she filled the tub with hot water and helped him into it. Only when he was shaving did she leave the bathroom—and that was only to give her time to lay out clothes for him. She laid out a tweed jacket for him, and a heavy wool turtleneck sweater, explaining that much of the house wasn't heated.

She didn't lay out the harness that carried the Lahti. But he slipped Thijn's 7.65 mm Mauser into a pocket of the jacket.

They went first to the breakfast room, a glassed-in sort of porch filled with potted plants and brightly lit by fluorescent lamps that gave the plants the light they needed in winter.

After a breakfast of eggs and sausage, toast with marmalade, and more coffee, Bolan felt his strength returning. He suggested to Marilyn that they take a walk on the grounds. Moving around was important. He would take a walk now and another this afternoon.

It was no colder outside than it was in most of the rooms of the house, so they walked in their tweeds, without overcoats or raincoats. As Bolan and Marilyn walked down toward the woods, four curious deer approached them and stood a few paces off, trying to decide, apparently, if these were people who would offer them something to eat.

"Peaceful," said Marilyn.

He nodded.

"The kind of world Sir Alexander Bentwood wants—where animals aren't afraid to approach people."

Bolan glanced curiously at her. It seemed a strange thought.

She went on. "Where you can distinguish the animals from the people." She had sensed his questioning reaction to her last words, apparently, and was trying to define her thought more specifically. "You fought crime for a long time," she said. "Lately you've fought something worse. What I'm trying to tell you is that Sir Alexander is working to make a world where what you've been fighting would simply cease to exist."

"You respect the man, don't you?"

"Yes. He understands things that— He understands what others should understand but don't. Does that make any sense?"

"Of course," said Bolan.

She seized his arm. "Suppose there were a thousand Mack Bolans instead of just one," she said enthusiastically.

"There are," he said.

A CAR SAT in the crushed-stone drive before the door to Oaks. Blue. A BMW. Bolan and Marilyn had returned through a grove that bordered the house from one side, not back up the main driveway, so they hadn't seen the car arrive. They came around from the north and didn't see the car until they were almost on it.

Bolan was tired. His wound didn't ache; he was just tired, as if he had expended too much energy in the walk to the pond and back through the grove. He moved slowly as they trudged along the crushed-stone path toward the drive and the main door to the house. The BMW made no impression on him at all. Oaks was a big estate.

The two great wooden doors curved into a pointed arch. They were bound with old wrought iron. They were heavy, yet so perfectly balanced on their hinges that they swung easily. Marilyn grabbed the big handle of the left-hand door, squeezed up the little lever that released the latch and pushed the door inward.

"John!"

Bolan's arms were around her, and he snatched her back outside before she could fall to her knees beside the body of the dead servant. His blood spreading across the stone floor of the entrance hall was evidence enough that he was dead.

Marilyn shuddered. "John..." she gasped. "Who...?"

"He got in somebody's way," said Bolan grimly.

They crouched just outside the door. From inside, no movement, no sound. John's murderers hadn't heard Marilyn's cry, didn't know she and the Executioner had returned.

Bolan ran to the BMW. He opened the door and pulled the release to unlatch the hood. Then he ran to the front of the vehicle, lifted the hood and jerked out the distributor. Whoever was inside or on the grounds wouldn't be able to start the car.

He pulled the Mauser as he returned to Marilyn. "You have your Beretta?" he asked her.

"Only the little one," she said, meaning the .22 in the little holster between her legs. She lifted her skirt and pulled out the tiny automatic.

"I've got one clip in this damn thing," he said, looking at the Mauser.

"We've got one advantage," she said quietly.

"Which is?"

"They don't know we're outside. They're inside looking for us. Also, it's just possible one of the other household staff has phoned the police. Even if nobody has, whoever killed John has to suspect somebody has. They've got to be in a hurry."

"Two of them?" Bolan speculated.

She glanced at the car. "Maybe three," she said.

"We don't have to go looking for them," Bolan said. "When they don't find us, they'll come back out."

"And?"

"And one of us waits inside," he said. "One out here. I'll wait inside. One of them—or more—will panic and run out."

"Mack—"

"Do it!" he said curtly. "Behind the car. I'll be—"

"The door to the right inside is a little empty room," she said. "It was once the estate telephonist's office, when there was only one telephone in all of Oaks. There are no windows. No one can get to you from behind. On the other hand . . . you'll be trapped in there."

Bolan nodded.

Holding the Mauser ready, he eased into the doorway. The big house was silent. The assassins were somewhere inside. He slipped across the stone-floored entrance hall and tried the door of the office.

As Marilyn had said, it was a small room. There was still a telephone there, an old-fashioned candlestick phone sitting on a table. Facing the table was a straight wooden chair.

Anyway, it made a good place to wait for the killers.

Bolan left the door open a little, knelt on the stone floor and took a moment to check the clip in the Mauser. With a cartridge in the chamber, it held eight shots, 7.65 mm. The shot that had hit Hermie Myrer, fired from this pistol, had bounced off bone. It had failed to penetrate and kill him. What was more, these slugs wounded, but didn't shock. They didn't knock a man off his feet. You could bet whatever the triggermen were carrying would have shocking power.

And Marilyn, outside, had nothing but a tiny .22 automatic, a pistol so small you could almost conceal it in the palm of your hand.

A door slammed. Upstairs, he thought—though sounds echoed strangely through this old stone house, and it was difficult to tell where a sound originated. But someone had slammed a door. Good. Someone had become impatient. That meant they were getting careless.

Now voices. Three of them, it sounded like. Okay. The three were working together. Stupid. They would have been much more dangerous if they had separated.

They spoke. What was it? It wasn't English. Or German. It wasn't French, either.

The second floor of the house—what Marilyn called the first—was reached by a broad oaken stairway that went up the right side of the big entrance hall, reached a landing, then turned and went on up to a balcony that looked down on the hall. The stairs were carpeted.

Five doors faced the balcony. Bolan hadn't been up there. Obviously four rooms opened on the balcony. Maybe more bedrooms.

The center door opened. Okay, that one opened on a hallway that ran back through the house. A man walked out and looked over the balcony, down into the entrance hall.

Figured. He carried an Uzi. He looked down on the body of the servant John, which lay facedown, blood still spreading over the stones. It didn't disturb him. Not in the least. He spoke a word back through the door, in that guttural language he spoke, whatever it was.

Another one came out. He had an Uzi cradled in his arm, too. He lit a cigarette.

Hardmen. They wore cheap short coats, maybe of nylon, lined with sheepskin or more likely some plastic meant to look like sheepskin. They wore cheap little hats. Cheap coats. Cheap hats. Cheap men. Hired to kill. Glad to do it for a little money. The kind of animals Marilyn had been talking about.

And there on the floor lay John, a decent man who'd been doing his job, had come to the door and probably had tried to deny entrance to these animals—and they had killed him.

Now here was the third. A different sort. A long raincoat, this one. A tweed hat. No Uzi. Erect. Graying. Obviously in charge.

One of the hardmen spoke to him.

"Speak English, goddamn it!" he snapped.

The hardman flipped his cigarette over the balcony and let it fall to the stone floor of the hall. "He's gotten away," he said. His English was good enough, accented in some way Bolan couldn't identify, but understandable.

"No, he hasn't," said the tall, older man in the raincoat. "When you fired your goddamn submachine gun at the butler, you alerted everyone in the house. But he's here, I tell you. Or on the grounds. And you better find him."

The hardman spoke to the other hardman, using again the language Bolan couldn't identify.

The two of them began opening the other doors that faced the balcony. From one they brought out—roughly leading her by the hair—a wailing young housemaid.

"Bolan!" the tall man in the raincoat yelled at her.

The girl only shrieked.

"Where is Bolan?" he shouted in her face.

She wept and shook her head.

"A big man, dark hair. He's here, isn't he? In the house!" The girl nodded.

"Where?"

"I don't *know*!" she shrieked. "I haven't seen him but once. Last night, it was! I haven't seen him today!"

She saw John's body lying below, and fainted.

They'd opened the four rooms and found no one but the cowering girl, who now lay at their feet whimpering.

"Outside," said one of the hardmen.

"No doubt," said the guy in the raincoat. "A brilliant conclusion. So *find him*! If you value your lives, you'll find him."

They started down the stairs, the two hardmen ahead, the man in raincoat behind.

When they reached their car, they'd see Marilyn. Bolan had watched where she'd gone. She was crouching behind the car. She hadn't backed away into the woods.

He steadied himself on his knees, aiming with the Mauser clutched in two hands. He chose the first hardman and took aim on his face. He squeezed easily.

The little Mauser cracked authoritatively, almost as if it fired a big slug, and bucked sharply. The little bullet struck the hardman at the bridge of his nose, penetrating, then blowing away the back of his skull and spraying the one behind him with gore.

As he fell, the hardman convulsively closed his fingers on the trigger of the Uzi, and it blasted a stream of slugs into the stairway, then, out of control, sprayed the stone floor before the dead fingers failed and the trigger sprung back. Ricocheting bullets whined off the floor and walls.

The second man had a good idea where the shot had come from. He let loose a burst on the door to the telephone room. Oak splinters flew into the room, and Bolan was forced to duck back.

Bolan moved to take another look, another shot. The guy in the raincoat had shoved his way past the second hardman and was running toward the open door to the driveway and the car. He had pulled a pistol, and as he ran past the door to the telephone room, he fired two shots into the room. The second hardman fired another long burst from his Uzi. The slugs shredded the oak door, chopped up the table and candlestick telephone and chipped the stone wall at the back of the room.

The hardman would have to change magazines, Bolan knew. He was too enthusiastic with his fire.

The man in the raincoat staggered back into the entrance hall and stumbled over the body of the dead servant. Bolan hadn't heard the shots, but he knew Marilyn had hit the guy with at least one, probably more than one, .22 slug. The man in the raincoat fell, but he rolled and fired into the driveway.

The surviving hardman fired a burst out there, too.

And that left him dry for a brief moment. Bolan threw himself against the doorframe and aimed a shot at his head.

The hardman was alert and wary. He threw himself to one side, and Bolan's shot tore off his ear. He howled but shoved his loaded clip into the Uzi and rolled over to fire. Bolan's second shot at the rolling, twisting man tore away his lower jaw. In agony he jerked the trigger. The Uzi spat slugs at the ceiling, off the walls. Bolan fired once more. That slug punched into the hardman's chest and silenced him.

The man in the raincoat rolled over and fired a shot at Bolan. The slug went wild.

Marilyn was in the door. She leveled the tiny Beretta at the last gunner and shot him in the throat. He dropped his pistol and clutched his neck, his eyes bulging. His lips moved. Blood oozed between them. Marilyn took calm, deliberate aim and fired a .22 slug between his eyes.

After the sounds of gunplay died away, Marilyn telephoned MI6. When the local police arrived, they were deferential and didn't ask many questions.

Bolan was exhausted. As soon as he could, he went to his bedroom. He slept the middle part of the afternoon and woke to find Marilyn at his bedside.

"What language were they speaking?" he asked her.

"Gaelic," she said. "Irish hoodlums. Learned terrorism with the IRA but decided to use it to earn money instead of promoting a cause."

"Who was the guy in the raincoat?"

"That's going to be a secret for a while," she said. "The government is going to have a bit of difficulty explaining his death. The official explanation will be that he died of a heart attack."

"His name was?"

"Oscar Cobden. MI5, retired."

"White Front," said Bolan.

She nodded. "Probably. He retired from MI5 under a cloud of scandal. You understand that MI5 is domestic counterintelligence, as MI6 is foreign intelligence—though the lines are very much blurred. In a very broad way we might say MI5 is like your FBI, whilst MI6 is like your CIA."

"Not really," said Bolan.

"Well . . . very broadly. Anyway, Oscar Cobden was with MI5 for thirty years. But it seems he had a bad habit. He tortured prisoners. His speciality was hanging them up by the heels, quite naked, and poking at their sensitive parts with the tip of his umbrella. Later, he used an electric prod. Became a scandal. But his death—here, this way—would become a worse scandal. In fact, I must tell you it might damage my career."

"It might," said Bolan sternly, "if anyone but me had seen you put a bullet into his head when he was down and helpless."

"That was for John," she said.

"It is intolerable, I tell you," said Sir Alexander Bentwood to Doktor Johann Kleist. "It is intolerable, and I won't allow it. It was insubordination. It was stupidity. It was emotional. It was a disaster."

Doktor Kleist lifted his glass of whiskey and soda and regarded the angry Englishman.

They were in the library of Sir Alexander's London town house—Sir Alexander, Kleist, Edward Holmesby-Lovett and Aldo Vicaria.

"Cobden," said Holmesby-Lovett. "Every reservation we had about him turns out to have been more than justified."

"He was trusted only on your recommendation," said Vicaria, glancing back and forth between Sir Alexander and Holmesby-Lovett.

"*You* authorized this," said Sir Alex to Doktor Kleist.

"Not exactly," said Kleist calmly, not troubled by the accusation. "On the other hand, when he talked to me about it, I did not discourage him. I tell you, Bentwood, this man Bolan must be destroyed!"

"Not destroyed," said Sir Alex. "Why destroy a man who has the greatest potential of any man in the world to promote our cause?"

"We can't turn him, I'm afraid," said Holmesby-Lovett.

"We don't have to turn him," said Sir Alexander Bentwood. "The man is committed to our cause already. He has been at war against terrorism as long as most of us have. Which of us has destroyed as many of them as he has?"

"If he walked through that door right now," said Kleist, pointing at a door, "he would kill us all."

Sir Alex sneered. "If he walks through that door two months from now, he will greet us and offer us his services. Two *weeks* from now."

"He hates us because—" Vicaria began.

"We made an error," Sir Alex interrupted. "We should have confided in Brognola, from the beginning—"

"No," snapped Kleist angrily. "You can't trust the Americans."

"*If,*" said Sir Alex, continuing as if he hadn't heard the interruption, "we had brought Brognola to our side, he could have brought Bolan. We could have explained ourselves to Brognola, and he could have convinced Bolan. I wanted to do it. It was a mistake not to."

"The man has rid the world of many vicious terrorists," said Vicaria.

"The only point on which he differs from us," said Sir Alex, "is on the question of whether or not you *use* terrorism to fight terrorism. We debated that a long time ourselves."

"His answer to us," said Holmesby-Lovett, "would be that he is willing to use terrorism against terrorists but not against anyone else. He's not willing to accept casualties among the innocent."

Sir Alex sighed. "A sticky point."

"I went ashore on D-Day," said Holmesby-Lovett. "June 6, 1944. Tens of thousands died, many of them innocent French civilians who just happened to be in the way. But because of what we did that day and in the murderous weeks following, millions of innocent people were freed from Nazi tyranny. Sometimes—"

"Sometimes," interjected Kleist, "you hurt a few of the innocent in the cause of the many."

"Shiites..." mused Sir Alex. "Palestinians. IRA. Red Brigades. ETA." He slammed the palm of his right hand on the table. "Goddamn them all! Who cares what their causes are? And goddamn all those who have lost the courage to strike back!"

"Including Bolan?" asked Kleist.

"Bolan hasn't lost his courage," said Sir Alex. "We're fools if we think our victory will eliminate the brutes. They'll still be out there. And we'll still have to send out men to fight them. I—" He drew a deep breath. "I want to be able to send out Bolan."

"I remind you," said Kleist, "that he was in the NUG office building the night when we met there. That close... with explosives. I still wonder why he didn't throw that bomb into our meeting."

"That is immaterial," said Holmesby-Lovett. "The question is, how much did he know? What did he learn that night? Which of us did he see? Which of us would he recognize?''

"Not I, obviously," said Sir Alex. "He chats with me amiably enough. He's accepting my hospitality. He doesn't know—''

"It is *dangerous*," Kleist insisted.

"Not for the moment," said Sir Alex. "Mr. Bolan is quite comfortable at Oaks. He's being given small doses in his food and drink to keep him lethargic. He has Miss Henry there to keep him placid. It helps that the dear girl has fallen quite in love with him."

"Your 'lethargic' Bolan and your lovesick girl shot down Cobden and his two experienced professional gunmen," said Kleist.

"How very fortunate for Cobden," said Sir Alex. "He dared invade my estate and murder one of my servants—not even to mention his insubordinate attempt to kill Bolan. It was Miss Henry, incidentally, and not Bolan, who killed Cobden. If she hadn't, I should have done it myself—only I should have used Cobden's own favorite technique, and he would be hanging upside down in my cellar right now."

"You think you have him under control," said Kleist. "Obviously you have not. He remains the chief threat."

"And potentially our chief asset in the future," said Sir Alex. "In any event, we need neutralize him only for another week or ten days. In another week...well, you know."

"I believe he should be disposed of," said Kleist, "and I have people capable of doing it. Do not speak to me of 'insubordination,' Sir Alex. I am not your subordinate."

"Bolan is under my protection at Oaks," said Sir Alex coldly.

"Very well," said Kleist. "At Oaks. I will not allow any of my people to invade your estate. There he is under your protection. Anywhere else—'' He smiled.

"That seems fair, Sir Alex," said Vicaria. "If you can control him, we need not fear him. If he leaves Oaks—"

"He will be disposed of immediately," said Doktor Kleist.

CHAPTER NINETEEN

The Foxbat was a MiG-25. Very few of them had been seen in the West. In September 1976 Soviet Air Force Lieutenant Viktor Belenko defected and flew a Foxbat A to Japan. A Syrian arms dealer delivered one, dismantled and stripped of its engines and electronics, to a Greek dealer in 1979. The dealers never revealed where they got it, but Israel bought it and shipped it to Tel Aviv, where Israeli engineers fitted it with General Electric engines and flew it in sub-mach tests. In 1984 another Soviet defector flew a Foxbat to the West. This one was a MiG-25U, a Foxbat modified to serve as a trainer. It carried no arms or radar, and an additional cockpit had been installed in the nose for the student pilot. It also carried modified engines, more powerful than the ones in the aircraft flown out by Lieutenant Belenko.

The Foxbat U was dismantled, then reassembled, chiefly by American engineers working at the U.S. air base at Mannheim. It was test-flown a few times, then stored in a hangar on the air base. Western engineers thought they had learned all they could from it, but it was kept in flying condition at the insistence of several intelligence agencies who said it might someday prove useful.

Security around the hangar where the Foxbat sat was provided by United States Air Force personnel. Security, actually, wasn't so much for the hangar as for the base itself. It was a fighter interceptor base, shared by the Air Force and the West German Luftwaffe. A dozen F-15s sat on the flight line. On down the line were fifteen Panavia

Tornados marked with the iron cross insignia of the Luftwaffe.

Responsibility for base security was shared by Major James Dugan, commanding officer of the military police unit assigned to Mannheim AFB, Hauptmann Gerhard Vogel, commanding the German military police unit, and Major Douglas McInenny, commanding the Air Force Intelligence office on the base.

Base security was exceptionally tight this month. The new wave of terrorism required that. In fact, after the Paris station chief of the CIA was murdered, Major McInenny had put his wife and two children on a flight to the States, had closed their house and was living in base officers' quarters.

The arrival of Colonel Jefferson Salisbury was wholly unexpected. He simply appeared at the gate and presented his credentials. The sergeant who received them through the window of the colonel's staff car thought them important enough to carry them inside for inspection by the lieutenant on duty. The lieutenant examined them closely. Colonel Salisbury, his credentials said, was an officer with Air Force Intelligence. The lieutenant told the sergeant to pass the colonel and his adjutant and driver onto the base, and he called base headquarters and told them who was coming.

When the Ford pulled up at base headquarters, Colonel David Finch was waiting in the reception hall—a gesture he thought appropriate.

"Strictly preliminary, Colonel," said Salisbury. "A courtesy call. I'd like to say hello to Major McInenny, maybe also to your Air Police commander, and I'll be on my way. Just in from the States. Just having a look around. We're tightening up all security. You know why."

"Glad to see you," said Colonel Finch. "Come on back to my office. I've had Major McInenny called."

"Okay. I'd like to send my adjutant and driver on for some breakfast," said Salisbury.

"Have them come in," said Finch. "We'll take care of that."

"Well . . . my driver will feel more comfortable in the noncoms' mess. And the lieutenant can pop into the officers' club. I wouldn't be surprised if he wants a screwdriver for breakfast."

Finch chuckled. "Whatever. Come on in."

The driver was Sergeant June Tracy, the adjutant Lieutenant Gene Mobley. They didn't go to the officers' club or noncoms' mess. They had something very different in mind.

Hangar K.

Sergeant Tracy drove the Ford directly to Hangar K and pulled up to the tiny shack where Corporal Bob Skinner was trying to keep warm with an electric heater. She got out and opened the door of the shack.

"My officer wants to see the Foxbat," she said. "It's in here, right?"

"Right. But you gotta have all kinds of authorization to get in there."

"I've got it," she said.

What she had was a small pneumatic pistol, which she now pulled from her pocket and fired point-blank at the corporal. He was struck by a dart, loaded with a quick sedative. He reached for the telephone, but before he could lift it he slumped.

The key to the padlock on the small door to the hangar was on a hook above the little desk in the guard shack. Sergeant Tracy lifted it, went to the door, which was just outside the shack, and opened the padlock.

Corporal Skinner wasn't unconscious. He mumbled his protest as the man and woman carried him into the hangar. They lowered him to the floor and left him sitting with his back to the wall.

"My God..." Sergeant Tracy whispered as she looked around. The Foxbat was unmistakable—a narrow fuselage between the two immense, gaping, slab-sided, flat-topped airscoops; thin, flat wings; fins angled outward and so far forward that they were actually over the wings; engines like two great open barrels on the rear. The aircraft looked like nothing more than two enormous flying engines; it looked as if it would just blast away into the air rather than fly like an airplane.

There were other planes on the hangar floor—a MiG-23, which NATO called a Flogger and a French Super Etendard.

While Sergeant Tracy stared at the aircraft, Lieutenant Mobley returned to the car and came back lugging a small trunk.

"Not much time," he said nervously. "Get an Uzi."

She, too, returned to the car—and came back carrying an Uzi submachine gun.

The lieutenant had opened the trunk and was pulling out an assortment of tools.

In base HQ the two colonels, Salisbury and Finch, sat over coffee, amused with each other's stories of service in various parts of the world. Salisbury had never flown in combat, he said. Thank God for small blessings, said Finch. I can fly a briefcase and navigate a desk, said Salisbury. Well, I'm learning, said Finch.

Major McInenny tried to seem as amused as the two colonels. He couldn't. He was uncomfortable. No one had told him an intelligence colonel was coming, and that could only mean one of two things. One of them was that somebody was unhappy with some part of the way he had been doing his job and he was about to be relieved.

Colonel Salisbury glanced at his watch, which he had done often during their meeting. "Well," he said. "I think I'd better be moving on."

Uh-oh, thought McInenny. Now it comes.

The colonel rose. He smiled warmly at Colonel Finch and shook his hand. Then he turned to McInenny and did the same, just as warmly.

McInenny followed the two colonels through the outer office. He watched Colonel Finch help Salisbury with his coat. They walked out and along the corridor to the entrance hall. McInenny could see Salisbury's blue Ford waiting outside the glass doors. He had a woman driver. The colonels shook hands again, and Colonel Salisbury waved and grinned at McInenny, and then he was gone.

Without saying a damn thing.

Colonel Finch started back toward his office. "Sir," said McInenny. The colonel stopped. "What was that all about, if I may ask, sir?"

Colonel Finch shrugged. "Damned if I know. Desk colonel from Washington. I suppose he'll report that he inspected security arrangements here."

"Well, I—"

"Major McInenny!" The sergeant behind the reception desk interrupted. "Call for you, sir. Urgent."

Major McInenny listened for a moment to the voice on the other end of the telephone line, then grabbed up a red telephone and gave curt orders. "There's a blue Ford with a colonel and two others on its way to the gate. Stop it! Hold those people."

"What the hell?" blustered Finch.

"Colonel, I take responsibility," said McInenny. "If I'm wrong, I've got egg on my face. But I put through a call to Frankfurt when that colonel arrived. They've been checking for me. There is no USAF colonel named Salisbury."

Outside, the woman—she wasn't a sergeant, and she wasn't June Tracy—shoved the accelerator to the floor. The Ford charged the gate and the guard who had stepped out and raised his hand. The younger man, who wasn't Lieutenant Gene Mobley, shoved an Uzi through the right window and swept the gate area with 9 mm slugs. The older man, who wasn't Colonel Jefferson Salisbury, aimed another Uzi at the gatehouse and chopped it with successive short bursts. The guard who had signaled a stop fell wounded. The lieutenant inside the gatehouse was thrown to the floor by three slugs in his shoulder. The Ford hit the gate and broke through.

As sirens shrieked all over the air base, the Ford lurched from side to side on the highway. It dragged a tangle of fence wire on its right fender, which was torn half-away from its body. The woman fought the wheel, but the car careened back and forth on the road. An approaching van blinked its lights. The woman jammed down the brakes.

The three scrambled out of the Ford and into the van through its back doors. The van swung around and sped away just as an explosion blew out the doors and windows of Hangar K.

"FRIDAY, THE EIGHTEENTH," said the President of the United States.

"Is it a problem?" asked the secretary of state.

"No, no," the President said, laughing. "If it's agreeable to the general secretary, it's agreeable to me."

"All right," said the secretary of state. "Cast of characters—President, secretary of state, director of Central Intelligence, director of FBI, national security adviser."

"And Hal Brognola," said the President.

The secretary of state raised his eyes from his notes. "And Hal Brognola," he said dryly. He knew better than to object, so he looked down and added the name with his pen. "We may have to divide the airplane into compartments to keep some of this cast of characters away from others."

The President shrugged. "Add the chairman and vice chairman of the Senate Intelligence Oversight Committee," he said.

"We'll build a brick wall across the middle of the airplane," said the secretary of state without looking up from scribbling his notes.

"Politics is the art of building walls when you need them, tearing them down when you don't," said the President.

The secretary of state nodded to the national security adviser. "Floor's yours," he said.

The national security adviser had been staring out into the famous Rose Garden during much of this talk—though he had been listening—and now he nodded, began to rub his hands together and started to talk.

"Officially you're in California," he said to the President. "You and the First Lady leave the White House late Thursday afternoon—being seen boarding the helicopter for Andrews. Air Force One takes off for California, carrying the First Lady. A little later the Presidential party boards another Air Force 707. Exact takeoff time and route will be decided when we get the weather forecast. There'll be time in-flight for a thorough briefing, a comfortable dinner, and six or seven hours' sleep. We'll land at Stockholm at noon. The first meeting with the general secretary is set for two in the afternoon. Our scheduled departure from Stockholm is nine Sunday morning, which is 3:00 a.m. Washington time. We arrive back at Andrews about noon—as does Air Force One. You and the First Lady are seen climbing out of the helicopter on the White House lawn early in the afternoon. When and whether you announce that you have been to Stockholm for a meeting with the general secretary is entirely optional."

"And since no one knows we're going, we need not worry about the new terrorism," said the President.

"Right," said the national security adviser. "We'
thought about giving the 707 a fighter escort. You coul
pick up escorts at Iceland, then fighters out of norther
Scotland, and finally some others out of north Germa
bases. We decided a 707 coming in with three or four fight
ers in escort just notifies everybody in Europe with acces
to a radar screen that something big is up. That word coul
get all around damn quick."

"The general secretary—"

"Is coming on a plane marked Aeroflot."

"Okay," said the President. "Sounds good."

"One thing more, Mr. President," said the national se
curity adviser. "We haven't told the cast of characters tha
they're going. The director of Central Intelligence doesn'
know. The director of the FBI doesn't know. Obviously w
haven't yet told the two senators or Brognola. I suggest w
don't tell them until a day or two before."

"I agree," said the President. "What no one knows, n
one can leak."

"On the other hand," said the secretary of state, "w
have to advise allied governments."

"A day or two before," said the national security ad
viser.

"A day or two before," the President echoed.

TWO HOURS LATER the president of Yogomuchi America
transmitted a coded cable to the president of the paren
company in Tokyo, via the company's satellite link. Thi
cable traffic was occasionally monitored by the Nationa
Security Agency. The code had been broken, and NSA
could read any cable it wanted to. Since the Yogomuchi ca
ble traffic between New York and Tokyo was so pedes
trian, so boring, it was only sampled occasionally. NSA
didn't realize that any cable that used the word "cryo
genic" in its first paragraph was not a business message and

wasn't to be decoded further by the ordinary decoding clerks in Tokyo but was to be forwarded coded to the office of the president of the company.

The cable from New York to Washington read:

> By express from New York I am sending you a copy of an article on cryogenics and magnetic phenomena, written by Dr. Howard Feldbaum. I recommend it to your immediate attention. The flight about which you inquired will depart approximately 1900 hours local time on Thursday the seventeenth and will arrive approximately noon. It is a nonstop flight via an aircraft of the regular carrier. I think you will find it most convenient.

If the cable had been decoded, it was unlikely anyone would have understood the significance of the second paragraph. No one who might have seen it would have known the significance of a nine-hour flight departing on the evening of the seventeenth. No one would have guessed that the reference to "an aircraft of the regular carrier" meant that an Air Force plane was being used, but not Air Force One.

"THE EIGHTEENTH," said Sir Alexander Bentwood to Edward Holmesby-Lovett. "Good. As predicted. Damn shame, isn't it, that we have to tell the krauts, frogs and wops? Damn shame!"

"We couldn't have done it without them, Alex," said Holmesby-Lovett. "No point in thinking how we could have done it without them."

"I suppose not. Still—"

"We've bet everything, Alex. Everything. I shudder to think of the reaction of Vittorio Muro and his group if their money fails to produce anything worthwhile."

"I can deal with them," said Sir Alex. "One could always deal with them. Their interests are defined and limited and—"

"And are not so very different from our own," Holmesby-Lovett interrupted with a puckish little smile.

Sir Alexander Bentwood nodded. "I accept your little witticism, Edward," he said, "if you mean what I think you mean—that we are working to preserve, or I should probably say restore, a world in which men could deal with other men."

"White men with other white men," Holmesby-Lovett interrupted again.

"Not at all," said Sir Alex tartly. "I've dealt honorably with men of all races."

"Uh, well, then. Friday. God help us."

"God help us indeed," said Sir Alex. "But let us not rely on him."

"IN THE NAME OF ALLAH, the Compassionate, the All Merciful," Major Alani murmured as he studied the chart of likely routes between the States and Stockholm.

There weren't many. Which one the pilots and controllers chose on the night of the seventeenth and eighteenth depended on the weather. The 707 could come in south of the Faroes and north of the Shetlands and cross the Norwegian coast about Bergen. Or, in the event of bad winter weather on that northern route, it could come across direct from Newfoundland to Scotland, then across the North Sea and the Skagerrak, flying over the watery part of Sweden and into Stockholm from the southwest. The second course was longer, but the weather might favor it.

The Foxbat, coming in from its base in northern Finland and clinging to the Russian frontier to accomplish its deception, would not have enough fuel to go hunting. Someone would have to identify the target they were calling Too

Bad before the Foxbat blasted into the air and streaked toward its fatal rendezvous.

Provided, of course, these Russian peasants could make the damn thing fly between now and next Friday...

IN HIS OFFICE at the Justice Department in Washington, Hal Brognola was reviewing a group of messages that had come in by satellite overnight and had been decoded by the night clerks and locked in his office safe until he arrived. The first one read:

> Thorough examination of the wreckage of the Foxbat in the Mannheim AFB hangar discloses that one subassembly was removed, a part of the mechanism that opens and closes in airscoop and controls the amount of ram air reaching the engine associated with that scoop. The subassembly appears to have been removed by someone familiar with the mechanism and equipped with the necessary tools. The three persons involved in this action remain unidentified, and there is no trace of them. No MiG-25 Foxbat in flying condition is known to exist outside the boundaries of the Soviet Union and its allies. None has been delivered in the West within the past two years. No known Foxbat is missing any element of the airscoop mechanism. No engineer or any other personnel identifiable as having worked on a Foxbat is missing.
>
> Baker, USAF Intel

A message had also arrived from Telpuchovski:

> The inventory contained in your cable of all MiG-25 aircraft in the West corresponds to our own list. None other is missing. We are missing, however, one Mikhail Nikolaievich Mikoyan, an engineer with exten-

sive experience working with MiG-25 aircraft. I am compelled to observe that it is not outside the bounds of possibility that a MiG-25 is missing from inventory, such fact having been concealed. We are engaging in a further investigation of this possibility. Mikoyan, thirty-four years old, was kidnapped in Prague while attending an international convention of aircraft engineers. This occurred about three months ago. Mikoyan would be capable of performing any kind of engineering work on the MiG-25 or any of a variety of sophisticated aircraft. Please oblige with any information of his whereabouts.

Finally Brognola frowned over a message from the CIA station chief in London: The person of whom we are only unofficially aware remains where you said he was, so far as we can discover. There is a complete blackout here on any word about him.

Brognola picked up his telephone and placed a call to Sir George Harrington.

CHAPTER TWENTY

Bolan couldn't shake the nausea and lethargy. The doctor came to see him, and he couldn't explain it. The shoulder was healing satisfactorily, he said, and the last of the anesthetic should have been out of Bolan's body; what was more, he couldn't find any infection, so he suggested Bolan force himself to be active, take cool baths and limit his intake of food and any alcohol.

Mr. Bradley should be patient. After all, only two days had passed since the bullet had been removed.

Yeah. Two days.

On the first of those days Cobden and his Irish thugs had invaded the house.

On the second someone raided the United States Air Force base at Mannheim, wounded three Americans and blew up a hangar. The story told on British television was incomplete. The raid on the base hadn't been just a terrorist shoot-up. No one had died. The raiders had come to destroy a specific hangar or something inside it, had set their bomb, but had been identified before they'd gotten away and had been forced to shoot their way out. Bolan could read that much even behind the simplistic report carried by the BBC.

When on the third morning after his operation he woke still feeling peculiarly weak and nauseous, his reaction was to be annoyed. Annoyance generated in him a determination to be away from Oaks, back to London.

"Marilyn," he said over breakfast, "I can't stay here. I've got to get back to London. I want you to drive me up there today."

"Mack . . ."

He raised both his hands. "I know. The doctor says this, common sense says that. But I—"

She smiled. "Haven't I been taking good care of you?"

"Too good," he said. "I could get used to this kind of life. But I can't stay. There's no doubt in my mind that the raid on the base at Mannheim was a White Front caper. They're on the move. They're getting ready to do something, and I can't just sit here and wait to find out what."

"Do me a favor," she said. "Let me drive into town and see if there are any messages from headquarters. Don't make a decision until we have the latest intel."

"Good enough," he said.

She could be back in twenty minutes. Encoded messages from London, addressed to Oaks, were held at the local post office. Since the death of John, Marilyn was the only one in the house authorized to pick them up. She was the only one who could decode them.

EVA ZHULEV STOOD on a low hill half a mile from Oaks and studied the great stone house through powerful binoculars. Sitting in the silver-gray BMW behind her, Fabian Hastings watched her and worried that she might violate their orders and approach the estate. Fortunately maybe, she seemed to see nothing, just the house. And the cold winter rain falling on her head discouraged her from taking up a station here and watching all day.

Fabian Hastings was afraid of Eva Zhulev. He was afraid, in the first place, because she wasn't afraid of Herr Doktor Kleist. She hadn't been intimidated by what they had done to Joop Thijn; she had come within a centimeter of the same thing herself, she said; and she said, too, that if she let herself by intimidated by something like that, then she deserved to be treated the same way. The White Front wouldn't be served by people easy to dominate, only by people with reckless courage.

Bravado, Hastings thought. No. Her eyes were cold. Her voice was cold. *She* was cold. She demanded that he satisfy her every night they were together, which had been no easy thing for him to do; and even when he did, it made her warm only for a moment, after which she was again as cold as a snake.

She had removed the bandages from around her throat, though the bruise there was still visible, and her voice had returned. She was an exquisitely beautiful young woman.

She lowered the binoculars, seated herself in the car and began to wipe rainwater from the binoculars with a white cloth. "I don't think he's in there," she muttered irritably. "They've put guards around the house since those fools tried to assault the place the day before yesterday. But I think it's a show. I don't think he's in there."

"Everyone thinks he is."

Eva sneered. "Who is 'everyone'? Damn!"

"They haven't confided everything in us, Eva," he said.

"What do you mean by that?"

"There's some reason why we can't enter that estate. It's part of the overall strategy fixed by the Council. If we went down there and succeeded in killing Bolan, I think we'd wind up like Thijn, or worse. Anyway, they don't tolerate insubordination."

"Don't use that word with me! I am nobody's subordinate."

Fabian Hastings had the courage to smile lazily. "Tell me something, then, Eva. You appeared before the Council. Who are they?"

"You are not allowed to know," she said.

"And neither are you," he said. "You and I know one
member—Herr Doktor Kleist. When you appeared before
the Council, you were blindfolded. He told me."

"Did he tell you—"

"Yes, he told me you were naked. And in handcuffs."

She tossed her head. "Did he tell you I was intimidated?"

Hastings frowned and thought about what the Herr
Doktor had said. "No..." he admitted. "He didn't say
that."

She nodded. And grunted. "He told me not to kill the
woman. But I will. I will, after Bolan is dead. If I see her."

"If he ever comes out of there," said Hastings, nodding
toward the house.

"He'll come out," said Eva. "If he hasn't already."

Eva raised the binoculars and studied the little blue Fiat
that was pulling away from Oaks.

"Damn! That's *her*! That's the bitch that almost broke
my neck."

She tossed the binoculars into the back seat. Trotting
around to the rear, she opened the trunk and pulled out a
MAT submachine gun. By the time Fabian Hastings understood what she was doing, she had pulled back and set the
telescoping butt and had unfolded the forward handgrip and
magazine. As he reached her, she was chambering a cartridge—the deadly French weapon was ready to fire.

"Eva, for God's sake!"

"She's off the estate," said Eva grimly. She was setting
herself in position behind the car, where she could hide from
the driver of the Fiat until she was ready to rise, steady herself against the BMW and let loose a stream of 9 mm slugs.
"Off the estate is—"

He seized her arm. "Bolan is in there!" Hastings yelled,
pointing toward the big stone house. "Plus MI6 and maybe
Special Branch types, God knows how many. You do

this—'' He sighed loudly and shook his head. ''At the very least, you'll alert Bolan. You'll foul up what we were sent here to do. And you, if not both of us, will wind up hanging like Joop Thijn. If you're not afraid of that, at least be motivated by our mission.''

Eva's eyes settled coldly on his hand gripping her arm. He let go.

''She's not our target,'' he muttered.

Eva glanced past him toward the lane that led from the house to the road. The Fiat had reached the road and was turning toward them.

She grabbed the handle of the rear door of the BMW and angrily climbed inside, with the MAT still in her hands.

Hastings got in behind the wheel, started the car and pulled into the road as the Fiat climbed the hill. The driver blinked her lights and sped past.

''It's *her*,'' Eva growled.

''Proof that he's in the house,'' said Hastings. ''There's his weakness. That woman. Dead, she's no good to us. Alive—''

Eva's grimace diminished into a leer. ''An idea...You may be worth something after all, Hastings.''

STANDING AT A WINDOW, Bolan saw Marilyn in the blue Fiat pass the silver-gray BMW. He didn't like the way the BMW pulled out into the road just before the Fiat reached it. Marilyn was an experienced intel agent, and something like that should alert her. He hoped it did.

As soon as she was out of sight, he walked into Sir Alexander's study and picked up his telephone. Getting through to Sir George Harrington at MI6 in London wasn't easy, but he managed it.

''Ah, Bolan! Good to hear your voice. I assume you don't have a secure line there, so we must be careful what we say.

In any event, how are you? I hear your recovery from the surgery is a bit slower than we expected.''

"A little," said Bolan. "Even so, I plan to come up to London sometime today."

"I'm glad to hear it. I won't mention the name, but a certain friend of yours asked me to put you in touch over a secure line. He was hoping you could be back in London today."

"I will. She resists the idea of driving me, and if she won't drive me I'll manage my own way."

"Tell her I authorize it, specifically."

"I'll do that. We and our friend have things to talk about."

"I'm looking forward to seeing you."

Bolan returned to the room where he and Marilyn had eaten breakfast half an hour ago. The maid had cleared away the dishes, but the coffee remained in a heated pot. He had been going back to it from time to time, thinking that the caffeine would counteract his wobbliness. This time, on some impulse, he turned away from it. He walked to the kitchen and asked the maid to make him a cup of tea.

"I'm glad to have a chance to talk to you, Mr. Bradley," she said. "The way I see it, you saved me life. I owe you—"

"No," he said. "No, you don't, Martha."

"Well. A nice cup of tea. A biscuit? Some fruit?"

"Just the tea, please."

She had water hot already, it appeared. She spooned tea leaves into a china pot and poured boiling water into the pot from a larger copper teakettle.

"I'll bring it wherever you wish, Mr. Bradley," she said. "As soon as it steeps a bit."

"I'll sit here," he said, pulling out a chair from the kitchen table.

"Oh? American, aren't you, sir? I mean, no English guest would sit down in the kitchen for his tea. Actually, now that I think on it, Miss Henry might. Democratic-like lady, she is. Stays and chats while I make the coffee."

"Which she doesn't drink," said Bolan.

"Well, she likes hers decaffeinated," said the maid. "Personally—"

She was interrupted by one of the young men MI6 had sent down from London after the attack by Oscar Cobden. "Excuse me, sir," he said to Bolan. "Sir Alexander's on the telephone."

Bolan took the call in Sir Alexander's study.

"All's quiet, Bolan," he said. "There's no need for you to come back now. All hell may break loose in a day or so, and then we'll want you strong, with all your faculties sharp. Right now... well, if you'll take my advice, you'll recuperate at least another day."

"Thank you for your concern," said Bolan, "but I feel I have to get back to work."

"Coming up to London, then, are you?"

"I think so. I have to talk with Marilyn about it."

"If you do, I'd appreciate your being my guest for dinner tonight," said Sir Alexander. "We didn't have a very good chance to talk when you were just out from under the anesthetic."

"I appreciate the invitation," said Bolan.

"Let's plan on, say, eight," said Sir Alexander. "I'll leave word at your hotel as to where. Marilyn, too, of course. You may tell her."

"Well, thank you again," said Bolan before Sir Alexander hung up.

Odd. Sir George was anxious that he should come; Sir Alexander was anxious that he shouldn't. Obviously Marilyn had called Sir Alexander from the village. She'd wanted him to apply his powers of persuasion, too.

Bolan went back to the kitchen for his tea. Then he went to his bedroom and packed his few things in his bag. He hung the Lahti in its harness. As soon as Marilyn returned, they would go.

MARILYN WOULD HAVE preferred that Sir Alexander make his argument to Bolan in the form of an encrypted message she could carry back to Oaks and decode. That would be more impressive, more persuasive, she thought. But Sir Alexander had said there wasn't time for that; he would have to call.

By the time she returned to Oaks, he would have talked to Bolan, and Bolan would know she had suggested the call.

The rain had slackened off, but the black pavement of the country roads remained slick. The Fiat clung to dry pavement very nicely, but it was a little dicey to drive when the roads were wet. She liked the little car. She enjoyed shifting it through its gears and demanding of it all it could give. She pushed it to its limit as much as she could.

Half a mile short of the entrance to Oaks, she saw ahead the same silver-gray BMW she had seen when she'd left.

Why was that car still parked by the side of the road? Marilyn pulled her Beretta from its holster under her raincoat.

The BMW pulled into the center of the road. Both doors opened, and a man swung out from the driver's seat, a woman from the passenger seat. They crouched behind the open doors, and it was obvious they had heavy-duty weapons.

Whipping the wheel around, she stabbed at the brake pedal. The Fiat went into a turning skid. It spun 180 degrees, winding up with its rear toward the BMW.

As the skid ended, she jerked the hand brake, grabbed for the door handle and rolled out of the Fiat as a burst of fire from the BMW ricocheted off the pavement. Marilyn leveled the muzzle of the Beretta at the pavement under the right door of the BMW and fired twice. The slugs spanged off the asphalt and whined away. She did the same toward the left door. Unless she was wrong, she caught somebody in the leg.

Another burst of automatic fire from the BMW ripped through the top of the little Fiat. Glass exploded.

What *was* this? They were spraying slugs everywhere but where she was crouching. They meant to disable her car, apparently—not to kill her but to capture her.

Well, to hell with that.

Marilyn took aim squarely at the nose of the BMW and fired. Three 9 mm slugs crashed into its radiator, which burst and spewed steam and water.

Marilyn rolled back into the seat of the little car. Crouching low, she shoved it in gear and jammed down the accelerator. It was damaged badly, but it staggered forward; the Fiat shook, and gears rattled, but it roared down the road.

The BMW roared, too, and charged after the Fiat in pursuit.

Marilyn glanced at the gas gauge. Down. The tank was ruptured by a ricocheting slug and was losing gas. A tire was broken and flapped, making the Fiat fishtail. Even so, she kept the accelerator down, and the little car zigzagged down the hill.

Another burst of fire shook it. Slugs broke through the sheet metal of the trunk and rattled around behind the seat. A slug hit the dashboard and shattered the clock.

But the Fiat kept rolling.

Suddenly there was a shriek of tires behind. Marilyn looked back. The overheated engine of the BMW—its cooling water blowing out and up—had stalled. The car stopped and sat in a cloud of angry steam.

Marilyn kept the accelerator down, and the Fiat ran on for two hundred more yards before it, too, stopped.

She huddled in the front seat and pushed a new clip into her Beretta.

Slipping out, she looked back at the stalled BMW. Taking careful aim with the Beretta, she fired all the cartridges in the new clip. She saw her slugs shatter the windshield.

By the time the pair in the BMW were out on the road and began to spray automatic fire in the direction of the Fiat, Marilyn was on her belly in the ditch. The Fiat blew up in a sudden flash of fire, but she was ten yards from it.

She shoved in her last clip and waited for the pair from the BMW to come. They didn't come. She saw them running. They had left their weapons as well as the car. One of them limped, was maybe hit. All they wanted to do now, obviously, was to put as much distance as possible between them and their car before the police arrived.

"VERY GOOD TO SEE YOU, Mr. Bradley," said the clerk at the Green Park Hotel. "Your account is quite in order, but we would appreciate something further if it's your intention to retain your room and be gone for extended periods."

Bolan dug into his pocket and handed the clerk five hundred-pound notes. "That should cover a few more days," he said.

Even so, Bolan concluded, he would have to call on Brognola for more money.

The Uzi he had taken from the Germans in Bloomsbury was where he had left it, in the suitcase under his bed. He had measured the case's distance from the wall, and as far as he could tell it hadn't been moved.

He felt stronger. Maybe the attempt to kill Marilyn had set his adrenaline going. Certainly it had infuriated him. She had come back to Oaks, shaken and pale. The local police had said that they couldn't help but welcome his announcement that he and Miss Henry were leaving the area; their visit had generated all the excitement one small country town could bear in a year.

Marilyn had gone home. She needed a change of clothes, she'd said. She had come into the lobby of the hotel with him long enough to share his message from Sir Alexander Bentwood; that they would meet for dinner at 8:30 at Wheeler's Sovereign, a restaurant within easy walking distance of his hotel and convenient for him.

Marilyn believed he would sleep in his room until their dinner date. Because Sir George Harrington had been anxious for him to return to London, while Sir Alexander and Marilyn had been anxious that he shouldn't, he saw no reason to tell her he was meeting with Sir George that afternoon. In fact, he saw no reason why people at MI6 generally should know he was meeting Sir George. He telephoned and suggested Sir George meet him in the bar at the Green Park Hotel.

At 4:00 p.m. they sat down at a table to one side of the bar.

"I feel," said Bolan, "that I'm no closer to the governing personalities of the White Front than I was when I first came to London. I feel I've rattled them, but I haven't penetrated their inner circle."

Sir George Harrington pursed his lips and brushed his mustache with one finger before he lifted a glass of straight Scotch to his lips. "I share your feelings," he said.

"I think there's a leak somewhere," said Bolan.

"I agree," said Sir George.

"At MI6?" Bolan asked.

"Possibly," said Sir George. "We've ceased to share anything with Jean Henriot since you reported seeing him in Düsseldorf. I'm not quite sure any longer with whom we may share."

Bolan nodded. "Then you understand me better."

"I've no difficulty understanding you, Mr. Bolan," said Sir George. "I've none with admiring your work. You will perhaps not object, however, if I tell you we can't run the entire free world's counterintelligence and counterterrorism operations as you run your part. Valuable as you are to us, we can't generally operate the way you do."

"I know you can't," Bolan conceded. "In some ways I'm a very lucky man."

"And in some ways quite unfortunate," said Sir George. Bolan nodded.

"I've a few words for you from Hal Brognola," said Sir George.

"I need to talk to Hal," said Bolan.

"You shall. He will be here tomorrow or the day after. In the meantime, he wants you to know that the President will meet with the general secretary next Friday, the eighteenth. You know where, he said. Frankly, *I* don't know where. I'm not sure the prime minister knows where. No matter."

"The raid at Mannheim," said Bolan. "That's what I want to know about."

Sir George nodded. "A clever operation. A deception that survived just long enough to achieve its purpose."

"Which was?"

"To allow the destruction of a MiG-25 that was stored in a hangar at Mannheim."

"A Foxbat," said Bolan.

"This one happened to be a MiG-25U, the trainer in which pilots were taught to fly the aircraft," said Sir George. "The miscreants who penetrated the security of the Mannheim base planted a powerful time bomb in one of the airscoops of the Foxbat and blew the aircraft to pieces. Difficult to understand why. The aircraft had been disassembled and reassembled by engineers. It had been flown by Western pilots. We had supposed we had learned everything there was to learn about it. Now... what point in blowing it to pieces now?''

"Not an ordinary terrorist attack," said Bolan. "Not a peacenik demonstration, either."

"Oh, no," said Sir George. "They actually carried the corporal they had drugged out of the hangar—apparently not wanting him to be killed in the explosion."

"Maybe someone was getting ready to fly that Foxbat for some reason? What insignia did it carry?"

"United States Air Force, I believe," said Sir George. "Of course, that could be changed in minutes."

"A Foxbat... with Soviet insignia. But what could it do, flying out of *Mannheim*?"

MARILYN CALLED from the lobby of the hotel. They would walk around the corner and through Shepherd Market to their dinner appointment with Sir Alexander Bentwood.

Her long coat covered her dress, and not until the attendant at Wheeler's Sovereign took the coat did Bolan see what she was wearing—a tiny, simple, black velvet dress with a short skirt and no sleeves. Her arms and shoulders were bare; her legs were displayed in dark sheer stockings. She wore a necklace of glittering stones, not diamonds Bolan judged, and her smooth blond hair was entangled in the necklace.

"Marilyn," said Sir Alex, "you're a vision."

They sat in an oaken booth, she beside Bolan, Sir Alex opposite.

"An American martini," said Sir Alex, raising his drink. "They make a good one here, my American friends tell me. Can you testify on that point, Mr. Bolan?"

"I'm no expert on martinis," said Bolan. "But when you get a bad one, you damn well know it, whether you're an expert or not."

"May I order two more? Perhaps we should compare our impressions."

He did order two more, one for Bolan and one for Marilyn—and gave the waiter instructions to bring another round as soon as he saw these finished.

"I understand someone tried to kill you this afternoon," Sir Alex said to Marilyn.

"I don't think so," she said. "Mack and I talked about it on the way to London. They *could* have killed me. Two submachine guns at fifty yards." She shook her head. "They fired under the car, around it—but never directly at me. I think they wanted to capture me."

"Kidnap you?"

"Yes."

"Did you get a look at them?"

"Yes. A man and a woman. A blonde."

"Eva Zhulev," said Bolan dryly.

"What? Surely that's a guess," said Sir Alex.

Bolan shrugged. "Maybe."

"I hope," said Sir Alex, "that both of you will accept protection. That's chiefly why I wanted you to stay at Oaks. We are right now under the care of three agents in this restaurant. I can assign them to the Green Park Hotel or to Marilyn's flat."

"Send them to protect Marilyn," said Bolan. "I can take care of myself."

Sir Alex smiled. "Am I to suppose you're not interested in spending the night in her flat?" he asked. "I can hardly believe it of you, Bolan."

Bolan glanced at Marilyn and couldn't subdue a grin. "Well, I . . ."

"At the very least, you can stay with her as much as possible, to protect her," said Sir Alex.

Marilyn smiled. "I'm like Mack," she said. "I can take care of myself."

"Perhaps. But you could have been killed this afternoon. Maybe even worse, you could have been kidnapped. I should be very grateful to have cooperation from both of you on this."

"Mack can't be turned into a baby-sitter," she said.

"I believe he has no pressing duties between now and tomorrow morning," said Sir Alex. "Incidentally, Hal Brognola will arrive in London in the morning. We shall have a conference. Both of you should be available at, say, ten."

CHAPTER TWENTY-ONE

They left the Sovereign a little after ten. Marilyn had a car that belonged to MI6, a red Porsche 911. It was in the garage at the Hilton Hotel. So was the gray Ford that belonged to the three men who were supposed to follow them to her flat on Lincoln's Inn fields and set up guard for the night. So was Sir Alexander Bentwood's Jaguar. They all stood around for a few minutes as the cars were brought up—the three guards keeping a respectful distance.

"What could they do with a Foxbat?" Bolan asked Sir Alex one last time. "That's what I want to talk about in the morning. The destruction of that MiG-25 at Mannheim is a key."

Sir Alex laughed. He had given Bolan the impression that his two martinis, white wine with dinner and brandy afterward had been too much for him. "We'll worry over that in the morning, Bolan," he said. "Enjoy a good night."

Marilyn drove the Porsche with authority. She roared around Shepherd Market and into Curzon Street, then cut into Half Moon Street and south to Piccadilly. The gray Ford kept up, though she seemed to Bolan to be challenging the MI6 driver.

"Let's have some fun," said Bolan. "Get rid of them."

"Seriously?"

"Seriously."

She cut sharply into Old Bond Street, sharply again into Stafford, then into Dover, then into Hay. Bolan lost track of the streets, but she accelerated as they rushed past

Berkeley Square, and after a moment he recognized the Roosevelt statue on Grosvenor Square.

She switched on the radio. It was set to the MI6 scrambled frequency and was equipped with an unscrambler, and they could hear the gray Ford and the dispatcher.

"Pussy Cat's run off from us. I say again, run off. Turned from Piccadilly into Mayfair. We've lost her. That's the red Porsche, if you want to issue an alert."

"Uh, understood, Tag Three. Proceed to Lincoln's Inn Fields and wait for Pussy Cat. Report contact when you have it."

Marilyn turned to Bolan and grinned. "Where to?" she asked.

"Back where we started from," he said. "There'll be street parking now."

"Your hotel."

"My hotel. I want to change clothes."

"And then?"

"I want to go hunting."

"For?"

"Eva Zhulev. She's the only connection we have that might lead us to the leaders of the White Front. And her cover for being in this country is that she's employed as a secretary at the East German Trade Mission. Maybe it's time we violate their diplomatic immunity."

"I can't do it," said Marilyn grimly. "That requires authorization, all kinds of authorization. If you want to take it up in the meeting tomorrow morning—"

"Then you never heard me say a word about it," he interrupted. "Just drop me off at the hotel, and I'll work this one alone."

"Mack—"

"She tried to kill you this afternoon, Marilyn. Or kidnap you. She's made me mad."

"What are you going to do? You can't just go crashing into the Trade Mission. Anyway, she wouldn't be there tonight."

"You speak German fluently," said Bolan. "Would it violate their diplomatic immunity if you went in, said you're a friend of Eva's and asked for her address?"

"I'm not sure they're open at this time of night. In fact, I doubt it."

"Are you kidding? That's the London headquarters for MfS—their Ministerium für Staats-Sicherheit. It's like supposing the CIA station is closed. They're open."

"Just hearing the name Zhulev will ring an alarm for them," said Marilyn.

"They'll deny anyone by that name works for them," said Bolan. "Then I'll go in and find out my way."

"At which point, I don't know you," she said. "Never heard of you."

"Good enough."

Marilyn sighed heavily. "Well, what first? How do we start?"

"What I want you to do is drive me to the hotel. I'll get out and go in the front door. You go around Shepherd Market and park on one of the darker streets. I'll find you."

"All I've got is the .22 in my purse," she said.

Bolan grinned. "Right. You could hardly hide a Beretta in that dress."

Five minutes later he was in his room. No one had entered while he was out. He could be sure of that. The old bent match trick was so obvious that it could never betray an entry anymore. His own simplest trick was to close the door on a tiny wad of tissue, then use a credit card to push it back out of sight between the door and the jamb. Even if the intruder saw it fall, he wouldn't know where to replace it. And Bolan, returning, could probe for it with the same credit card and see if it was exactly where he had left it.

He changed quickly into his blacksuit, pulled the Uzi from the suitcase under the bed, shoved a clip into it and secured the extra clip under his belt. Five minutes after he had arrived in the room, he went out the window and up to the roof—dressed in the blacksuit, watch cap, belt with knife and pistol, and carrying the deadly Israeli submachine gun.

Shortly he tapped on the window of the Porsche.

Marilyn's mouth fell open.

"My working clothes," he said.

"Where'd you get the...?" she asked, pointing at the Uzi.

"A guy was careless and left it lying around."

Marilyn glanced up and down and across the street. The night wasn't entirely dark, nor was the street entirely deserted, and she wondered how a passerby would react to this black-clad apparition with a submachine gun under his arm.

"Get in," she said.

"The hotel's clear," said Bolan. "I've been on the roof, looking around. The roofs are clear, also the alleys, doorways... If Eva and her pals are looking for us, they're looking somewhere else."

"Mack, this is crazy."

"The DDR Trade Mission's in Pimlico," he said.

She said nothing more during the drive. She had learned—as people did—that when Mack Bolan said he was going to do something, he did it. Right now he said he was going to the East German Trade Mission, and there wasn't any point in arguing against it.

She pulled the Porsche to the curb in front of the red-brick Georgian building with the little forest of antennae on the roof.

"I'll ask," she said curtly.

Pulling her coat around her, Marilyn walked to the door and spoke to the guard. Bolan watched. After a moment she was admitted.

"Nothing like effective lying," she said when she returned five minutes later. "Eva Zhulev has a flat in Wapping."

Wapping was a strange, oddly spectacular neighborhood. Just east of the Tower of London and on the river, it was the site of the old London Docks, now no longer in use.

Here, when the tide was out, the mud flats of the Thames River were exposed; and when the tide was in, the swift waters lapped against brick walls that had held the river back for two centuries. Muscular new industry and bright new housing rose above falling-down decay.

Marilyn shouldn't have been with him. She was dressed for dinner in a good restaurant and had no weapon but the .22 Beretta that normally she carried between her legs but this evening carried in her purse. Bolan would have liked to send her home, but he doubted she would accept the suggestion.

"I want you to keep a distance," he said to her. "I know you're good—damn good, in fact—but there's nothing you can do."

"Sit and wait," she muttered.

"It's not your way. But this time it has to be."

He surveyed the building she had pointed out. The night duty officer at the Trade Mission had given this address. It was a five-story brick building, its overall squareness relieved by arched tops on all the windows.

"Let me check the mailboxes at least," said Marilyn. "You walk into the lobby dressed like that, somebody's going to call the police."

Without waiting for him to agree or disagree, she swung out from under the wheel and walked across the street and into the building. Bolan didn't like it. Someone at the Trade Mission could have called ahead a warning, and Eva Zhulev's target this afternoon had been Marilyn, not him. He followed her across the street and waited outside the door in the shadows, ready to go in blasting if anyone came near her.

She came out. "Eva Zhulev," she said. "Flat 3D. That's on what you Americans call the fourth floor. I'm going to do you one more favor, whether you like it or not. I'm going to open a door at the rear of the building and let you in."

"Marilyn—"

"Then I'll sit in the car and wait for you."

"Not here," he said. He pointed to the end of the street. "Around the corner, there."

Carrying the Uzi, he jogged around to the rear of the building while she walked through. When he reached the rear door, it was propped open with a scrap of a fast-food carton, and when he opened it and stepped in, Marilyn was gone. He heard her heels on the floor beyond the next door, but he didn't see her.

He was in a service area. Big trash cans stood around. A steel-and-concrete stairway led to upper floors. He opened the door into the center hall and checked for a guard or watchman. Nobody. The hall was silent except for the muffled sound of music playing in one of the apartments.

Civilians. Probably children, too, in some of these flats. He'd have to be careful.

He climbed to the third floor, as the English counted floors. Flats up there had a view of Tower Bridge, if they were on the west side of the building. The window in the stairwell, where he was, just looked back into Cockney London.

There was one more floor above. And Bolan sensed that someone was in the stairwell up there. He wasn't sure how he knew. He didn't hear anyone, exactly. Maybe a man breathing in a confined space, like this stairwell with its hard walls, changed the air pressure, which the ears might sense and yet not communicate to the brain as a sound; or maybe a man who had sharpened his senses to a fine edge, as Bolan had, could pick up the magnetic signature of a living creature as an electronic sensor could do. It made no difference how he knew—he knew.

With his back to the door into the hall, he turned the knob. A quick retreat out of the stairwell might become abruptly critical.

He slung the Uzi under his arm by its black nylon strap and drew the Lahti. A burst of automatic fire inside this apartment building was out of the question.

Okay. I'm ready. Make your move up there.

The move was a surprise. It bounced down the steps, a clanging steel ball spewing smoke. Or maybe spewing a gas. Whatever it was, Bolan didn't take a sniff of it to find out. He threw himself against the door behind him and onto the floor of the hall.

A slug punched through the door just above him. His instinct for getting down in dangerous situations had saved him. For an instant. Whoever had fired so impatiently, without waiting to see just where he was, could fire again. But he had already rolled. The second shot crunched into the floor and ricocheted up, the tumbling, distorted bullet cracking a fist-size hole in the door.

The pistol was silenced. It was firing subsonic cartridges. If there were innocents behind the doors to the flats on this floor, they didn't know someone was trying to kill a man in their hallway.

But they were going to find out. Bolan didn't intend to take a third shot without returning one. Still rolling, he spun into firing position and leveled the muzzle of the Lahti.

Maybe his attacker knew how deadly accurate Mack Bolan was when he fired a weapon. He extended the silenced pistol in both hands, but without firing a shot ducked through the open door of one of the flats and slammed the door.

Bolan held his fire.

It could have been Eva Zhulev in a sweater and slacks. Whoever it had been, it was a slight figure. But he hadn't seen the blond hair.

Behind him. He jerked the door open. A man stood there, startled. He had a pistol, but the muzzle was down. Bolan swung at him with the Lahti. The heavy automatic cracked the man's cheekbone. Blood flew. He staggered back and fell down the steps.

Smoke. That was all he had thrown, a smoke bomb. Clever. The idea had been to drive Bolan to bolt carelessly into the hall, to take the fire from the silenced pistol. Teamwork.

So they had known he was coming.

A bullet punched through the wooden door. Then another. He threw himself over the rail and landed on the steps below.

The man he had hit across the face with the Lahti lay doubled up on the steps, moaning. Bolan kicked his pistol away from him. It clattered down the steps.

The people above began firing their silenced pistols wildly into the stairwell. Slugs spanged off concrete and steel, bouncing dangerously everywhere.

Bolan pulled open a door and ran the length of the center hall of the building. He ran down the carpeted main stairs toward the lobby where Marilyn had checked the mailboxes.

Now he realized that in the forty-five minutes it had taken them to drive from Pimlico to Wapping, the forewarned gang in 3C—and likely occupying other apartments besides—had turned the building into a trap. As he entered the brightly lit lobby, the glass doors dissolved in an explosion of automatic weapon fire. The nervous triggerman had fired impulsively, as soon as he saw the black-clad figure, and the shots that blew away the glass sprayed the lobby too high.

Bolan hurled himself to his right and down, bringing up the muzzle of the Uzi and returning a burst of 9 mm slugs. He crawled across the lobby. More fire blew away the windows above him, but he was below the level of the window-sills, protected by the brick wall, and the stream of slugs and explosion of glass were well above him.

Whoever was firing cared nothing for people in the building. Bullets punched through the plaster of the wall behind Bolan. Terrified people screamed.

Bolan threw a chair through a window at the end of the lobby and dived through it.

He landed on the hard pavement of a parking lot, rolling over two or three times and coming up with the Uzi aimed.

And he saw her. It was Eva Zhulev. She was the trigger-man outside. She stood, legs apart, skirt hiked high, moving her submachine gun from side to side, looking for a target.

Three weak little pops sounded behind her, from across the street, and Eva staggered.

Marilyn was firing the .22, and she had hit Eva.

Eva turned and sprayed a burst of fire into the darkness behind her. Then she ran down the street.

Two men ran through the shattered doors of the building. Another came around. They stood, peering into the dim light of the street. One of them pulled the clip from his pistol and replaced it.

Bolan searched for Marilyn. He thought he saw her, though he couldn't be sure. He thought he saw her run after Eva.

The men in front of the building thought so, too. They set off toward the end of the street, where Eva had gone, where maybe Marilyn had gone after her.

Marilyn . . . Not with that .22 popgun, after a woman armed with whatever that was that had blown the glass doors out of the building. Courage was one thing; reckless foolishness was another. And now, with the three hardmen going down the same street, she—

Bolan moved out of the shadows of the parking lot and followed.

Shortly he was following no one, he realized. All of them—the two women and the three hardmen—had disappeared in the night. He rounded the corner at the end of the street. The Porsche was parked there. No one was in or near it.

Ahead was a wide street, then the river. He ran to the wide street and across it.

The Thames lay before him, visible between two old, dark buildings. He walked cautiously between them to the top of the wall. The Pool of London, the river was called here. Upstream a mile away—Tower Bridge. Beyond it in the distance—the old cruiser *Belfast*, moored in the river, and beyond that other bridges, all busy with traffic. Across the river—the lights of a commercial and residential section of the city. The tide was out. It was running. The river was low and flowing swiftly.

Yellow light. Enough to see by, not enough to cast shadows. He looked down at the mud flats exposed by the receded tide. A litter of debris. Gleaming, sandy mud.

You could get down there, down brick stairs slimy from being submerged half the time.

Bolan looked around for a deep shadow, saw one and disappeared into it. He held himself rigid there, listening, his eyes searching the flat, littered ground behind the wall and the mud flats.

He heard nothing. He saw nothing.

He ventured out of the shadow and stepped forward to the edge of the wall. He looked down.

It was fifteen feet from the top of the wall to the bottom on the mud. And there, edging cautiously along the foot of the wall, was Marilyn.

She was stalking. He peered into the darkness ahead of her. Maybe she could see somebody. He couldn't. He could see that she had her .22 in her right hand. Her feet were sinking into the mud. He could see her pulling them out with every step, and clearly she had long since lost her evening shoes. She moved slowly.

He stared at the shadows fifty yards downstream, trying to see whatever she saw. And maybe...light flickered off the swirling water—dim flashes, lasting only an instant—and twice he thought he caught sight of a figure at the base of the wall.

One stairway went down. If he went down that way, he would be no help to Marilyn. If he could get well ahead of her and go over the wall behind the figure she was stalking...

Bolan trotted east, alert to anything lurking or moving in the shadows all around him. He went on until he was fifty yards or more from where he had seen Marilyn. He stopped and peered over the wall.

Now he saw nothing, neither Marilyn nor her prey.

But he couldn't see very well. It was dark down there. He found a rusty old stanchion, doubled his rope through it and in a few seconds had dropped quietly to the mud at the base of the wall. He pulled down his rope and recoiled it over his shoulder—all the while peering into the darkness to both sides.

Nothing. But Marilyn had to be down here somewhere. Didn't she?

Had that *been* Marilyn? In the dark, at a distance...it could have been Eva. But—

In Marilyn's coat!

They could have taken her! God knows how many of them there were, and where. She had run down the street after Eva. Maybe Eva had faked being hit by a .22 slug.

Someone could have jumped Marilyn from behind. Maybe the trap—

Possibilities. To hell with possibilities. Two people were down here on the mud flats, and one of them was a woman—Marilyn or Eva. He unslung the Uzi, checked it and began to work his way along the foot of the slimy brick wall.

It stank. This was the mud of a river that sluiced out one of the world's major cities. Twice a day the saltwater from the North Sea filled the Thames nearly to the top of this wall, carrying with it whatever sea life could live in such waters, and then it went down, leaving its dead. As it retreated, the Thames carried tons of the city's debris—not sewage, just detritus, whatever a careless population saw fit to throw into the river, everything from soiled mattresses to plastic beer cups. In past centuries they had chained pirates on these flats and left them to drown in the rising tide.

Police horns hooted on the streets above. Someone in the apartment building had called them. When they found a lobby blown apart by automatic weapons fire, they would come in great force.

He held himself flat against the wall. There *had* to be someone down here.

And there was. He spotted three of them. They had stationed themselves where they supposed he had to come down—at the foot of the brick stairs. They were waiting, crouched in the mud. One was upstream from the stairs. Two were downstream. They were focused entirely on the stairs. It hadn't occurred to them, apparently, that he might have come down another way.

Three men.

No Marilyn. No Eva.

Bolan picked up a short piece of waterlogged scrap lumber. He set himself and tossed it high in the air. His judgment of the distance was good. It landed where he had wanted it to land—on the brick steps near the top of the wall—with a loud clatter.

All three fired.

Their silenced pistols made almost no sound, but the bullets cracked hard against the bricks.

Okay. No question. Civilians didn't fire silenced pistols at the noise of a board on the water stairs. They were hardmen. They were the ones who had tried to kill him. They were stationed to kill him now.

Bolan leveled the Uzi and fired a burst.

He got all three. One stumbled back into the water and fell. One doubled over at the foot of the wall. One collapsed into the mud. The one in the water drifted downstream, facedown.

The police would be here in a minute. Bolan backed away along the bottom of the wall.

VERY DELICATE BUSINESS, the men from Scotland Yard concluded immediately. The two men they had found in the mud were armed with silenced Czech pistols. They carried no identification, no money, no keys. Their clothes were without labels. Their pockets were heavy with extra clips of ammunition. The chief inspector put in a call to MI6.

Sir George Harrington arrived on the scene a little after 2:00 a.m.

"No one injured in the building, Sir George. Frightened badly but not hurt. One of the flats is rented in the name of Eva Zhulev, a secretary at the Trade Mission of the German Democratic Republic. She wasn't at home this evening and hasn't returned. We've entered the flat, but to no good purpose. Nothing there in particular. A woman's clothes. A few books, magazines. Food in the fridge. A telly. Nothing out of the ordinary."

Sir George nodded. He knew who had been shooting, and why.

"There's a rather good-looking Porsche parked around the corner," said the chief inspector. "Registered to MI6."

"I know," said Sir George.

"Then you'd like it all kept quiet, I suppose."

"I should be grateful, Chief Inspector."

The detective nodded. "Very well. We'll tell the news chaps it seems to have been a shoot-out among some suspected cocaine dealers."

"I'm concerned about the whereabouts of two women," said Sir George. "Eva Zhulev and another, a blonde, very attractive. She was driving the Porsche."

The chief inspector shook his head. "We've seen no women other than the ones identified as living in the flats in this building. No attractive blonde, for sure."

"The attractive blonde is an agent of MI6," said Sir George.

"We have two bodies," said the chief inspector. "Both men. No automatic weapons, though automatic weapons were fired here. Everyone who survived whatever this was, escaped."

"Is your investigation complete, or nearly so?"

"You want us to leave?"

"I have a sense, Chief Inspector, that once your men are gone someone will appear whom I very much want to see."

BOLAN HAD WATCHED for a long time from a warehouse roof. Now, as the police got into their cars and vans and drove away, he stayed where he was, still watching.

Sir George Harrington remained. He stood for a while just outside the shattered doorway of the apartment building. He lit a cigarette. Then, after another minute, he walked away, with that peculiar, characteristic limp of his and moved slowly along the street toward the corner. Bolan could see both streets. Sir George went to the red Porsche, unlocked it with a key from his pocket and sat down inside it. He sat and smoked. He didn't start the engine.

Bolan used his rope and let himself down from the roof. He walked directly to the Porsche.

Sir George reached across and opened the door on the passenger side of the car.

"Get in, Bolan. Where is she?"

"I don't know."

"She hasn't called in, which she would do if she could. I'm afraid they've got her."

CHAPTER TWENTY-TWO

After the meeting at MI6, attended by Sir Alexander Bentwood and Sir George Harrington, Mack Bolan and Hal Brognola walked to Piccadilly and across into the royal parks. They walked in silence for the most part. After crossing the Mall, they walked down to the edge of the pond and sat on one of the benches facing the water.

Even on a cold December day, people strolled along the pond, tossing bits of bread to the waterfowl. It was a Saturday. Children weren't in school, and families had come to the park. Toddlers ran unsteadily after the birds. The ducks and geese were bold and rose for a short flight, or swam out into the water, only at the last moment before the children reached them. On the grass behind the bench where Bolan and Brognola sat, a father and his small son kicked a soccer ball back and forth.

"You love her, don't you, Striker?" said Hal.

Bolan didn't answer. He stared at the water and the birds.

There had been no word from Marilyn. MI6 had issued its special alert—agent in trouble—last night. Scotland Yard's Special Branch had assigned twenty men to the case. MI5 had twenty men looking for her. Every MI6 agent considered Marilyn Henry a special responsibility, and many had reported in this morning—they would join the search even though they were on vacation, or it was their weekend off. Two agents who had been injured in the line of duty and were recuperating at home arrived at headquarters and volunteered to join the force searching for her.

There was goodwill, but not much more. No one had a clue as to where Marilyn was. No one had a clue as to where Eva Zhulev was. MI6 had four resources inside the East German Trade Mission. None of them could come up with any word as to where Eva Zhulev had gone. Bolan had reported he believed she was wounded by a .22 slug, but no physician or hospital reported any case of gunshot wound.

Bolan remembered what he had seen of Eva Zhulev in that conference room. The ruling council of the White Front was marked with a streak of sadism. The image in his mind as he sat staring at the green water of the pond was of Marilyn in the hands of sadistic men, undergoing God knows what.

"Don't try to kid me, big guy," said Brognola. "I know what you feel. I've got a wife, remember. Thanks to you. You saved her life when she was kidnapped. But I know what you're going through. I went through it myself, remember."

Bolan nodded.

"As far as I'm concerned, you can make Marilyn your assignment. It's the White Front who has her anyway. You're entitled to—"

"No," said Bolan curtly. "We've got to talk about the Foxbat and all the rest of it. We can't be sidetracked. We may not have much time."

"Striker...damn it, you're entitled to a personal life. You're entitled to think like a man, *feel* like a man."

"I *do*," said Bolan. "Look at that."

"Look at what?"

"Look at that little girl chasing the geese. Look at her laugh. Look at that boy back there, kicking the soccer ball. Look at his father, for that matter. Half an hour from now they may be in a store back on Piccadilly, or in a crowd on Trafalgar Square, when some animal sets off a bomb. I do feel, Hal. I do care."

"Marilyn—"

"Marilyn's an agent. Marilyn's a soldier in the war against the animals. She took a risk—an unacceptable risk, if you want the truth, and one I told her not to take. Sure, I want to save her. You bet I do. But I have to keep my priorities in order."

"And you don't want to talk about it anymore," said Brognola quietly.

"No."

"You can change your mind," said Brognola. "You're entitled."

Bolan nodded, but it was a nod of dismissal. "I was glad you didn't say much in that meeting this morning," he said. "I'm pretty sure MI6 is leaky. GIGN is. Dutch security was and maybe still is."

"I didn't tell them what I've got to tell you," said Brognola.

"I've been thinking about that explosion in the hangar on the Mannheim AFB," said Bolan. "Why did somebody want to destroy that Foxbat? I can think of only one good reason—which is that they wanted a part off it, and they got in there and took the part, then blew up the Foxbat to conceal what they'd done."

"You're exactly right," said Brognola. "Only it didn't work. When the experts examined the wreckage, they found that a subassembly had been removed from the Foxbat. Not only that, Telpuchovski reports that a Russian aircraft engineer who would be entirely capable of doing any kind of repair to a Foxbat is missing. He was kidnapped in Prague about three months ago."

"Is there a Foxbat missing anywhere?" asked Bolan.

Brognola grinned wryly. "I find this hard to believe, but our Soviet friends run so clumsy an inventory system that a sophisticated interceptor aircraft could be missing and they wouldn't know. I've been in touch with Telpuchovski. He's trying to find out."

"The White Front," said Bolan.

"We don't know that," said Brognola. "It could be an entirely independent operation."

"From what I've seen of White Front operations," said Bolan, "I don't take it for a group that's going to be satisfied just setting off bombs and assassinating intel agents. They've got to have something big in mind."

"Like what?"

"Like shooting down Air Force One with a Russian interceptor."

Brognola nodded. "Great minds run in the same channels," he said. "That's what I've been thinking."

"When the President comes over to meet with the general secretary."

Brognola nodded again. "We're in tune, Striker."

"Destabilization," said Bolan. "We'd be at the brink of nuclear war."

"If we didn't actually go over the brink."

"Fear," said Bolan. "Panic. Governments would fall."

"Affording the White Front an opportunity to move into positions of power," said Brognola. "That's my analysis, too."

"That's what they want," said Bolan. "That's what Joop Thijn talked about—how strong men would take over and put what he called the weaklings out of power. The assassination of the President, apparently by a Soviet interceptor firing a rocket at Air Force One, would be a triumph for them. In the mess that would follow, they could move in France, Germany, Britain—even the States."

"In the Soviet Union, too," said Brognola. "The end of the general secretary. The return of the old hostiles."

Bolan frowned, then nodded. He turned his head to watch a little girl shrieking and retreating as a big goose walked out of the water and advanced toward her, hoping for a morsel of the bread she had been throwing to the birds.

"If they've got a Foxbat," said Brognola, "where is it?"

"Assuming our speculations are right," said Bolan, "it has to be somewhere in Russia. When it comes up to take a shot at Air Force One, it's going to be on radar. It has to come from inside the Soviet Union. What's its range? Do we know?"

"About a thousand miles," said Brognola. "Five hundred miles out from its base and five hundred back. It could reach Stockholm from Leningrad and return. It could do it from any base near the Baltic or the Gulf of Finland. Or, of course, from almost anywhere in Finland—anywhere south of the Arctic Circle."

"A lot of territory," said Bolan. "And if he refuels, or if he's not going back—that is, if it's a suicide mission—you're looking at four times as much territory. There has to be a thousand airstrips where he could take off."

"Not a thousand hidden ones," said Brognola.

"You can hide bigger things than that if you've penetrated a nation's security agency," said Bolan.

"Even so..."

"Even so, we need to know where the base is," Bolan admitted. "I only know one way to find out."

"Get your hands on a member of the White Front," said Hal Brognola.

"And I only know one possible," said Bolan bleakly. "Marilyn hit Eva Zhulev with a .22 slug last night. I saw it. I *know* she hit her. It didn't kill her, didn't stop her, but somewhere in London she's holed up nursing her wound."

"How can you find her?"

"I've got a couple of ideas," said Bolan. "If necessary, I'll break into the East German Trade Mission and tear the answer out of somebody's throat. Before that, I've got another idea."

Brognola shook his head. "I've got to be back in Washington no later than Monday," he said. "I've been summoned to the White House." He opened his briefcase. "Here's two thousand pounds and a new passport," he said. "Notice the passport. Diplomatic, in the name of Frank Vinton. You've used that alias before."

Bolan looked at the "new" passport. It had been made to look long-used and dog-eared.

"You've got to be careful, guy," said Brognola solemnly. "This is a big one, and there's something wrong, damn wrong."

"You don't have to tell me," said Bolan.

"IF WE'D RECEIVED a note, a threatening call, anything... Unhappily we've not," said Sir George Harrington.

Bolan had returned to MI6 headquarters to ask if there had been any word about Marilyn.

He stood at the window of Sir George's office, staring down at the street. It was two weeks before Christmas, and the rain that had begun to fall that Saturday afternoon hadn't discouraged the shoppers who were hurrying along the wet streets with arms full of packages.

"Is there anything at all we can do for you?" asked Sir George sympathetically.

"You can issue me a couple hundred rounds of 9 mm parabellum," said Bolan.

"Of course. But two hundred rounds? We issued you a Lahti Two—"

"Somebody was careless enough to leave an Uzi lying around," said Bolan.

"Ah, then we shall issue it to you in Uzi magazines. Thirty-two-round ones?" He picked up the telephone to order the ammunition. "In a holiday-colored shopping bag." Then he saw that Bolan was somber, and he issued his order crisply. "She's a resourceful young woman," he said. "Brave. Intelligent. If anyone can—"

"Wait a minute," Bolan interrupted. He was looking down at the street, where a rotund man was hailing a cab—having apparently just left this building. "Do you know that man?"

Sir George looked down. "Indeed I do," he said. "That's Edward Holmesby-Lovett, a very dear friend. Veteran of World War II. He waded ashore on D-Day in the first wave. Something of a national hero. Remained in service for many years. Intelligence. Retired about four years now. A fine gentleman. Do you know him?"

"No," said Bolan. "At first I thought he looked familiar, but now that I have a better look at him, I see he's not the man I thought he might be."

But he was. He had been at the table in the meeting in the NUG executive office building outside Düsseldorf.

HAL BROGNOLA WENT to dinner with Sir Alexander Bentwood and Sir George Harrington that evening. Bolan was invited, in fact, urged to come. He declined politely. By four in the afternoon he had left the Green Park Hotel. He paid for another week in advance and told the desk clerk he was leaving London on a business trip. He carried his bag, with the Uzi inside, also his blacksuit and equipment.

He rode around the city in cabs for half an hour until he was confident he wasn't being followed. Then Mr. Frank Vinton, bearer of an American diplomatic passport, checked in at the Dorchester. He took his room for three days and went to a car rental desk and rented a small gray Ford.

It was time to work alone. It was time to do things his own way again. He would get in touch with Brognola as soon as he could, to warn him that Sir George Harrington had a dear friend who had sat at the table in the Düsseldorf meeting. But it would have to be during a personal meeting; he couldn't be sure they hadn't bugged Hal's telephone.

He had some time to kill, and he used it sitting in his room, reviewing things in his mind. What he was going to try tonight was a long shot, but it was all the shot he had. In spite of what he'd said to Brognola, he really didn't think he could break into the East German Trade Mission and force someone to tell him the whereabouts of Eva Zhulev. Even if he could, they would call and warn her, just as they'd done last night.

He and Eva shared something. They had underestimated each other. He wouldn't make that mistake again. Neither would she.

About ten he took his rental car from the garage and drove to a well-remembered address in Bloomsbury.

"I IMAGINE YOU remember me."

She shuddered. "I didn't do anything to you. I didn't have anything to do with what they did to you."

"Well, that's about half-true. They called you Priscilla, right?"

"I've been called a lot of names."

Bolan was standing with his back to the door, and now he turned around and shot the bolt. He walked across the little parlor and sat down.

"Relax, Priscilla," he said. "I didn't come back to hassle you."

"Harper's dead," she whispered hoarsely. "You killed him, didn't you?"

"So's Schellenberg," he said. "Had it coming, didn't they?"

"I only worked for Bobbie Harper," she said. "Only took orders. I don't know what he was mixed up in."

"Who do you work for now?"

"I'm not sure. Some people. They haven't got it all straightened out yet. It's all I know, this business. I was a hustler from the time I was sixteen. Harper let me run this place for him. That was a good deal for me. Otherwise I'd have been on the street with nothing."

"All right, Priscilla," said Bolan. "No one knows I'm here. The lock on your front door will need some repair. I wanted a private talk with you. Very private. Permanently private. I'm going to ask you some questions. I want honest answers. If I get them, you'll be okay, because I'll never tell how I found out. If you don't answer, or you lie to me, I can make things very tough for you."

The woman began to cry. "I don't know nothing," she sobbed.

"Last night," he said. "Last night, sometime after midnight, Eva came here. She had a bullet in her. She needed some help. You're scared of her. You have good reason to be. So you helped her."

Priscilla shook her head. Her tears were dissolving her mascara, which was running down her cheeks in black streaks.

"Was she alone?" he asked.

"What makes you think she came here?"

"Priscilla, I *know* she came here. Don't try to kid me. You can be in big trouble. With me, which is bad enough. With the police. Or you can get out of trouble. So... which is it going to be?"

"You're an American," she sniffed.

"So? Tell me the story."

"She was here," Priscilla sobbed.

The bluff had worked.

"Go on. She was here. Alone?"

"A guy was with her. She wasn't badly hurt. She didn't even need a doctor. We took her up to a room. All we had to do was clean her up and bandage her. She didn't have a bullet in her. The bullet had just touched her, just barely. Ripped the skin along her ribs. She'd bled some, but she was okay.''

"Another woman, Priscilla. Was there another woman with her?"

Priscilla shook her head. "No, just this guy. Kind of a dumb-looking guy, talked with an accent. German maybe. You know that Bobbie Harper was mixed up with Germans some way. Eva is German, too, I think."

"All right. Where is she now?"

Priscilla shook her head. "I don't know."

"The hell you don't."

"Please . . ."

"She's upstairs," he said, another bluff.

"She's got a gun. She'll shoot up the place if you go near her. It's a bad gun—some kind of little machine gun, like. The police will—"

It made sense. It had been a long shot, but it had made sense. Eva had two places to go to ground—the flat in Wapping, the Trade Mission in Pimlico. She couldn't go back to the flat. She would figure the police would be watching the Mission. Also, she might have contacts in London, but a wounded woman, showing blood, might not be able to go where her contacts were—maybe in a hotel. She knew this house. She knew Priscilla would be terrified of her. Yeah, it made sense.

"I'm not going up to see if she'll try to shoot me," Bolan said. "But I want to know—is she alone up there?"

"Right. The guy that brought her didn't stay. Even last night, he didn't stay. Another guy came to see her this afternoon. Different type—one hundred percent English if you know what I mean. He was in and out."

"You sure she's up there? Not out a window?"

Priscilla shrugged. "I don't know anything for sure anymore."

"Okay," he said. "Just one more thing. You don't tell her I was here."

"God forbid," croaked Priscilla. "The sooner she's out of here... The sooner I never see any of you again, the better I'll like it."

BOLAN GUESSED Eva would leave the whorehouse before morning. Instinct would tell her to move while it was still dark, when there was little traffic. That was a silly instinct—she could walk the streets of London all day if she wanted to with almost no chance of being recognized and stopped—but it would govern her, likely. He crossed the street into the darkness of the little park that faced the house and sat down on a bench to wait.

His guess proved right. About one o'clock a small blue van backed into the narrow alley beside the house—just as had happened the night when he'd escaped naked over the roofs. He walked quickly to his car, got in, started it and pulled it around the corner and along the street opposite the entrance to the alley. No question. There was Eva, climbing into the passenger seat.

The van pulled out of the alley in no great hurry. Bolan let it get fifty yards ahead of him, then followed it.

He didn't know the streets, but fortunately traffic was light, so he had no difficulty keeping the van in sight ahead of him. He recognized Oxford Street and knew they were heading west. As they entered Bayswater Road and drove along the northern boundary of Hyde Park, he wondered for a moment if they weren't going to the house on Craven Hill where he had found Schellenberg. Instead they drove the entire length of the park, then turned south. And now he didn't know the streets or neighborhood at all, but they entered an area not unlike Bloomsbury—solid, blackened old brick houses on streets where homes and commerce lived together.

The driver finally pulled the van to the curb, and as Bolan drove past he saw Eva standing on the doorstep, pressing the bell, and waiting to be admitted after hours to the reception room of a tiny hotel. He drove on. The van pulled away behind him. He drove around the block and returned. Eva was inside. He could see her just inside the door, talking to the elderly woman who had let her in.

So. Was it a safehouse for MfS operatives, or for White Front agents? Not likely. If it had been that, she could have come directly here last night. More likely, someone had located the place for her and rented her a room. Likely she was alone.

Well . . . not alone. The driver had parked the van somewhere and returned on foot. That was why Eva and the old woman still stood inside the door—she had told her that her friend would arrive as soon as he parked their car. Shortly the old woman switched out the light, and Bolan had to assume Eva and the driver had gone to a room.

He didn't believe Marilyn could be inside. If he had thought so, he would have gone in. But if they had brought Marilyn here last night, why had Eva gone to the whorehouse to have her wound cared for and spend the rest of the night and the day? If this was a rendezvous, a safehouse, she would have come here directly. In fact, she had taken a risk to go to the whorehouse—and would have taken none to come here. He, Bolan, knew where the whorehouse was. He didn't know about this little hotel.

He wished he could trust someone. He wished he could let someone watch this place part of the time. Eva and the driver would now sleep. He couldn't. He had to sit here in his Ford, awake, until she came out.

Well, he had something to do besides sit and wait. He left the Ford and went looking for the van. He found it. It was locked, but he knew how to overcome that. Within a minute he was inside.

What he found was no surprise. Or maybe it was. He had expected to find an Uzi. Instead, he found something just as deadly, a French MAT submachine gun. A 32-round clip, loaded with 9 mm parabellum. Eva and her friends weren't short of lethal weapons.

He could take the MAT, or he could disable it. But if he did, it would be a warning. They would know somebody had been in their van, and they could guess who.

On the other hand . . . He pulled the clip. One by one he thumbed a dozen cartridges out into his hand. Then he re-loaded. But he put three cartridges in backward—that is, slug to the back, case and primer to the front. The second from the top, particularly. If she pulled the clip to check it, she wouldn't notice. If she fired a burst, the weapon would quickly jam. Dangerously. The action driving shut would clamp down on a reversed cartridge and might explode it. If nothing like that happened, and if she cleared the jam, the gun would jam again as soon as the next reversed cartridge came up. She would have to unload the whole clip to straighten it out. She wouldn't know that all the reversed cartridges were among the first dozen.

A dirty trick. Eva and her buddies deserved worse.

SUNDAY MORNING DAWNED bright. A white sun rose into a sky obscured by a thin layer of haze. A small restaurant opened for breakfast, and Bolan was able to pick up coffee and a sweet bun, also the morning papers. He sat in the car, ate, drank his coffee and read the papers—always keeping an eye on the door of the little hotel.

He had walked around it before dawn. There was no way out except by the front door. Bed and breakfast. London had hundreds of these little places. Cheap. Obscure. Yet clean and decent. He doubted Eva and the driver were oc-cupying the same room. Little hotels like this were anxious not to become hot-sheet operations. She had probably offered some plausible justification for her wee-hours arrival without luggage.

This was a *neighborhood*. People knew one another here. They walked their dogs. They stopped to chat on the street. It was a neighborhood of old people; he saw no children. The little restaurant did a lively business in morning tea with cold toast and marmalade.

The man coming along the street made himself obvious by his purposefulness. He alerted Bolan from the moment he saw him. Like Bolan himself, he was here on some business and was anxious to be about it and have done with it. He walked briskly, stiffly, like a soldier marching. He wore a gray overcoat with a black velvet collar, a maroon paisley silk scarf around his neck, with a black homburg, black leather gloves; and he carried an old-fashioned leather briefcase. Focusing his attention on him, Bolan guessed the man would go into the hotel. And he did.

It would be well to have a better look at him when he came out. Bolan started the Ford and drove it fifty yards down the street. It had sat in one place too long. He locked it and walked back to the little restaurant, where he bought another paper cup of coffee, and he returned to the street and stood close to the wall of the house next to the hotel, where he couldn't be seen from a hotel window.

He waited.

The man came out. Bolan had guessed he would return the way he came and had waited on that side of the hotel. He was right. As the man walked past Bolan, he glanced at him and obviously didn't recognize him.

But Bolan recognized the man. He was another one of the men who had sat around that conference table in the NUG office building outside Düsseldorf. In less than twenty-four hours he had seen two of them—Edward Holmesby-Lovett and this man. In London. What was more, he guessed this man wasn't English. Holmesby-Lovett conspicuously was.

This man conspicuously wasn't. Bolan took him for a German.

In any case, he was far more important than Eva Zhulev. Bolan turned and followed him.

The German, if that was what he was, walked with complete self-confidence, never turning to see if he was being followed. Bolan crossed the street and followed on the opposite side, but it wasn't necessary. The man wasn't worried.

He couldn't be going far, if he was walking. He walked past an underground station, so he wasn't taking a underground train to some other part of the city.

They came to a main street, and Bolan recognized the Natural History Museum. Now something made sense. In his hotel room yesterday afternoon he had checked the telephone directory for the address of Edward Holmesby-Lovett. It was in Kensington. This was Kensington.

The man walked on three more blocks. Then abruptly he walked up the three steps and rang the bell at the door of one of a row of handsome Edwardian houses. And sure enough, Holmesby-Lovett appeared in the door and let him in.

Now what to do? Maybe the White Front was meeting. Maybe he could find a way into the house, to see them, better yet to listen to them. Maybe if he just stood here he would see more of them come. Or he would see them when their meeting broke up and they left.

Maybe he would see Sir George Harrington. Maybe some American. It would be great to know who was involved. He could tell Brognola.

And maybe Hal couldn't do anything about it. Anyway, it wasn't the Executioner's mission just to get intel and pass it along for others to take action. He had to get into that house.

In the middle of a sunny Sunday morning, two weeks before Christmas, the Kensington street was busy. People strolled to the churches, others to the parks. To enter a house without being noticed was going to be difficult.

He was reluctant to leave the street, for fear of missing the arrival of another White Fronter—or perhaps of missing the departure of the German. Still, he couldn't enter the house from the front. That was clear. There had to be a rear entry.

To get to the rear, he would have to go all the way to the end of the block, apparently. The houses joined. They shared walls. There was no passage between them.

He walked toward the end of the block. At the corner he paused. The way to the rear of the houses would be through a narrow alley he could see from there. As he followed the German here, he had noticed how these were arranged in this neighborhood. The alleys were bounded by high brick walls with gates in them. Going over a wall, a man would almost certainly be noticed.

Suddenly Bolan spotted the blue van. It had entered the street and stopped opposite the house where Holmesby-Lovett had received the German. Eva. And her driver. What were they up to?

Bolan walked up onto a door stoop, so as not to be seen from the van.

The German—probably a German—came out of Holmesby-Lovett's house. He crossed the street and spoke briefly to the people in the van. Then he hurried away and around the corner.

For two or three minutes all was in suspension. Bolan wanted to follow the German but would have to walk past the van to catch up with him. Anyway, what was Eva about to do? Something was going down. He had to know what.

The suspense ended abruptly. The door swung open on the passenger side of the van, and Eva swung out. She strode across the street toward the door of Holmesby-Lovett's house, wearing a raincoat that very likely concealed the MAT and probably a pistol, too.

Bolan emerged from the doorway and walked toward the house. She didn't see him. She was at the door, ringing the bell. Holmesby-Lovett answered the bell. Bolan saw him step awkwardly back from the door. He knew her, of course. Probably she had shown him a gun.

Bolan ran for the door. He reached it in ten strides and kicked it open.

But he was too late. He heard the guttural burp of the submachine gun and heard Holmesby-Lovett scream. But he also heard Eva grunt. Sure. The MAT had jammed!

He heard a heavy step behind him. Eva's driver. The man burst through the door and straight into a quick, solid punch to the breastbone, then another to the nose. He dropped, and Bolan smashed his foot down on the hand that held a pistol, then kicked it away. The man—a wiry, muscular, English-looking blond guy—groped for his pistol, and Bolan kicked him in the jaw. He rolled over onto his back, clutching his broken jaw with both hands.

Eva and Holmesby-Lovett were in the living room to the right of the entry. She stepped into the doorway, still fumbling with the action of the jammed submachine gun. Bolan had the Lahti in his hand.

"*You!*" she screeched.

She dropped the submachine gun and went for a pistol, then suddenly thought better of it and ducked back into the room. Bolan flung himself through the door, stumbled over Holmesby-Lovett and recovered his balance just in time to see Eva throw a chair through the big window of the dining room and jump out after it.

Bolan ran into the dining room. Behind him, Holmesby-Lovett screamed. Bolan turned. The driver had recovered his pistol and staggered into the living room, pointing it unsteadily at Holmesby-Lovett. Bolan fired. The driver's head burst like a melon.

"Bolan..." muttered Holmesby-Lovett.

Bolan knelt beside the old Englishman. Eva had intended to cut him in two with a long burst from her MAT, but it had jammed after the second shot, and Holmesby-Lovett had taken only two shots, through his upper abdomen.

"Bolan..."

"You know me?" Bolan asked.

"Of course I know you," Holmesby-Lovett whispered hoarsely. "Help me, Bolan. Help me. I don't want to die."

Mack Bolan had seen these kind of wounds before. Edward Holmesby-Lovett was going to die. He had maybe five minutes, maybe ten. The man was bleeding to death internally. Bolan had seen it in Nam too many times.

Bolan stiffened. "Why should I help you?" he asked. "You're a victim of what you started. Just one more victim, of hundreds."

"No...you don't understand. Help me, Bolan. Help me!"

"I want some answers first," said Bolan coldly. "You answer my questions, then I'll do everything I can for you."

"Time..." Holmesby-Lovett whispered. "Maybe I don't have much time."

"We'll take the time to save other lives first," said Bolan. "Then yours."

It wasn't going to make any difference for the old man. And maybe, just maybe, he would tell enough to save the world.

CHAPTER TWENTY-THREE

Eva had gotten off two shots from the MAT before it jammed. Bolan had fired one from the Lahti. Eva had smashed out a window at the rear of the house. But the police didn't come. The old brick house was solid; even so, Bolan supposed no one was home in the houses to either side. He had no time to ask Holmesby-Lovett anything like that. He could see the life fading from the man.

Edward Holmesby-Lovett was carefully dressed in three-piece blue suit, white shirt, tightly knotted tie. He lay on his back. There was little blood on his vest. It was pouring out inside. If Bolan hadn't known this man and his confederates were directly and personally responsible for the assassinations and bombings that had been happening in Europe for the past two months, he could have felt great sympathy for him.

"First, very quickly, where's Marilyn Henry?"

"I don't know, Bolan. I had nothing to do with that."

"I saw you in Düsseldorf," said Bolan. "In the meeting with Herr Voss and the others. I was hanging on a rope outside the window. I—"

"Oh, good show," murmured Holmesby-Lovett. "They told me you're one hell of a man. You belong on our side of things, Bolan. I wish I could make you understand that."

"The woman who shot you is Eva Zhulev. She was there that night, too. Quite a sight."

"Psychological warfare technique," said Holmesby-Lovett. "Nudity. Spatial disorientation, through blindfolding or hanging upside down. You know—"

"Who was the man who visited you just before Eva came?"

"Doktor Johann Kleist," whispered Holmesby-Lovett. "Long, distinguished career in the BND. A bitter man. A fanatic, I'm afraid."

"Why did he order your death?"

"Don't you know? Because of *you*, Bolan. He wants you dead. Some of us don't. He thinks we've protected you. In fact, we have. From him. From others, too. The East German Ministerium für Staats-Sicherheit—" Holmesby-Lovett coughed. His face blanched. "Minis—"

Bolan recognized the signs. He had held good men in his arms through this ordeal. It was hard to believe that Holmesby-Lovett, who'd had combat experience, didn't realize what was happening.

"Where's the Foxbat?" Bolan asked.

Holmesby-Lovett's lips were now stained with fresh blood coming up from his stomach. Still, he smiled. "You know about that, do you? You're a good man, Bolan."

"Where is it?"

"This answer, and you'll help me? I mean, Bolan, time is running out. You know how to stop some of the bleeding until the doctors get to me. You will—"

"I'll do everything I can. Where's the Foxbat?"

"Finland. A few miles north and east of a town called Purumavaarra. Just west of the Soviet frontier. Aircraft flies down the border at hilltop altitude, then climbs and reaches altitude where radar will notice it. Will look like it's coming out of the Soviet Union. Then...Bolan...it's *fast*! It can launch missiles from a hundred miles away."

"And shoot down the President's plane as it approaches Stockholm for the secret conference."

Holmesby-Lovett nodded. "You know everything. I'd like to know how you learned—"

"You really don't know where Marilyn Henry is?"

"No. God, Bolan. Help me now."

He stripped the old man's abdomen, examined his wounds and confirmed what he'd thought. There was no chance. Even so, it wasn't how he would have gotten intel if he could have gotten it any other way.

He telephoned the police before he left the house. Then he returned to his rented Ford and drove back to the Dorchester.

Every damn bit of it was what he'd thought. He tried to call Brognola to set up a meeting, but Hal's flight for the States had left at noon. He'd left a message—call me before ten-thirty—but of course it hadn't been possible to call him. What was more, it wasn't possible to reach him. Whose line was secure?

Holmesby-Lovett had been hand-in-glove with MI6. So far as Bolan could guess, he might be British security's public enemy number one right now, with Holmesby-Lovett found dead. He guessed they had raided his room at the Green Park Hotel by now. He'd left them nothing to think about—or plenty to think about, if you wanted to consider it that way.

All right, he was on his own. Finland. At least they didn't know how much Holmesby-Lovett had told him, and they couldn't be sure he was going to Finland. In fact, they might not suspect it at all. On the other hand, they'd be checking the passenger lists of flights from London to Helsinki. He would have to go another way.

SUNDAY WAS OBSERVED rather strictly in London. You could do little business. He wanted a map of Finland, some clothes for arctic wear and so on. Not on Sunday. Well...he needed sleep.

He slept. He couldn't even call MI6 to ask if they had any lead on Marilyn. At this point he wasn't even sure they were trying to find Marilyn. So what could he do? He slept. He ate. He would need his strength tomorrow and after that.

In the shop on Jermyn Street on Monday morning he purchased special supplies and clothing for cold weather.

In a bookstore on Piccadilly he found an array of books on contemporary jet fighter aircraft. Two included extensive descriptions of the MiG-25 Foxbat. He bought both of them.

He flew to Denmark. And from there to Stockholm, and only from there to Helsinki. Brognola's thought of giving him a diplomatic passport had been brilliant. Without it he wouldn't have been able to carry the Lahti or the Uzi through the several inspections.

As it was, he was glad to retrieve the Lahti from his luggage in his hotel room in Helsinki. He hadn't been comfortable traveling unarmed. He had no doubt that Eva was somewhere looking for him—on the orders of her superior Doktor Kleist. Kleist would guess that sooner or later Bolan would come to Finland. At any rate, Kleist would take that precaution.

Marilyn. If he hadn't left the Green Park Hotel, if he had kept his contact with MI6, he might have gotten the message—give up, go home, if you want to see her alive again. It wasn't an option. He couldn't trade her life against what the White Front meant to do to humanity.

He lay alone on his bed in a hotel room in Helsinki and thought about her. Somebody was going to die for taking Marilyn from him. His mission to stop the Foxbat wouldn't last forever; and when it was over, somebody was going to die.

How do you get from Helsinki to Purumavaarra?

Apukka, the man behind the desk in the little travel agency told him. "Flights go there all year round. There you can rent a car and drive to Purumavaarra. It's farther than Tauormanen, but the roads are better."

Bolan told the agent that he had to be there the next day.

The man shrugged. "I can arrange for a pilot to fly you. That will be expensive. You will be in Apukka tomorrow and can drive to Purumavaarra on Wednesday. I can arrange a car for you. You should not start out from Apukka without good arctic gear."

It was arranged for sunup the next day. A two-hour flight. Bolan was told that the pilot would be at his hotel in the morning.

The sun set about three. When Bolan returned to the hotel, it was dark outside. A light snow was falling. The snow silenced the streets. At four o'clock it was as dark as it would have been at midnight in London or New York. He hurried in out of the cold. Beginning tomorrow he would wear the arctic gear he had bought in Jermyn Street.

At the door of his room he inserted a plastic credit card in the crack between the door and frame. Working it up and down, he came to a small wad of tissue. But—

But it wasn't where he had left it. He had tucked the tissue in three inches, exactly, below the lock. It was four inches below now. The room had been entered.

Not only that. Whoever had entered it was almost surely in there. An intruder who had come and gone wasn't likely to have replaced the tissue. Why bother?

Bolan pulled the Lahti. He rapped firmly on the door, three times. "Guruk," he said, affecting a high-pitched voice. "Guruk."

Guruk meant nothing, so far as he knew, but if the person inside spoke no Finnish, either, he might take the nonsense word as something from a bellboy.

It worked. The latch turned and—

Bolan kicked the door inward, into the face of the man working the latch. The hardman was staggered, but he was ready with a big revolver. Bolan didn't want to have to explain gunshots to the Helsinki police, so he swung the Lahti in a sweeping backhand and crashed it against the hardman's ear. The hardman's skull cracked. He buckled over and fell sprawling.

No identification. Nothing. Just a .44 revolver and a jacket pocket filled with ammunition. A set of lock picks. A hired hardman. Nobody much. Maybe the White Front was running short of personnel.

But Bolan didn't need a corpse in his room. He needed to get rid of him.

Bolan explored the hotel room. He could stuff the body in the closet. The maid would find it no later than midday tomorrow. In the bathroom he found a hatch in the ceiling. Access to the pipes and heating ducts. With the rope he carried with his blacksuit, he could raise the body of the hardman through the hatch. The body would be found of course. But not for a few days. Not until Frank Vinton was no longer in Finland.

But how had this guy gotten here? How had he known? Not on his own. He had worked for someone. Kleist. Eva. And he was the first try. Somebody else would be along when the dead guy failed to come out saying he had killed the American.

Bolan stripped the outer clothes from the body. He pulled onto the corpse a white shirt from his bag. He propped him in a seated position on the toilet and balanced him with his head down. Then with the rope, he climbed through the hatch in the ceiling and waited, leaving the hatch open so he could see what happened.

He didn't wait long. Within half an hour he heard the faint scratching in the lock that told him someone was entering his room.

He had left the light out in the bathroom, one lamp on in the bedroom. Whoever had entered was quiet. After the inevitable scratching at the lock, his burglar was silent.

A pro. Not a burglar, either. A murderer. Being above the ceiling wasn't a bad advantage.

Slow. Methodical. Careful.

Bolan leveled the muzzle of the Lahti on the bathroom door.

What followed was finished in the space of a second. A man's senses can obtain a lot of images in a second, gain them and hold them for later review like a film that can be run at a slower speed.

The door swung back slowly—kicked gently. Eva. She stood in the bathroom door, dressed in heavy black winter clothing, a stubby submachine gun in her hands—maybe another MAT, but this one looked like an Uzi. Her face was distorted with tension, also with hatred as she saw the figure sitting on the toilet. She fired. The gun was set on semiautomatic, and it was thoroughly silenced. Close as Bolan was, all he heard was a staccato slap-slapping, as if someone were clapping hands. But the body of the hardman was lifted off the toilet seat by the impact of half a dozen slugs. It fell away to the side, and Eva backed out of the door.

She didn't know she hadn't killed Bolan. He could be sure. One of the images he retained was a sneer of utter satisfaction that had come over her face as her slugs slammed into the body on the toilet.

He could have killed her. But better this way. This way she would go back to Kleist and report she had at last killed Mack Bolan. The hardman had taken their money and run, but she had succeeded. They would find out in a day or two that she had failed again. They would inquire about a police investigation into a killing in the hotel and would learn that nobody had found a body or called the police. By then he would be at Purumavaarra and beyond, his business there maybe finished.

It took two hours to hoist the body into the crawl space above the trapdoor and clean every trace of blood from the bathroom.

LEO TUOMINEN WAS the name of the pilot. He was taciturn, maybe because his English was limited. Fifty-five years old at least, he wore a leather jacket, breeches and boots and seemed conscious of his image as a rather romantic flying character.

The high-wing, single-engine Cessna was equipped with skis as well as wheels. So far as Bolan could tell, Tuominen navigated by compass and not much more, but he seemed confident he knew what he was doing and where he was going. They flew northeast over snow-covered forested land dotted with lakes large and small—though many lakes, Tuominen explained, were obscure because they were covered with ice and snow. He didn't climb high. His altimeter was calibrated in meters, and Bolan noticed that he didn't climb much above one thousand meters.

They landed at a lakeside airport called Kajaani to refuel, use the bathroom, buy sandwiches and refill a big thermos with near-boiling tea. When they took off from there the sun was already low and white. It was all but set when Tuominen brought the airplane down on its skis on a runway Bolan found invisible.

"Apukka," he said.

Apukka had the aura of an Alaskan gold rush town— Lapps in furs seemed disinterested in going in out of the cold. Tuominen insisted that there was only one place to stay. He would show Bolan. What he emphatically recommended as the best bar-restaurant-hotel in town, in a log building, was also, surprisingly, a bordello staffed with Lapp girls with happy, shiny faces. Tuominen was accustomed to it. He ordered rooms for both of them, since he could speak the language, and offered in English to sit down to dinner with Bolan and order for him—if, of course, Bolan would stand the expense of their two dinners and their drinks.

Drinks proved to be a liter of vodka. Dinner was platters of greasy meat with potatoes.

Tuominen wasn't displeased. He was a small but muscular, bald, gimlet-eyed man. He arranged early for one of the Lapp girls to spend the night with him.

"You stay here?" he asked Bolan skeptically. Obviously he couldn't believe any American in his right mind would stay any longer than he had to in Apukka. "I fly back tomorrow. Could fly back the next day, for the money."

"Tell me," said Bolan. "Can you land at Purumavaarra?"

Tuominen shook his head. "Purumavaarra. No landing strip there."

"You have skis on your plane."

Tuominen shook his head again. "Very dangerous. Hit rock or stump under snow. It's dark all day there, this time of year."

"Can you land any place nearer Purumavaarra? Nearer than here, I mean."

"Oh... maybe. What you have in mind?"

"Suppose you could find a place where you can land, somewhere close to Purumavaarra. What would you charge to fly me there?"

Tuominen shrugged. "You pay in English pounds, huh? Say two hundred and fifty."

"Let's say four hundred, and you keep it a secret."

"Good. Deal."

"I'm looking for a base camp an oil company has established somewhere north of Purumavaarra, maybe northeast. I'm not sure just where it is. I want you to fly me up there tomorrow. I want to fly around looking for it."

"In the dark you think you find it?"

"Maybe better than in the light. They have to have light, don't they?"

Tuominen shrugged. "If you think so. I can't promise to find anything. Big country." He shrugged again. "Of course . . . if you see something, probably it's what you're looking for. Not many camps out on that tundra."

"If we find it, I want you to land as near as you can and let me out."

"Let you out? In that country? You pay in advance."

"Right. And for another four hundred, you come back and get me."

"Oil . . ." said Tuominen skeptically.

"Why not?" asked Bolan innocently. "They found it on the North Slope in Alaska."

TUOMINEN WAS WHAT in North America would have been called a bush pilot. He watched without comment but with a critical eye as Bolan loaded his arctic gear into the back of the airplane. It was ten in the morning. He would take off before sunup, so they could be north of Purumavaarra before it got its hour of weak sunlight, a little before and a little after noon. The sun wouldn't rise there, really, but the sky would lighten, and he would be able to scan the ground. If he couldn't see the lights of the base, maybe he could identify the runway. If a Foxbat was to take off on the tundra, someone had to have cleared and leveled a runway.

At an altitude of one thousand meters, they could see the lights of tiny villages as they flew northeast from Apukka. That was because Tuominen had chosen to navigate by following a highway. After half an hour, when the cold gray gleam of the sun had begun to appear off the right rear of the airplane, Tuominen banked and turned to the right. From then on he was obviously flying with the compass.

At first there were village lights to the right and left at a distance; and then there were no lights at all, and they were flying over bleak, empty land. It was lowland, tundra, with little vegetation. Although it was covered with snow, plainly the snow cover was light, for Bolan could see bare patches where the wind had blown all the snow away. Endless, endless gray.

Tuominen opened his big thermos of scalding tea and poured two tin cups half-full.

"Lucky with this weather," he said. "Wind not bad."

It was bad enough, Bolan noticed, that Tuominen had the nose of the airplane turned about twenty degrees north of the course it was making over the landscape. This was robbing them of speed and of the little light they would have to scan the landscape beyond Purumavaarra.

Tuominen pointed a little right of the nose. "Purumavaarra," he said.

Bolan was glad he hadn't tried the drive from Apukka. The road coming up from the south to Purumavaarra was a winding single track, partly drifted over with snow. The village itself was a cluster of low, dark buildings, huddled together in the cheerless cold. White smoke drifted away from a dozen chimneys, then was caught by the wind and dispersed.

"Northeast," said Bolan.

"Not much east," said Tuominen. "Soviet frontier, thirty-five kilometers. Murmansk, two hundred. You fly across that line, MiGs come out of Murmansk in a swarm, shooting."

"Then north of Purumavaarra," said Bolan. "And a little east."

Tuominen nodded. "You run out of tundra just a little north," he said. "Higher ground. Two river valleys."

"I expect they've built a landing strip," said Bolan. "I want to look for land flat enough for a long landing strip."

"Ah, CIA man."

"*Not* a CIA man," said Bolan so firmly that Tuominen decided it would be discreet not to suggest it again.

Tuominen pulled back the throttle, and the little airplane lost altitude, coming down quietly over the forbidding land. There was not much area to search. The Soviet frontier limited them to the east. Tuominen knew the area and followed a small frozen river north from Purumavaarra. The land to either side wasn't suitable for a landing strip, but Tuominen followed the river for a few minutes. To the north it made a sharp turn to the east and then looped back to the south, almost paralleling its former course. Tuominen pointed to the northwest, to another river that flowed away to the west. Between these two rivers there was a divide, three or four miles of higher land—flat, suitable for an airstrip.

Bolan understood. Without words Tuominen had said, if you are going to build an airstrip in this area, there is the place for it.

Bolan had read of the Foxbat that it was designed to require a hard-surfaced runway three thousand feet long. Obviously there could be no such thing there. On the other hand, frozen earth, scraped smooth, was as good as pavement; and a skilled pilot who knew what he was doing could sharply cut the normal takeoff roll of any aircraft.

"Buildings," said Tuominen.

Yeah. Buildings. One long, low shed, surrounded by a cluster of half a dozen huts. And beyond— Sure. The runway. Two thousand feet, maybe twenty-five hundred. Flat. Narrow. But absolutely without trees or rocks. If you flew over at ten thousand feet, you didn't have a chance of noticing it. If you flew over at a thousand or so, as they were doing now, you would see if it you knew what you were looking for.

Something else Bolan had purchased in the Jermyn Street store was a set of binoculars, small, with a restricted field of view, but very powerful. Bolan scanned the base. The shed was a prefabricated hangar. The huts were support buildings, living quarters and the like. A litter of cans and trash lay around some of the huts.

And the clincher. What made it certain. In an open space a few yards from the shed—a wind sock.

"No closer to the Soviet Frontier," said Tuominen. "Too close now. They're not always very careful about drawing the line."

"So where can you put me down?"

"West. Northwest. You'll have to cross river to get back. But it's small, frozen."

"How far?"

"I have to find place to land. Say, thirty-five, forty kilometer. Sorry. Can't do better."

"Good enough," said Bolan.

He was already reading the airplane's compass, noting the reciprocal of the course Tuominen was flying. He glanced around for landmarks. Little point. Everything looked alike. He'd have to rely on a compass heading to return to the base.

"You read the *magnetic* compass," said Tuominen. "It's all off in this latitude, but so is the one you'll be carrying. Off more than twenty degrees. Look at chart."

So the old bush pilot carried a chart after all. It was a low-altitude chart, showing terrain landmarks such as rivers, lakes, villages and the international boundary. Bolan located Purumavaarra and then the flat, high land between the two rivers, where the base was laid out.

The last daylight was failing when Tuominen let out his wing flaps and cut his engine. Bolan was always surprised at how slowly these small planes settled to the ground. Tuominen had chosen the frozen surface of a pond for his landing. The wheels and skis worked together. The plane partly slid, partly rolled, over rough ice. Tuominen held the nose high, for braking, and the Cessna at length skidded gently into a bank of snow and light brush at the end of the pond.

"Rendezvous," said Bolan.

Tuominen nodded. "When?"

"Saturday. Noon. If you don't see me here, don't land. I'll try to make a signal for you, maybe a fire. Look out for helicopters. Don't let them see you land. Can I keep the chart?"

"Sure. You're going to need more than that. You sure you want to stay here?"

Bolan nodded. "Wish me luck."

"That's what you're going to need. Luck. I wish you a lot of it."

CHAPTER TWENTY-FOUR

Bolan had been to the Arctic before. One of the worst things about the Arctic was isolation, a sense that you were a thousand miles from another human being, maybe miles from anything that lived, because the environment was so hostile no one and nothing wanted to live there. He was gripped by that sense of isolation as he watched the little airplane lift off the ground, bank to the north and climb away to the west.

He was on the ground. It was dark. The temperature had to be forty degrees below zero. A brisk wind whipped ice crystals off the ground and stung his face.

He had the Lahti, the Uzi and the knife, plus some cold-weather equipment—a tiny propane stove, matches in waterproof containers, goggles against the wind and stinging ice, fatty rations, tea, coffee, salt and excellent cold-weather clothing. He slung the Uzi inside his parka, where it would be protected against the worst of the cold. He wore the knife outside and the Lahti in a fleece-lined holster at his waist.

Okay. He had twenty-five or thirty miles to go, as the crow flies—more if he had to circle the river Tuominen said he could cross. He had a day and a half—and a little more—to do it.

Light and darkness were no measure here. Instinct said it was dark and time to think of making camp. Reason said it was only midafternoon and time to cover some miles before making camp.

Anyway, it wasn't entirely dark. A crescent moon hung low and gave some light. The aurora flashed eerily. Bolan shot the little beam of a penlight on his compass, fixed his direction and identified a low hill with a distinctive stand of small trees as his target for half an hour's walk.

He set his pack comfortably on his shoulders and set off, trudging purposefully but carefully toward the hill.

He couldn't judge distance except by the time it took him to walk to a landmark. He kept his eyes on the hill and trees and established a pace. It took him three-quarters of an hour to reach the low ridge and the trees. From there he chose a more distant goal, a saddle in another ridge, and he set off again.

He walked into lower land between the two ridges, so low in fact that the saddle was out of sight and he had to use the compass to make sure he wasn't wandering off course.

Looking back from where he had come, he saw he was making a track. Studying the track, he saw that it disappeared maybe a quarter of an hour after he moved on. The wind blew snow into the marks of his footsteps and obscured them.

In the lowland between the ridges he realized he was walking over ice sometimes. In the short summer this land probably thawed into a sticky marsh. Now it was frozen solid. He kept an eye on the ground and sometimes saw the tracks of small animals. He was alert for wolves. He knew there were packs of them in this country.

He was surprised at how little he felt the cold. Even his feet, which pounded the frozen ground, weren't cold. His clothes weren't heavy enough to be an encumbrance, to restrict his movements. In fact, he felt good. It was good to walk in the clean, cold air under a rising moon with the aurora flashing overhead, putting the miles behind him.

The simplicity of it appealed to him. He had thought that while he was out here on this trek his mind would fill with dark images. In fact, the exertion of the hike was just enough to dominate his attention. He watched where he was going, tried to keep track of time and distance and covered ground. And that was good.

It cleared his mind. He forgot nothing. But he was able to focus more on what he had to do.

He covered six or seven miles, maybe even ten, and then he judged it was time to make camp and rest.

A part of his kit was a nylon tarp, so thin it had folded into a small packet, but close-woven and impregnable to the wind. That was its purpose, to afford a man a shelter from the wind and whipping ice. He spread it over a pair of stunted pines and weighted its corners and edges with rocks. He cut the branches off other pines around the area and spread them over the frozen ground to give him some insulation from the cold below.

When he was huddled inside his makeshift tent, he struck a match and lit the little propane stove. He put a tin cup of snow on the flame and soon had hot water for tea. He made strong tea and laced it with sugar. That was good for energy. He opened two of his cans and ate the greasy meat.

It was odd how little a man needed to be comfortable and content. He took off his gloves and warmed his hands before he turned off the propane, and when he weighted down the last gap in his makeshift tent and shut out the wind and ice, he was cozy and drowsy. He doubted he would sleep long, but he would sleep and renew his strength, and whenever he woke he could start out again.

WHEN HE WOKE he was cold, and he had a vague sense that something had wakened him—something threatening. He sat still and silent for a time, listening.

Nothing.

But he was cold. He lit the propane and made another cup of hot tea. The heat and the sugar revived him.

It was after midnight. The moon was setting. The aurora would provide a little light, but it was going to be dark.

He struck his little tent, took a compass bearing on still another hill or ridge, and set out again.

The river. Tuominen had said he would have to cross a river, or hike around it. And here it was. In the States it would have been called a creek. In many parts of the world it was a river. Here, for him, it was a problem.

He knelt at the edge and struck at the ice with his knife. Solid. Safe to walk on. But out there a little, black ice. Under that ice the water was flowing. An inch of ice? Not enough. Two inches? Maybe. But if he went through, it was death. For sure.

River ice was always treacherous. No matter how cold the air was above, the water flowing beneath the ice was above freezing. The bottom of the ice was constantly swept by a current of water a few degrees above freezing. If the current was slow, the cold above would penetrate and prevent its being gradually scoured away. If the water ran swift, it would weaken the ice and create deadly traps.

The river was less than twenty yards wide, but he dared not chance it.

Bolan sat on the bank and studied Tuominen's chart in the thin yellow beam of the penlight. Right here this river ran east and west. To the east it ended in the tundra, the lowland that probably fed it. To go there, to try to find its source and cross the tangle of little streams that fed it, would detour him ten miles, maybe more, according to the chart.

He checked the compass. The base was south of this river. He had to cross it. He began to move upstream, exploring.

The problem was, there were no big trees here—even if he had an ax to fell one. He couldn't make a raft. He couldn't make a bridge. The best he could do was look for a narrower place, where maybe he could crawl out on the ice gradually, testing and slipping forward and maybe making the crossing without cracking through.

The river widened. For a distance it flowed between low banks and spread out to more than a hundred yards wide. Very likely it was shallow. Likely if he cracked through the ice he wouldn't be in deep water. But at this temperature, water up to his waist could be fatal.

There were tracks on the ice. Big animals. With hooves. Also wolves. Maybe the big animals used their hooves to crack the ice and drink, and the wolves came to hunt. And not long ago, either. Tracks didn't last long here.

Bolan moved on. The country ahead was higher. Maybe the river ran through a narrow valley, even a gorge.

The moon set. But the sky wasn't entirely dark. Apart from the aurora, the sky was never entirely dark. It glowed faintly, and made enough light for a man to move carefully. Then—lucky for him—the aurora shimmered spectacularly; a curtain of red and green glowed across almost the whole sky. It persisted and made it easier for Bolan.

He had to keep track of where he was going. When he came to the river, he had estimated the base was twelve or fifteen miles away and at 160 degrees magnetic. Now he had moved more than a mile to the east. The base would be at about 165 degrees.

He climbed into the higher land, where the wind swept almost all snow off the rocky ground. The river had cut through here. It ran in a little valley, and the rocks on both sides confined it to a narrower course. In the valley, protected from the wind, the snow lay a foot deep. It was marked with the tracks of dozens of small animals. He was leaving a permanent track, he noticed. There were little evergreens in the valley, with some other small, tough vegetation he couldn't identify.

And now he saw water. The river, running swiftly through a shallow but narrow gorge, coursed along an ice-free channel, black water gurgling and pitching. The rocks to either side were covered with slippery ice.

Bolan looped his nylon rope around the base of a four-foot evergreen. He tested it. Then he began to let himself down the slippery rocks toward the edge of the water. When he was as close as he dared go, and on a flat place, he used his knife to carve out a secure place to plant his feet before he pulled the rope down. Standing there in the dark valley, he appraised his situation. He could get across here. It was risky, but he could do it.

The distance to the rocks opposite him was no more than four feet. He could jump that distance, easily. The problem was that he would come down on ice and slip back into the water. The solution was to anchor the rope on the opposite side and use it to hold himself from slipping when he jumped across.

Four feet. A little beyond, a scrub pine. Make a loop. Lasso that pine.

He made the loop and tossed. The loop missed the tree. He tried again. The loop flattened as he threw it and wouldn't drop over the spread of the little tree. He tried again, and again.

He realized that he could toss the lasso all night, and it would never fall over that tree. This kind of rope was too flexible. A cowboy's hemp rope had a stiffness to it that held the loop open as it flew. The nylon didn't.

Bolan stood at the edge of the water, breathing heavily. He wasn't even sure how he could get back up the bank he had come down.

As he stood thinking, trying to figure a way, he began to untie the slip knot he had put in the rope. It didn't untie easily. He'd dragged the rope back through the water, and the knot was frozen.

Frozen . . . Hell, yes! He pulled a wide loop and dropped it in the water. As he pulled it out and held it in the air, the nylon stiffened. The loop became stiff as wire.

He began to toss again, and the loop stayed open. All he had to do was hit the target with it. On the tenth or twelfth try, the frozen nylon noose fell over the little pine. Bolan tugged. The loop and knot were so stiff the loop resisted closing. But gradually it slipped and tightened on the trunk of the pine. He had his way across.

He tightened the strap over the Uzi, then closed the flap over the Lahti. Next he checked the straps on his backpack. For insurance, he tied the nylon rope around his middle.

He looked up at the sky and waited for the glare of the aurora to give him a little extra light. When it did, he jumped.

His boots came down on solid ice, frozen an inch or more thick on a sloping rock, and Bolan slid backward. He grabbed forward on the nylon rope, but as he did he fell forward. His chin struck the ice, and for an instant he was stunned. His hands loosened on the rope, and he slid instantly back into the cold, rushing water.

To his chest.

His clothes were waterproof, but not against immersion; and he felt the shock of the frigid water.

He gripped the rope as his body shuddered in protest against this violent invasion, and with desperate exertion he hauled himself out of the water—onto a crazily-tilted sheet of ice and into air far colder than the water. He crawled up, tugging on the rope, until he reached the little pine that had saved his life for the moment. Above it the land sloped upward, a rough bank of ice and snow and rock.

Bolan scrambled up, searching for a flat place. The skin on his face and throat burned as the water there froze. His hands, inside soaked mittens, turned numb. He felt himself weakening. He had challenged the Arctic, and it was having its revenge.

He rolled over the top of the riverbank onto a terrace five yards wide, a place nearly flat before the land sloped steeply above. He threw himself down on the snow and jerked off his backpack.

The stove. The propane stove. He yanked it from the pack and set it before him. His hands were almost too stiff to strike a match, but he managed after four tries to strike one and move it into the stream of gas he had already started. The gas lit. A hot blue flame stood over the stove.

For a moment he put his hands in the heat, then his face. But the wind blew around him, and the stream of heat from the little blue flame was quickly dissipated in the cold air.

He had to have a fire. A big fire. A wood fire.

There were evergreens around. Desperately he hacked at branches. In a minute he had a small bundle of branches covered with green needles. He held them to the propane flame, and they caught. He put them down, burning, and hacked at others.

The evergreen brush, rich with oily resin, crackled into hot, smoky flame. But it wasn't enough. Trembling, still feeling his strength ebb, Bolan scrambled on his hands and knees to a larger scrub pine. For a minute he hacked at it with the knife before he realized it would take him ten minutes or more to cut through the tough trunk. Breathing in gasps, he drew the Uzi from under his wet parka. He set it to fire full automatic, thrust the muzzle at the trunk of the tree and fired a burst of six or eight slugs. A couple whacks with the knife finished the job, and he was able to throw the whole tree on the fire.

Alternating between pressing himself as close as he could to the flame and shooting down evergreens, he took another fifteen minutes to build the roaring, lasting fire he needed. Only then did he dare begin to undress.

He wrapped himself in the nylon. He propped his wet clothes—now crackling stiff with ice—on extra trees that would be thrown on when needed, and he huddled close to the red, sparking fire.

He held the Uzi close to the fire until the ice that had formed on it melted and the water dried. Then he did the same for the Lahti.

When his body was dry, he found he could make short dashes to a small tree, blast if off and bring it back to throw on the fire, covered only with the nylon, or even without it. He relit the propane stove and made tea. He drank hot, sugary tea and ate another can of the fatty meat.

Maybe the smell of the fatty meat brought the wolves. Or maybe they were attracted by their curiosity about the fire. In either case he became aware of them. He saw their eyes first, filled with reflections of the fire. Then they stepped boldly out of the brush and stood staring at him, no more than ten or fifteen feet away.

Man and beast, both hunters, watched each other warily—judging. They were small and wiry, not the great gray animals he had thought wolves would be. They demonstrated their family instinct for working in packs. One alone would have been no great menace to a man. A dozen were— and they knew it.

He understood something of their tactics. He knew how they attacked. He set the Uzi on semiautomatic and waited.

After maybe ten minutes a leader advanced closer. He came away from the pack and walked boldly up to within five feet of Bolan.

"I'd rather not have to kill you, old boy," Bolan said.

He threw a smoldering stick of wood toward the wolf. It hit him, actually, and he sidestepped and turned for a moment to regard it with resentful curiosity. Then he moved forward another foot or two—and now the pack moved out and came closer, too.

"Okay."

Bolan shot the leader. The big slug threw the wolf back, and it fell into the snow and died silently.

The others growled and pawed the ground. One, bolder than the others, trotted forward and sniffed at the dead leader. He broke away, snarling at Bolan. He circled then, twisting his neck to keep an eye on the man in the light of the fire, snarling as he moved. He was the new leader, and this was a tactic.

Bolan couldn't let them move in from all sides at once. He had to break their tactic. He shot the new leader.

And suddenly, as abruptly as they had appeared, the wolves were gone. They went silently. He couldn't judge how far. But from what he had heard of wolves, they had abandoned this menacing intruder and gone their way.

His fire burned for four hours before his clothes were dry. He wearied himself scampering into the brush, blasting off and carrying back small trees to burn. When at last he let it die down, and prepared to move again, he could be sure of one thing—no other human being was working the area; if anyone had been, he would surely have come to see who was firing short bursts of automatic rifle fire and keeping an immense blaze streaming sparks into the sky.

Reaching the high ground above the valley of the little river, Bolan estimated that the base was now at 170 degrees. He chose a distant hill, maybe five miles away, and trudged off toward it.

A man couldn't walk at anything like a normal pace in this country. The darkness slowed him down. He came to small feeder streams he had to cross, each one carefully. The first hint of daylight—daylight that would never really materialize—revealed details of the horizon. He wasn't within sight of any habitation.

As he reached the hill he had guessed was five miles away, and climbed it, he hoped from the crest he would catch sight of the base. But no. Not yet. He checked his compass, identified a new goal and set out for it.

Maybe he and Tuominen had underestimated the distance they had flown yesterday afternoon. It was frustrating to have to walk over miles that he had flown over in a few minutes. Yet he could see the pilot had been right; he couldn't have landed anywhere short of the place he had chosen. The land was like rough corrugated steel, rolling ridges and valleys—except that the ridges and valleys didn't lie in neat parallel lines but crisscrossed, punctuated with outcroppings of rock and stands of stunted trees.

Bolan stopped and scratched a set of triangles in the snow, using the compass heading they had flown yesterday afternoon and the distance they had estimated as one leg, his eastward walk along the river as a base line, and angles to the base as alternative third sides. He remained convinced that the compass heading from where he stood to the Foxbat base had to be roughly 170 degrees.

There was nothing to do but set off at 170 degrees magnetic and keep walking.

It wasn't as invigorating as it had been. Falling in the water, nearly freezing, the struggle to build the fire and keep it blazing the long time it took to dry his clothes, plus the discouragement of mounting ridge after ridge without any sign of the base—all this was sapping his strength. He could understand what he had learned in survival school so many years ago, how the Arctic gradually bore in on a man and wore him down.

He had the remainder of this day and all night to reach the base. He remained confident he would make it, if he had no more accidents and didn't get lost. But by noon, eleven hours after he had last slept, he decided it was time to stop and rest.

He made camp against a rock that sheltered him from the wind. The nylon tarp broke it from the other side. He

checked the fuel level in the propane stove. It was holding
out nicely. He made tea. He decided, too, that he would fry
some of his canned meat, as the instructions on the can said
he could. He spooned it into his mess kit, put that over the
flame, and in a minute the fatty meat was sputtering and
giving off a savory smell. He wished he had a few eggs.

He slept three hours, more than he had expected to sleep.
He woke to something encouraging—the distinctive slap-
ping sound of helicopter rotor blades.

He couldn't see the choppers. He had slept through the
hours of gray daylight. But he could hear them. Three helicopters, maybe four. They landed somewhere near, somewhere within a few miles. The base.

He left his tarpaulin tent and climbed the nearest ridge,
hoping to see the helicopters lift off, to confirm his idea of
the direction of the base. But he never saw them. After they
had been on the ground maybe twenty minutes, they lifted
off again, one by one. He could hear them distinctly, but
they showed no lights, and they kept to a low altitude. Obviously they had swept into the base, keeping low to avoid
radar detection, and now they were sweeping out the same
way.

Okay. Now he knew. For sure.

He broke camp, set out at 170 degrees, and as the moon
rose and the aurora began to light the landscape, he
marched another mile, then another, and so on.

About midnight he spotted the base. So obscure was it, so
well did they conceal their lights, that he walked down the
side of the ridge that faced it and started across the last mile
of frozen ground before he realized he was upon it.

It had taken him more than thirty hours to find it.

He had time. The way he figured, the Foxbat would stay
in its hangar another ten hours.

He had read up on the Foxbat. It was fast. It was capable of intercepting the President's plane, flying into Stock-

holm from Washington, and shooting it down with a long-range air-to-air missile.

Holmesby-Lovett had said the Foxbat would fly south along the Finnish-Soviet frontier at hilltop level, to avoid radar. Then it would climb to its operational altitude and streak across the skies of Finland toward its rendezvous with the President's 707. When it first appeared on radar, it would be climbing west, just at the frontier. It would look like a Soviet interceptor off a base inside the Soviet Union, violating Finnish airspace.

No one would guess, probably, that it was on its way to assassinate the President of the United States. Only after it had completed its mission would the nations of the world reconstruct the radar evidence—that a Foxbat interceptor had flown from a Soviet base and murdered the President. It lacked the range to return. The pilot would eject somewhere over the Gulf of Bothnia, probably; the Foxbat would be destroyed by a powerful explosion; then let somebody try to identify it more fully from the shreds that would fall into the deep, cold water.

By the time anyone could possibly discover the Foxbat hadn't flown out of Russia, the damage to international relations would have been done. If the world wasn't at war, it would be near it.

The President's plane was due in Stockholm about noon. The Foxbat had to fly, first, about three hundred miles down the border. That was bad duty for a MiG-25. Three hundred miles at a low altitude where none of its special capabilities could be used. Probably it wouldn't break the sound barrier for that three hundred miles, to make it more difficult to detect as a supersonic interceptor. So it might take forty minutes to fly that distance. Then it would climb and accelerate to its optimal speed, mach 2.5 or above, and it would cover the remaining six hundred miles in a little more than twenty minutes. It could make the intercept in an hour. Since it might have to hunt a little and might want to make the intercept a little west of Stockholm, likely it would take off around 10:30 a.m., maybe even a little sooner since the President's plane might be early.

If he could somehow enter the hangar, he could destroy the Foxbat with a few carefully placed shots to vital parts. More likely he would have to fire on it after it was rolled out, maybe even as it made its takeoff run.

He had studied the structural drawings of the Foxbat. To destroy one with sixty-four rounds from an Uzi—and that was all he would have—would require careful shooting. As he saw it, he had two options—to fire into the fuel tanks contained in the wing nearest to him, so cutting the aircraft's fuel supply significantly and maybe shredding the wing so much as to interfere with supersonic flight, or to shoot at the tires as the Foxbat rolled down the runway. The cockpit would be a more difficult target. Also, it might be armored.

He had time. He sat down and checked the Uzi to make sure its action wasn't frozen. He checked the Lahti. It was made for this climate, and its action worked smoothly.

He put the binoculars to his eyes and surveyed the base.

Doors opened. Men came and went between the huts and the hangar. He couldn't identify them at this distance. That is, he couldn't tell technicians from hardmen—and it would be important to know, after a while. But there was no question about what was there. The prefab building was a hangar.

Time to move closer.

With the Uzi in hand and ready, he walked down the last slope and began a march across the flat land. Tuominen had guessed this one right. Damn! what would he have done if he hadn't accidentally found that pilot? Tuominen had identified this shallow valley as the only mile-long stretch of flat land within a twenty-five mile radius of Purumavaarra.

He found it difficult to believe what the White Fronters had done. In this narrow, shallow valley, in an impossibly remote area of Finnish tundra, they had somehow managed to scrape a flat runway and haul in—unquestionably in pieces—a MiG-25 Foxbat.

If that was what was in that hangar. If he wasn't here on a fool's mission.

There had to be security. They couldn't be doing what they were doing without guarding it. Sensors, he figured. Mounted around. Sensors listening for sound, seeking infrared, seeking magnetic anomalies. People who spent what somebody had spent to establish this base and bring here what they had, didn't skimp on security.

He stopped often and scanned the base through the binoculars. Hardmen. It figured. They stayed inside mostly, but when they came out, their submachine guns were evident.

He made a head count and identified half a dozen. Probably there were three times that many.

The hours of night and day didn't mean much here, but the base was alive and active in the hours after midnight. Sure. It *would* be. In a few hours they were going to send their bird south and west to kill the President of the United States. Yeah, and make it look like the Soviets had done it. They had a lot of getting ready to do.

He found it odd that their perimeter security didn't extend out very far. He'd supposed he would trip something when he was two or three hundred yards out. But so far nothing.

A dozen hardmen. Maybe twenty. Half of them asleep. What would happen if he just charged the place, Uzi spitting? What if he hit the Foxbat with a clip of 9 mm parabellum before they knew what was happening?

He'd die, that's what would happen. He might make it, but it would be the end of Mack Bolan. And if so, maybe that was what it had to be, to stop this thing.

On the other hand, what were the odds? The hardmen would be defending a restricted perimeter, one they had rehearsed defending. Their devices would be concentrated around the hangar. Maybe he'd do better to attack the Foxbat after it was rolled out, when they had to disperse in the cold and dark and—

Choppers again!

Bolan turned over and looked up. They swept across the valley, no more than fifty feet above the ground. As he stared at them—three of them—brilliant lights burned from the bottoms of the three helicopters, catching him in a glare of blue-white light.

He huddled on the ground, trying to make himself invisible, tense against the bursts of fire they would—

But they swept right on over.

The lights had been to find the ground, not to find an intruder they still didn't know was there. The three choppers stopped, hovered over the ground, their rotors whirling the light snow into a cloud, then settled to the ground.

What were they bringing here now? Surely every gallon of fuel, every rocket, every—

Men! Men in hats and raincoats.

Yeah. The same men who had been in the meeting in Düsseldorf, likely. Here to make sure everything was done right.

Bolan peered at them through his binoculars. He recognized one, the one who came out to greet the others. Sure. Black hair flying in the wind, gold-rimmed spectacles, red nose—Jean Henriot. He had been at Düsseldorf.

The arrival of the helicopters meant more hardmen on the ground. He watched them milling about, stamping their feet, anxious for permission to go inside, then going in, permission or no.

One by one the doors were closed. The base was dark. Bolan crawled forward, testing the security.

The closer he got, the more apparent it was that the area around the hangar was covered. His best—maybe his only—chance of hitting the Foxbat would be on the runway.

He checked the wind. Even a Foxbat would take off into the wind. The runway ran east-west. The wind was from the west. The pilot would taxi to the east end, then shove in his throttles and charge down the runway east to west. Bolan moved eastward.

So IT ALL CAME down to these few minutes. He studied it all through the binoculars and did everything he could to make himself ready. He waited the remaining hours. After the Foxbat was towed out and everything he had suspected was confirmed, a hardman had taken a shot at him.

So there were perimeter guards. There was one less.

The pilot taxied the Foxbat east. Bolan checked his watch. Ten-thirty. On schedule.

The damn thing was a beautiful airplane. A work of art. Of the engineer's art, something created to serve a purpose and designed for that purpose alone. Useless for anything but what it was designed to do.

Like the Uzi the Israelis had designed to do what he was now about to try to do with it.

Now at the last moment the hangar doors opened. Twenty men stepped out into the cold to watch the Foxbat take off. Bolan would have liked to study their faces through his binoculars, but his attention had to be focused on the Foxbat. He glanced at the huddled men in their big coats, then turned his attention to the aircraft.

It swung around and faced him. He imagined—though he knew his imagination deceived him—that he could see the face of the pilot in the cold electronic glow of the lights on the instrument panel.

Very abruptly, the whine of the engines rose to an intolerable level, and the Foxbat moved toward him.

Bolan unslung the Uzi and rose to his feet.

It would lift from the runway at a 150 miles per hour. It would be rolling at eighty or ninety when it reached him. He knew that from his reading; he would have only seconds to pump bullets into it as it raced by.

He chose to shoot at the tires.

He lifted the Uzi to his shoulder, intending to shoot with sights instead of from the hip.

The Foxbat roared toward him.

Fifty yards. Thirty. The nose wheel was already off.

Bolan squeezed the trigger.

His 9 mm slugs chopped the frozen ground just ahead of the Foxbat's left main gear. The wheel rolled into the stream of slugs. The tire exploded. The strut collapsed. The missiles under the left wing dropped and dug into the ground. One of them flew into the air and detonated in a great yellow-white flash. The wing hit the ground and broke off. The airscoop dug in, and the Foxbat cartwheeled.

It skidded along the remainder of the runway, turning, breaking up. Another missile, left behind, exploded on the ground behind it. The fuselage split. The nose and cockpit veered away while the heavy engines skidded forward.

A thousand miles away the President's 707—not Air Force One, as Bolan supposed, but another Air Force 707—cruised toward the Norwegian coast. Hal Brognola sat in the executive compartment with the President and discussed the problem of the White Front.

THE EXECUTIVE COUNCIL of the White Front didn't understand that their Foxbat had been stopped by a stream of 9 mm slugs. They thought it had struck a rock in the runway.

But they abandoned all pretense at secrecy, turned on all the lights and ran to the wreckage. They even dragged their stunned pilot out of the cockpit.

Bolan watched through his glasses.

"YOU DO THAT?" Tuominen asked as he turned the Cessna around the black scar on the snow and the wreckage of the Foxbat. "Those oil fellows had some funny equipment. Somebody burned it all up."

Bolan studied the scene through his binoculars. Finnish paratroops remained on the scene in force. He had seen them drop a few hours after he had retreated from the base. They had arrived too late to find the helicopters. The three choppers had been long gone.

CHAPTER TWENTY-FIVE

For a moment Bolan thought the woman was Marilyn. She lay on the floor among the men's chairs, strapped tightly inside a white canvas straitjacket. Her ankles were bound together by a leather strap. A red rubber ball, held in her mouth by a tight strap, gagged her. Bolan tensed, but then he saw she wasn't Marilyn. She was Eva Zhulev.

"I guess we shouldn't be surprised," said Sir Alexander Bentwood.

Bolan had just stepped into the library of Sir Alexander's handsome Belgravia town house. He was wearing his blacksuit. He held the Uzi with its muzzle leveled on the men sitting around the fireplace.

"The evening would hardly have been complete without you," Sir Alex went on. "We've met to analyze our disaster, and how could we have done that, really, without a word or two from the man who caused it?"

Bolan stood with his legs apart. His face was hard. His finger lay heavily on the trigger of the Uzi.

"I may as well introduce you," said Sir Alex. He nodded to each of the men seated in leather chairs, as he pronounced their names. "Herr Doktor Johann Kleist. Monsieur Jean Henriot, I believe you've met. Signor Aldo Vicaria you haven't met. And Gospodin Lavrenti Potopova."

"And Eva Zhulev," said Bolan coldly. "We've met."

"Ah, yes. Eva."

"Let her out of that thing," said Bolan, gesturing with the muzzle of the Uzi.

"I'd be happy to," said Sir Alex. "It is Doktor Kleist who has the flair for the dramatic and brought her here in that condition."

Bolan turned the Uzi toward Kleist. "Unstrap her," he said. *"Now."*

"Do you think you are in command here, Herr Bolan?" asked Kleist.

"I am for the moment," said Bolan, "wouldn't you say?"

Kleist fixed his eyes on the muzzle of the Uzi. "For the moment," he said. He knelt over Eva Zhulev and began to unfasten her straps.

"Bolan..." said Sir Alex, watching Kleist loosen the buckles and straps of the straitjacket. "It *was* you...? I mean, out there in the dark, north of Purumavaarra. That was you."

Bolan allowed himself a faint smile. "Your men never came near me. They didn't seem to have any training for Arctic hunting."

"Then you knew. You saw—"

"I saw *you*. Through my binoculars. The Foxbat fell apart, and all of you came running."

"We couldn't believe we had been attacked," said Sir Alex.

"It was Major Alani, our pilot," said Aldo Vicaria, "who insisted a man had risen from the snow by the runway and fired at his aircraft." Vicaria seemed able to tell this serenely, as if none of it made any difference to him. "For a while we didn't believe him. And we didn't send anyone to hunt you, Mr. Bolan. Then Major Alani showed us the bullet holes in the magnesium wheel."

Bolan looked at the floor where Eva Zhulev sat dazed, rubbing her wrists and shifting her eyes to Bolan, then back to herself. She was dressed in a short black skirt and a gray sweatshirt. She looked up at Kleist, pleading.

"Failure," he sneered at her. "Useless."

"She tried," said Bolan. "You can't fault her."

Kleist smiled sarcastically. "We do not honor failure, Mr. Bolan," he said. "We *do* fault failure, whatever its cause. Nothing can—"

"Then commit suicide, Herr Doktor," said Bolan, "because *you* have failed repeatedly. She's no more a failure than you."

"That's *my* decision to make," snapped Kleist.

"No, it isn't," said Bolan. "Not anymore. Get up, Eva. Pull up a chair for yourself."

"Thank you, Bolan," she whispered.

Bolan lifted his chin. "Where's Marilyn?"

"Miss Henry? She's here," said Sir Alex. "Ah, yes. I know. You and she—"

"I want to see her."

Sir Alex shrugged. "You will have to allow one of us to go get her."

"Is she in a straitjacket, too?"

"Not at all. With your permission..." Sir Alexander Bentwood rose from his chair, went to a door and called, "Marilyn! Marilyn! Please..."

Bolan stood rigid, holding the Uzi on Sir Alex, alert for a trick.

Sir Alex returned to his chair and sat down, leaving the door open. A moment of silence. Then Marilyn appeared in the doorway.

"Mack!"

She wasn't harmed. She was wearing a yellow sweater and a pair of tightly tailored gray wool slacks. She stood in the door, obviously astonished. Her eyes darted from Bolan to Sir Alex and back again.

"Your hero," Sir Alex said to her dryly. "Come to rescue you."

She closed her eyes and shook her head. "Mack," she murmured. "God . . ."

"Mr. Bolan," said Sir Alex, "you haven't been properly introduced. Allow me to present Fräulein Lili Gürtner of the Ministerium für Staats-Sicherheit."

Marilyn still stood in the door, facing Bolan. Her face had first drained white, then flushed. She stared at Bolan. She licked her lips and dabbed at her eyes with one finger.

"You will want the whole story," said Sir Alex.

"I believe I'm entitled to it," said Bolan.

"I do care for you, Mack," she whispered. "I really do."

"Which rendered her ineffective," sneered Kleist. "Worthless." He shook his head at Eva. "Worse than that one."

"Come in, Lili," said Sir Alex. "Stand by the fire." He looked at Bolan, his face a mask of calm amusement. "She does care for you, Bolan," he said. "It's true. So do I, in a different sense. You'd be dead if we didn't."

Marilyn—Lili—walked to a sideboard and poured herself a generous drink of Scotch. She carried it to the fireplace, where she leaned against the mantel, took a swallow and lowered her eyes.

"She's brave," said Sir Alex. "Beautiful. Intelligent. And she is—I suppose I should say was—an agent of the East German intelligence organization, MfS. Anyway, she was sent here ten years ago with the cover name Marilyn Henry and a contrived biography that was supposed to make her appear a native-born Englishwoman. She exceeded MfS's highest expectations and became an agent of MI6. Only she wasn't exactly an agent of MfS any longer."

"A double agent," said Bolan.

Sir Alexander Bentwood nodded. "Let us say a triple agent," he said. "Unknown to MfS or MI6, she became an agent of the White Front. It's been a very agile balancing act. MfS still doesn't know. MI6 doesn't know—"

"If *you* know, then MI6—" Bolan began.

"Doesn't know," Sir Alex interrupted. "Doesn't know about me. Didn't know about Edward Holmesby-Lovett. Didn't know about Oscar Cobden. Didn't know about Sir Michael Lansdowne. Just as BND doesn't know about Doktor Kleist, GIGN doesn't know about Jean Henriot, SISDE doesn't know about Aldo Vicaria, the KGB doesn't know about Lavrenti Potopova, and so on."

"Then—"

"Explain it to him, Lili," said Sir Alex.

Marilyn took another great swallow of Scotch. She glanced at Sir Alex, then focused on Bolan. "Where do I start?" she asked dully, as if explaining was really more than she could do.

"I know what the White Front is, if that's any help," said Bolan. "What it *was*."

"What it *is*," said Marilyn. "Don't suppose it's dead, Mack. It isn't."

"Anyway—"

She sighed. "All right. Doktor Kleist killed Friedrich Hohnzecker. Jean Henriot killed Claude Crillon. That is to say, he arranged it. Aldo Vicaria killed Galeazzo Bastianini. Lavrenti Potopova killed Grigori Parotikin. And Sir Michael Lansdowne killed Richard Vauxhall. You see the pattern."

"I've seen it for quite a while," said Bolan.

He shifted the Uzi from one arm to the other. Marilyn stiffened, as if she were afraid he would shoot her.

"All of them were traitors," said Kleist.

"This is true," said Jean Henriot.

"Who was Schellenberg?" asked Bolan.

Sir Alexander nodded at Marilyn, and she continued. "The Front is highly placed in many governments," she said, using skillfully the voice and accent Bolan could hardly believe belonged to a German woman named Lili Gürtner.

"Only one government has officially cooperated—that of the German Democratic Republic. That government—*my* government—doesn't like the cozy little pseudofriendship that has been built up between West and East. It—"

Sir Alex raised a hand and picked up the story. "I turned Lili a long time ago," he said. "Over the years she has kept MI6 well-informed of MfS operations, not just in Britain but all over Europe. Imagine my amusement, Bolan, when the East German government advised me—in conspiratorial secrecy—that it had an agent working in London named Marilyn Henry. By that time Lili wasn't only a traitor to the MfS. She was also a traitor to MI6, having become one of the most valued agents of the Front. MfS advised me that it had sent orders to Miss Marilyn Henry to cooperate with me and follow my orders. Of course, the East Germans expected her to report back to them on everything she learned about the White Front."

Marilyn allowed herself to show Bolan a faint smile. "It has been what Sir Alex suggested," she said. "A difficult balancing act."

Kleist complained. "Whose orders has she been following? Whose? MfS? MI6? Sir Alex? Her heart?"

"Unfortunately," said Sir Alex, "the White Front is composed of a consortium of strong-willed individuals. Different members of the governing council have gone off on their own, doing this, doing that, working at cross-purposes. It—"

"Who wanted to kill me—and who didn't?" asked Bolan.

"*I* wanted to kill you," said Kleist. "From the beginning. I'd heard of you. I thought you were a menace. And—" he glanced around at the others "—I was right."

"There were three attitudes toward you, Mack," said Marilyn. She walked back to the sideboard and poured herself more Scotch. "Doktor Kleist wanted to kill you.

Cobden wanted to kill you. Sir Michael Lansdowne wanted to kill you. My government wanted to kidnap you and use chemicals to drain your head of every idea and every bit of information you had picked up in the past ten years. Those were Schellenberg's orders, and those were mine—from East Berlin. And Sir Alex and I wanted to keep you alive and maybe recruit you. If we would just keep you from spoiling everything, for a few weeks, then we would have accomplished what we wanted to do. And after that we would have been the legitimate force against terrorism in the world, and you might have joined us.''

"You didn't know me very well, Marilyn," said Bolan sadly.

"I thought of us as allies," she said. "Working together. In a good cause."

"Joop Thijn said something like that," said Bolan. "How could you have thought I'd work with people who used bombs to kill hundreds of innocent—''

"Spare us your good morals, Bolan," Sir Alex interrupted. "Finish the story for him, Lili."

"Schellenberg kidnapped you at Heathrow on orders from Berlin," she said.

"And from me," said Kleist grimly. "I was willing to go along, for the moment, with the idea of draining your mind."

"But you killed his hoodlum and escaped from Schellenberg," said Marilyn. "Now we knew you were more dangerous that we had thought. Anyway... a shot was fired at you from a rooftop on Half Moon Street, the first night you were in London. You might have been killed if I hadn't screamed a warning. Right? Not right. Our sharpshooter never meant to hit you. It was an act, something we cooked up to make me look good. Your introduction to me as an agent of MI6.''

"Sir Michael, though, really meant to kill you from that same roof," said Sir Alex. "Working on his own, against my orders. You caught him and threw him off the roof. You executed the man who killed Richard Vauxhall—Mr. Executioner."

"The man who shot at us from Lincoln's Inn Fields," said Marilyn, "was an East German agent, working for me. The idea was to make you think someone had tried to kill *me*—and you had saved me. Bind us together, you know. I didn't want you to kill that man."

"All right," said Bolan darkly. "And in Paris you caught up with me on that motorcycle on the streets of Montmartre—"

"Not because I could ride so fast," Marilyn interrupted. "Because I knew where you were going. That is, I knew where Schmidt was going. I knew where he would lead you if you could catch up with him."

"We didn't have to kill all those people," said Bolan.

"*You* didn't," she said. "*I* did. If you had taken Aimé Rafil alive, she would have told you all she knew. Or she would have told GIGN. She was a professional bomber, and she would have betrayed anyone to get a lighter sentence."

Eva Zhulev had kept her eyes down during most of the conversation. Now she looked up at Bolan. "The night we caught you in Harper's bordello," she said, "I should have killed you. I could have. Schellenberg was acting on orders from Berlin. So was I. We *did* have to pretend at least that we still took our orders from MfS. Who could have guessed that another agent of the Ministerium für Staats-Sicherheit would betray—"

"Not betray," said Sir Alex. "She acted on my orders."

Marilyn nodded at Bolan. "Schellenberg called me and bragged that he had captured you. The chemists were coming to inject you. I called Sir Alex. He told me to try to save you. If I couldn't, Front forces would have assaulted the whorehouse.''

''*You* threw the key. . .'' Bolan murmured.

She smiled. ''I knew you rather well by then, Mack. I knew your powers. I figured if I could come down between those walls and toss you the key, you could climb out. I disabled the charming Eva with a chop across the throat—''

''She killed Schellenberg,'' said Eva.

''And Harper,'' said Marilyn. ''He knew too much. He couldn't be trusted.''

''Of course not,'' said Bolan. ''I understand. And you shot Oscar Cobden between the eyes at Oaks for the same reason you shot Aimé Rafil in Montmartre—to keep him quiet.''

Marilyn tossed back another swallow of Scotch. ''He was expendable,'' she said coldly.

''*You were drugging me!*''

She nodded. ''A little something in your coffee. To keep you from becoming too frisky. The smallest possible dose.''

''Don't think too badly of her, Bolan,'' said Sir Alex. ''When she helped you in Amsterdam—I mean, when Joop Thijn's motorcyclists were shooting at you—she was acting on her own. Even contrary to orders. The dear girl had fallen in love with you, you see. In all these years, Lili never did that before. Interest in men, yes. Close friendships, yes. With me, of course—especially. But never in love. Never so much as to risk anything for a man. You are to be congratulated on that, Bolan. I should like to know how you did it.''

Marilyn glanced at Sir Alex. ''Don't worry about it,'' she said. ''You will never understand, Alex. Certainly you will never duplicate—''

''The night you disappeared?'' Bolan asked Marilyn.

Marilyn sighed. ''You insisted on going to the East German Trade Mission,'' she said. ''I knew I couldn't stop you.

But I couldn't let you get your hands on Eva, either. While I was inside, I simply telephoned her, told her you were coming, *and* told her to get out of that building in Wapping. Instead, she decided to try to kill you. And kill me. Eva wanted to kill me, too.''

Eva lifted her chin defiantly and spoke to Bolan. ''I knew what they'd do to me if I didn't manage some way to kill you. I understand you saw me in the NUG conference room in Düsseldorf. It was because of *her* that I was there. And tonight. You saw...do you have any idea what they've done to me, Bolan?'' She began to cry. She pulled back the sleeves of her sweatshirt and showed him the raw bruises on her wrists, evidence of handcuffs locked on too tight and left that way for many hours, maybe for days. ''Take me with you when you leave. Please. They're going to kill me.''

Kleist sneered. ''He won't take you. You think he's a fool?''

''Please...'' Eva whispered.

''I was in Wapping that night,'' said Sir Alex. ''Lili had called me, too. She got off a shot at Eva and wounded her slightly. Then she was overwhelmed by superior firepower, as we say. She ran to my Jaguar, and we left Wapping.''

''I went down on the river flat,'' Eva whispered. ''In a raincoat that belonged to one of the men. We thought you would look down there sooner or later, when you couldn't find Lili. And you did. And we had another chance to kill you.''

''And failed again,'' muttered Kleist.

''The next day you disappeared,'' said Marilyn.

''And I took off for Helsinki,'' Eva whispered hoarsely. ''I wasn't authorized, but I did. I was afraid you had learned too much from Holmesby-Lovett and would go there. And I was right.''

''She reported she'd killed you there,'' said Kleist. ''That misinformation lowered our guard at Purumavaarra.''

"Who could have killed Bolan?" Eva shrilled. "We all tried. He is invincible! Why is my failure worse—"

"Shut up, Fräulein," said Kleist curtly.

"Why Holmesby-Lovett?" Bolan asked.

"Doktor Kleist," said Sir Alexander Bentwood, "decided to take over the White Front. He went to Edward to recruit him to his side, and when he failed he ordered Eva and her friend Fabian Hastings to kill him. I was next." The handsome Englishman smiled at Bolan. "A little disagreement among friends, you see. And, being a onetime Nazi, Kleist wanted to solve his problem as one of his old heroes would have solved it."

"Another failure of yours, Fräulein," Kleist said to Eva.

"The gun jammed. It *jammed*!" she shrieked.

"But this one won't," said Sir Alexander calmly.

Watching Kleist and Eva, Bolan hadn't noticed the Englishman reach inside his jacket and withdraw a Walther PPK. He swung the muzzle of the Uzi toward Sir Alex. But the Walther wasn't pointed at him. It was aimed at Kleist, and Sir Alex calmly squeezed the trigger and fired four quick shots into Doktor Johann Kleist. The German's body jerked as each shot broke through his ribs, and he slumped gently to one side.

Sir Alex put the pistol aside on the table by his chair. "Good show, Bolan," he said. "You're a calm man not to have pumped a burst into me when you saw the pistol. That was something I had to do, you understand. *He* was the source of our failure, not Eva Zhulev."

Bolan could hardly believe what he saw. The others—the Frenchman, the Italian, Eva and the woman he now had to identify as Lili—witnessed the death of Kleist without a ripple of emotion.

"It had to be done, Mack," said Marilyn—Lili—stoically.

"It simplifies things a good deal," said Bolan. "When Special Branch arrives, they'll have a murder charge. A whole lot simpler to prove in court than—"

"Nothing is going to come to the attention of Special Branch," said Sir Alex. "Much less a court."

"Think not?" asked Bolan.

"Mack..." said Marilyn-Lili quietly. "Mack. *Think*. He's deputy foreign secretary. All of us—even Eva, now that Kleist is dead—that ... well, something. All of us. We'll all testify to something."

"Besides, Bolan," said Sir Alex. "You're not unaware that we've penetrated many agencies. We lost the Foxbat and all that, but our people are still in place. They'll take care of us. Surely—"

"I don't think so," said Bolan. "I don't think you've got it under control. Right now you're bluffing. So I call in Special Branch. Let's see how well you've penetrated."

He reached for the telephone that was on a small table to the right of the fireplace.

"Mack!" cried Marilyn-Lili.

"Bolan—" said Sir Alex.

The Frenchman pulled a pistol and fired a shot past Bolan into the wall before Bolan let loose half a dozen slugs into his throat and face. The Russian, too, and the Italian jerked pistols from under their jackets. Bolan had jumped to one side as he fired on Henriot, and the Russian's shot, accurately fired, passed squarely through the space Bolan had occupied until an instant before. Bolan's next burst took his head off—literally, exploded it and took it off, into the leather chair behind him. Then the Italian. He didn't get off a shot, but he meant to. A short burst of Uzi slugs caught him in the upper chest. Sir Alex grabbed for his Walther, but slugs from the Uzi caught him as he lunged, and he fell to the floor, one shot having caught him in the ear.

Eva Zhulev cringed on the floor, whimpering.

Marilyn-Lili calmly picked up Sir Alex's Walther. She stood with it in her hand, facing Bolan.

"Can you do it, Mack?" she asked quietly.

His eyes were on the pistol more than on her face. If she moved to—

"*I* can't," she said.

He shook his head. "No... I suppose not."

She nodded. "Goodbye, Mack Bolan," she said. "You're the most wonderful man I ever knew. I wish it could have been different. Uh, if you have to. A long burst, please. Quick."

She turned and walked through the door. Bolan watched her go.

THEY SAT TOGETHER in a small, separate dining room in Tiddy Dol's. Neither Hal Brognola nor Sir George Harrington understood that the place had an emotional impact on Bolan, because it was there he had had a romantic dinner with Marilyn—which he still preferred to call her—only three weeks ago. He had nothing to do for a few days, so he let them order drinks and wine and heavy food, and he relaxed.

"We will never be free of their kind," said Sir George, "but the White Front died in Sir Alex's townhouse the other night. There are many strings to be followed to their ends, but you put an end to the Front when you disposed of the last of their governing council."

"They infiltrated—"

"Yes," Sir George interrupted. "MI6. GIGN. BND. And so on. But we've been alerted. We're rooting them out."

Bolan shook his head. "You'll never root them all out."

"No, Striker," said Brognola. "We won't. You're absolutely right. We won't be rid of their like anytime soon, any more than we'll build a perfect world anytime soon. But you won a major victory for us."

"We called in the right man," said Sir George.

"They came close to ending my checkered career," said Bolan bitterly.

"It was a particularly tough one for you, we know," said Brognola. "The President knows. He's been thoroughly briefed. He's been in touch with governments through diplomatic channels, and whatever complaint any of them had is dead. They understand. In fact, they're grateful."

"Am I going to be inducted into the Legion of Honor?"

"Do you want to be?"

Bolan smiled. For the first time he lifted his drink—a tough, dry martini—and took a big swallow. "What was it Napoleon said?" he asked. "That men are motivated by baubles? Why didn't he say *olives*?" He stabbed an olive from his drink and popped it into his mouth. "More value."

Brognola sipped from his drink. "Couple of things," he said. "Eva Zhulev has settled nicely into the routine of a British prison. She had better. She won't be leaving soon."

"And—"

Brognola sighed. "Lili Gürtner—Marilyn Henry— crossed through Checkpoint Charlie day before yesterday. Tonight she's either being toasted at a heroine's banquet in East Berlin, or she's lying in a cell in an MfS prison."

Bolan lifted his glass again. "Who cares?" he said.

Nui Ba Den. Charlie holds the mountain stronghold until
Special Forces takes it back.

VIETNAM: GROUND ZERO..

STRIKE

ERIC HELM

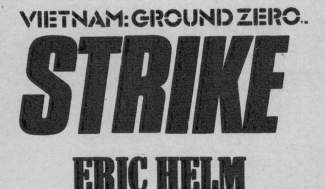

An elite Special Forces team is dispatched when heavy traffic in
enemy supplies to Nui Ba Den has intelligence in Saigon worried.
Primed for action, Mack Gerber and his men wage a firefight deep
inside a mountain fortress, while the VC outside are poised for a
suicide raid against an American political delegation.

Take
4 explosive books
plus a
mystery bonus

Mail to **Gold Eagle Reader Service**

In the U.S.
P.O. Box 1394
Buffalo, N.Y. 14240-1394

In Canada
P.O. Box 609,
Fort Erie, Ont. L2A 5X3

YEAH! Rush me 4 free Gold Eagle novels and my free mystery bonus. Then send me 6 brand-new novels every other month as they come off the presses. Bill me at the low price of just $14.94— an 11% saving off the retail price - plus 95¢ postage and handling per shipment. There is no minimum number of books I must buy. I can always return a shipment and cancel at any time. Even if I never buy another book from Gold Eagle, the 4 free novels and the mystery bonus are mine to keep forever. 166 BPM BPS9

Name   (PLEASE PRINT)

Address   Apt. No.

City   State/Prov.   Zip/Postal Code

Signature (If under 18, parent or guardian must sign)

This offer is limited to one order per household and not valid to present subscribers. Terms and prices subject to change without notice.

4E-AD1